LETHAL
LIES

PRAISE FOR
REBECCA ZANETTI'S NOVELS

DEADLY SILENCE

"Zanetti balances the adventure and menace of Zara and Ryker's lives with a relatable romance. The result is a story that's sexy and emotional, and filled with a rich look at love in all its forms."

—Washington Post

"TOP PICK! 4½ STARS! Emotionally charged and sexy action-packed thriller. It doesn't get better than this!"

—RT Book Reviews

"Budget your time, readers, because this is one that's hard to put down."

—HeroesandHeartbreakers.com

TOTAL SURRENDER

"Top Pick! 4½ stars! Bravo and thanks to Zanetti for providing stellar entertainment!"

—RT Book Reviews

"*Total Surrender* is action packed, thrilling, and heart-stopping romantic suspense at its best."

—Harlequinjunkie.com

"*Total Surrender* is in a word…WOW!"　　　　—FreshFiction.com

"Brava on a book (and a series) beautifully imagined and artfully delivered!"

—GraveTells.com

"*Sweet Revenge* is like a locomotive barreling at you at full throttle! With amazingly well-developed characters, the romantic tension, and a plot so full of subplots, this escape from reality is one of those books that you keep saying just one more page…just one more page…until it's 3 a.m. and there are no more pages left!"

—TomeTender.blogspot.com

"The magic Zanetti creates when she puts pen to paper results in my kinda romance. The basis of the Sins Brothers series is one that captivates the reader; it's fresh, unique, and I absolutely love it!"

—KTBookReviews.blogspot.com

FORGOTTEN SINS

"4½ stars! Top Pick! The rich world of romantic suspense gets even better with the first in Zanetti's tremendous new paranormal-edged series…[A] rapidly paced, clever thriller…Zanetti pulls together a heady mix of sexy sizzle, emotional punch, and high-stakes danger in this truly outstanding tale. Brava!"

—*RT Book Reviews*

"Lord, I loved this book. From the first page to the last, this one left me trying to catch my breath after each action-packed page…Zanetti will always be a fixture on this reader's bookshelf!"

—Ramblings from a Chaotic Mind
(nikkibrandyberry.wordpress.com)

LETHAL LIES

REBECCA ZANETTI

FOREVER

New York Boston

Copyright © 2017 by Rebecca Zanetti
Excerpt from *Twisted Truths* copyright © 2017 by Rebecca Zanetti
Cover design by Brian Lemus. Cover copyright © 2017 by Hachette Book Group, Inc.

Forever
Hachette Book Group
1290 Avenue of the Americas, New York, NY 10104
forever-romance.com
twitter.com/foreverromance

First Trade Paperback edition: May 2017

Forever is an imprint of Grand Central Publishing. The Forever name and logo are trademarks of Hachette Book Group, Inc.

The publisher is not responsible for websites (or their content) that are not owned by the publisher.

The Hachette Speakers Bureau provides a wide range of authors for speaking events. To find out more, go to www.hachettespeakersbureau.com or call (866) 376-6591.

Library of Congress Control Number: 2017932185

ISBNs: 978-1-4555-9429-0 (trade paperback), 978-1-4789-7010-1 (audiobook, downloadable), 978-1-4555-9427-6 (ebook)

Printed in the United States of America

LSC-C

10 9 8 7 6 5 4 3 2 1

To Michele and Brian on December 3, 2016. In life, there are many Once Upon a Times. Here is to your Happily Ever After! Best wishes and congratulations!

Acknowledgments

I'm delighted we're writing a spin-off series for those Sin Brothers, and I hope readers enjoy this new band of lost and wounded men. This series found a wonderful home with Grand Central Forever, and I'm grateful for the opportunity to work with so many wonderful, talented, and hardworking people.

Thanks to Michele Bidelspach for being such an amazing editor. She works so hard and sees the depths that can be found in each and every character. I don't know how she does it.

Thanks to Brian Lemus for the absolutely awesome covers in this series. They're amazing, and I love them. Thanks also to Jodi Rosoff, Michelle Cashman, Jessica Pierce, Yasmin Mathew, Dianna Stirpe, and Kallie Shimek from Grand Central Forever for their hard work.

A big thank you to my agent, Caitlin Blasdell, who does an amazing job across the board. Thanks also to Liza Dawson and the Dawson gang for the hard work and support.

Thanks to Jillian Stein, Minga Portillo, Rebecca's Rebels, Writerspace, and Fresh Fiction for getting the word out about the books.

Thanks also to my constant support system: Gail and Jim English, Debbie and Travis Smith, Stephanie and Don West, Brandie and Mike Chapman, Jessica and Jonah Namson, and Kathy and Herb Zanetti.

Finally, thank you to Big Tone for being Big Tone. I love you. Also, thanks to Gabe and Karlina for being such great kids. I love you both!

PROLOGUE

Twenty years ago

The car smelled like leather and something fake. Heath had never been in a new car before, but he'd seen advertisements for "new car smell" fresheners on television a couple of times. Last month, he would've liked exploring the car. Now, who cared? Why bother?

His head hurt, and his chest ached. The doctors had just finished poking at him, real doctors, which was weird. "Why did I have to get a physical?" he asked the driver.

She looked at him in the mirror, her blue eyes sharp. "We like to have a complete medical history at the boys home."

Boys home. Yeah. What a shithole. Heath had arrived there yesterday, tried to save a mangy kitten, and then had taken a beating from the owner of the place. Ned Cobb was an asshole.

But hey, Heath had saved the cat. It had been his first day, and it had sucked. Then this lady had shown up early in the morning to take him for a routine physical. The doctors had believed him about falling on his bike to get the bruises.

Like he'd ever had a bike. "How long do I have to stay at this place?"

"Until you're an adult."

That sucked. His mom's boyfriend had killed her and then disappeared more than a week ago. Heath had been trying to find him, but the police had caught his ass, putting him into the system.

At just eleven years old, he didn't know much about the system except he didn't want to be there.

The car smell was kind of cool, but he'd give anything to smell his mom's lotion again. Her scent had been soft and sweet, kind of like he imagined pink roses would smell. If he'd been stronger, smarter...he could've saved her. Tears pricked the back of his eyes, and he ruthlessly shoved them away.

It hurt, but he kept his gaze blank, especially since the lady driving the car kept watching him. She had really sharp blue eyes and too-red lips, and she'd known his name.

"Do you work at the boys home?" he asked, shifting on the leather seat.

"No. I just consult," she said, her eyebrows rising as she looked at him in the mirror. Her voice sounded like the ex-lawyer who'd lived next to Heath at one time. The guy had swum constantly in a vodka bottle but had been all right and even helpful with geometry homework. This lady probably had a bunch of degrees, too.

Heath didn't have words, so he nodded at her, not really giving a shit about a home or whatever a consultant did. Without his mom to take care of, he didn't have anything to do, since Spyder, the fucking killer, was long gone. His mom had been sweet but so lost with the meth. Sometimes she'd loved the dangerous crystals more than him, but he got it. Drugs sucked. He rubbed his chest, picturing her pretty bluish green eyes when they'd been clear. Drug free, she'd loved him a lot.

That was more than most kids got.

She had always chosen losers to live with, and Heath had been getting just big enough to protect her. But he hadn't gotten there fast enough and she'd died. He clenched his fingers into a fist and fought not to cry in front of the lady driving the car.

"You'll like it at the home," the woman said. "And we'll get to know each other."

Why would the lady want to know him? "Humph."

She smiled, and her teeth were really straight. "Do you remember my name?"

He scratched a scab on his elbow. "Sylvia Daniels." He never forgot anything and could even recite the first page of a book he'd read years ago. "You're a social worker studying smart kids." At least that's what she'd said when she'd picked him up to take him to the doctor. Something told him she wasn't giving him the full truth, but grown-ups usually didn't. So long as they left him alone, he didn't really care. But she probably wasn't going to leave him alone.

"Did your mother tell you anything about your father or family?" Sylvia asked.

"No." Heath picked the scab off, and his elbow bled a little. His mom had seemed afraid of somebody—maybe family—and was always looking over her shoulder. "Do you know anything about them?"

"I do not," Sylvia said, her voice changing in pitch.

He leaned his head back on the seat. Grown-ups always fucking lied. He'd gotten the feeling more than once that he and his mom were running from something. Maybe his dad was a total asshole who wanted to kill them. Made sense, considering the men his mom had ended up loving.

Well, except him. She'd loved him. Maybe he was an asshole, too. He frowned.

Even if he came from a jerk of a father, his mom had been a good person. Maybe he was half good. That'd be okay. If he'd had a chance, he might've been all good and made her proud. Gotten her help somehow.

Now he'd never get the chance. His bottom lip trembled, and he bit it. Hard.

Sylvia pulled down a long dirt road by a sign that said LOST SPRINGS HOME FOR BOYS on it.

The name had an odd ring to it, and he shivered at seeing the sign again. They reached the main building, and she stopped the car.

Heath slowly slid out and scanned the area. He'd hadn't had a chance to really look around the previous day. Now the place seemed busy. A bunch of bigger boys messed with a scruffy dog over by a stand of trees. Assholes. Some smaller kids played with a soccer ball in a dirt field a ways away. His gaze caught on a boy sitting on a log fence by himself just watching everyone. He was frowning at the big kids.

Sylvia followed his gaze. "That's Ryker. He's another boy I study." Her voice had a low tone Heath couldn't quite read, but a shiver wound down his back.

He swallowed. Nothing in him wanted to be studied. Did he have a choice? Probably not. "Do you study a lot of kids?"

"Only the two of you."

The shiver got bigger. What did "study" mean? He didn't want to wonder, but he couldn't help it. "Why the two of us?"

She turned to face him full-on. "You're special, Heath. Both of you are."

He tried to smile for her and play the game, but his mouth wouldn't work. Did she know all about him? About the way he could hear things other people couldn't? His eyesight and memory were weirdly good, and he could move really fast if he had to. There was nowhere to hide from this woman, so he didn't try. "How are we special?"

"We're going to find that out."

Maybe she didn't know what he could do. He sure wasn't going to tell her. Heath looked back at Ryker. There was something about the boy that called to him. Did Ryker have freaky skills, too? Why else would Sylvia study him? Heath's heart beat faster.

Sylvia smiled. "I'll go get Ned Cobb so we can discuss your plan here. I know you met him yesterday. Why don't you introduce yourself to Ryker?"

Heath didn't move. What if Ryker punched him in the face? Then he'd punch back, and he'd be in a fight right off the bat. But maybe Ryker knew a way out of the boys home. Heath had known bad people during his life, and when the hair on the back of his neck rose, it was time to run. Was there anywhere to run?

He rubbed the back of his neck.

Sylvia disappeared into the building.

Heath watched Ryker, and Ryker had turned his full attention on Heath. Then the older boy moved toward Heath, and he walked like a tiger Heath had seen on television one time.

Heath hunched his shoulders but didn't back up. He planted his threadbare tennis shoes that were a size too big.

Ryker had bluish green eyes and fresh bruises along his jaw. "I saw you save that cat yesterday."

Heath blinked. He hadn't realized anybody had been watching. That was rare for him. "He was alone and scared." The scruffy little thing had just wanted food, and Heath had peanuts. "Um, I'm Heath."

Ryker eyed him.

Heath cleared his voice. "Who hurt your face?"

Ryker didn't even twitch.

Yeah. That's what Heath had thought. How far did the woods go? He could run that way. "Sylvia said she studies you."

Ryker's eyes flared and then shut down. Jumbled emotions came from him and bombarded Heath. "You her new pet?"

Acid crawled through Heath's stomach. "I hope not," he blurted. He shoved his hands into his pockets and looked around the perfectly clean place with no litter anywhere. The sun was too bright. Most of the *clean* in his life was just on the surface. This home…had dirty all over it. He could feel it. "Is this a good place?" His voice was too high, and he blanched.

"No."

That's what he'd figured. One beating from Ned Cobb was all he was gonna take. "Then I'm outta here." He turned for the road.

"You won't make it." Ryker sighed. "Not today, anyway. Don't try it."

Heath paused. "Sylvia said she wants to study me, too."

Ryker's gaze narrowed. "Did she say why?"

"No." Heath swallowed over a lump in his throat. The kid didn't seem to want a friend. "Do you like being studied?"

"Fuck no." Ryker took a rock and threw it across the dirt.

Heath's shoulders slumped. "Yeah. I kinda figured that."

Ryker cocked his head. "I'm leaving as soon as I can."

Heath's knees wobbled. "Maybe I could come with you?" The two of them would be stronger together.

The boy studied him as if he could peel Heath's skin back and see all the way to his bones. Finally, Ryker nodded. "Are you a dickhead who tortures animals?" he asked, jerking his head toward the bigger boys.

Heath breathed out, his lungs finally relaxing. "No. Like the kitten yesterday, I try to save 'em." It seemed like Ryker needed to be saved a little. Maybe they could be friends. If nothing else, they could cover each other's backs. "You?"

"I don't torture, but *saving* seems a waste of time." Ryker's mouth turned down.

Heath leaned against the shiny car. His chest puffed out. He could help Ryker get the hell out of this place. Maybe not be so alone. Then Ryker could help him find the dick who'd killed his mom.

The bruises on Ryker made Heath's stomach clench again. They would survive. He'd make sure of it. "It's gonna be okay, Ryker. I promise."

The dog yelped from a bigger boy throwing a rock at its legs. Heath's body heated, and he pushed away from the vehicle.

"Where are you going?" Ryker asked.

"To save the dog."

CHAPTER
1

Present day

Pictures of dead girls lined the east wall of the small home office, their eyes somehow accusatory. Anya Best paced the new carpet in the temporary apartment in Snowville, Washington, trying to avoid looking at the faces. On the west wall, a corkboard held the layout for an article she was writing on the criminal mind and how it related to social media. Being on sabbatical from her job as a professor should have made it easy to write. The other wall held a murder board. Pictures of viciously killed redheads with neatly typed notes beneath each victim. She'd profiled their killer, but it was their faces that haunted her at night.

They all looked a little like her. Red hair, youngish, bright eyed. Before they had been strangled to death.

Her cell phone rang from the makeshift desk, and she jumped for it. "Hello?" she asked breathlessly. Was her sister finally checking in?

A male voice cleared. "Is this Anya?"

She drew up, her breath heating. It wasn't Loretta. Her temples thrummed. "Who is this?"

"Heath Jones of Lost Bastards Investigative Services. We met briefly last week in Salt Lake when I, ah, collaborated on the Copper Killer case with Loretta." His voice was low and authoritative. Smooth and deep.

She exhaled. "Right. I remember." She and Loretta had been in Salt Lake with the serial killer task force, tracking down a lead. Another missing girl. "How did you get my number?" Heath had spent an hour with Loretta, who was a special agent with the FBI, and they'd compared notes. Anya had been working in the other room.

"I'm a P.I. We get numbers," he said, the tone lacking humor.

"Oh." Anya swallowed and turned away from the murder board. "Loretta isn't here."

Silence. "Ah, what do you mean?" he asked, his tone dropping. Tension slammed through the line.

"She's undercover and has been for nearly two days." Anya should probably be watching her words, but Loretta had trusted the guy, at least a little. "Do you have any updates on the case? I've been profiling the killer and could use any new information." She didn't reveal the rest of her involvement.

"You're, ah, a profiler?" he asked, almost as if gathering his thoughts.

She frowned. "Criminal psychologist." Sure, she just taught at the college, but she had the skills and knowledge. She'd been forced to use them.

He was silent longer this time.

"Mr. Jones?" What in the world was going on? She'd met Heath only once, very quickly, but she remembered him well. Tall with broad shoulders wide enough to play professional football. Stunning green eyes with gold flecks, and an intensity that had given her pause. Danger.

Finally, he spoke. "I need to see Loretta's files again. Can you bring them to me?"

Clearly Loretta hadn't shared all of her files with him. "No," Anya said. The agents guarding the entrance to the apartment building wouldn't let her leave anyway. She was under lockdown until Loretta returned from making herself bait for the damn killer. "Sorry." A sharp rap sounded on the door. "I have to go. Bye." She clicked off and turned to run through the narrow living room for the door. Was there news on Loretta?

She flung open the door. Two men stood in the bright hallway.

"Anya Best?" The first guy had brown eyes, wavy dark hair, and a charming smile. He stood like he could handle himself. A jacket covered his large frame, and a slight bulge showed at his waist.

Gun. He had a gun at his waist. She gulped. All right. She stepped back. "Who are you?"

The guy dug out a badge holder and flipped it open. "U.S. Marshal D. J. Smithers."

She blinked. "The FBI agent downstairs let you in?"

"Of course," he said smoothly.

The other guy, much shorter than his buddy, nodded soberly. He had nearly black eyes, adult acne, and a slight paunch over his dress pants. "We just need a moment of your time."

"Why?" If this was about the task force, the FBI would be present. "I don't understand. Is this about the Copper Killer case?" She needed Loretta to be there. Where was her sister, damn it?

"No." Smithers tucked his badge back into his coat. "It's about Heath Jones and the Lost Bastards detective agency."

Anya's mouth dropped open, and the phone felt heavy in her hand. She'd just disconnected the call. Like, seconds ago. "Um."

Smithers kept her gaze. "We have your phone bugged just in case. We've been watching the Lost Bastards, and we know that Heath met with your sister last week. When he just called—"

Air burst out of Anya's lungs. "Bugged? My phone?" Her mind spun. "This doesn't make sense. I mean, what does this have to do with the Copper Killer case?"

"Nothing," Smithers said calmly. "This is about Lost Bastards."

Her lips trembled. "How—I mean, why—No, how are you here so fast?"

"Oh." Smithers relaxed. "That. We were scouting the area when the call came in. Happy coincidence that we could get here so quickly."

There wasn't any such thing as a happy coincidence. Anya's stomach started to hurt. Something was off. She turned toward the other guy. "I didn't see your identification."

He straightened and then solemnly drew out a badge.

Her body relaxed. The cops were the good guys. "I'm sorry to be so suspicious. This is just weird." She looked closer at the badge. Her stomach dropped. It was a good fake, but a fake nonetheless. She'd seen the genuine thing just a week before. Why have a fake badge? There was no way he had made it past the FBI guard downstairs. Somehow they'd snuck in.

These guys wanted Heath Jones, and all she'd done was talk to him on the phone. If she screamed, would anybody hear? Most people were at work right now and not in their apartments, and the FBI agents only covered the entrances to the building. What kind of mess was Heath in? Did it have anything to do with Loretta's case? God. What if it did? She had to get out of there. So she forced another smile. "I don't really know Heath Jones or his business. What's this really about?"

Smithers didn't miss a beat. "We're concerned about them. It looks like they've gotten caught up in a dangerous case with Colombian drug cartels, and we're concerned for their safety."

Colombian drug cartels? Seriously? Who was this guy? That was the biggest load of crap she'd ever heard. At the moment, she had more important issues to deal with. Heath and his agency would have to handle their own problems, and if she had to throw him under a bus, she would. She moved closer to Smithers to show trust. "Do you have a card? I'm happy to call you if he contacts me again."

Smithers nodded. "Actually, we're hoping you can arrange a meeting."

She glanced down at her phone and clicked a button. "His number didn't come up when he called." She turned the phone toward Smithers. "See?"

His eyebrows drew down in the middle. "That's unfortunate."

"It sure is." She reached for the door. "I'm sorry, but I have a case to work on right now. I'll contact the Marshals Service if I hear from Heath again."

His body straightened, and he planted a hand over hers.

She coughed, her body stiffening. Adrenaline shot through her veins.

"I think we need to make a plan," he said, his face lowering toward hers.

She squinted. Were those colored contacts? Looking closer, she could almost make out putty along his jawline. She tried to jerk free. The man was in disguise? Why?

He held her in place.

"Let go of me," she gritted out, looking frantically around.

"No," he said easily, also scanning the area. "Quiet little apartment building, isn't it?"

His buddy laughed.

Thunder rolled outside.

"I have a feeling you're the key to getting the Lost Bastards where we want them," Smithers said, pivoting and tugging her down the hallway.

"No." Anya pulled back, setting her feet. She opened her mouth to scream just as Smithers turned and clamped a hand over it, easily dragging her toward the stairwell at the end of the hall. She fought hard, trying to yell into his hand.

He lifted her and carried her down two flights of stairs to the basement. Unbelievable. It had been that easy to get into the building and avoid any guards? She struggled, but before she could harm him, they were on the back street next to a black sedan

The FBI agents were out front, damn it.

Snow smashed into her face, and the wind pierced her. She was about to be kidnapped because of a phone call? She shrugged back and shot her elbow into Smithers's gut. He grunted and dropped her to her feet, still keeping a tight hold.

Tears filled her eyes as she battled against his strength.

Suddenly, an engine roared down the road, and a battered Chevy truck barreled close, smashing hard into the sedan. The sedan collided with a parking meter and metal crumpled with a loud crunch.

She yelped and jumped back, finally freeing herself. Her breath, heated, shot out of her in a loud exhale. Her heart thundered wildly. What in the world?

The truck swung around, and the passenger door was thrown open. "Get in," bellowed a low voice.

She blinked at seeing Heath Jones, the detective from Lost Bastards. Her knees felt like jelly. D. J. Smithers scrambled beneath his jacket, yanking out a shiny gun. She had about two seconds to go with her instincts, so she did. She ran across the snow, leaping through the passenger side of the truck and slamming the door.

Heath punched the gas, and the truck fishtailed as it roared away from the sidewalk.

Bullets struck the side of the truck with an odd pattering sound. She screamed, curling forward.

"Get down." Heath grabbed her neck and shoved her further down, sliding lower in the seat but not losing any speed. His hand was rough and his voice tense, but he didn't hurt her.

She blinked, her heart thundering. The glove box fell open, and a gun dropped onto her knee. She grabbed it and held on tight. With a cop for a dad, guns weren't foreign to her, but she'd never actually shot one.

The truck fishtailed again, around a corner and then several more. Finally, Heath released her neck. "Are you okay?"

"No," she bellowed, shoving herself to the bench seat. Her ribs hurt from the rapid beating of her heart. "How?" She looked out the back window at an empty and snowy road.

Heath glanced her way. "How what?"

She swallowed and surveyed him. At least six foot four, tightly muscled, definitely strong and fast. Brown hair waved over his collar, and his greenish gold eyes pierced right through her. While the fake marshals had been shooting guns, there was no doubt this guy was twice as dangerous. What had she done, leaping into his truck? "Um." She fumbled for the door handle.

"I'm driving too fast for you to jump out." He kept his broad hands on the steering wheel.

She blinked, and her shoulders trembled. "What is going on? Why were those guys bugging my phone? Why do they want you?" she yelled.

His frown drew down his dark eyebrows. "That's a very long story about a different case that has nothing to do with you, and I'm sorry. I had no clue they were getting close enough to start bugging phones of people I barely know."

"They shot at you," she whispered, her mind reeling. Good guys usually didn't have people shooting at them.

Heath glanced her way once more. "Yeah. Again, sorry about that."

She leaned her head back. Somebody had just shot real bullets at her. Bile rose in her throat. God, this was getting too confusing, and she was having trouble breathing as her adrenaline ebbed. She hadn't slept in two nights. Every time she closed her eyes, she saw an image of her sister, in danger and hunting a serial killer. What had Loretta been thinking to set herself up as bait for a murderer? Even though she was an FBI agent, she was still human. Still vulnerable.

Anya yanked herself back to the moment. She had to think. "Why are those fake cops chasing you and now me?"

He looked at her again, really looked this time. "How did you know they were fake?"

Being his sole focus heated her whole body. Man, he was something to look at, but bad boys had never drawn her. "I met a real U.S. Marshal last week who's a friend of my sister's. Saw her badge." Plus, her instincts were fairly decent at knowing when people were lying, considering her background as a criminal psychologist. "There was something not quite right about them."

Admiration glimmered in Heath's stunning eyes. "Nicely done."

"I guess." She shrugged back inside herself. Something about him made her feel feminine and yet strong. Must be the bad-boy lure. She knew better. She eyed the snowy trees flashing by outside. "Why are they after you, Heath?"

"It's a totally different case from the Copper Killer case. Don't worry about it. They'll leave you alone since I know they've been bugging your phone. As a lead to me, you've been blown."

She swallowed, cold clacking through her. That was weird, right? "Who are you?" she whispered. What had she been thinking to jump into his truck?

"Just a private eye, Anya."

"This is crazy. It's all so crazy." Her voice sounded hysterical, so she tried to calm herself, rubbing her hands on her jeans.

He covered one of her hands with his as if trying to offer comfort.

She frowned and grasped his hand, turning it over. A long scar ran along his lifeline. "What happened?"

He glanced down. "I formed a family." At her tilted head, he smiled. "Blood brothers for life." Past hurts and strong ties lived in his words.

"Oh." Her entire body ached. This was out of her experience. God, she needed her sister. Why hadn't Loretta called in? Tears gathered in her eyes, and she turned away from Heath for a moment. She cleared her throat. "Family is what matters."

His voice roughened. "I need the files your sister had."

"No. You can ask her when she gets back from her undercover op." It had to be soon. Loretta had said she might not be able to call in. But two days was long enough to wait.

Heath pulled the truck into the empty parking lot of an abandoned gas station. A rusted sign swung in the wind, clapping against the metal siding. He turned toward her. "I'm so sorry."

Her body tensed before her mind could grasp his meaning. "What?" she breathed.

He looked at her, obviously weighing his words. His eyes darkened and deepened. "They should've told you, Anya. The FBI had no right, and you have to be careful who you trust."

The FBI didn't even know she'd been taken from the apartment. She swallowed. Her chest tightened in denial. "Told me what?" Her voice trembled.

He inhaled deeply, moving his broad chest, as if trying to gather strength. "I'm so sorry. Your sister was taken by the Copper Killer Monday afternoon. Two days ago."

CHAPTER
2

Heath had spoken the words as gently as he could.

Anya's body recoiled as if he'd punched her. She shook her head as her face turned a stark white. "No. That's not right." She looked frantically around the empty lot and reached for the door handle.

"Wait." Heath wrapped a hand around her bicep. "Just wait a minute." It hurt to see her in pain. Why the hell hadn't the FBI told her the truth about Loretta's kidnapping? Sure, they'd kept the information out of the news, but they should've told Loretta's sister.

Anya shook her head again, her red hair spinning. She lifted his gun and pointed it at him. "Take me back. Now."

Training kept his body calm. A gun barrel elicited an instant reaction, and the moment narrowed his focus. "Okay. Listen. Your sister is smart, and she knows how to deal with criminals. Even though she's been kidnapped, you can't lose hope that she's alive."

Anya audibly gulped. "I know. She has to be alive."

Heath released her and maneuvered the vehicle back onto the road. He kept his hands loose on the steering wheel as he drove through town and watched the woman out of his peripheral vision. Dark and straight red hair, determined green eyes, delicate features. Shock and pain in those eyes. And terror. Fear for her sister.

Her aim was direct to his neck, and her arm shook. The weapon was a Sig Sauer, fully loaded with one in the chamber. No safety on the gun. "Loosen your grip, sweetheart. You might squeeze off a round accidentally, and I'm still recuperating from my last gunshot wound."

Anya's grip tightened until her knuckles turned white. "You are?"

The concern on her face nearly stopped him cold. Who was this soft woman? He'd only met her once, but at seeing the bruises on her face that day, he'd wanted to kick the shit out of the person who'd caused them. Immediately. "Yeah. I was shot on a job and got between an asshole who didn't want to pay child support and the loud woman demanding it. Took a bullet to the shoulder." It had been just a graze, and he was fine. Denver, his brother, had gotten shot the same week but was also fine. That had been one shitty week.

Her eyes widened, but her jaw kept a stubborn tilt. "I don't want to shoot you."

"Then we're in agreement." His calmness was serving to throw her off balance, and he needed her to relax before she shot him, damn it. "Lower the gun, and we can talk about it." Snow billowed down, and he twisted the windshield wipers into faster action while turning left toward the apartment building. "I've given you a shock. You doing okay?" It was a stupid question, but he had to offer some comfort.

She shook her head. "No. I keep wondering what's happening right now to Loretta. What is she going through?"

"She's tough and smart. She's hopefully getting free." He wanted to hold on to the hope. Badly. He tried to turn Anya's focus so she'd calm. "Last time I saw you, you had bruises on your neck." He'd wondered who had dared to hurt her.

"Yeah. I shifted right when I should've gone left. Loretta's partner was training me." She looked out the window, her body one tense line. "I'm not so good at the physical stuff."

"Really?" he barked out before he could stop himself, his gut dropping. "I've heard many an excuse and lie, but that's a new one. Most battered women go with the 'I fell down the stairs' explanation." He winced. That hadn't been nice. "Sorry."

Instead of getting angry or cowering away, Anya seemed to focus on him. "Wow. That was a serious leap in logic, buddy."

He paused.

Her chin lowered. "You sound as if you have experience in that area."

Now he stiffened. "What are you? A shrink?" he muttered.

"Well, kind of."

He turned her way. "Do you practice? With patients?" If anything, she became more intriguing every time she talked.

"No. I'm a professor of criminal psychology at Ocean City College. So I could've been a shrink."

The stunning redhead was a professor? "Tell me the truth about the bruises."

Her shoulders settled and her arms stopped shaking. "Loretta's partner was teaching me some self-defense moves, and I honestly moved the wrong way. He pulled the punch, but…"

But delicate skin like hers bruised easily. It sounded like she was telling the truth, but he knew from experience how often victims lied. "Right."

She blinked. "What's your deal? You have definite issues, don't you?"

His chest hurt in an old ache. He sighed and took another turn, correcting when the truck fishtailed again on the black ice. "My mom was killed by an abusive boyfriend when I was a kid. She was addicted to drugs, and we never stayed in one place long, but she always managed to find the biggest dickheads in the world to fall for. The last one finally killed her." His tone had remained low and matter-of-fact, even as pain exploded in his solar plexus.

"I'm sorry," Anya whispered, her eyes glassy. "That's terrible."

His phone rang.

She stiffened, her hands shaking more. God, she really was going to shoot him.

He gingerly pulled out the phone to read a text. His entire body tightened. "My brothers have a lead on your sister. I have to go."

"What's the lead?" she asked, her voice unsteady.

"I don't know. They just said to suit up." He took another turn.

"Brothers?"

"Lost Bastards Investigative Services is owned by the three of us—Ryker, Denver, and me. We're brothers." They were all he had in the world, and if something happened to either one of them, his heart would be cut out. So he understood her need to find her sister. He really did. Everything inside him wanted to gather her close and provide shelter.

Her gaze turned to the deserted snowy road. "I'm going with you."

Hell, no. "I can't have you with me if I find the guy." Not only would she be in the way, he didn't want her to see Loretta if the serial killer had finished with her. The guy had a pattern, and it wasn't pretty. Considering Loretta was an FBI agent, the killer would probably want to make a statement. A nasty one.

"My sister might need me." Her voice had trembled on those words. "If you're telling the truth. If not, then I'm shooting you."

His chest ached. He'd only met Special Agent Loretta Jackson a couple of times, but he liked her. They'd collaborated on the serial killer case, and Loretta's sharp intelligence had impressed the heck out of him. In fact, she'd been whole and strong—the complete opposite of his mother. And yet...she'd been taken by a killer. The unfairness of that fact nearly made him choke. "I respect your sister and know she'd want me to keep you safe. Let's do this my way."

Anya set her other hand on the gun. "I don't think so."

Even from across the cab, he could see the rapid rise and fall of her chest. If she didn't calm herself, she was about to go into a panic attack. "You need to calm down, Anya."

"I'm calm." Her voice had come out an octave higher than it had earlier.

He had to get through to her somehow and get her to concentrate on something other than the gun and him. "When I talked to your sister the other day, she implied you two had just recently reconnected."

"Yeah. We've always stayed in touch but not as much as I wish we had. Loretta's mom was, well, what my dad fondly called a serial wife." Anya squinted out into the storm.

Heath frowned. "What does that mean?"

"She married a lot of men, including my dad. Loretta was ten when they got married and had me, and she was fifteen when they split." Anya's tone lowered. "We knew of each other but didn't really bond until earlier this year." Her hand started shaking again. "We have to find her, Heath. She has to be all right."

So she did believe him. Imaginary weights slammed onto his shoulders. "The FBI won't stop looking, either. She's one of theirs." How had the Copper Killer gotten an FBI agent?

"The FBI should've told me." Tears choked her voice.

"Agreed." Heath would use every skill he had to find her still alive. First, he had to get Anya safely back to the FBI so he could get to work. "Give me the gun."

"No."

All right. Enough was enough. He pulled over next to a snowbank at the side of the road and put the vehicle into neutral. Then he turned toward her, facing the barrel of his own gun and keeping calm like always. "Last chance, Anya."

A frown marred her smooth forehead. "I have the gun."

Yeah, but he had reflexes that were definitely beyond the norm.

He blew out air. Man, she was pretty. Her eyes were the color of a misty forest and nearly glowed against her pale skin. Totally inappropriate for the moment, but his interest in her grew. "Listen. If I get the gun from you, it's because I have unreal training, okay? It has nothing to do with strength or you. You are not weak, and you are not a victim."

She blinked. "I already told you that I'm not a victim. You're across the truck from me, so you might want to watch your ego. I'm keeping the gun."

"Right. Just say you heard my words, okay?" God, he didn't want to do this.

She rolled her eyes. "All right, tough guy. I heard your words."

He lifted his left hand and twisted, smoothly taking the gun with his right.

Her mouth gaped. Even in the cloudy day, the highlights from her dark red hair glinted with life.

He tucked the gun into his waistband at the back. "Thanks for not shooting me."

"You moved impossibly fast."

"Yeah." That was a minefield he wasn't entering with her. "I'm sorry I had to take the gun." He set the truck into DRIVE and moved back onto the icy road.

"You apologize a lot," she murmured, turning to face the front window. Her shoulders slumped.

He blinked and warmth bloomed in his chest even though she was shrinking his head. "My brothers wouldn't believe you about that." They thought he was one stubborn bastard.

"Bad guys don't apologize. You must be okay." She sounded thoughtful and a little sad. Scared.

She was also wrong. "I'm not a good guy. Trust me."

"Right." She shoved that glorious red hair away from her face.

"Loretta thought you were good at your job, and that means something."

"I'll do my best to find her, and I promise I'll call you if I find out anything."

She rubbed her hands down her jeans. "Good enough. Check in the second you have news."

"I will." He slowed the truck around a chunk of ice in the road. "You do the same."

"Sure."

That didn't sound like the truth. Man, she really didn't trust him. Oddly, all of a sudden he wanted to prove her wrong. Yet his instincts bellowed for him to get the green-eyed beauty somewhere safe and definitely away from him. Her skin tempted him to explore, and her mouth looked delicious. He couldn't be distracted like this—especially when he had a job to do.

Her apartment came into view. The front entrance was empty, but he'd seen an FBI agent inside the lobby and out of the storm. "Hey. Do me a favor and don't let the FBI know about the fake marshals, would you? That's a private case, and we really need the FBI to concentrate on your sister and not lose traction by following irrelevant leads."

She studied him. "I'll think about it."

That's all he could ask her to do. "Let the FBI keep you safe." As if they could.

She nodded. "Where are your offices located?"

"They were in Cisco, Wyoming, but we've closed those down. We're working on relocating to the Pacific Northwest," he said easily. They hadn't found a place as of yet.

Her face was still too pale. "Promise you'll call if you find out anything. And if you're lying about Loretta..."

"I wish I were. But I'll find her." He studied Anya. Delicate bone structure, bruised skin, terror-filled eyes. After she exited the truck, snow dropped onto her flaming hair, and with the gray building behind her, she was all light and color. "I promise."

She shut the door and turned to run into the building.

He waited until she'd reached the agent inside, looked around the quiet area to make sure nobody had followed them, and then took off.

Leaving her didn't feel right.

CHAPTER
3

Anya settled back in her seat as the too-silent female agent drove her through Snowville toward the FBI offices. The woman had barely confirmed that Loretta had been kidnapped. For any more information, Anya needed to speak to a superior.

Kidnapped. Anya leaned her head against the window, not minding the chill. Where was Loretta? Was she hurt? Scared? Still alive?

Closing her eyes, Anya said yet another prayer. Heath's cece filled her mind. Strong lines, intelligent eyes, determined jaw, sculpted lips.

What would those lips feel like? With that thought, she flashed back to almost five months ago, when her life had started to unravel.

"Leave me the hell alone, Carl," she snapped, struggling with both the lock on her apartment door and her luggage. Her laptop case fell off her biggest suitcase, landing with a thunk on the plush carpet of the long hallway. How was her taste in men so terrible when she'd been raised by a single father who had been an amazing person? "Damn it."

Carl sighed and stepped away from her. "We have to talk about this."

Talk about this? She whirled on him. "You're kidding me. You're actually kidding with me right this second."

His sizzling blue eyes dimmed. "I'm sorry. You have to know how sorry I am."

"I don't care." She turned and unlocked her door, heat and hurt filling her chest. They'd dated for nearly six months before they'd won a grant to study abnormal psychology at an institution in southern Washington and had taken sabbaticals from Ocean City College in western Washington, where they both taught. It had seemed like such an adventure. "We're through."

"Come on." He shook his head. "It was one mistake."

"Right." They'd been on a research sabbatical for two months, with ten to go. She'd do her own research without his help. She struggled to shove her suitcases inside. Was it only the night before that she'd found him in bed with his research assistant? The idiot should've never given her the key to his temporary apartment. The bastard must've broken speed limits to get here so quickly.

He cleared his throat and reached for her laptop bag.

"Don't," she hissed, shoving his hand away and grabbing it herself.

He sighed. "You are so dramatic. Listen. We've been dating for months and there has to be a way to salvage this."

She bit her lip. "You should worry more about your career, considering you just slept with a nineteen-year-old student. Your student. We're done." Slamming the door in his face, she leaned against it. Tears prickled in her eyes. "Jerk," she whispered.

"I'll call you tomorrow. We're not done," he said through the door.

The man was crazy. Tripping over her suitcase, she moved through her front hall to her wide kitchen with its cheerful whitewashed cupboards and granite countertops. Dust and a sense of emptiness surrounded her. God, she had to have some wine somewhere. She dug through the cupboards and drew out a bottle of

Shiraz. Perfect. Opening it took a second, pouring a few more, and by then, she decided to get over Carl the asshat and now.

She took a deep gulp. Spice and warmth exploded in her stomach.

Her living room stretched before her, the leather furniture and bright pillows welcoming her home to her bachelorette pad. She'd always be alone. Her heart ached. A picture taken of her with her father around her seventeenth birthday caught her eye. He'd received a commendation for stopping a robbery and stood so proudly next to her in his police uniform, his strong arm over her shoulder, his green eyes a perfect match for hers. "I am never going to find a man like you," she murmured, letting the room blur for a moment.

What she wouldn't give to be able to call him right now. Of course, if he were still alive, he'd drive to her small Washington coastal town and beat the shit out of Carl. The thought made her smile.

She eyed the round table in the wide nook, piled high with magazines and mail. Mrs. Polansky from next door had done a good job of sorting it all into piles.

With another gulp, Anya strode toward the table and sat. With ten months still to go on her research project, she would give anything to be able to return to teaching the next day. To get on with her life without Carl. She angrily shoved away tears.

She took the mail and organized it further, into garbage, somewhat interesting stuff, and bills she'd already paid online.

Four envelopes—the regular white kind—caught her eye. Her name and address were scrawled in strong handwriting across them. No return address.

She frowned and pushed the wineglass away. Then she opened the top letter.

A picture fell out.

Squinting, she lifted the snapshot to the light. A girl of about eighteen looked into the camera. Tears filled her pretty blue eyes, and her long red hair was splayed over her shoulders. What in the world? Chills clacked down Anya's arms.

She reached for the letter to unfold and read it. The scent of lavender filtered around her.

Dear Anya,

This girl tried to be you, to make us, and she failed. Nobody can be you. I'm afraid she'll have to be punished.

XO
Me

Anya's stomach roiled. "Punished"? Was this some kind of sick joke? She grabbed another envelope and ripped it open. Another photograph spilled out. This one was of another redhead, who appeared to be in her midtwenties with brown eyes. Tears glimmered on her face, too.

Dear Anya,

Did you like my last present? I haven't heard from you, but that's okay. We'll have plenty to talk about soon. This girl also tried to be you...she tried so hard. But she failed as well. Her death is deserved. They're calling me the Copper Killer now. How cute is that? Until we meet in person, my love.

XO
Me

The psychologist in Anya roared to the forefront. Either this was an incredibly sick joke or something horrible was going on. Her hand shook as she reached for the third envelope. She bit back a scream when the picture fell out.

A totally different redhead looked blindly at the camera, her eyes dead, her mangled neck bruised.

Anya cried out as she stood and shoved away from the table, falling against the edge of the counter. Her hands shook. That quickly, her gaze caught on the stack of newspapers next to the mail. The top headline read: COPPER KILLER TAKES ANOTHER LIFE.

Oh God. She backed out of the kitchen, her hands trembling, her breath panting. What was happening? She looked wildly around the quiet apartment. Help. She needed help. So she turned and ran for the room she used as an office, flipped through her address book, and quickly dialed.

"Special Agent Jackson," her half sister answered with authority.

"Loretta?" Anya breathed, tears sliding down her face. Her entire body had gone cold. "Loretta?"

"Yes? Anya?"

Anya paused. They didn't speak as much as they should and only exchanged e-mails or Christmas cards once in a while. Yet Loretta worked for the FBI. "Yeah. It's me." She should've probably called the police.

"Oh." Loretta was quiet for a moment. "Are you all right? You sound funny."

Anya bit her lip, her mind spinning. "I don't think so. I mean, no. I think I need help."

The car slid in the snow, and Anya came back to the present with a gasp. Her head pounded.

It was her fault. Loretta hadn't even been working the Copper

Killer case until Anya had asked for help, and now she was in the hands of a brutal psychopath.

* * *

Heath shrugged off unease at leaving Anya with the FBI and picked up speed, quickly dialing the only other number programed into his phone.

"Where are you?" Ryker, his brother, snapped.

"Snowville," Heath said. "Long story. For now, what do you have?"

"Big news. Loretta wasn't taken from her temporary quarters in Snowville. She was on her own in a small town called Gold City in the northwest corner of Idaho. Not too far from where you are, though. Probably there to draw out the killer."

Heath bit back a snarl. "The FBI kept that a secret."

"Actually, they think she was taken from the decoy position in Snowville," Ryker said. "But they'll figure it out shortly, I'm sure."

Heath slowed down. "Do I need to get back to the airport?"

"No. It'd be faster for you to drive there." The sound of typing came over the line. "We caught a picture of Agent Jackson in Gold City the day she was taken, so she might still be in Idaho."

Almost two days ago. Heath punched the gas and headed north. "What was she doing there?"

"If you ask me, she was setting herself up as bait without backup," Ryker said evenly, still typing.

"Stupid," Heath muttered.

"Desperate," Ryker countered. "The video was from the camera at a small post office, so I tracked around town and found one more shot, this one from a small bank."

"Okay." So they'd found Jackson before she'd been kidnapped. "How does that help us?"

"The same truck is in the background in both shots. Ran the plates and nothing. We think Jackson disappeared right after visiting that bank. So, ah, Denver hacked into some satellite feeds—don't ask about the legality."

"And?" Their brother Denver was a genius at hacking governmental technology. Heath's breathing sped up with the scent of a trail.

"We've tracked the truck to a farm about two hours from your current location." Ryker sighed. "Well, we think we have. Satellite had the truck for a while, but there's a colossal storm over the Northwest, and cloud cover is too thick. We then used Google satellite images to find what looks like a farm—the only one with structures in that area."

"Most farms in the area grow crops?" Heath sped up on the icy road, his shoulders stiffening. They'd found her.

"Yeah. Some wheat. But this place, at least from the images, doesn't look like a working farm. There aren't enough structures. Another satellite picture from two years ago shows it to be abandoned. There's a large crumbling barn and two more outbuildings that might not even exist now."

It was a long way to drive for an unlikely place, but it was all they had. "Send the coordinates to my phone."

"Denver is heading over from the Montana-Idaho border where we've been working from a block of cabins. If we found this lead, the FBI should have it soon, so be careful."

"I will. Also, two guys bugged Anya Best's phone, looking for us." Heath increased the speed of the wipers against the pelting snow.

"All right. Are you free of them?"

Considering he'd smashed their car to bits, yeah. "I'm free."

"Good. One thing at a time. Let's find Special Agent Jackson and go from there," Ryker said.

Heath flipped on the heater. "We have to find her before he kills her." The Copper Killer took delight in torturing victims before killing them, and he hadn't left a clue with the eight previous kills. "She has to be okay."

"Shit, Heath. You need to keep a distance here." Concern wove through Ryker's tone.

"I'm trying. Loretta is strong and smart—and he'll attempt to strip that away from her." That's what bullies did. Who knew who his mother could've been if just one loser boyfriend hadn't kept supplying her with drugs? He couldn't fail again. "The killer might not be prepared for a trained FBI agent. He might have to kill quickly with Loretta. The bastard."

"I know," Ryker murmured. "But you have to keep cold and sane. Any woman in trouble pushes your buttons. You need to be smart and distant for this fuckin' case."

"Got it." His brother had always tried to protect his psyche, and Heath knew to listen to him. "I'll stay clear thinking. I promise."

"Good. Wait for Denver before going in." Ryker clicked off.

Heath tossed the phone onto the seat and glared up at the heavily overcast sky. He hadn't liked leaving Anya by herself, but she'd be safer with the FBI for now. He dialed his brother again.

"Yeah?" Ryker asked.

"Do a search on Anya Best, Loretta's sister. I want to know everything about her," Heath said.

Silence ticked over the line for a moment. "The bruised one?"

Heath closed his eyes for a moment and then reopened them to watch the road. "Just do it. I need the info for this case." He clicked off, knowing he hadn't fooled his brother a bit. The last thing he needed right now was another lecture on his penchant for trying to save lost souls.

Anya wasn't lost. Hell, the woman had even held a gun on him. He grinned.

Soon sleet mixed with snow and made him slow down for the two-hour drive. He had the rural roads to himself and quickly climbed through a series of forested ravines.

Scrub brush, rocks, pine trees, and snow surrounded him. A chill slithered down his back. The turnoff came into view, and he followed a barely there trail, parking about a half mile from where the barn had been two years ago. He took several precious moments to wipe down the truck and any evidence either he or Anya had been inside, just in case he had to leave it behind.

His body thrumming, he jumped from the truck, and cold assailed him. He zipped his coat, tugged the collar around his neck, and turned to dodge through snowy pine trees. Within minutes, the barn came into view.

Heath reached for his phone and dialed Ryker. "I've found it."

"Wait for backup. Denver will be there in fifteen minutes," Ryker ordered.

Even with the storm, the air was too quiet. Tension hung over the entire area. Heath had to go in. "Tell him to hurry. I'm finding her now." He shoved the phone back into his pocket before Ryker could argue.

Taking a deep breath, he closed his eyes and zeroed in with his odd senses.

One heartbeat, barely, could be heard from the crumbling barn.

He launched into a run for the building, reaching it quickly and pressing his back to the chilled wood of the barn, trying to see through the swirling snow. Visibility was nil, so he closed his eyes and tuned in. Nothing. He centered himself and tried again, barely making out a slow heartbeat. Maybe.

Drawing his gun free, he inched toward the door, keeping his steps light on the icy snow. His gloves were thin enough so he could easily control the weapon.

The wind blew an angry aria through the pine trees, scattering even more snow. Cold slashed into him, and he ducked his chin into his coat.

If Loretta was inside, she'd be freezing.

He nudged open the door and listened. The storm increased in force along with the wind, banishing all other sounds. Damn it. His body bunched to move, but his mind and training took over. Slowly, he finished opening the door and slipped inside a narrow tack room. Threadbare leather halters hung from rusted nails, and a ripped saddle had been shoved against the widely spaced wooden slats at the far end.

Dirty hay covered the concrete floor and had been kicked into clumps. Had there been a struggle?

The smell of blood hit him hard enough to catch his breath. Metallic and thick. His body short-circuited, and his mind went blank. Panic threw him into action.

He shoved through the room and charged into a sprawling barn area. A woman lay on the ground, her head turned away, blood pooling around her. He moved toward her, and a slight whisper of movement came from behind him. He turned, and something hard struck his head, shooting sparks in front of his eyes.

His brain slammed against his skull, and he went down. Darkness claimed him a second later.

CHAPTER
4

Anya thanked the junior agent who dropped her at the front door of the FBI offices in Snowville. The storm had made the fifteen-minute drive last about half an hour. She barreled through the storm to push open the door. The woman behind the counter and Plexi-glass wall pressed a button, and Anya strode down the hallway. She waited for another door to open and then walked into the main bullpen.

Instant heat and activity surrounded her.

"I don't give one damn about the storm. We're getting those heli-copters in the air right now," Special Agent Frederick Reese bellowed, shoving papers into a manila file at a wide wooden table. By far the tallest man in the room, he overwhelmed his entire area.

Agents scurried around him, several talking on phones. Two of-fices sat off to the side, both manned by agents typing furiously on computers.

Anya rushed to him. "What the hell, Reese? How could you not tell me?" Without thinking, she punched him right in the gut.

He barely bent over. "We didn't want to scare you."

"You complete dick," she breathed, clutching her purse tightly. "Where's my sister? What do you know?"

"We have an update." He looked down at her, his brown eyes swirling with emotion. "Your sister was taken from a small town called Gold City in Idaho. We found surveillance videos, and we might have an idea where she is." He scoured the room, and his voice rose. "But we need the helicopters in the air."

Anya took a step back, her heart thundering.

Reese was six feet of pure male muscle with deep brown eyes and thick brown hair. Wildness and fury lit his eyes.

She caught her breath, heat rushing through her head until her ears rang. "You have to keep it together," she whispered. She'd yell at him again later. Right now, he had to find her sister. If the FBI discovered he'd been dating Loretta, they might take him off the case. Anya grabbed his arm. "It's okay. We'll find her, Reese."

The door in the back of the room burst open, and a fifty-something agent with silver hair hustled inside. "We have another letter and photograph. Already dusted the envelope, paper, and picture for prints. Nothing."

Anya's legs gave way. Her mind numbed.

Reese grabbed her and pushed her into a chair, reaching for the stack. "Fuck. When?"

"Mailed yesterday," the agent said, stepping back.

Anya shook her head to clear her brain, leaning over to see her name and address scrawled across the front of the envelope. The FBI had issued a forwarding order for her mail after the first few notes. The familiar handwriting made her gag. "Oh God. Reese—"

"Hold on," he bit out, flipping the paper over. "We don't know she's dead."

A tear slid down Anya's face, feeling cold. "He sends me a letter after he kills them." This was the ninth letter.

Reese flattened the letter on the table.

Anya shifted to read it.

Dearest Anya,

Your sister tries to be you, but she can't. I'm so sorry, but she can't be you. I should've known...but I had to try. And she tempted me, wanting me to take her. It was almost a dare. Her hair isn't red like yours, not really. I haven't heard her scream yet. Truly, I don't want to hurt what is yours. I'll try not to.

XO
Me

"She's still alive," Reese said, his hands shaking.

Anya panted out air. "Yes." There was no alternative. Not really. She tried to stand taller as her knees trembled. More than ever, she wished for her dad. For that security.

A man in jeans and a dark sweater hustled in from one of the offices, a computer tablet in his hands. "The storm is too wild. Even if we took the birds up, we wouldn't be able to see anything or land, Reese. We have to wait."

"I'm not waiting." Reese grabbed a coat off a rack. "What's the nearest SWAT team to where we think she was kidnapped?"

"Spokane," a woman spoke up from one of the offices.

"Fine. Somebody is taking me via air. Get SWAT from Spokane to get their asses up there right now," Reese bellowed, motioning to several agents as he strode for the door.

Anya grabbed his arm. "I can't stay here. Please let me come."

He halted midstride and glanced down at her hand.

She released him. This was all her fault. She had to do something.

Reese's gaze darkened. "Whatever you're thinking, stop it. You are not responsible for any of this."

Tears filled her eyes. "Yes, I am. Loretta is involved because of me. It's my fault. I called her."

Reese shook his head. "Loretta always makes her own decisions, believe me. She got involved in the case because she wanted to be in the center and help you. You're sisters. That's what family does."

"I know," Anya said, clasping her hands together. "So I should help now, too."

"You have. Your insights into his mind have been invaluable."

"Yeah, but I haven't figured out his connection to me. Not yet." The guy wanted her for some reason.

"Might not be a real one. He could've just seen you on the street one day." Reese zipped up his jacket. "This isn't my first serial, Anya. They're all nuts."

"I need to help," she implored.

"How did you find out she was taken, anyway? Do we have a leak?" He scanned the room.

She winced. "A private detective who had been working with Loretta told me." Now wasn't the time to discuss Heath's problems or the fake marshals. Loretta was more important.

"Do you trust him?"

Trust Heath? The guy had people shooting at him, for pete's sake. Life was black and white, good or bad. The gray area didn't really exist for her. "I don't trust him, but I do think he's a good detective, based on what Loretta said about him."

Reese breathed out. "Give all of his information to one of the agents while I'm gone, and I'll follow up with him. I want to talk to anybody who has seen Loretta in the last month."

Anya blinked. "He's not the Copper Killer, Reese." While a few things about Heath didn't quite ring true, he'd seemed way too angry about the killer. Why she felt the need to defend him, she'd never know. "He might be helpful in finding my sister."

Reese frowned. "Give us his contact information so I can talk to him. Thanks." He turned for the door.

"Wait. Please. What if Loretta needs me?" Her voice had risen in the plea, but she didn't care.

He paused and then shook his head. "I'll call you with any update." His voice gentled. "I can't take you into a combat situation, Anya. Your sister will kill me if I do." His smile was halfhearted at best but did reveal a dimple in his left cheek.

Why hadn't she trained as a profiler or a police psychiatrist? The rules probably didn't allow for Reese to take a civilian. "Call the second you know anything, and I'll go through the files again." For the zillionth time. Maybe something new would leap out at her.

"Agent Dingman?" Reese called.

The woman from the side office approached, her hair a wild mass around her broad shoulders. She was about thirty and had sharp brown eyes. "Yes, Reese?"

"Make sure you get Anya's statement about the private detective." His gaze didn't leave Anya's. "Keep her here until we bring back her sister. You know, so Loretta doesn't stab us both to death."

Anya tried to give him a smile.

"I'll go get Loretta." He patted her shoulder and strode again for the door, quickly disappearing.

Dingman cleared her throat, showing stress lines at the sides of her mouth. "I just got here. Do you mind catching me up to speed?"

Anya swallowed. "Absolutely. Why don't you tell me what you know so far?" She moved toward the big table in the center of the room. Perhaps talking about the case again would make something stand out to her. It was a long shot, but she had to do something. Anything.

Dingman's eyes lit as she scanned the files on the table. "Okay. The Copper Killer kidnaps redheaded family members of folks involved in law enforcement. We've traced this guy's movements from women he has taken to where we've found the bodies." She turned and pointed to the far wall, where pictures of the victims had been taped up. The victims ranged in age from seventeen to thirty, all with reddish hair and all related to either a cop or a private detective.

Anya's chest ached at seeing a picture of Loretta taped up there. "Right," she murmured quietly. A lump settled into her stomach. She had her own set of pictures and notes at her apartment. She turned back toward a map on the table. "Based on the timeline, we think he's still in Idaho or maybe Washington State. He seems to like the Northwest."

Dingman nodded.

"Do you know my sister?" Anya asked quietly.

Dingman's face fell. "Yeah, I do. We both usually work out of the DC office, but Loretta travels for cases a lot."

Yeah. The second Anya had called, Loretta had headed to Snowville and joined the serial killer task force there. "So you were brought in to crunch data now that she's been taken," Anya asked, her throat going dry.

"I volunteered. I look at the data and try to find patterns. I also read the notes from the behavioral science experts from the FBI."

Anya frowned. "The profilers?"

Dingman's lips twitched. "They don't like being called that, believe it or not."

"I've already read their files. Did you learn anything?" Anya studied the map with carefully marked locations of abductions.

"This guy has a serious problem with both authority figures and redheads." Dingman shrugged. "Maybe his mother was a crazy redhead who abused him, and his father was a cop who beat him or didn't care. It seems like the profiles are kind of obvious, if you ask me. Unless they're wrong."

Anya breathed out. "That's what I found as well. My dad was a cop—the best. We've factored that into the profile since the killer has focused on me."

Dingman studied her. "His fascination with you is interesting, but tracing your past, we've found nothing." She opened a file that held copies of the letters the killer had sent to her. "It does seem as if he knows you."

Anya shivered. "Maybe. There's nothing specific to me or my past in any of the eight letters, so it could be he saw me and became fixated. Or perhaps he found me on the Internet on the college website." Many serial killers created connections where there were none. "I shouldn't have called her."

Dingman patted her arm. "Of course you called your sister when a serial killer started sending you letters. Who wouldn't?"

"Yeah, but Loretta wasn't on this case." Anya swallowed, her throat feeling like she'd swallowed glass. "We need to find this guy." Before he killed her sister.

"Yeah." Dingman shoved curly black hair away from her face. "One of the profilers thinks the killer might have a partner, just based on timelines and how quickly he moves. He's also able to subdue some trained women pretty easily."

"Like Loretta." Tears pricked the backs of Anya's eyes.

"Right. So maybe he has help?"

That didn't fit with Anya's profile. Her phone buzzed in her pocket, and she yanked it out to press to her ear. "Reese?" she asked, her adrenaline spiking.

Quiet fizzed across the line for a moment. "Who is Reese?" came next.

Anya's heart sank. "Excuse me," she whispered to Agent Dingman before hurrying into the smallest conference room for privacy and shutting the door. The instant quiet surrounded her, and she put her back to the brick wall. "I asked you not to call me, Carl." Her voice shook and she quickly calmed it.

"Where are you?" he asked, ignoring her words.

"None of your business," she all but snarled. "We're over, we're done, and you need to leave me alone before I file a complaint against you."

Carl snorted. "You already had your badass sister come and threaten me. Isn't that enough?"

Anya swallowed several times. "Loretta visited you? When?" She dug her nails into the phone.

"Put a gun in my face and told me she'd blow my head off if I came near you again, which is both a battery and an assault, you know. I'm thinking seriously about lodging a complaint with the police. Agents can't go off half-cocked like that."

He was such a weasel. "When?" Anya snapped. She'd had no idea Loretta had tracked Carl down. "When did you see her, damn it?"

"Saturday night. Why?"

Loretta had disappeared on Monday, and Anya had seen her Sunday night. So Carl the asshat hadn't hurt Loretta. "Did you see anybody following her? Any odd vehicles or people around?" Anya gripped the phone tighter.

"No. Why? What does that have to do with anything?" Carl hissed.

Anya drew in a deep breath. The FBI had kept Loretta's kidnapping out of the news. It was doubtful Carl knew anything, but she'd give the FBI the information anyway so they could question Carl. "Nothing. Just stop calling me." The last time he'd called, she'd gotten upset and cried all over Loretta. So her big sister had apparently visited southern Washington in her spare time. Every bone in Anya's body began to ache.

"Listen, Anya." His voice turned low and soothing. "You and I dated for months, and I made one little mistake. I said I'm sorry, and you need to let me make things up to you."

She bit her lip. "Not a chance."

"It was once. Cathryn came on to me," he cajoled.

Anya shook her head, her stomach hurting. How had she ended up in a situation with such an asshole? To think she'd wondered, even once, if they could make a go of it. "You don't know me, Carl. One mistake like that is all you get."

He was silent for a moment. "Please."

She dropped her chin to her aching chest. "Sorry, pal." The curt words actually sounded like Loretta, and Anya stood straighter. She knocked her head gently against the wall. "No. For the final time, no."

A ruckus set up in the main room. "I have to go. Don't call me again." She clicked off and yanked open the door, rushing inside. "Is there any news?" she asked.

Dingman stared at the photographs of the murdered victims. "Yeah. Reese called in and he's about thirty minutes out from some abandoned barn in the middle of nowhere. It's the only structure anywhere near the town where we think Loretta was taken." Dingman didn't turn around. "He'll call as soon as the helicopter touches down."

"Do you think we've found the place?" Anya whispered.

Dingman turned and looked over her shoulder. Her face remained calm, but her eyes sizzled. "I really do."

CHAPTER
5

Cold trickled down Heath's back. Pain pounded through his head, and he winced as he opened his eyes, blowing hay out of the way. He was flat on the barn floor, and his head pulsed like his skull had met the metal end of a hammer. The concrete beneath him felt like a solid block of ice. He uncurled his fingers inside his gloves, his bones aching. "Loretta?" he croaked.

The storm bellowed outside, and the worn barn slats clacked against each other.

He lifted his head and fought nausea, shoving up from the rough concrete to find her. Ah shit. She lay on her back, head turned to the side. A coarse burlap sack covered her from thighs to upper chest, stained with blood. He crawled over to her, his movements jerky. "Agent Jackson?" he whispered, moving to her other side and smoothing the hair back from her face.

His breathing stopped when his vision cleared and he could actually see her.

Her pretty brown eyes were glassy in death.

God. She was dead. He touched her cheek, and the skin felt unreal. Not alive. Just there.

That quickly, he flashed back to another dead woman covered in blood. His mother's startling hazel eyes had also been glassy, and the smell of her blood still haunted his nightmares. Why did they always die and keep their eyes open? Were they looking for something? Somebody to save them?

He was too late again.

"Fuck, I'm sorry." His chest contracted as if he'd been kicked by a horse. Every muscle in his body tightened to the point of pain. He levered up onto his knees and reached out to close her eyes, his hand shaking. "Go somewhere nice, Loretta," he whispered.

His entire body shuddered. While he didn't know how to pray, he could offer silence. The floor chilled his knees, and a sense of urgency slammed into him. Outside, the wind whistled angrily, but inside, death kept silent.

He had to get out of there. His faculties returned, and he quickly looked around the otherwise empty room. Whoever had hit him had taken off.

He swallowed, and dots swam across his vision.

While he already knew the answer, he needed to double-check. Gently, with his hand shaking, he tugged down the burlap sack enough to read the letters M-I-N-E carved into her upper chest.

Fucking Copper Killer.

Rage ripped through Heath so quickly his ears heated. He sucked in air to calm himself, wavering slightly.

Reaching out, he smoothed the burlap back into place and fought the urge to wipe the blood off her temple. The killer liked to knock his victims out with a hit to the temple and then revive them. Closer scrutiny proved Loretta had likely been strangled to death. Heath didn't want to know more than that and moved away from the body to stagger to his feet.

Tears pricked his eyes, and he rapidly wiped them away. Failure settled in his stomach and swelled like a sponge until it filled him. The woman had been dead for at least a day, and he hadn't been even re-motely close to rescuing her. The idea of the strong and proud agent being reduced to a naked woman in burlap made him want to puke. Bile rose in his throat, and he ruthlessly swallowed it down. How frightened she must've been.

Even now, he could hear his mother pleading for mercy from the asshole beating her to death so many years ago. Heath had tried to save her and had caught a backhand to the face, a slam into the oven door, and then unconsciousness.

There was no mercy when monsters harmed women.

He gagged. Here and now. He had to focus on the here and now...and remember his mother later.

Cases involving women usually took him back to the night his mother died, but not like this. Not like razor-sharp claws ripping into his chest to slash at his heart. He tore off a glove to wipe his cheek.

The blood brother scar across his palm caught his eye. Family. Brothers. He had to call his brothers. He reached for the phone in his back pocket to find nothing. Damn it. A quick glance around showed the killer had taken not only Heath's phone but his gun, too. Neither could be traced to him, but the idea burned anger through him. He felt his other pocket. Ah hell. His wallet with the real picture but fake ID was also gone.

He shivered. It was freezing in the barn. His gaze went once again to the silent victim.

Cold. The woman on the ground was so cold. He didn't give a shit that she was dead and wouldn't feel the chill. She needed to be covered up. To be protected, even though he'd been too late. He yanked his glove back into place.

A side door he hadn't noticed burst open, and he dropped into a fighting stance.

"Heath?" Denver asked, the storm swirling in with him. Snow covered his black hair, and his hard face was set in stone. His thick boots clomped across the concrete.

Heath blinked twice at his brother and straightened. The chill took over his bones. "She's dead," he whispered, his voice hoarse.

Denver swallowed, surveyed the area, and finally walked toward the deceased agent to look down. His scruff-covered jaw tightened, and his bloodshot eyes widened. "Oh."

"Yeah." Heath's vision blurred again.

Denver glanced at Heath's hands. "Good. Gloves." Then he leaned to the side, frowning. "Holy shit." Rushing forward, he grabbed Heath's head and tugged, scrutinizing his temple. "How bad?"

Agony lanced through Heath's skull. "Not too bad. Minor concussion."

"Knocked out?" Denver leaned in to study the wound above Heath's right ear.

"Yeah. Not sure for how long." The room took on a surreal glow, and Heath slowly went numb. No more pain—no more cold. He moved on autopilot and tugged his gloves up his wrists.

Denver released him. "Somebody actually got the drop on you? I thought that was impossible. Who is this guy?" Snow clung to his black leather jacket and faded jeans. The blue in his eyes overtook the gold flecks, darkening with concern. "Did you lose any blood?"

Heath looked toward where he'd fallen. Blood was everywhere, but it was probably all Loretta's. "Not sure."

"Not good." Denver rushed over and kicked hay out of the way, scowling as he studied the barn floor. "Don't see any."

Yeah, but one drop would get them screwed. "We have to cover her up," Heath said, his chest compressing. He hadn't saved her. The woman deserved protection. Safety. Warmth.

Denver's mouth gaped for a second, and he slowly focused on Heath. "No."

"Yes." Heath looked frantically around. There had to be a horse blanket somewhere. He moved toward one of the three stalls on the north wall.

Denver intercepted him with a hand against his chest. "We need to go, brother. Now."

"No." Something rose in Heath, something dark and fluid. "We're covering her up. Period." He couldn't just leave her on the floor like that. Not cold and alone. Damaged. Destroyed.

"No." Denver's voice strengthened, and he leaned into Heath's face until their noses were inches apart. "The police are coming, and we have to get the hell out of here."

Heath caught his breath and tried to think through the rage. Rioting thoughts filled his mind, all with violence. The only thought he could grasp was that he needed to help Loretta. To protect her even though it was too late. He shoved Denver out of the way and strode toward the tack room. Had there been a blanket in the far corner?

Denver wasn't the type to attack a brother, ever, so Heath didn't see him coming. Within seconds, Denver had him in a headlock and was dragging him toward the side door.

"What the fuck?" Heath wheezed, digging his gloved fingers into Denver's rock-solid forearm.

"Gotta go." Denver's breath brushed Heath's hair.

Heath struggled, scattering hay in every direction. He never would've thought Denver would grab him from behind, or he wouldn't have turned his back. "Let go."

"Nope." Denver continued relentlessly dragging Heath toward the door, his arm exerting enough pressure to restrict breathing.

Heath struck back and hit Denver in the thigh. Hard.

Denver grunted, stumbled, and kept on moving. "Need you to settle back into yourself. The smooth and in-control Heath. Need him now."

At well over six feet tall and muscled, they were evenly matched in a fight. But a headlock was a fucking headlock. Heath tried to get enough leverage to dig in his boots and toss Denver over his head, but Den was just as well trained as Heath and kept him off balance. They reached the door, and Denver flung them both outside into the storm. With a twist, he shoved Heath away from the barn.

Wind howled through the trees around them. The storm was getting worse. Fire roared inside Heath's chest even as freezing snow slapped his face. He dropped his chin and charged.

"Stop." Denver held up one hand. "We can't disturb the scene if we're gonna catch this guy."

The scene. Loretta was just part of the scene. Heath kept moving toward his brother, his hands clenching. She was more than that. She was so much more than that, and the killer had taken that away. Had taken her away.

"She's gone, man. Not here any longer." Denver always could read his mind somehow. "Dead and gone. There's nobody left here to save. Except us." He coughed out. "We have to get out of here if we're going to find this guy. And protect Ryker."

Heath blinked. The haze across his vision wavered. Police were on their way. If he and Denver got caught by them, they were screwed. He sucked in frozen air. It was too late for Loretta, and he'd deal with that failure later. Right now he had to get his brother to safety. It was Heath's fault Denver was out in the open like this. "You're right."

Denver's face cleared. He hunched in his coat and headed down the road and through inches of new snow. "I parked close."

Heath leaned into the piercing wind and followed his brother into the snow-filled dusk, concentrating to keep his balance on the ice. The smell of blood stayed with him somehow. Coppery and intrusive.

They reached a stand of fir trees, and Denver shoved branches aside to reveal an older Volvo. He slid into the driver's side. "Stole it."

Heath ran around the other side to jump in. "Move, Den." The

FBI couldn't be far behind. "We've been running for too long to get trapped now."

Denver ignited the engine, pulled around, and drove quickly down the barely there lane. He reached Heath's truck and let out a low whistle.

"Son of a bitch," Heath muttered, taking in the slashed tires. The killer had used precious moments to make sure Heath couldn't follow him. Thank goodness Denver had hidden his ride better than Heath had. "Keep going."

"Wiped down?" Denver asked, punching the gas pedal.

"Yeah." Thank goodness. "There's no way to trace it to us." Though he didn't like the thought of the FBI being distracted for even a second from Loretta's case, and they'd work hard to locate the owner of the truck. Good thing he'd stolen it, too.

Something buzzed, and Denver yanked a cell phone from his pocket. "Yeah?" He pressed the speaker button.

"The FBI is on the way. They should be there any second. Where are you?" Ryker asked, his voice low.

"Just leaving." Heath naturally spoke up so Denver wouldn't have to. "Almost off the property."

Denver fishtailed down the road and quickly corrected. "Sorry."

Ryker breathed out loudly. "Did you find Agent Jackson?"

Her name was like a punch to Heath's gut. He grunted. "Yeah. I was too late."

Ryker was silent for a moment. "I'm sorry."

"Me too." Heath stretched his neck to look out the window at the blustering storm. His body felt heavy. "We have to get out of here."

"Turn right at the end of the lane and not toward town," Ryker said. "Your only option is to head into the mountains."

Denver reached the end of the lane and slid right, corrected, and hit the gas.

Sirens sounded in the distance.

"Shit," Heath said, buckling his belt. "Buckle up, Den."

"No time." Denver leaned over the steering wheel and stared into the swirling white evening.

Heath unbuckled and leaned across his brother to grab the seat belt. He quickly strapped Denver in and then refastened his own belt. "Faster."

"The storm is too bad for additional air support," Ryker said evenly. "So keep going, be careful, and you'll actually end up in the northwest part of Washington State. Ditch the car and find something else as soon as you can."

Denver's knuckles turned white on the steering wheel. "Road might be closed."

Yeah. Mountain passes were rarely kept open during storm season. They'd have to risk it anyway. Heath wiped snow off his forehead and then planted a hand on the dash to balance himself. "Ry? See if you can trace my cell phone. The killer took it, my wallet with the fake ID but real picture—and my gun."

"Are you okay?" Ryker asked even as he started typing loud enough to be heard through the speaker.

"Fine. Little headache." Heath gingerly touched the lump above his right ear. Why hadn't the killer taken him out completely? Was the guy only into killing redheads? "Find it?"

"Yeah. It's back at the farm somewhere." Ryker fell silent. "Are your prints on it?"

Heath shook his head. "I'm not sure. They're on my gun for sure." He winced. Would the Copper Killer somehow use those? Probably. "I'm sorry, guys." He rubbed his aching eyes. What had he done? He'd rushed in and now had put his entire family at risk of exposure. The hollowness in his chest actually hurt.

He was the smooth and calm brother, and yet he was acting like an emotional jackass. His issues with female victims had to be kept under control or he'd hurt the few people in life who were his. "I'm so damn sorry."

"We'll figure it out," Ryker said. "Don't worry. Chances are the killer took the gun and left the burner phone somewhere to be found by the FBI. I know you. You regularly wipe down everything, and if you're wearing gloves, you're okay. We're okay."

Yet were they? Heath had been in such a rush to find Jackson, he wasn't sure. A sour taste filled his mouth, and he slowed his speech to regain control. "I don't know, Ry."

Denver increased the speed of the windshield wipers. "Worry about now."

"Agreed," Ryker said. "One catastrophe at a time. For now, you guys have to get through the mountain pass in this storm before the FBI is able to get birds in the air and conduct surveillance."

"Before they block the roads," Denver muttered quietly.

Heath stiffened. "You're right." Once the FBI found the agent's body, they'd put up roadblocks in every direction. "Hurry, Denver. We have to get out of here."

CHAPTER
6

Anya stood in the snow, her black skirt covering her boots, her gaze on the casket slowly being lowered into the ground. She'd cried for five days straight, and she felt empty. Her sister, the strong and vibrant FBI agent, was dead. Tears filled Anya's eyes, but she couldn't look away from the smooth, polished wood.

Dead and gone—found on a barn floor.

Why had Anya called Loretta for help? She could've just called the closest FBI office, which happened to be in Snowville and had been already working on the case. She pressed a hand to her chest; it felt like somebody had punched her.

The FBI had found Loretta dead on the floor of the barn in Idaho. The killer had left her there in the cold.

Loretta was gone.

The sister she'd only just begun to really know. The woman who'd dropped everything, relocated to Snowville, and put herself on a dangerous serial killer case just to protect a sister she talked to only a few times a year. The big sister Anya had needed and had already admired so much. The only family she'd had left in the world.

Dead.

The priest's voice droned on, and several people cried silently, so silently around her. The agents were quiet in their pain.

She drifted, her mind numb and sliding back three months to
when she'd opened her door to a sharp knock right after dawn.

*"Loretta," she said, stepping back and trying to wake up. "What in
the world are you doing here?"*

*"Took a night flight from DC." Loretta shoved curly brown hair
away from her face and pushed inside, a small bag over her shoulder.
Her chocolate brown eyes took in the entire apartment in seconds.*

*Anya looked into the hallway and nodded at the uniformed police
officer who had shown up right after she'd called her sister. He nodded back.*

"Where's your luggage?" Anya asked.

"Here." Loretta dumped the small bag. "I travel light."

*"Oh. Okay." Anya shook her head and blinked several times.
"What are you doing here?"*

*Loretta paused. "You're in trouble. We're sisters." Then she'd en-
folded Anya in a warm hug. "I promise I'll take care of it, An. I
promise."*

*Safety surrounded her. She hugged her sister back, feeling the
sense of family once again. "I'm so glad you're here," she whispered,
drawing Loretta farther into the apartment. "Are you hungry?"*

*Loretta released her. "Starving. Let's eat, and I'll take a look at
those pictures. The Snowville team will be here in about an hour,
and then I'm thinking we move there for a bit. We can work this case
together." She shrugged, shifting her feet. "I thought we could use a
few minutes together first."*

Tears pricked Anya's eyes. "It's so good to see you."

Loretta grinned. "You too. Now. Do you have ice cream?"

"For breakfast?" Anya choked out.

*"Sure. If you cook like our mom did, I want something from a
carton."*

Anya shook her head, her gaze catching on Loretta's gun at her hip. Her sister was a badass. "I can cook. I hope you really are hungry." She headed for the kitchen. "What's new?"

"Besides finding out a serial killer has focused on my baby sister?" Loretta asked, stretching her neck.

Anya jolted. "Funny. Very. How's work?" She pulled out a couple of pots.

"Great."

Anya turned to open the fridge. "Are you dating anybody?"

"Yep. Long distance…but maybe not so much now. You'll meet him soon." Loretta moved toward the table. "You?"

"No. Definitely no." Anya paused as Loretta lifted her eyebrows. "Long story. I'll tell you over breakfast."

"Do I have to kill anybody?" Loretta asked, seeming to be only partially joking.

Anya snorted, feeling the bond she'd always remembered settling right back into place. "That might be something to discuss." She laughed.

A sneeze brought Anya back to the freezing graveyard and stark reality.

Her heart hurt so deeply inside her chest. She couldn't rub the pain away. Even her temples ached. Anya's parents were both gone, and she was tired of being alone. For a brief time with Loretta, she hadn't been.

She wavered, and Reese set a hand on her shoulder.

"You're doing well," he murmured, his normally bronze face pale. His intelligent eyes scanned the scores of agents, DC cops, and civilians all standing in the cold to say good-bye to Loretta. "I'm so sorry, Anya."

"So am I." She patted his hand. Reese had found Loretta dead and had had an angry hollowness in his eyes ever since. The FBI coroner had performed an autopsy, and now Loretta was being laid to rest in a peaceful cemetery outside Washington, DC, where she'd lived.

Anya looked around at the multitude of mourners. "Loretta was loved," she said. The pain in her chest lessened a little.

"Yes, she was," Reese said quietly. The casket finished lowering, and he turned toward her. "You need to return to protective custody until we find this guy. I owe Loretta that much."

Not a chance. There was one good opportunity to catch this guy, and Anya was the key. He would not be allowed to continue. She purposefully let fury shove away the agony.

For now, she had a mission. Everything she'd learned, everything she truly knew about criminal psychology, told her exactly what to do. She dug deep for resolve and said a quick prayer for her sister to watch over her. She looked at the news vans and reporters being held back by a wide rope and several police officers. They seemed too far away across the icy snow. Could she get there before Reese stopped her? "How did they find out about Loretta's death?"

Reese glanced over her shoulder. "I don't know. It's big news. Death of an FBI agent at the hands of a serial killer."

The words sliced like a knife. Anya brushed snow off her coat and straightened her spine. "The service was beautiful." The priest had been eloquent and had known Loretta well. Anya hadn't even known her sister was Catholic. She focused on Reese, whose brown eyes were swirling with emotion. "Does anybody else know you were together?" she whispered. She'd known the second Loretta had introduced her to the man.

He concentrated on her. "No. It's against Bureau rules, so we weren't together." His voice sounded clipped and almost robotic.

Anya sighed. "I'm glad you guys broke the rules."

He blinked. "Why?"

"Because I'd like to think she found love during her life. That she'd found somebody." Anya clasped her glove-covered hands together.

Reese lifted his head. "I wanted to go public, but she was a stickler for the rules." He smiled a sad smile. "I actually liked that about her." The agent's pain was almost palpable and barely drowned out the tension emanating from the many other FBI personnel. They'd lost one of their own, in the most heinous scenario possible. Many were pale, most had set jaws and determined eyes. They were going to find this asshole. The words weren't said, but they flowed throughout the group.

Anya swallowed and tried to find comfort in the fact that these people would stop at nothing to avenge her sister. But it wasn't good enough. Her hands shook and her lungs heated. Standing on the sidelines wasn't enough. *She* would find the asshole.

He wanted to include her in his psycho plan? Fine. She was smart and trained. He'd regret it. He'd regret everything.

A light snow began to fall, and a shiver wound down her back. The hair at the nape of her neck stood up, and her body tensed. Instinctively. She looked around slowly, trying to find movement in the dark shadows hovering around trees and headstones.

Nothing.

Yet she *felt* something. Eyes on her.

She hugged her coat tighter around her torso and kept searching. Who was watching her?

A serial killer was out there…focused on her. Was he close? Did he want to see Loretta's funeral? Bile rose in Anya's throat. Before she could completely panic, a figure stepped away from a stand of snow-covered pine trees.

Heath Jones.

She drew in a sharp breath and took him in. Tall and broad, he stood in a battered leather jacket with long jean-clad legs encased in thick motorcycle boots. Aviator sunglasses protected his eyes from the meager sun, and snow fell unchecked onto his dark hair. A dark scruff covered his hard-cut jaw, and even though those odd eyes were covered, she could feel his gaze on her.

Tingles exploded unexpectedly in her abdomen. Her breath heated and quickened, the feeling not unpleasant but definitely a warning of some sort. Every inch of her wanted to run for him, to seek a risky shelter with him. What was wrong with her?

He seemed to be the opposite of her father, and yet…

As if acknowledging that she'd seen him, he raised a hand and then stepped back into the shadows.

Within a second, she couldn't tell where he was.

Why had he wanted her to know he was there? She'd already given Reese Heath's information, so it was too late to stop her there. Although she hadn't told Reese about the kidnapping or the fake marshals. The detail on her had been light before, and if she told him, they'd definitely increase their forces. Of course, the light detail was how she'd ended up with the fake marshals briefly. They didn't have anything to do with Loretta's case, and that was all that mattered right now. So why was Heath there? The man had seemed to have a healthy respect for Loretta, so perhaps he attended just to pay respects.

Yet why stay in the shadows and away from the FBI?

There was no doubt in Anya's mind that Heath Jones had a plethora of secrets, but that was his problem, not hers. In fact, couldn't she use that? A man like Heath, one so definitely dangerous and mysterious, would be a huge insult and challenge to the serial killer. If she focused her attention on Heath, wouldn't the killer take it as an insult? That she'd chosen Heath instead of him? A plan formed in her mind so quickly she nearly stopped breathing. If she had to use Heath's secrecy and masculinity to avenge her sister, she would. Her vision narrowed to a tunnel, and she straightened her shoulders.

She patted Reese's hand. "Excuse me for a moment."

He glanced down and then was distracted when two agents approached him with what sounded like meager updates.

With another hard look into the shadows, she turned on her high-heeled boot and maneuvered very carefully through the snow to the roped-off area. The reporters scrambled toward her along with several camera operators.

"Anya," she heard Reese call from behind her.

She gave the cameras a sad smile, her mind rapidly turning over the facts of the profile she'd created on the killer. Oh, she could get into his head. Make him show himself. "I'm Anya Best, and Special Agent Loretta Jackson was my older sister. She was brave and proud, and she served her country with passion and dedication." Tears pricked Anya's eyes, and she blinked them back.

Deliberately, she flicked her red hair over her shoulder to bring attention to the bright color. Then she leaned toward the closest camera. "Stop courting me, asshole. I'm tired of your game and am getting bored. In fact, I'm recently engaged to a real man, unlike you. My fiancé is Heath Jones of Lost Bastards Investigative Services out of Snowville in Washington State. You don't like anyone in law enforcement, right? I'm *marrying* a guy who chases down jerks like you." The guy preferred his victims to have living relatives in the law enforcement arena. He probably got off on the pain he caused family members.

"Snowville?" one of the reporters yelled.

"Yes." The location was perfect, considering the Copper Killer Task Force was actually operating out of Snowville. Heath had said he was looking to relocate to the Pacific Northwest, right? Snowville could be the next office site for him. Whether he liked it or not.

The reporters started shouting at once, asking questions about the investigation.

She held up a hand and they went silent. "I think the Copper Killer is a stupid, weak, pathetic name that actually fits you, dickhead. I'm too much for you, which is exactly why you've never made a move on me." She lowered her chin and let her eyes blaze, defying everything the killer thought she was. "You can't get me. I want you to understand, we know what a coward you are, and we'll get you. *I'll* get you." Then she smiled and drove in the final nail, even as her stomach rolled over. "I don't want you. Never did and never will. In fact, I can't even remember when we first met. If we even have met." The ultimate insult, considering the man was obsessed with her.

Without another word, she turned on her heel and headed back to Reese.

His face was pale, his mouth pinched, his eyes swirling with shock. "What in the world did you just do?"

She blinked and clenched her fingers into fists. "I set myself up as bait for the asshole—right in your hometown, no less." In addition to turning the psycho's attention onto Heath, which he wouldn't like. The killer would have no choice but to make a move on her instead of some other helpless victim. It was time to set a trap. "Now do your job and find this guy."

CHAPTER
7

Even from a distance, Anya could feel fury coming from the stand of trees beyond the many gravestones. She had to be imagining that, right? No way could Heath be angry enough that she could feel it. She took several deep breaths and tried to convince herself.

Reese grabbed her arm. "You're crazy. Seriously crazy."

She gently extricated herself. "No. This guy is fixated on me, and it's time to take him down." Her sister had been brave, and she could be, too. The killer wouldn't get the chance to kill another woman. It was time to end this.

For Loretta.

"You're going back into custody right now." Reese motioned her toward the row of cars.

"No." She planted her feet. "Loretta had the right idea."

"Loretta was abused and strangled," Reese burst out, his handsome face blooming red. "She was trained and dangerous, and this guy still got her."

Anya's knees wobbled. The images cut into her sharper than any blade. "I know." But she had one shot to help find her sister's killer, and she was taking it. "I respectfully decline your offer of custody."

Reese shut his eyes as if trying to keep his temper fully in check. Mourners moved around them toward the cars. "Listen. I get it. I really do. But if I let anything happen to you, Loretta will haunt me till I die. So work with me. And by the way, you suddenly have a fiancé?"

She kept her face calm. "Heath and I had a whirlwind romance, and he proposed quickly, but it'll stick. We'll stick." She lied through chilled lips. "Heath is a detective, so we definitely fit the profile." Part of the killer's motivation was the pain he inflicted on the living…not just the redheaded women. The family members of his kills were his victims, too. She'd used every bit of her education to work up the profile on him. "The killer will think I just betrayed him in his bizarre fantasy by getting engaged to another man. It'll infuriate him."

"You're crazy," Reese muttered.

"Yeah, but time is short. The killer is probably looking for his next victim now." The guy waited anywhere between one and five weeks before striking again.

Reese shook his head. "The killer also goes after cops now. Maybe he has his sights on another cop."

"Maybe, so let's get busy." The chill attacked her, and she shuddered. "I'm not being stupid here. Heath really is a private detective, and I've hired his firm to help with this. They were working with Loretta, so I'll keep them on retainer in a protection detail while this is going on." Was it called a protection detail? She'd seen that on television somewhere.

Reese shook his head. "I don't think so."

"I'm not giving you a choice." She was fairly certain the FBI couldn't force her to remain in custody since she was neither a witness nor a suspect. "You know I'm the best bet to find this guy."

"Only because you just set yourself up on every damn news channel," he snapped.

"He started it." God, what had she done? For the first time in her life she was taking a huge chance to the point of being reckless…but she wasn't stupid. "This is our only way of getting this guy, and you know it." When she did get him, she'd make him pay.

Two agents motioned for Reese, one of them talking rapidly on the phone. Reese furiously waved Agent Dingman over. "She doesn't go anywhere."

Dingman nodded and clutched her worn wool coat around her body.

Anya dipped her chin at the agent and moved toward the gaping hole in the ground. "I just want a moment," she said.

The woman's eyes softened. "I'll be right over here. Take your time."

Anya stepped lightly over the ice to reach her sister's casket. "I'm sorry I got you involved with this," she whispered, tears finally flowing freely. "You were everything strong and good in the world, just like my dad. I love you, big sister." How had this happened? How could Loretta really be dead? A sob rolled from Anya, and she bit her lip.

"Anya?"

She turned suddenly and looked up to see her ex. "Carl? What are you doing here?"

He brushed snow from his sandy blond hair. "I saw the news and came right away." He gingerly grasped her arm. "I'm so sorry for your loss."

Anya's mouth dropped open and then shut quickly. She shook her head at Dingman's questioning look. "It's okay," she mouthed.

Dingman lifted an eyebrow but remained in place.

Anya kept her face placid as fury flowed through her veins. How dare he just show up? "It's nice you came, but I don't want you here," she said under her breath. "There are FBI agents everywhere, and if I throw a fuss, they'll be on you in a second."

Carl shook his head, standing straighter in his gray suit with a tailored overcoat. His blue eyes sizzled through the storm. "Listen, I know you're angry, and I deserve that. But your sister has died, and I'm here to be with you. We dated for months, sweetheart."

Yeah, they had. She looked up at his smooth shaven face, one she'd once thought was so handsome, and just felt sorrow for the time she'd wasted. "I'm not the nice person you thought I was, so let's leave it at that. I'm happy to forgive you for cheating on me, but we're over." There weren't many other ways to say those words. Plus, considering she now very publicly had a fiancé, Carl was only going to get in the way.

He tightened his hold until she had to bite back a wince from the pain. "Let go of me," she hissed through gritted teeth.

His expression remained concerned, but he leaned in until his face was an inch from hers. "I'm in trouble, and I need your help." Desperation darkened his eyes.

She frowned. "Trouble?"

"Yeah. Cathryn has filed a complaint with the dean."

"Oh." Anya pursed her lips, her attention already moving back to the serial killer case. "It's a mistake to sleep with a student, Carl."

"One mistake," he almost whined.

What a jackass. She had to keep him from causing a scene. Agents and reporters were everywhere.

She shook her head. "You made your bed, buddy."

"Please, just tell the dean that she's lying." He leaned in, his gaze intense.

"Excuse me." Without warning, a rough hand ripped Carl's grip away and then a muscled body stepped between them.

She swallowed. "Heath?" she whispered. Where had he come from? How had he moved so quickly? Glancing around, she took in several FBI agents suddenly looking her way. Oh man, she had to control this. She grasped Heath's arm and tugged him to her side while plastering on a small smile. "Everyone is looking."

Heath slid an arm around her shoulders and faced Carl directly, although Heath had at least four inches on the professor. "You touch her again and you lose a hand." His voice was low and rough while a tension all but rolled off him that stopped Anya's breath completely.

Carl looked down at Anya, his face turning red. "Who the hell is this guy?"

"I'd like an answer to that question as well." Reese was immediately there, with Dingman right behind him. "Who are you people?"

Anya tried to answer, to defuse the situation, but Carl talked quickly. "I'm Professor Carl Sparks, and I was dating Anya until very recently."

"I see." Reese stepped even closer. "I'm glad you're here. We've been meaning to discuss Special Agent Jackson's visit to you."

Carl paled.

Anya coughed. Apparently Loretta had informed Reese but not her about the little visit. God, she missed her sister.

Reese turned on Heath. "And you?"

Anya swallowed and tried unsuccessfully to step free of Heath's protective hold. "Well, he's, ah…"

Heath smiled, showing none of the tension he was communicating to Anya with his body. "I'm Heath Jones. Anya's fiancé."

* * *

Heath ignored the itch between his shoulder blades that warned of imminent trouble—he'd already jumped into the boiling pot of water. He'd avoided the law for more than fifteen years, and now here he was, surrounded by FBI agents.

All because one tiny redhead had looked frightened for a moment.

He'd seen the guy grab her, and he'd noticed the tightening around her eyes. At that point, the confrontation had become inevitable. For goodness' sake, he was the calm brother. Ryker and Denver would be pacing with concern. Especially if they had just watched the train wreck Anya had created on the news.

He'd deal with her next.

For now, the agent staring at him so directly needed to be defused. Heath forced his most charming smile. "You must be Special Agent Frederick Reese. My Anya has told me all about you."

She stiffened slightly beneath his arm at the possessive tone, so he pulled her into his warmth for effect. The woman had brought him into this mess and could just play along. Plus, even through his jacket he could feel the chill from her coat. She needed a thicker coat. He held out his other hand for the agent. "It's very nice to meet you."

Frederick Reese had a strong hand and firm handshake. He held on a second too long, his gaze piercing and seeking. "I'd like to interview you about Loretta if you don't mind."

"Any time," Heath said smoothly. "We formed a friendship while exchanging information about this case during the last several months. I respected her greatly." Too bad Ryker wasn't dealing with this agent—he was the most cop-like of them. At least it wasn't Denver caught in this disaster. "She was a hell of an agent."

"She was," Reese said, emotion in his tone he tried to hide.

Ah. Was it personal? Either way, they had been partners. Heath lost his smile. "She seemed very dedicated, and I admired her upon meeting her."

Reese nodded. "Agreed. So you discussed the case?"

Heath slid his hand down Anya's arm, pushing snow off her soft coat. "Yes, and we sort of bonded over rotten coffee. Her mind was amazing. I was hired by the family of the fourth victim to find her, and I crossed paths with Special Agent Jackson. She was open-minded enough to work with a private detective, and she was deter-

mined to find the killer. To bring him to justice. She was my friend."
The words were true, and his gut ached. She should still be alive.

Reese's face cleared. "She was a good friend to many."

Had the guy been afraid he and Loretta had gotten busy? Heath
turned his head to press a kiss to Anya's temple to dispel any such fear.

Anya sucked in air.

Heath fought an inappropriate grin at her discomfort. She had no
clue what she'd unleashed.

The blond frowned. "I'm Carl. Up until recently, Anya and I were
dating."

Heath gave the man his best *You're about to get your ass kicked* look
and then smiled. "Anya and I dated last year and broke up. My fault.
I wasn't ready for a commitment, realized my mistake, and have been
working hard to win her back."

"You cheated on me?" Carl hissed.

The FBI agent watched the exchange with sharp eyes.

"No," Anya said, pressing her hand to Heath's chest. "Heath and I
have been talking only. After I discovered you in bed with a student,
he, ah, found me and we decided we belong together."

What? Heath burst out with a short laugh and then remembered
he should probably already know about the situation, considering he
was her fiancé. "I can't believe you were stupid enough to cheat on a
woman like this."

Anya smiled up at him.

Carl took a step toward her, and Heath reacted, instantly setting
the redhead behind him. "Put your hands on *me*, asshole. Try it."

The agent moved between them, facing Heath. "I'd like to interview you tomorrow in my office. Where are you staying tonight?"

"The Morningstar," Heath said smoothly. Well, he was now.

"Excellent. Be at FBI headquarters at nine in the morning. Are you
capable of keeping Anya safe for the night?" Reese asked.

"I can keep myself safe." Anya grabbed Heath's coat from behind.

Heath kept the agent's gaze. "Yes. She'll be safe tonight."

"Good. We'll talk long term tomorrow if I don't arrest you," the agent said.

Anya moved to stand at Heath's side. "Why would you arrest him?"

"We'll see." Reese's gaze encompassed them all.

"When are you returning to Snowville?" Anya asked.

Reese shook his head. "Shortly." He gave Heath a hard look. "It's a bit of a coincidence that you just opened up an office there. You need to be interviewed, Mr. Jones, and then I want you to stay out of my way. Leave the case to the FBI."

Heath smiled. "No problem."

Reese pivoted. "Mr. Sparks? I think I'll interview you tonight. Morons who sleep with students don't get leeway with me." He pierced Carl with a hard stare. "I already know the story, and you're lucky the student was of age."

Anya shoved forward. "Reese, really. He's not—"

A snarl erupted from Heath's mouth, and the woman fell silent. He turned on her, keeping his hands to himself. "Don't even think of helping this jerk out." Any man who'd caused her pain should be dropped to the bottom of a very deep well.

She narrowed her gaze.

Ah hell. They needed to get a couple of things straight and right now.

The agent paused. "Anya? You're free to come with me tonight. I'll keep you safe." He turned a glare on Heath.

Heath shook his head. "I'm a total dick, but I'd never physically harm a woman." He paused. "Or emotionally or psychologically. Never."

The agent leaned in. "See that you don't."

Heath grinned. "You're a decent guy, Reese."

The man's expression didn't waver.

Anya partially moved in front of Heath, and he let her since her ex was still behind the agent and couldn't reach for her. "It's okay, Reese. I'm fine, and I'll accompany Heath to the FBI offices tomorrow. I hope we can work together in Snowville, or at the very least I hope you keep me informed. Get some sleep tonight." She placed what appeared to be a gentle hand on the agent's forearm.

Reese's nostrils flared and he lowered his voice. "You know we'll work together. Your insight and profile has been invaluable. We need to go through *all* of your files again."

"Definitely," Anya said.

Heath drew in air. Unable to stop himself, he lifted her thick hair away from her collar and wiped off the snow before it could slide beneath her coat—acting like a fiancé. He'd wanted to touch her hair since the first time he'd met her, and she'd given him very public permission to do just that. "Let's go, sweetheart."

She allowed him to turn her.

He took her hand and walked partially in front of her. She'd put herself into the line of fire with the news cameras. While the killer would never come at her head-on, Heath couldn't help but provide a shield.

Every instinct in his body flared alive. She was dangerous to him, and he knew it. Not only was she beautiful, she was fragile and so determined to find justice. He was more than aware of his trigger points, and she hit them all. Plus, the sensual tilt of her lips had provided more than one wild dream for him since he'd met her.

How fucked up was that?

He kept his hold gentle but firm, guiding her toward the SUV he'd left at the curb. Good thing he'd rented this one under the Lost Bastards account and not stolen it, considering Agent Frederick Reese was already copying down the license plate number. Without a word,

Heath helped her into the passenger side, then rounded the vehicle to slip in and start the engine.

Slowly, he pulled away from the curb.

Her scent of strawberries filled the interior and nearly made him groan. Even though the engagement was fake, there was something about having somebody—a woman—that appealed to him. This woman. This strong, smart, and savvy woman, who *so* did not trust him. What would it be like to have her to call his own? To earn her trust? His jeans tightened, and he started to recite basketball stats in his head.

Anya cleared her throat. "I'm staying at the hotel at the corner of First and Hanover."

"Put on your seat belt." He maneuvered out of the cemetery and turned toward Virginia.

She fumbled but did as he said. "Did you hear me?"

He turned then and took her in. Wide green eyes, rioting red hair, pale skin with faded bruises. Small and fragile...and she'd just challenged a deranged serial killer on national television. Anger and a desperate need to protect her rose hard and fast inside him. "Oh, I heard you, sweetheart. As my fiancée, you're not going anywhere by yourself until this guy is caught. Period."

CHAPTER
8

Anya stared at the male predator holding her gaze so directly. Okay. So she'd chosen the most dangerous guy she'd ever met to stand in as her fiancé—and one who would definitely anger the serial killer by just looking manly. Yeah, part of that had been self-preservation, and Loretta had trusted the guy. Yet Anya hadn't given him a choice, now, had she? "I'm sorry," she murmured.

One of his dark eyebrows rose.

Her eyes teared up, and she couldn't hold his gaze. She brushed snow off her legs to the floor, watching the white fall and melt almost instantly. "I just did what I thought I could to catch the guy who murdered my sister. Not once did I consider what it would mean to you." Guilt heated inside her as she realized she would've done it anyway. "I'm sorry."

"Jesus." He turned back to the snowy road outside the windshield. "Don't start being sweet now."

She looked at him again. In profile, his face was sharp angles and hard lines. "I'm not. It's just, I had an idea, and I ran with it. I've studied killers, and I think I know how this one thinks. He hurt my sister, Heath." Her voice broke. "I got her involved."

He turned toward her. "About that. What don't I know, Anya?"

She blinked.

"The things you said to him. About him courting you...What has the FBI kept out of the news?"

Heath was no dummy. Anya bit her lip. "The killer is focused on me and has been since the beginning. He sends me a letter after each kill."

"You've been his focus since the beginning?" Heath turned back to the road, his shoulders looking tight. Tension rolled through the vehicle. "So you called your sister?"

"Yes." Pain flushed through her, pricking every nerve. "I got her killed."

"No. A psycho killed her," Heath said, reaching out to press his hand over hers. "Not your fault, Anya."

Yet it was. "She was my sister, and I owe her. I can't sleep until we catch her killer."

"Agreed." His shoulders slowly relaxed beneath the worn leather jacket. "I have two brothers, and if anything happened to either one of them, I'd lose my fuckin' mind. There's nothing I wouldn't do to save them, and if I couldn't, nothing would stop me from seeking vengeance."

"Are these genetic brothers or the ones who probably have matching scars on their hands?" She hadn't been able to get his hand out of her head. That scar he'd shown her had provided insight into him, and she wanted more.

"Those two are blood brothers. But I do have a genetic one," he said, his voice thoughtful. "He's a good guy. Just met him."

There were more out there like him? He was being incredibly fair, to see her side and admit his own motivations in life. "Man, you guys hit the genetic jackpot."

He barked out a laugh. "Oh, darlin'. You have no idea."

What did that mean? "So you'll help me and pretend to be my fiancé?"

He tilted his head and blew out air. "I promise I'll hunt this guy down no matter how long it takes."

She stiffened and leaned back against the leather seat. "That wasn't an answer."

He looked her way again, his eyes a startling green and brown tinged with goldish flecks. "It was an answer—just not the one you wanted."

The snow thickened outside, lending a sense of intimacy to the vehicle. His natural masculine scent filled the cab, and her body softened. She studied his implacable face—where there was no softness. "If you want in on this case, you have to work with me. Also, do you know where I can get a gun?" She should've gotten one in the Pacific Northwest.

"No. How about we make a deal? I'll send you to an incredibly safe place for a while, and then I'll find this guy. I promise." Heath turned back to the icy road.

She sighed. "I'm not weak, Heath. I've been assisting the FBI with a profile, and I can get into this guy's mind."

He leaned his head back. "Why me?" he asked quietly.

She blinked. "Huh?"

"Why did you choose me as your fiancé? You had the agent and maybe even your ex to choose from. He's not in law enforcement, but as a professor, he is an authority figure. Does he also teach psychology?"

"Yes," Anya said. "Abnormal psych." How perfect was that? "The jerk."

Heath kept his hands light on the wheel, but every line of his hard body showed capability and command.

She swallowed and ignored the warming of her abdomen. She had to stop looking at those hands. He'd shown her honesty, and she owed him the same thing. "Well, everyone in the FBI would've known I wasn't Reese's fiancée. Plus, I think he could've had me arrested or put somewhere for impeding an investigation or something like that—if he knew for sure I was lying." Reese would've done it to keep her safe for Loretta's sake.

"And the ex?" Heath's hands tightened on the wheel.

"Not a chance." She crossed her arms. "I don't trust him, and I don't think he'd be a match for this killer anyway."

"You're done with him?"

"Definitely." She slowly turned her torso toward Heath and dug into his mind. Oh, he was definitely living in the gray area, and he wasn't telling her much about himself. Yet there was a hint of sweetness in him, the promise that he'd die to protect somebody he perceived as weaker than him. "Please work with me."

He sighed. "You're killing me here."

Yeah, he definitely had trouble saying no to somebody asking for his help. She should feel badly about manipulating him, but this was too important. "I'm sorry. But I can handle this. I'm not weak or breakable, Heath. You and I can do this." She looked at him beneath her lashes.

He switched on the heater. "You're definitely breakable. Don't charge into danger without knowing that one fact." His low rumble filled the vehicle and then zinged right through her body.

She shifted her weight on the seat. Was he warning her about the case or about himself? Why did this guy intrigue her so? That was the other reason she'd chosen him for her fake fiancé, and she was aware enough to admit it to herself. She'd wanted to see Heath Jones again. "I suppose from an analytical standpoint, we're all breakable."

"Uh-huh." His phone buzzed, and he ignored it.

"Are you going to answer that?" she asked, more than a little curi- ous. Panic flared in her breast. "Oh no. I didn't even think. You don't wear a ring, but are you married?" God. What if he was married? She'd just caused him a world of hurt on national television.

"No."

She should be embarrassed by the relief that flowed through her. "Girlfriend?" She held her breath.

He cut her a look. "*Now* you ask that?"

Heat filled her face.

He sighed. "No girlfriend. Apparently I now have a fiancée."

Warmth bloomed through her chest. What would it be like to actually date somebody like him? A man so tough and seemingly strong? "I said I was sorry," she muttered.

"If you were sorry, you'd let me get you somewhere safe so I could go to work."

She reached out and grabbed his arm, almost desperate to make him understand. "I don't want to be the scared little girl hiding somewhere while you go after the bad guy. I'm the key to this guy's obsession, like it or not."

"The key." He shook his head. "Do you have copies of the letters?"

"Yes. I made copies of the entire file." She winced. "Don't tell the FBI. At least come to my hotel and see what I've put together." Oh man. Heath in her small hotel room. She bit her lip. The bed was right by the small desk area. The bed. Heath. A bed. What in the world was wrong with her? Sure, she'd known desire before, but he was just so much—so much muscle and strength and hard good looks. When had she become attracted to bad boys?

Did he have ripped abs? She'd always wanted to see ripped abs.

"Why are you blushing?"

She coughed and released his arm. "Sorry. Just got overwhelmed for a moment."

His head lifted as if in understanding. "Ah. I'm sorry, sweetheart. You have to be feeling her loss."

Anya blinked. For a few minutes she'd actually forgotten. Her sister was dead. That quickly, raw emotion tore through her. "I'm okay." She set her shoulders back against the seat. "In fact, I'm determined. We're going to find that bastard, Heath, and we're gonna make him pay."

"No." He turned, his face implacable. "I failed to protect your sister, and this guy has killed nine women already. If you're a halfway decent shrink, you already know that there's no way in hell I'm allowing you to be bait. We'll get the files, and then you're going underground."

Her mouth gaped. Oh yeah? That's what he thought.

CHAPTER 9

The snowstorm increased in force, so Heath sped up the SUV's windshield wipers. His phone buzzed in his pocket again; he ignored the insistent demand. Ryker would have to wait until later to yell at him about his suddenly very public involvement in the case.

"All right, Anya. Here's the deal." Heath kept his voice low and commanding, hiding both his concern and anger. "We'll get your stuff from your hotel and take it to the one I told Reese I was staying at. Guess I should check in. Then you can show me the letters."

"Why a different hotel?" she asked.

God, she was naive. "Because you challenged a serial killer about an hour ago, so I'm thinkin' we should get you somewhere safe."

"Hmm." She rubbed her chin. "Good idea, but he knows your name now, too."

Heath shook his head. "I'll register under a false name. We detectives use those, you know." He said the last with wry humor.

She turned to study him. "I'm thinking that's only half the truth."

Man, she was quick. And by the drawing down of her brows, she didn't like that about him. His phone buzzed again, and he ignored it again.

"Damn it, Heath," boomed suddenly from a speaker above the rearview mirror. "What the holy fuck of a holy fuck have you gotten yourself into?" Ryker yelled through the satellite system provided by the rental agency.

Heath winced. "Hacked into the satellite, did you?"

"Denver did. What the hell? Your name is all over the news with the press conference. Do you have any idea how quickly—"

"I'm not alone," Heath cut in before Ryker could reveal all their secrets.

His brother fell silent for about two seconds. "Oh. Of course not. I take it your fiancée is with you?" The sarcasm cut through the suddenly thick silence in the vehicle.

"Um, yes," Anya said, her eyes narrowing at the speaker. "You are Heath's brother, right? I'm really sorry to have dragged you and your agency into this. I just wasn't thinking after I buried my sister." Her voice trembled and sounded thick with tears.

Anger roared through Heath. "Damn it, Ryker."

"Shit, Heath," Ryker returned. He sighed loudly. "I'm sorry I swore, Anya. Heath? This ain't a good idea."

No kidding. "I'm still figuring things out."

"What is there to figure out?" Ryker bellowed again. "Get her ass to the Montana safe house, and we'll go find this killer."

Anya crossed her arms next to him.

"That might be a problem," Heath returned. Not one part of him wanted to force her somewhere else while she blamed herself for her sister's death. The pain of that must be excruciating. Her sister had been murdered, and she deserved a chance to find the bastard who'd done it. While he wanted to get her to safety, hearing somebody else order it made him want to defend her. To help her. "Besides. Do you really think the Montana, ah, contingent will allow the target of a serial killer to stay there?"

"They're family. If we ask for help, they'll cover her as nobody else could. The killer won't have a clue she's there." Ryker sounded like he was losing what little patience he actually owned. "Heath, this is an easy answer."

Heath looked at Anya. Her chin was up, her eyes burning. "That's what you think." God, she was sexier than hell when facing him like a spitting cat. No way could *they* happen, though. She seemed like a forever type of girl who followed the rules, and he was an on-the-run type of guy who had no problem breaking them. The smartest thing for him would be to force her into safety.

Yet what would that do to her?

"I'm about to speak really frankly here," Ryker warned.

"Don't," Heath returned evenly. "I know exactly what you're about to say."

Anya looked on, her gaze turning curious.

"Do you, now?" Ryker asked, his voice going low.

"Yep. Heard it a thousand times before. Trigger points. Bad past. Mistakes now." Heath kept his words vague for Anya's sake, but there was no doubt Ryker was about to lecture him on his penchant for saving every wounded animal or shattered woman. "I've heard it, I know it, and that's not what this is about."

"Really? What is this about?" Ryker asked, his tone turning concerned. "Vengeance?"

"No. Redemption." Heath reached up and disengaged the satellite feed, turning toward Anya. "Maybe for the both of us."

She studied him, her eyes darkening. Finally, one corner of her mouth quirked. "You're a *beneath the surface* kind of guy, aren't you?"

He couldn't help but grin back. "I'm the deep one in the family." Well, not necessarily true. Denver had untold depths—he just never talked. "Sorry my brother yelled at you."

"It's okay. Are you all from Montana?"

"No." He searched for the right words. "We have relatives there, but we don't know them well. The ranch is a safe place if you ever need safety." No way could he go into deeper detail, even if the truth was believable, which it wouldn't be.

"You live in the gray area—no black or white?" she asked softly, an odd sadness curving her bottom lip.

He drove into the hotel parking lot, wanting to soothe her but not sure how. While he couldn't tell her everything, he could be honest with what he said. "I think that's safe to say. Why? You don't?"

"No," she said. "My dad was a cop, a good one, and I've always walked the line."

"Yeah, I figured that about you already." He quickly rolled the SUV to a snowy stop. "Not all cops are good." He knew that first-hand, unfortunately.

"Most are," she countered.

Whoa. Talk about different lives and realities. Maybe it was fine that she believed right always won. He fucking knew better.

Enough with philosophy—they had a killer to catch.

Heath studied the bright pink doors against the solid white building. "Which room?"

"One-oh-three."

He jumped out and scouted the nearly empty parking lot. The hotel was small but quaint looking. Raised voices from one room caught his attention. A man and woman fighting about somebody named Bonnie. "There's an argument going on in room one-twelve. If it escalates, somebody might call the cops. Let's hurry."

She paused and looked toward the room. "I don't hear anything."

My senses are a little above average." At her raised eyebrow, he smiled. "Okay, a lot beyond average." It felt right to share a truth with her. But a sense of urgency took him by the throat. "We have five minutes. Let's move."

She gave him a look but hopped from the SUV and led the way to her room. He allowed her to unlock the door and then set her aside to enter first, quickly scanning the entire area. "Clear."

Her snort showed she wasn't taking the danger quite seriously yet.

He stepped inside and walked immediately to her notes and pictures spread all over the small table. His whistle filled the silence. "Where in the world did you get all of this data?" He turned to see her blushing a very pretty pink. Fascinated, he could just stare.

She shuffled her snow-covered boots. "I, ah, may have copied Loretta's file right after she was taken and before Reese confiscated everything."

Smart. Illegal, but smart. Talk about untold depths. "So much for right and wrong."

Her lips firmed. "Catching this asshole is the right thing to do."

He studied the woman. She'd set herself up for a serial killer to avenge her sister. While reckless, that was strong. That realization had the unfortunate effect of stirring his cock to life. *Down, boy.* "I'm fairly certain stealing FBI files is a felony, darlin'."

She twisted her mouth and studied the wall. "Probably, though I didn't actually steal anything. Just made copies. Since I'm working as a consultant on the case, it's okay."

Probably true. "Start packing." His phone buzzed and he lifted it to his ear. "No lecture."

"Just turn on the television," Ryker said.

Heath moved for the battered set and twisted a knob to ignite the TV. It sizzled and then a picture formed of Anya talking to the reporters. He turned the channel. Same scene. "Damn it," he murmured. The killer would certainly see it. Even on the crappy screen, Anya's determination and dare came through bright and clear. "You're on every channel."

She stepped up next to him, her hands full of pictures and notes. "That was my plan." Her voice shook, and her skin paled.

Her pallor concerned him. "That was very brave, darlin'." He could give her kudos before he argued with her.

"I'm not brave." Her sigh held pain and sadness. "I'm scared to death of this guy and definitely don't want to end up alone in a room with him."

That was the very definition of bravery. "You won't."

"Hey," Ryker snapped from the phone.

Oh yeah. Heath had forgotten his brother was even there. "Sorry. I saw the live version, Ry."

"I know, but now we're in a shit-storm. She gave your name and the name of the agency. We've been exposed."

Heath took a deep breath and let his mind clear. "I'm sorry."

"Don't be sorry—just be safe." Ryker sighed. "Do you really want to open an agency in Snowville?"

"Yes." The plan was already in place. "Listen, Ryker. I know we have to lie low, so how about you and Denver just stay in the cabins? I'll handle the Snowville office on my own until we catch this killer." Heath ignored the intense curiosity filtering across Anya's pretty face.

"Not a chance, brother. If you're in the line of fire, we're right beside you," Ryker said, his voice low.

Heath's chest warmed. "You have too much to lose, and you know it." His brother had recently fallen in love and needed to keep his woman safe. "Let me do this."

"Nope. We're all in. That's the whole point of family, and you know it. I guess we're moving to Snowville." Ryker rustling papers came across the line. "Denver is giving me his best *This is fucking crazy* expression, just so you know."

"So long as Denver doesn't say the words, he's not really concerned," Heath countered. "Our entire purpose for opening that physical office in Cisco was to draw the killer out. Setting up an office in Snowville is just a continuation of our own plan."

"I agree, but we don't need Jackson's wounded sister as bait," Ryker said.

Heath winced. "She's no more wounded than the rest of us."

Anya paled but didn't speak and then started gathering her notes into a big file folder.

"Fine. But are you seriously thinking of putting that untrained woman into the line of fire?" More curiosity than censure filled Ryker's voice.

"No," Heath said shortly. "I don't want her anywhere near danger. We'll meet in Snowville and come up with a plan that finds this guy without really putting her in front of a killer." He wasn't quite sure what the plan would be, and he was positive Anya would argue, but there had to be a decent way to make this work and let her take part. "Loretta was her sister, and she deserves to be involved."

The gratitude that shot into her stunning eyes shouldn't warm him so intensely. He'd have to watch his emotions around this woman. Without question.

"Are you sure you've got this?" Ryker asked quietly.

Damn mind reader. "I'm fine, Ry. Stop worrying and get back to your own life. Gone ring shopping yet?" Heath couldn't help but grin. His brother had recently fallen hard for an amazing woman named Zara, and he was sweating bullets trying to find the right ring for her.

"Yes, but I haven't found the one. I mean, I proposed already. Kind of."

"It doesn't count until you ask with a ring in your hand," Heath said, biting back a laugh. Like he knew one thing about proposals.

"That's what Denver said."

Denver didn't know shit about them either, but this was fun. "Yep. You need a ring and the whole down-on-one-knee moment," Heath said.

"Fine, but she already said yes, so I'm holding her to it. There has to be the perfect ring out there, right?" Ryker asked in a low growl.

"Hell if I know." He'd never even considered buying an engagement ring for a woman. At the thought, he frowned at Anya.

Ryker chuckled. "I guess we can go shopping together now."

"Funny," Heath said, not finding the idea totally unpleasant. Whoa. He was not getting engaged for real. Probably ever. "I think the hit to the head last week is still giving me issues."

"Keep telling yourself that." Ryker hung up before he could answer.

"Good plan," Heath muttered, sliding the phone into his back pocket. "Got everything?" He glanced around to see her bag already packed and the bed made. The little redhead was a neat freak. He liked that.

The bed was small for a hotel room. Yet she'd look stunning draped across it. He cleared his throat.

"Yes." She finished shoving all the paperwork into a worn blue laptop bag. "Why do you and your brothers need to lie low?" She straightened, her gaze serious. "Does it have something to do with the fake marshals who shot at us?"

"Yes." He met her gaze in a silent battle of wills.

She gave in first. "Well? Who are they?"

He rubbed the whiskers on his jaw. "Listen, Anya. I'm willing to help you catch Loretta's killer because I liked her. In addition, I like you. But my life is my own."

Her eyes darkened to the color of a pine forest. "None of my business?"

"Exactly." His secrets were shared by his brothers, and he'd never betray them. But he wanted to level with her. There was a tension between them, one he could almost taste.

She looked around and then back at him. Awareness lived in her gaze. She felt him on a similar level—he could see it. "Like you said before, you're not exactly a good guy."

"Nope." As soon as she truly realized that fact, they'd be on much better ground.

She looked at the bed and then blushed. "There's a lot of emotion going on right now."

Yeah, there was. It was all jumbled up, and part of it was sexual attraction. He'd felt it for her the moment he'd laid eyes on her. From her pink cheeks, she felt it too. "I know," he said softly.

She gave a slight shudder, which moved her pert breasts. "This is confusing."

"It doesn't have to be." He didn't like games or subtext. It was time to lay it all out there for her to make a decision about the ridiculous attraction between them. It was getting too difficult to concentrate around her, and they both needed to let off some steam. "While I might not give you the full story, I'll never lie to you. So here it is. I want you."

Her eyebrows rose toward her hairline. Her breath quickened.

"And I think you want me."

Now her chin lowered. She drew in air and slowly let it out. Her nipples hardened until he could see them beneath her shirt. Clearly.

"I thought we should get that truth out of the way and decide what to do about it. If you want something physical, I'm definitely in. If not, we're still going to do this job. I can give you my time and expertise and anything else you want as we do this job. But then I'm gone." Would she want to do more than just work together? Maybe have some fun if possible? Relieve some of the pressure and escape reality for a short time?

Her forehead wrinkled. "You're hitting on me."

He finally settled into the moment and let his mind clear. Let his emotions relax after the shitty last couple of days. "Yes."

She licked her lips.

He groaned.

"I'm not sure what to say, but I'm glad we're tackling the issue." That slight pink color traveled from her cheeks down her neck.

He'd like to tackle her right into the bed. The storm pressed against the windows, lending a sense of intimacy to the bedroom. "No problem. I'm better when everything is out in the open. What do you think?" he asked easily, discreetly adjusting his jeans.

She cleared her throat and focused on a spot near his left shoulder. "The whole fiancé thing and going to your hotel tonight. Then returning to Snowville and working this case together—I get why you'd want to make the most of it. I mean, thank you for the very up front offer, and I know we have to be around each other, but I don't want to get things muddled up, you know?"

He bit back a grin. She was as cute as she could be. "Not really. I'm better with a yes, a no, or a maybe."

"Maybe?" She slung the laptop bag in front of her, the pink turning rosy. "Just what would you do with a maybe?" Curiosity filled her eyes, and her head tilted just enough to be adorably flirtatious.

He shoved his hands into his pockets to keep from reaching for her. "I guess with a maybe I'd be charming and irresistible so you'd change that to a yes."

She swallowed and met his gaze. "All right. Let me get this straight. We're going undercover to flush out a killer who's obsessed with me, and you're offering to play at being my man for real with no strings or future?" She hoisted the bag onto her shoulder. "That's some ego. Are you that good in bed?"

"Yes." And that was definite interest in her eyes.

She clicked her tongue. "I'll keep your offer in mind."

"You do that." He maintained a low and calm voice. "While you're considering, let's look at the situation. You have publicly made me your fiancé in order to draw out a killer, which means I have to act as such. Any halfway intelligent law enforcement officer or private investigator would keep his redheaded fiancée very close after the stunt you just pulled. If you're not with me, the killer is going to be very suspicious."

She stilled, expressions crossing her face rapidly. "That's a good point," she said slowly.

Yeah. Sometimes reality helped him out a little. Plus, the killer had a hard-on for her, and he must already have plans to take her at some point. She'd just upped the timeline. "In addition, you need protection around the clock now, and I'm willing to provide that. So while you're keeping my offer in mind, we'll be staying in the same hotel room or same apartment." He made sure he had her full attention. "While we plan the wedding, of course."

Her challenging smile thrilled something inside him. "That's fair."

He stepped back to give her some space. "Good. Are you ready?"

"Yes." She looked around the room. "I do have to ask. What if I didn't agree with you about your keeping secrets from me? Considering people shoot at you, and I'm going to be at your side, it seems fair that you tell me who these people are." She cocked her head to the side and focused back on him.

"I have more immediate concerns than being fair," he said smoothly. "You brought me into this mess."

A frown drew down her eyebrows. "Listen. I want an answer about you."

"I just gave you one." At her mulish expression, he searched for better words that wouldn't end in an argument.

Suddenly, the door blew wide open and bounced loudly off the table. "Anya!" he yelled, jumping for her.

CHAPTER
10

Anya yelped as Heath tackled her to the floor, rolled her behind the bed, and leaped back up in a span of seconds. Her ears rang, and her breath came out in short bursts. The sound of flesh hitting flesh filled the air.

What was happening?

She grabbed the bedcover and forced herself to stand. Wind blew snow to swirl inside as Heath fought with a man hand to hand, both hitting hard and furiously. The guy wore all black, with a dark ski mask covering his face, and he moved as quickly as Heath did. A series of punches and kicks came from them both.

God, they were fast and brutal. Her knees shook.

Heath's face was a mask of savage concentration with an odd calmness. No anger, no fear. Just raw intensity. He punched the other guy in the jaw and pivoted to land a kick on the attacker's chest. The guy flew back and shattered the cheap mirror on the wall. Glass crashed down.

Faster than possible, he leaped up and kicked Heath in the jaw. "That one is from Sheriff Cobb," the guy said, his voice low and hoarse.

Heath's head snapped back and he fell onto the bed, then rolled backward and stood. With a ferocious roar, he shot forward and hit the attacker in the midsection, the momentum plowing them both into the wall. "Give him this in return," Heath muttered. Sheetrock cracked and powder flew in every direction. The guy reacted with a chop to the throat and a knee to the gut.

Heath let out a pained *oof* and dropped to one knee.

"Heath!" Anya screamed. A weapon. There had to be some sort of weapon around there. Maybe a fork from dinner last night?

Even as she scanned the room for anything she could use, Heath jumped straight up and hit the attacker beneath the jaw with his head. The guy's skull flew back into the wall with an ominous crack.

Heath finished with a flurry of punches to the middle of the guy's body and then pivoted to kick the guy's knee. The guy bellowed and swung an arm, nailing Heath in the jaw with an elbow. Who was this guy?

How were they both standing? The blows they'd both taken would've knocked out a buffalo.

The men breathed heavily, circling each other, eyes missing nothing.

She had never in her life seen such purposeful violence. They both fought with no emotion and didn't seem to feel pain. How was that even possible? Her knees weakened, even as her fingers tightened into a fist. Her breath panted out. She should run. Man, she should run.

Sirens sounded in the distance. Somebody in the hotel must've called the police. Thank God.

The guy stiffened and yanked out a gun.

"Shit." Heath leaped over the bed and straight into Anya. It was like being hit by a truck. Her body recoiled and the air whooshed out of her lungs.

She dug her fingers into his torso and screamed. Heath's hands clamped around her back and landed on the carpet first. His big body covered her in one long line of rippling muscle, pressing her to the floor.

Bullets ripped into the wall above their heads.

He grabbed her head and tucked it into his neck, holding tight.

She whimpered against his skin.

He shoved her half under the bed and moved into a crouch.

She tried to clutch him, to keep him safe, but he dislodged her hold. Moving silently, he crab-walked to the end of the bed and took a deep breath. Then he jumped.

Nothing. No sound.

"He's gone. Get up and move. Now." Heath's voice held a sharp command.

She reacted instantly and hustled up, grabbing the laptop bag. Heath already had her suitcase in his hand and was heading for the open doorway. He more than filled it with sheer male size. She stopped. "Wait a minute. The police are coming."

The look he gave her dried the spit in her mouth.

His chin lowered, and his eyes sizzled green through the goldish brown. "Move now, Anya. Now."

She launched into motion, her body moving before her brain could catch up. At the door, he grabbed her hand and pulled her into the snowy day, keeping his body in front of hers. He looked around and then started jogging for his SUV. She had no choice but to keep up. Within seconds, they were in the car and speeding out of the hotel parking lot.

The sirens increased in volume, and Anya turned around to see police cars skidding into the parking lot. "Why didn't we wait for them?" she breathed, her heart pounding sharply against her rib cage. The day fuzzed. Her head ached. She started gasping for breath.

A large but gentle hand grasped her nape and pressed her face down to her thighs. "Deep breaths. You're going into a panic attack. Shut your eyes and take deep breaths," Heath said, turning the vehicle.

She followed his orders to keep from passing out. "I…can't…breathe…" She gasped.

"You can." He rubbed circles between her shoulder blades. "Shut your eyes." His voice was low and soothing.

She shut her eyes and concentrated on his warm palm with the scar.

"Good. Breathe out and then in evenly. Don't worry about filling your lungs. Just breathe a little."

She followed his advice, and soon the buzzing in her head subsided. Slowly, she lifted her head to see houses and snowy trees flying by outside. "Oh my God. Slow down."

He sped through the streets, one hand on the steering wheel, easily controlling the vehicle on the icy roads. "I will in a minute. You're strong enough to put on your seat belt."

She eyed the door handle, every instinct in her body yelling at her to run, and now.

"Don't even think about it," he said, taking a corner at a terrifying speed.

She turned and eyed him, her breathing quickening again. "Who are you?" she blurted out, her voice hoarse.

He cut her a look. "Somebody you're gonna want to obey for the next hour or so. After that, I'll make sure you're free to go wherever you want."

Obey? Did he just say *obey*? He'd just gotten in a brutal fight and then fled from the police. Why would he avoid the cops? Fury filled her. Who was he to order her to do anything? She opened her mouth to argue.

"Now, Anya."

Her nostrils flared, and emotions rioted through her. One might be fear. Another one was certainly anger. "Listen—"

"If I have to pull over to secure your belt, you're not going to like me very much." He pierced her with a hard look.

"I don't like you at all right now," she spat, pressing back against the seat. The world sped by too quickly outside for her to escape, even if she could get the door open before he stopped her, which she doubted at the moment. The smart thing was to put on the belt in case he crashed, but the word *obey* sat like a hard lump of rock in her stomach. Her fingers inched toward the door handle.

"Damn it." He hit the brakes and went into a skid, spinning the SUV in a full circle. The world swirled by in a nauseating blur. She shut her eyes and held on to the dash, trying not to scream.

He swung them around almost easily and stopped in a small parking lot of a suburban park.

Silence fell fast and hard.

She gingerly opened her eyes to see snow falling onto the windshield. Her mouth gaped and she turned to face him. He was a brutal fighter. She should be scared of him. Yet all she felt was completely overwhelmed and hugely defiant. What was up with that?

He studied her, no expression on his rugged face. "You have me between a rock and a hard place here, darlin'," he drawled.

She blinked. "Huh?"

"Yeah. I can't leave you here without protection, and it doesn't suit my purposes to take you back to your hotel with the cops there. We need to keep going until I can get you somewhere safe, and I plan on driving like a bat out of hell. To do so, and to keep my concentration where it should be, on the icy road, I need your seat belt on." He had spoken clearly but with a definite threat of tension through every word.

"So?" She tried to keep his gaze, but her eyes almost stung from the effort.

"So I'd rather not put my hands on you at the moment. Period."

Fire lashed through her. "Seriously? Try it. Definitely try it." Her voice had gone hoarse.

His lips compressed. "Life isn't always a clear path."

She pointed back the way they'd come, her hand shaking, she was so furious. "The police were coming. Sirens are good. Why would you run from them?"

"Because not all cops are good." His voice deepened and smoothed out, causing the hair to rise on the back of her neck. His eyes glittered an angry green/brown flecked with gold, and tension roiled in him like a steam engine bottled up. "Now put your damn belt on."

"Or what?" she challenged, more than ready to smack him in the face.

He turned back to her, and in the darkening vehicle, his face was all strong lines and dangerous shadows. "I'll put it on you."

Okay. Why did that intrigue her? Seriously. How could anger and attraction be melding inside her? The way he'd fought to protect her from the guy in the hotel room was frightening...and intriguing. Maybe even sexy. "Who is Sheriff Cobb?" she snapped.

"None of your business," he retorted quickly. "Anya—"

"I don't like being threatened," she burst out.

"I'm sorry." He reached out and ran a gentle knuckle down her cheek.

Yet he didn't back down. The simple touch heated her throughout, and she shifted in her seat. "If we're going to work together, I need the full truth."

He studied her. "No."

She blinked. "Excuse me?"

"I said no." He rolled his broad shoulders. "That guy and my wanting to avoid the police all deal with a case that has nothing to do with you and never will."

The words kinda cut a little. She clenched her teeth. "I'm going back."

He sighed. "Fine. It'll be about a twenty-minute walk. Stick to the road."

Her jaw dropped. "What?"

He glanced at the clock on the dash. "This undercover op was your idea, and you dragged me into it without even asking."

"So?" she challenged.

"So?" Heat flared in his eyes. "You take your fake fiancé as you find him. We do this my way or no way."

She lost her voice but shook her head.

His chin lowered just enough to give him a predatory look, which appeared perfectly natural on him. "Yes. If you want to run back to the cops, feel free." His tone turned gravelly.

"You're not giving me a choice here."

He lifted an eyebrow. Intensity swelled from him. "All right, sweetheart. I'll give you a choice if you choose to stay in my vehicle." His smile was wolfish. "Either put on your belt or prepare to be pushed up against the door with my mouth on yours. I've had enough of being reasonable."

The words filtered through her anger to land hard in her abdomen. Tempting. Definitely tempting. The entire situation had leaped right out of her control. Oh, she'd wanted to challenge him and had wondered how long he'd let her. Now she knew.

Sirens echoed again.

"Looks like option B will have to wait. Either get out of the SUV or put on your belt." He set the vehicle into DRIVE. "Seat belt now."

Her hands clenched. If she left, she'd be giving up the undercover op to catch the killer. She had to catch Loretta's killer. Nothing else mattered. She snapped her belt into place and crossed her arms with a small huff. "Where are we going?"

He pinned her with a look. "Exactly where you told the killer. Snowville, Washington."

She blinked. "That's like a thirty-five-hour drive."

"Twenty-eight hours with me driving. I suggest you take a nap."

A nap? Yeah, right. Snowville it was, then. "I don't get it. Why not tell the cops about the guy who just attacked us?" Unease whispered through her.

He sighed. "You opened up an opportunity with the killer, and we don't have time to mess around. We have to get into place and now. Plus, the guy who attacked us is long gone, and since he wore a mask, I have nothing to give the cops. Why wait?"

It all sounded so plausible, and yet…"Are you wanted by the police?" she asked, her voice lowering and her breath catching.

He paused. "No."

She studied him, realizing how little she truly knew him. Was he telling the truth?

CHAPTER
11

Sheriff Elton Cobb finished rifling through the nearly empty desk drawers as wind beat against the building that had once housed his prey's detective agency. Why had they tried to settle down in Cisco, Wyoming?

He'd known the men as boys, and he understood them. He'd bet anything this office had belonged to Heath, however briefly. The desk was glass and a dark wood, as were the file cabinets. Ryker's probable office was chrome and glass, while Denver's was solid cherrywood.

Or he was dead wrong. Either way, the offices were fairly empty. Only furniture remained. Same with the apartments upstairs.

So the rabbits had finally tried to settle down. Dumb-asses. He'd never stop hunting them. There was no peace or comfort for them, and when he caught them, there'd be no life.

His phone dinged and he quickly read an update text.

Operative found Heath in hotel outside DC hours ago. Fight ensued. No capture.

Fuck. Cobb fought the urge to throw his phone across the room. No capture? To have Heath so close, almost in his grasp, made him want to hurt somebody. Bad.

He cleared his vision and looked around the stupid office. Why had the little shits decided to put down roots in Wyoming? Was it the woman? Apparently Ryker had fallen for some paralegal from the small town. A woman who was now on the run with him as well as the other so-called brothers. While Cobb didn't truly understand the science that had gone into creating those boys, he knew without a doubt they weren't really brothers. He'd had a brother who'd run the orphanage kind enough to take them in. He'd loved his brother...and they'd killed him. Heath, Ryker, and Denver had murdered Cobb's sole family member.

They'd pay, and they'd pay with their lives.

His phone dinged again, and he pressed it to his ear. "Cobb here."

"Hi, darling." Isobel Madison, the only woman he'd ever loved, purred through the phone. "Tell me you've found something."

At her words, something caught his eye in the bottom of the nearest drawer. He tugged out a penciled drawing of himself with a donkey coming out of his ass and the caption FUCK YOU, ASSHOLE above it. Rage swept through him, and he turned over the paper to see a two-headed serpent, both faces Isobel's. The caption read SYLVIA DANIELS OR ISOBEL MADISON? "I've found a little something."

"What?"

"There's a picture where they used both your names."

She chuckled. "I only have one name. Sylvia Daniels was a uniform I wore when studying them as children. They know who I am now. Did you find anything else?"

He'd never understood why she'd used a fake name anyway. "No. They cleaned the offices and apartments out, leaving just the furniture. They paid in cash for everything," he added before she could start questioning him.

She sighed. "Well, I did create them to be brilliant, so we shouldn't be surprised."

Brilliant, his ass. Sure, they had been genetically created in test tubes by Isobel, but intelligence couldn't just be created. "If you say so," he muttered.

"Any clues there? We know it was some sort of detective agency," she said, typing softly across the line. "But they didn't register it with the state or county."

"There aren't any business cards or letterhead here," he said. "I questioned the lawyer they worked with, and he didn't remember a name." Though gut instinct told Cobb that the lawyer had known more than he'd said. Apparently Heath and the boys had learned to create loyalty in the folks they met. "I could take another run at the lawyer but not if you want me to remain under the radar."

"No need. My boys have left Wyoming, and we know that Heath is outside of DC."

"The text I just received said that good old Daniel failed to bring in Heath," Elton retorted. The supersoldier was Isobel's pet, and he'd failed.

"Daniel will get the job done. Trust me. I will have those boys back here under our control by this time next year."

So she could return them to the labs and force them to work for her—as well as provide genetic samples for a new generation of engineered supersoldiers. Cobb shook his head. "Okay." He fully planned on killing them all before they could do shit. After he demolished anybody and everybody they loved. Isobel would just have to forgive him afterward.

"There are bigger issues at play than simple vengeance," she said, reading him with impressive accuracy.

That's what she thought. "They killed my brother."

"I know." She sighed. "But you and your brother shouldn't have beaten them for so many years. They were bound to fight back. It's in their very genes—I made sure of it." A barely veiled pride whispered in her voice.

Cobb shook his head. Those assholes were lucky enough to have had a roof over their heads and food in their bellies. They deserved every beating they ever got. "Any other news about the DC op?"

"Barely." Her voice had lost any semblance of pleasure. "Yes. Daniel said Heath protected a woman in the fight."

A woman? Excellent. A weakness for Heath. It was shocking Daniel had even noticed a woman. He was one of the few people on earth who gave Cobb the willies. If eyes could be dead, Daniel's were. "Where is Daniel now?"

"He landed at the Boise airport and should be arriving here at any moment." Isobel's new compound and lab were located several miles outside Boise, Idaho…a place where she could conduct her genetic experiments in private.

Cobb shrugged off unease about Daniel. "Who was the woman with Heath?"

"Her name is Anya Best, and she's the sister of an FBI agent who was taken by some serial killer. Had a very nice news conference during which she announced she was Heath's fiancée and they were moving to Snowville in Washington." Satisfaction put a lilt in Isobel's cultured voice.

His pulse rate picked up, and he sat forward. "We know where they're going?"

"I find it highly unlikely. It's possible she gave the location to throw us off track. It'd be the smart thing to do, and Heath knows we're looking for them. With Daniel finding them in DC, Heath has to feel the time for our reunion drawing near."

Cobb flopped back in the chair. "Good point. There's no way Heath would allow her to announce their location to the media."

"No. Unless it suits his purpose, which I can't imagine at this point. He has to know how vulnerable a dalliance would make him." Isobel chuckled the deep-throated sound that made Cobb's entire body hum. "I had no clue I'd created such a group of romantic fools when I spliced their genes."

Women made them weak, and Cobb would use that. "I take it you're tracking down information on Anya Best?"

"Of course. I'll know everything about her by tonight. She might have FBI protection since her sister was with the Bureau, so we'll have to proceed very carefully."

"If she's with Heath, she's not with the FBI," Cobb returned. "I'm considering filing a report on my brother's murder to get the entire U.S. law enforcement community after these assholes." The only reason he hadn't done so was because he wanted to extract revenge on his own without the court system. But after twenty years of searching for them, he was ready to let them just go to jail if that was the only way to make them pay.

"No. I need them for further research, and you need them to hurt for what they did to you," she countered easily. "I promise you'll get much more satisfaction from letting them live and suffer. Just think what you can do to their women in front of them."

His dick hardened. "That's a good point, my love." God, she'd be frightening if she weren't on his side. Hell, she scared the shit out of him sometimes, and he was a sadist. "How's the new lab coming along?"

"So well." Her tone evened out to pure pleasure. "About two weeks to go, and we'll be up and running. I have a few genetic samples left that look viable and just need female surrogates, which we can discuss later. Right now I'm receiving the proper equipment, and Daniel will get back to training the soldiers. I have only five still loyal from the past." Her pout sounded through the line.

"Five is a good number to start with," he returned. Especially since those five had been trained from birth to fight and kill.

"I wish I could get all my boys back here," she whispered.

He shook his head. "You'll make more soldiers, Isobel."

"Just find my boys for me. I need their sperm to start creating again." She clicked off the call.

He slipped the phone back into his pocket. Sperm? Right. Once he was finished with them, they wouldn't be able to produce shit—much less sperm. At that thought, he yanked out his dick and started stroking himself.

Might as well leave his mark on the office.

* * *

Dr. Isobel Madison kept her spine straight as she typed, her fingers flowing over the keyboard. Anticipation rushed through her. Changes were coming, and she could feel her creations drawing near, whether they liked it or not. Though once again she couldn't help but wonder why they didn't see their importance to science.

Her work was creating life in test tubes, and she'd nearly altered biology to get the boys she'd wanted. Then she'd studied those boys as they'd become men.

Several of her boys who'd created familial bonds—the bonds of brotherhood—had somehow escaped her. She would love to study them again and figure out how to break those bonds. To create truly unencumbered soldiers. It was her calling, after all.

A sharp rap sounded on the thick metal door. "Enter," she said, sitting even straighter. Now in her early fifties, she had to remind herself sometimes to continue good habits.

Daniel strode inside, snow on his broad shoulders and thick boots. "Dr. Madison."

She gestured toward a seat. "You failed."

"Yes." He stood at the back of the chair and made no move to cross around and sit. His brown gaze met hers evenly, the bruises cascading down the right side of his rugged face only enhancing his wolf-like good looks. He stood well over six feet, tightly muscled, and pleasantly relaxed most of the time. "Heath fought well."

Made sense. From an early age, Heath had exhibited faster reflexes than many of her creations. "Are you injured?"

"No. Just sore." Daniel flexed the bruised knuckles on his right hand. The man had always had broad and beautiful hands, even as a boy. "Heath was protecting the woman fiercely. There's something between them."

"She's his fiancée," Isobel returned.

Daniel looked around the feminine office.

She tilted her head to the side and began taking mental notes, unable to stop studying him for even a moment. "Do you want a fiancée, Daniel?"

He lifted an eyebrow and focused back on her. "Why in the world would I want entanglements, Dr. Madison? They make you weak and give your enemy a way in." He shook his head, and snow sprayed from his thick dark hair. "A soldier fights alone. You taught me that."

Yet he was one of the few who'd actually learned the lesson. She loosened her top button to watch his reaction.

Nothing. Always alert and paying attention, but nothing. She'd seduced many a soldier through her years training them, but Daniel had never given her more than a second glance. Sure, he'd been trained like the others in every sexual technique, and she knew he'd been with many women, but he looked upon her as a fellow soldier. As someone he trusted and took orders from, not as a woman. That had peeved her for years.

"I understand about entanglements, but what about sex?" she asked.

His lip twitched. "I have companionship and sex when I want, and you know it."

Yes, but what about sex with her? She eyed him. The man was hers and had been from the second she'd created him. He'd make a good ally should she ever need one, considering he could fight and kill easily. Could she get him to kill for her out of emotion instead of obedience? "I am rarely concerned with your private activities," she said.

He just looked at her.

So she looked back, wanting answers. True, it'd be smart to align herself with someone so young and strong. And it would be nice to be desirable to such a masculine specimen. Yet, as always, finding the answer to a question was so much more important than ego or feelings. Daniel would be more than satisfactory in bed. He'd certainly filled out in his late twenties, and he'd been trained by the best. So long as Elton Cobb didn't find out, why not have a good time?

"Do you think I'm pretty, Daniel?"

He studied her face for a moment, his gaze dropping to her breasts and back up. "Your beauty isn't a matter of opinion. You're just as stunning today as you were when I was a boy."

True. She smiled. "Yet you've never made a move."

He straightened even more, his eyes calculating and then veiled. "You're also the closest thing I have to a mother. Lines must be drawn."

Most women would feel old at the statement. She felt questions. Could she push him from that view into a different one? One from which he fought for her, for her affections, out of need and not duty? Or was he messing with her? Challenging her? She needed to spend more time in his head, because that was fascinating. The possibility of changing his mind, whether he liked it or not, aroused her.

One thing at a time, unfortunately. They had work to do.

"I'm pleased you find me attractive, and we'll explore that issue later. For now, can you tell me anything about Heath?" It had been so long since she'd seen her special boy.

Daniel shrugged. "He fights well, especially considering he wasn't raised and trained with us." For the first time, a look other than confidence filled Daniel's dark eyes. Curiosity? Yet he didn't ask.

She leaned forward. "You can ask me anything."

He paused. "All right. Why? Why did you have these other soldiers somewhere else and not with us in the compound? Not raised and trained like we were? Without the commander's guidance and gift?"

Oh. The sweet boy was still feeling loyalty to the commander, who'd been Isobel's partner for years. She'd handled the science, and the commander had dealt with the training and most of the discipline. Recently, he'd been killed by one of their own soldiers, and the wound was still somewhat fresh inside her breast. "All scientific research needs different parameters," she started.

Daniel frowned.

She continued, "Heath, Denver, and Ryker were sent out into the world and then relocated together as boys to a home where I could study them. They found each other, as I'd hoped, and their skills developed naturally, much like yours did."

"So we're all specimens to you." Daniel's voice remained level and merely curious.

"No. You're family to me—I created all of you." She clasped her hands together on the glass-topped desk. "Plus, my entire life I shared with the commander. It was nice to have a project that was just mine alone. All mine." Those boys owed her. Without her, they wouldn't even have life, much less each other.

"And Sheriff Cobb? You were his lover even back then. The commander didn't know about the good ole sheriff, now, did he?"

Isobel lifted a shoulder. "He might have—I'm not sure. We had an open relationship, as you know." The love of her life had had no problem seeking out other women once in a while, so she had seen no need to deny herself. She studied her loyal follower. "You deserve something for yourself, too. Think about it." With his training, he'd be amazing in bed.

His eyes flared for the first time, and he gave a short nod. "I will. After I hunt down Heath and return the beating, maybe I'll find something for myself."

Isobel smiled. "That's my boy."

CHAPTER
12

Anya jolted awake in the SUV and then winced as her neck flared in pain. "Ugh." The masculine scent of leather and male filled her head, and she glanced down at the heavy jacket draped over her chest. She breathed in deeply. Heath Jones. All Heath Jones. Her skirt had bunched up a little, and she pulled it down. She turned her head to see him looking at her from the driver's seat.

"You talk in your sleep," he said. "Something about cupcakes."

She blinked and sat up, focusing on a snowy parking lot in front of a ramshackle motel with worn red doors. Clouds covered the moon, expanding the sense of being alone in the quiet world. "Where are we?"

"Halfway." He held up a key—the old fashioned kind. "I need a few hours of sleep."

He'd already checked in? Man, she hadn't heard a thing. The wind rattled sleet against the window, which fogged quickly. "I can drive," she blurted out.

"No." He softened the word with a smile. "Sorry."

"Control freak." She handed his jacket over and drew hers up from her lap to shrug into. Her brain was still a little muddled, so maybe it was good she wasn't driving the big vehicle. She opened the door and dropped to the icy ground. A sharp, cold wind instantly assailed her, and she hunched inside her jacket.

She needed to change into jeans and get out of her funeral suit.

Heath jumped out and came around the car to grasp her hand and lead her through the storm to one of the cracked doors. His hand enclosed hers with a firm and definite warmth, which sent a shot of awareness to spark in her abdomen. He carried both her suitcase and a duffel bag in his other hand, while she kept a tight hold on her laptop bag.

Wait a minute. She drew back. "Um."

He quickly unlocked the door and pulled her inside, snapping the door shut. "It's freezing out there." Releasing her, he moved for a worn heater stretched across the wall and started twisting knobs, dropping into a crouch.

One bed. The minuscule room held one bed, a rickety table with two chairs, and a television console circa 1960. The carpet was an avocado green and the walls were yellowed. A very tiny bathroom lay off to the side. "I, ah, have a credit card we could use for a couple of rooms in a hotel with newer carpet," she murmured weakly. What kind of germs were hidden in the carpet?

He looked up and grinned. "This place takes cash and doesn't require identification." Heat blasted from the furnace, and he stood, dusting off his hands. Even in the dim light, he overpowered the room with the sense of maleness. Strength and masculinity.

"Why can't we use identification?" She swallowed. The bed was only a queen. Not even a king. A man his size needed a much larger bed. At least the flowered quilt appeared fairly new. But they could not share that bed.

"The case I can't talk about." He rubbed the dark shadow on his jaw. "Sorry about the one bed, but you're the one who challenged a serial killer and asked me to be your groom."

She shook her head and tried to find reality. Why was she so tired? "I did not ask you to be my groom."

He shrugged. "Same diff. We're engaged, baby. That means one room and one bed." His voice was a low rumble that caressed her already overexposed nerves.

She eyed the bed.

"I need a shower, sweetheart. We can fight about the one bed after." He grasped his duffel and disappeared into the bathroom. Within seconds, water started running.

Baby, *sweetheart*, and *darlin'*. The guy loved endearments. "You know my name, right?" she whispered with an eye roll. Even worse, she liked the endearments said in his deep voice just for her. She had to get a grip. The idea of his spectacular body all naked in the next room made her skin feel too tight.

Okay. Enough of that. This was a job. Maybe it would help if she considered him a job.

Man, she'd like to work him. She giggled to herself.

She ran a shaky hand through her hair. After the funeral, the fight, and then sleeping for hours, she just couldn't grab a thought. But a shower sounded nice. She lifted her suitcase onto the table and rummaged through it for yoga pants and a top. While she didn't want to look like a disaster in front of Mr. Dark, Deadly, and Sexy as Hell…she also didn't want to extend an invitation. They needed to get on track with the case and find the killer. Any complications would lead to problems.

Plus, her taste in men truly sucked lately. Carl had been such a prick, and it seemed like he wasn't giving up easily. She idly wondered how his interview with the FBI would go. What about the FBI? Heath had promised to meet with Reese. Would the FBI chase them?

Why was Heath running from the police? What kind of mess had she created by identifying him on television, and why was he working with her?

She knew. Not only her education but her instincts told her he wanted to find Loretta's killer. He needed to find him. So what was she to make of that? She had to get a grip on her thoughts.

She tried to concentrate on the small room. Yes, she could handle one night with Heath. They needed sleep, and they'd figure out everything in the morning. Good plan. Definitely a good plan.

Yet Heath was the sexiest man she'd ever seen, and now she was shacked up in a motel with him as a storm beat against the windows. But the poor guy must be exhausted. He'd gotten into a pretty bad fight and then driven through the storm for hours. No wonder he'd jumped into the shower.

Her mind returned to the fight. Heath had been brutal. Shouldn't that scare her, even a little? Yet it didn't. She felt safer with him—from bad guys, anyway—than she'd felt in much too long. Now all she had to do was control her libido and things would work out fine. She gingerly sat on the bedspread and waited, her thoughts scattering.

The door opened, and he stepped out with a towel wrapped around his waist, his thick hair wet and curling to his nape. Holy ripped abs, Batman. Her gaze dropped to the ridges in his abdomen, and her mouth salivated. Actually salivated. Then she noticed the folded up toilet paper he was pressing against the back of his rib cage.

"Do you have a sewing kit?" he asked calmly.

She leaped from the bed and moved toward him. "A kit? God. Why?"

Blood had seeped through the flimsy paper. He carefully peeled the paper away to reveal a long gash on his back. "I think I got cut from either the Sheetrock or the mirror when I fought with that asshole earlier. I can't get the right angle to sew it. Are you up for it?" He tried to twist and better see the wound.

Bile rose in her throat along with a healthy dose of panic. "Are you kidding me? You've been bleeding for hours? Why didn't we go to a doctor?"

"I pressed a bandanna against it all day. It just needs a couple of stitches." A frown drew down his dark eyebrows. "It's all right. Really."

Who the *hell* was this guy? Her legs wobbled when she walked back to her suitcase. "I have a traveling sewing kit, but it's for loose buttons." Not for flesh, for pete's sake.

Heat filtered along her back, and his breath stirred her hair as he looked over her shoulder. "That'll do. I can't get the right angle to sew it. Are you up for it?"

She shivered from his proximity. He was so damn big. "This just got weird. Really, really, really weird," she muttered. "Should we heat the needle or something?" Hadn't she seen that in a movie? She turned to face him and fought the urge to back up a little.

"Okay." He didn't seem to care. With deliberate movements, he shoved the toilet paper back into place. It stuck to the blood.

She coughed. Her stomach rolled over and shimmied inside her belly.

He grabbed the motel matches off the bedside table. "Now aren't you glad we're staying in a dive? A nicer motel wouldn't have good old fashioned matches lying around to promote the place." Lines fanned out from his eyes—from either pain or exhaustion.

"Though a nicer hotel would have a doctor." She tried not to wince as he ignited a match and turned the needle black. "Are you sure this is a good idea?"

"So long as you don't pass out or puke on me, we're good." He gently threaded the needle with bright yellow thread.

"Yellow?" she murmured.

He shrugged. "You have more yellow than the other colors."

"That's because I don't usually wear yellow buttons," she whispered. Could she do it? Actually draw the needle through his skin? Her stomach rioted.

"Hey." He reached out and cupped her chin to lift her face. "It's okay. If you can't do it, I'll just tape a shirt to it." His greenish brown eyes softened. How odd for such a huge guy to be so gentle.

She steeled her back. If he was strong enough to get sewn up without anesthetic, she was strong enough to stitch. "I can do this."

"Good girl." He leaned down and pressed a light kiss to her forehead.

The small touch ripped through her with the force of a dangerous tide. Her legs wobbled again. She blinked. "So. Maybe you should lie down?"

"Yeah." He handed over the needle and turned to sprawl on the bed, resting his face on his arms.

The towel dislodged enough to reveal the top of his very fine ass. His long legs hung over the edge of the bed, and even his feet were masculine and sexy.

Wow. She set a knee on the bed and gently began to pry the bloody paper away from the wound. It was a deep gash already filling with blood again. Her hands shook, and she took several deep breaths, forgetting about his butt. "Okay. It's okay."

He didn't move and seemed almost asleep. "Just take your time," he said drowsily.

How much blood had he lost? "I can do this." Her hands trembling, she pressed the sides together. He didn't so much as twitch, but it had to hurt. "I'm sorry," she croaked.

"I'm fine."

There was an intimacy in caring for him that gave her pause. Something feminine in her, something real, wanted to soothe him. Heal him. She gingerly slid the needle in, surprised by how much his flesh fought her. Her temples started to ache. Then she twisted and tried to draw it through. The angle was wrong. She shifted closer to him, her knee hitting his hip. Nope.

"You're gonna have to straddle me, darlin'."

She could've sworn that was amusement in his deep voice. Her gaze slid to his narrow waist and powerful back. "Right." Taking yet another deep breath, she shifted closer and lifted one of her legs over his hips. To avoid the wound, she had to shimmy back and sit squarely on his butt. Her skirt rode up her thighs and put her skin flush against the towel, which then rode up toward the wound. She tried to lever up and shove it down, but it was trapped beneath him. "Um."

He sighed, partially lifted, and yanked the towel free to toss on the floor. She landed on his bare butt this time. She gasped. God. His skin against hers. A totally unwelcome and insistent humming set up between her thighs. Heat flushed through her. All of him was so damn tight and muscled. Was he real?

"Anya? We'll have to pay extra if I bleed all over the bedspread," he said, his voice hoarse.

The poor guy sounded pained. "Right. Okay." She leaned forward and clasped the wound, drawing the needle through. From her new vantage point, it was a lot easier. A lump filled her throat. She blinked away tears.

He relaxed beneath her, and her hands steadied as she sewed the wound together. His skin fought her, but she prevailed. Man, he was tough. Who could take needles through their skin without flinching? His strength, his very masculinity, stole her breath.

Finally, she tied a knot at the end and snipped the string free with the tiny sewing kit scissors. "Done," she breathed out, sitting back. Sweat dotted her forehead, and she wiped the back of her hand across her skin.

"Thank you," he rumbled.

"No problem." As gently as she could, she slid off his body and tried not to stare at his stunning ass. Fights, blood, and stitches shouldn't be a turn-on. Yet there was something about his obvious maleness that made her feel soft. Needed. Feminine. "We should get a bandage or something."

"There should be something in my bag." He turned his head to face her, his hair rumpled, his eyes lazy, his body stretched out like a satisfied lion. "Make sure it isn't wet, though."

Wet. He'd said wet. Her nipples peaked. Man, she was out of her depth. "Sure." She rushed for his bag and almost kicked it out of the way before bending down and drawing out a dented box holding bandages, quarters, and a couple of condoms. Talk about prepared. She hustled back to him, securing the bandage against the stitches. She kept her movements gentle.

"Thanks," he said, his gaze warm on hers. Then his hand took over. "I've got it." He slowly started to roll over toward her, muscles rippling beneath his smooth skin.

Panic grabbed her. "No!" She lifted a hand and fell back, tumbling off the bed. Her butt hit the floor with a loud thump. Heat flared into her face.

He leaned over, just his head visible. "You okay?" Laughter made his eyes glow a deep green.

"Fine." She primly pushed herself to stand. "I, ah, just will take a shower now." Keeping her head high, she reclaimed her yoga pants and camisole before striding into the bathroom. Yeah. It would be a very cold shower.

CHAPTER
13

Heath gingerly stretched his side, making sure the stitches remained in place. His ribs ached, but he could live with the pain. The shower started in the other room. He forgot all about his wound as his mind flashed to the idea of Anya in the shower. Naked.

He groaned and turned his face into the pillow. Minutes before, she'd been straddling him. His groin tightened. Sure, she'd been stitching him up, but still.

His eyes ached, and he shut them. He wanted to stay awake until Anya returned to bed, but the earlier blood loss took its toll, and he dropped into an uneasy sleep. That quickly, he was right back in hell at the boys home.

The storage room, the one for beatings, had taken on a surreal glow. Ned, the owner, stood over a dead kid—Ralph—while Denver bled in the corner.

Ned rushed Heath, and he swung a bat the same second Ryker did, both of them hitting Ned in the head. The sound was worse than a watermelon bursting. Blood went everywhere, and Heath jumped back, his gut roiling.

Ryker dropped his bat, his face white in shock.

"He's dead," Heath said, looking around. There was no question.

Nobody could've survived that. The body lay contorted and was still twitching.

"We killed him," Ryker whispered. His jaw dropped. "What do we do?"

"Run," Heath said, tossing his bat toward the wall. His body vibrated and his head hurt, but they had to run. It was their only chance. He hurried toward Denver and pulled him to stand. "We have to go. Now."

They were gonna get caught. But if he could get Ryker and Denver to safety, then he could confess or something. "I have stuff stored on the other side of the woods. Clothes and some food." Tears pricked his eyes, and he shoved them away. No time. "We have to go."

Denver pulled back, his blue eyes so dark they looked black. Bruises covered his entire face and neck. "Fire."

Heath paused. "Fire?"

Denver slowly nodded, his shocked gaze on the dead bodies.

Heath sucked in air.

Ryker jerked back into himself. "He's right. Let's burn this place down."

Heath awoke with a gasp.

"Heath?" Anya murmured sleepily, turning toward him.

The old furnace blasted the crappy hotel room with meager heat, he was in bed, and Anya was next to him. He shuddered.

She brushed her palm over his chest. "Bad dream?"

"Yeah," he croaked out, his body slowly relaxing.

She moved closer and snuggled her face into his neck, wrapping an arm over his chest. "You're safe. I've got you." Her breathing deepened.

His heart rolled over, and he buried his face in her strawberry-scented hair. She had him. Yeah. He thought she did. Her kindness and vow of protection wound around him, through him. She was so damn special. Softly, so not to awaken her, he placed a kiss on her forehead. Then he drifted into a dreamless sleep.

Several hours later, he awoke with an indrawn breath and quickly surveyed his surroundings, tuning in with his extra-sensitive hearing.

No sounds out of the ordinary to worry about. Snow fell outside the motel room, a long-haul truck started in the parking lot, and a small woman was burrowed into his side, breathing softly.

The room was freezing.

He turned and glared at the too-silent heater. The thing must've given out during the night, and he'd been too tired to notice. After the fight and blood loss, he'd needed sleep. He barely remembered hearing Anya come to bed after her shower.

Anya in bed with him. His groin awoke fully.

She lay on her side with her nose pressed to his shoulder, her hand flattened over his heart, and her leg over one of his. It was as if she were trying to bind him to her during sleep. She felt small and delicate next to him...and warm. Sleepy and warm, sexy woman.

He took several deep breaths and tried to recite golfing scores in his head. Or golfing records. Anything to do with golf bored him, so he pictured green rolling hills and water hazards.

Nope.

She murmured something and slid even closer to him.

Why did she draw him so, especially when he knew better? His body and brain disconnected when he was around her, and he needed to get himself under control. Now. "Anya?" He partially turned toward her. "Baby? Wake up."

Her pretty green eyes slowly opened. Her mouth pursed into a silent O. "Heath?" She blinked several times and then drew back, her leg flying off him.

He grabbed her shoulders to keep her from rolling onto the floor again. "You're okay." He waited until she'd gathered herself and then released her when he wanted nothing more than to keep touching that soft skin. "Mornin'."

"Ah." She shoved rioting red hair away from her face. "Um. Morning." Frowning, she ducked further under the covers.

He grimaced. "The heater died."

"Oh." She snuggled a little closer to him without seeming to move. A tug centered low in his belly. Her hair caught his eye, and he reached out to wrap a wild curl around his finger. "Your hair is curly." He released it and watched it spring back up. The intimacy of the moment heated him throughout.

"Yeah. I usually straighten it but didn't after my shower." She swallowed, her gaze dropping to his neck, her voice throaty.

What would she look like in passion with that wild hair and her stunning coloring? Probably all red, green, and luscious pink. He bit back a groan, slowly exhaling to control his lungs. "I like it curly."

"Hmm." She yawned into her hand and eyed his bare chest. Awareness flitted across her pretty face. "This is awkward."

Amusement bubbled through him, and he grinned, the lightness turning him on even more. "Do you always blurt out whatever's in your head?"

She rubbed her eyes. "I find it's a lot easier than choosing words carefully, you know?"

God, he liked that about her. A lot.

She gingerly reached out and ran a finger along his biceps. "You must work out every day."

That one little touch rippled through his skin, filled his chest, and zinged right down to his cock. He pressed his lips together and fought for control. "I run and lift weights when I get the chance." And hey. Guess what? He was also a freak created in a lab to be superstrong—

wasn't that great? Plus, he was fleeing from a murder charge, and it was easier to run when in shape.

She pulled back her hand.

He tried to remain still, itching to have her hand back on him. Anywhere on him. "Are you afraid of me?" he asked.

She blinked. "No." There was a hint of uncertainty in her tone.

He swallowed. "I'd love to take this to the next level, but only if you're sure." Yeah, he was taking his lead from her honesty. If she could do it, so could he. "But I understand we're under pressure from chasing down a serial killer." It'd be more than nice to relieve some of that pressure.

Her gaze moved back to his chest. "I feel like I owe her, you know?"

He felt her stare like a burn. "Your sister?"

"Yeah." Anya's green eyes softened to the color of a spring meadow. "She was strong and so kind. The second I called her, she instantly moved into action to protect me." Pain sizzled in the air. "She was so good to me." Anya chuckled sadly. "I didn't know she'd threatened Carl, though. I wish I could've seen that."

Carl was really an idiot to hurt a woman like this. Heath reached out and gently rubbed along her neck. "I'll beat him bloody for you if you'd like."

She grinned. "That's a kind offer."

He hadn't been kidding. Not completely, anyway.

She shook her head. "I left him, and I win. I'm just sorry I wasted so much time and doubted myself. He's an insecure jackass, and I hope he loses all his hair and gets warts."

Heath slid his hand up into her glorious hair. "So no fear here?"

She licked her lips, and he felt it in his groin. "No. Although you sure can fight. I've never seen such precision."

He grimaced. "Yeah. It's a gift." Good thing he hadn't needed to snap the attacker's neck in front of her. Of course, that guy could fight, too. Really fight. He had to be one of Cobb and Madison's soldiers, which was the main reason Heath hadn't wanted to deal with the police. "I'll never hurt you, Anya."

She leaned into his touch, interest leaping into her eyes. "Let's make a deal. I won't be frightened of your scary fighting abilities, and you stop treating me like some fragile woman who shouldn't be here."

The feeling of all that silk around his hand was torturing him, but he couldn't release her. What answer should he give? He did have scary fighting abilities, and she was so fucking fragile and petite. Yet she'd given him an invitation. "Should we seal the deal with a kiss?" he murmured, his gaze dropping to her pink lips.

She visibly swallowed. "You think that's a good idea?" Her voice had gone husky fast.

No. It was a terrible idea. Disastrous. "Yes." He leaned in—carefully, to give her plenty of room and time to move away—and pressed his lips against hers.

With a low moan, she opened her mouth under his and kissed him back. Hard and fast.

His head nearly blew off. He'd expected tentative and sweet. What he got was powerful and dangerous. She moved closer and rolled right on top of him. The second her core came into contact with his, she stiffened and then settled in.

Both of her hands tunneled into his hair for a tight grip, and she kissed him, her tongue dueling with his.

In an instant, he went from curious to on fire. He allowed her to control the kiss for two more seconds and then let himself go. He tightened his hand in her hair and twisted, angling her head so he could delve deeper. Her heated sex cradled his cock, which jumped against her, wanting in. Her soft body tortured him. He flattened his free hand at the small of her waist, pressing down.

She moaned into his mouth, and he nearly lost the tight hold he had on his control. The woman was soft and round everywhere he was hard, and he wanted nothing more than to get lost in her.

With a low growl, he turned and flattened her beneath him.

She hissed a breath into his mouth, and it took a second for him to realize she was in pain. He lifted up, his mind clearing. "What happened?" His elbows held his weight, so he wasn't crushing her. Yet his dick was pressed rather insistently between her legs.

"Nothing," she murmured, tugging his head closer.

He stilled. "I hurt you. How?" He settled his knees on either side of her body and sat on his haunches, caging her.

She looked up, her eyes still cloudy with passion, and her lips a deep red. "It's nothing."

He studied her pale pink camisole over her dark yoga pants. Keeping her gaze, he settled his thumbs beneath the flimsy fabric and pushed up. "Holy shit." A bruise covered several of her ribs. "Tell me they're not broken." As gently as he could, he ran the pad of his finger across each rib.

She sucked in air but didn't flinch. "Not even cracked, I don't think. It's just a bruise, and it still hurts a little, and you caught me off guard when we rolled."

Jesus Christ. "This happened when I flattened you at the hotel room. When the attacker burst through the door." Heath looked at the bruises he'd caused. These were from *him*. What was he thinking to go along with this insane scheme? Her sister was already dead. Anya could be next. He pulled down the shirt and stepped off the bed. "I'm so sorry."

"It isn't your fault." Her eyes wide, she scrambled to sit up. She pulled her knees to her chest and wrapped her arms around them. "I'm fine, Heath."

"You are not fine," he exploded. She flinched, and it was like somebody had kicked him in the balls. Hard.

CHAPTER 14

Anya could've slapped her own head when Heath paled. "I didn't mean to flinch," she said weakly. He was a big guy with a temper, and he was beyond dangerous. Anybody would've taken note of his anger, but the raw pain in his eyes made her chest hurt. "I'm not scared of you." There were serious land mines in that man's head. In his heart, too. She cleared her throat and tried not to look so small against the headboard.

"I know." He ran a rough hand through his already disheveled hair, his gaze down as his face went stoic.

"No." She sat up straighter. "Don't retreat. Please."

He frowned, his focus moving to her. "Don't shrink me."

Amusement bubbled up through her. "Buddy, I don't think that's possible."

God, he was something to look at. Standing perfectly confident in his nudity, he was all predatory muscle. A shadow covered his jaw, and his eyes glowed a greenish brown in the light. Her body still hummed with need from his kiss, and for a moment, when he'd pressed her against the bed, she'd thought maybe they'd take it further. What would he be like hot with passion and fully engaged? Her nipples peaked even more.

He started, and then his shoulders seemed to smooth out. "I have a slight glitch with strong people hurting, ah, smaller ones."

It was nice that he'd said *smaller* instead of *weaker*. "You have a glitch with men hurting women," she said softly. "That's not a bad glitch, Heath. The fact that you are strong and could hurt somebody doesn't mean you will. It doesn't mean you're bad."

His head went back, just enough to show shock. "I don't think I'm bad." His voice lacked conviction.

She didn't want to be his shrink, but she did want to help. Wanted to soothe him. "Somewhere deep down you know you could hurt me. The fact that you won't, that you wouldn't even think about it, shows you're good." It was so easy for childhood trauma to mix up reality, even in adults.

He studied her, his gaze probing and lightening. "You're a smart one, now, aren't you?" Admiration and something darker filled his tone. Something masculine and...interested. Then his eyes leisurely wandered down to her body, no doubt seeing everything.

Tension rolled through the room. Wild and deep...even emotional with need.

Her gaze slid down the hard planes of his chest and even lower, as if she couldn't control herself. "Oh my God." Heat flashed into her face and burned her cheeks. While she hadn't really looked before, now she couldn't help herself. He was well outlined and definitely aroused. "Dude. You're huge."

His mouth went slack for a moment. Then he shook his head like a dog with a face full of water. "Jesus."

She winced and tried to focus on his face. Only his face. Not lower. Definitely not any lower. "Um. Too much information. Sorry. Brain and mouth are connected." Yet didn't guys like to hear that? In his case, it was certainly true. He didn't seem overly pleased with her observation, however. "Um. Sorry." She ground a fist into her eye. This was getting beyond awkward.

He sighed. "Let's get dressed and hit the road. We can grab something to eat on the way."

As if on cue, her stomach rumbled. "Good plan." Her cell phone buzzed from the side table, and she picked it up. "Hi, Reese."

Heath's head jerked back.

Her eyes widened. Oh no. She hadn't thought. Her mind had been on Heath's body and not on the moment. She wasn't even fully awake yet.

"Where the hell are you?" Reese snapped out. "You and Heath Jones are supposed to be in my office right now. As in right now, right now."

She bit her lip. "Well, we, ah, aren't going to make it."

Heath held out a broad hand for the phone. She gave him a look but handed it over. He pressed the speaker button. "Special Agent Reese? I decided to take Anya out of the jurisdiction and get her to safety, considering she all but put a bull's-eye on her red head."

"You think we can't keep her safe, asshole?" Reese's voice rose dangerously and filled the room. "We're the FBI."

Anya winced. The speaker on the phone was way too loud.

Heath nodded. "I don't care who you are because you'll use her. We both know you'll use Anya as a decoy, and I'm not gonna let you do that."

Silence ticked for a moment. "She made herself a decoy."

"Yeah, because she's emotional about this case, as are you. She's my fiancée, and I'm going to keep her safe whether you like it or not." Heath's emphasis on the word *my* sent funny tingles through her still-aroused body. "After I get her somewhere safe, I'll contact you, if you'd still like to interview me. I promise I don't have any information I didn't share with Loretta. There's nothing to learn from me."

"I think you're full of shit, Jones." Rustling came over the line. "If you think I'm going to sit here and not start investigating your ass, you're crazy. In fact, where were you the day Special Agent Jackson was taken? Have an alibi?"

Heath's face hardened. "I liked Special Agent Jackson, and I never would've hurt her. You know that, or there's no way you would've let me leave the cemetery."

As if anybody could've stopped Heath. Anya watched him, her instincts flaring. He was even more dangerous than she'd thought, but that didn't mean he was a bad guy. Unless he was, and since her instincts sucked lately, it was unfortunately possible.

Her hands shook as she rubbed her eyes again. God, she was tired. "I talked to Loretta after I met him one time, Reese." She tried to strengthen her voice. "Loretta said that she'd cleared Heath for at least two of the earlier murders and that she trusted him."

"She didn't know we believe there might be two killers," Reese shot back. "Where are you, Anya? I'll send a car to bring you to safety."

"Why do you think there are two?" Heath asked, frowning. "The M.O. fits one crazy bastard, not two."

"I'm not sharing with you," Reese returned evenly. "As of now, you're impeding an investigation."

Heath shook his head and glared at the phone. "You know I'm not. Why don't you do your damn job and find this guy? Have you interviewed Carl Sparks? That guy seems sketchy to me. He could be your guy."

"You know, maybe he is," Reese said thoughtfully. "He didn't show up for his interview, either. Maybe you and Carl are the killing pair I've been looking for."

Okay, so Reese was pissed. Anya breathed out, her mind clicking facts into place. Intelligence and not emotion would prevail. "I understand that you're angry, but come on. Heath has been cleared by Loretta, and while Carl is a jerk, he's not a serial killer. Frankly, I don't think he's savvy enough to have evaded the authorities for this many months, and there's no doubt the Copper Killer is a smart guy. Or guys."

"Either way, I scheduled two interviews and neither man showed up." Reese whispered something unintelligible to somebody. "If you ask me, Carl is on his way to find you. He seemed overly concerned that you left with Heath. And you're wrong about me, Anya. I have no intention of using you as a decoy. I plan to put you back into protective custody. I owe Loretta that much."

Anya shook her head, breath rushing through her. "I don't want to be hidden away. This guy killed my sister, and I'm his end goal. Why not use that?" She tried to sound sure, but the idea of the killer finding her sent chills skittering down her spine. She shivered.

"Because you're an untrained civilian," Reese said, whispering away from the phone again.

Heath disengaged the call. "Damn it. Get ready to go. Now."

"Why?" she asked, swinging her attention to him.

"They traced us. I heard a tech whisper that to Reese," Heath said. "We need to go. Now."

Okay. His super hearing was bizarre, but she'd figure that out later. She scrambled up and grabbed her suitcase, fully on board with his plan. For now. "I don't want to go into protective custody." The killer wanted her and would keep taking other victims that looked like her until she stopped him.

Heath reached for jeans on the floor. "Agreed. Frankly, the FBI didn't protect Loretta, and you are right. This killer is good. Brilliant maybe. I want you where I can watch you."

While there was nothing sexual about his tone of voice, the words still tunneled through her like a wild kiss. "You don't trust the FBI, do you?" she murmured.

"No," he said shortly. "Loretta was too easy to find. Maybe somebody in her team shouldn't be trusted."

Anya paused, shoving the phone into her bag. "Man, you really don't like law enforcement people."

He shrugged his massive shoulders. "Let's just say I want you with me and the few people in life I know and do trust. I'll have my brothers set up a safe place, several really, in Snowville. They should be set by the time we get there."

Speaking of trust. "Should we talk about what happened earlier?" What had almost happened?

He looked up from rummaging through his duffel for a faded green shirt. "There's nothing to talk about. We had a moment, it was a mistake, and that's the end of it." His expression remained neutral and his gaze veiled. "I'm sorry if I scared you, and I'll make sure to take better care from now on."

She clutched her bag closer to her chest. He had been taking great care of her, but she truly didn't know him, now, did she? "I'm asking one more time. Are you wanted by the law?" There was something off about him, but she couldn't quite put her finger on what. Her dad had been a cop, and she believed in the system. In the people working for the system.

"No. I'm just not a big fan of the police," he said.

"Just like the Copper Killer," she blurted. Her eyes widened. "Oh. I mean—Well, I know you're not the killer."

He grinned, but the smile didn't reach his eyes. "That's a relief."

CHAPTER 15

Snowville had a sweet charm that she'd discovered while staying there with Loretta, and Anya appreciated the nicely plowed neighborhoods they passed before reaching their destination. The building Heath's brothers had chosen as a safe haven was made of older brick, which looked crumbly but sturdy in an authentic early 1900s kind of way. There were garage doors on one side, which would allow them to park on the ground level.

The idea of a clandestine operation raised her blood pressure, and yet her focus had narrowed and she seemed to notice everything. The homeless guy shuffling along the icy sidewalk with a full shopping cart. The teenagers in their ripped jeans and puffy jackets strutting toward the stores. The mom with three toddlers and an empty stroller. Were they all who they seemed?

Anya glanced at Heath's calm expression as he circled the block. Watching him filled her with more than anticipation. Her blood sped, and her body tuned to his. The more time she spent with him, the more fascinating he became. He noticed everything, and that was quite a skill. And what was up with his super-hearing, anyway? What kind of a world had she just entered? Was she imagining things or was there more at play?

"What are we doing?" she asked, just having awoken upon entering Snowville.

"I'm taking note of alleys and escape routes from the building. You should look around, too." His voice remained calm and steady, but an alertness showed in the line of his strong shoulders.

She studied the buildings around them. Everything in her wanted to trust her instincts, but he was way beyond her realm of experience. "I know you're innocent, but you have traits the FBI might be interested in. You need to be careful."

He rubbed the scruff on his jaw. "What do you mean?"

That jaw looked made of stone. Chiseled and strong. "You are smart and trained, and you could take on a trained FBI agent easily. However, you do have definite triggers about women, and you've been involved in the case for a while. Don't many killers try to work with law enforcement in such cases?" she asked thoughtfully.

He cut her a look. "Yeah. Maybe I am a good suspect. If Agent Reese thinks about it, he'll start plastering my face everywhere in an effort to track me down. That can't happen."

"Why not? You have a good face." Truth be told, he had an amazing face. If she were a sculptor, she could spend weeks getting the lines and angles just right.

He flashed a grin. "Thanks. With the detective agency, I like to stay under the radar as much as possible."

It was a good explanation, but was it the truth? Besides being strongly good-looking, he was so alert and dangerous. What was she doing trusting him? If he turned on her, what would she do? She shivered.

He circled the building once more and drove up to one of the small garage doors, which opened immediately. "Cameras are already in place and functioning around the perimeter of the entire building." He drove into a cavernous parking area.

Concrete surrounded them, cracked and crumbling. Was the building sound? If Heath's brothers were as careful as he was, then the building would be perfect. Well, probably. That hadn't been a very straight answer about the law. She instinctively searched for another exit in the garage.

A sleek black truck and a nicely decked out Jeep were parked in the far corner. Heath cut the engine.

She released her seat belt and surveyed the garage area. Her breath quickened. "I guess we've arrived."

"You sure you don't think I'm a serial killer?" he asked quietly.

She tried to see beyond the surface with him. To understand. To stop feeling so vulnerable and out of her depth. "No. I'm a redhead, and you wouldn't be able to act so natural around me. Besides, if you were, you'd be trying to wear my skin by now, right?"

He chuckled at her lame joke. "I have no clue if that's right or not, but I'm not the killer."

"Loretta said you weren't, and she was good at her job." Anya clasped her hands together. "Based on my profile, you don't exactly fit." Yet where did he fit? Really?

"I don't?"

"No. Your attachment to your brothers gives you a hint of normalcy." She looked around. "So. What do we do now?" Her knuckles turned white as she tightened her hold on her hands.

"You're safe here." He stretched from the SUV and reached in for their bags, gaze sweeping the entire area. "We need to get settled in and then discuss a plan. And a contingency plan." He lifted an eyebrow. "And probably a plan C."

Why did she feel safe with him? She didn't know him and wasn't sure she should trust him. But as he scouted the garage for threats, she knew with a certainty born of instinct that he'd protect her. "I'm in on this plan," she said. The crazy plan to catch a deadly serial killer. Heath wasn't arguing with her or trying to force her into somewhere safe and hidden, as appealing as that was. "I'm playing a part."

He slammed the back door and came around to her side of the vehicle. "You're playing the most important part." He paused. "But if you've changed your mind, I definitely understand. We can move on to Plan D." His shoulders relaxed as if he'd been carrying a burden that had suddenly becoming lighter. "We could—"

"No." She turned fully toward him. "I want to do this. I mean, it's not like I'm going to just walk right up to the guy and say 'Take me,' you know."

Why couldn't she figure out who he was? There had to be some sort of clue somewhere. She'd gone over her own life, her entire past, so many times her head hurt.

Heath straightened. "Very true. It'll be more like you making a couple of public appearances with me and then being visible around town. We'll have you protected at all times."

"That was Loretta's downfall." Saying her sister's name hurt. "She tried to go out on her own." Shouldn't Anya have realized that aspect in her sister? Maybe her psychology skills had been dulled by her time in the classroom. Reading people and figuring them out was far different from teaching. She rubbed her suddenly chilled arms. "A team is needed to take down this guy."

"Exactly." Heath turned as an older wooden door opened behind him.

Two broad men strode out followed by a stunning dark-haired woman with nearly sky blue eyes. She was tall and nicely muscled in an ultra-feminine way.

Talk about an intimidating and strikingly good-looking team. Anya forced a smile and tried not to worry about her wildly curly hair and makeup-free face. Compared to the beauty in dark jeans and a red silk top, she felt like a hick cousin from *that* side of a family tree.

"You must be Anya." The woman strode forward and extended a hand.

They shook. "Hi."

"I'm Zara." The woman's smile made her appear even more beautiful. "We've scrambled to put together apartments on short notice." She motioned to the first guy, who had black hair, bluish green eyes, and a bad-boy vibe. "This is Ryker, and this is Denver." The other guy had dark hair, blue eyes, and a tight build.

Both men nodded and offered to shake hands, their expressions revealing nothing. After gently releasing her, without seeming to move, they quickly scouted the very empty garage area.

"Hi," Anya said weakly, noting scars on their palms. Blood brother scars. The scars were both sweet and somehow threatening. A vow in blood—what wouldn't they do for each other?

They were a solid wall, without question. What would it be like to want to form a family with somebody? With men like these who seemed so indestructible? She suddenly studied the very put-together Zara. Her gaze was direct and intelligent, and she stood like she could take care of herself. But even now, both Ryker and Denver remained close enough to jump in front of the beauty instantly.

And beautiful she was. It was all Anya could do not to fix her own hair. Why hadn't she brought her professor clothes?

"Status?" Heath asked his brothers.

Ryker leaned to the side to survey the SUV, his gaze intense. "We need to dump this vehicle and return it to a rental agency since you rented it with our business account. I'll take care of it. For now, this building is secure. Motion sensors, cameras, a couple of hidden devices if necessary."

Devices? What was a device? Anya looked toward Heath.

"This is a good headquarters, guys. Thanks. What about the decoy offices? Are they ready?" Heath turned toward Anya. "We have two sets of offices and quarters. This one is secure and secret, while the other one is public and will draw out the killer. We hope."

Tension suddenly swelled through the room, filling the huge space. Anya's legs trembled.

"This is not a good idea," Ryker said, his voice a low rumble.

"Nope," Denver agreed, his gaze moving to Anya.

She fought the urge to squirm. Heath moved toward her as if sensing her discomfort, and the heat from his body washed over her. While he didn't touch her, just having his solid form near calmed her rioting nerves. A little.

Ryker cut Denver a look and sighed.

Anya frowned. What were the weird undercurrents going on? Her face heated. She'd had no right to involve these people in a battle with a serial killer. They seemed to already have enough going on. "I know I've created danger with the Copper Killer, and if it's a problem, I can go work with the FBI."

"Good idea," Ryker said bluntly.

Denver just studied her. She'd seen a wild bear once on a refuge, and Denver's gaze was similar, somehow. She rubbed her suddenly freezing arms.

"No," Heath said. "The FBI will store you somewhere they think is safe, and I doubt their security at this point. This guy has outmaneuvered them before."

Denver rubbed his chin. "True."

"The decoy offices?" Heath repeated without much patience.

Ryker slipped a hand into his pocket. "Across town. Just for show, but we made a good effort. Fully protected with the same measures, along with one large apartment upstairs that we can make look like we use it. Very similar to what we have here, but this place is our safe zone, and it's untraceable. The other is a decoy zone," he said evenly. "We need to discuss how far and how public we want to go. The more visible we become, the faster we'll need to get out of here. It's a hit-and-run op, or we're dead."

Anya shook her head, her stomach aching. The apartment she'd temporarily shared with Loretta was all the way across town. She didn't know this neighborhood at all. "You guys are talking weird lingo here. What are you saying?"

Nobody spoke.

Ryker cleared his throat. "Also, we, ah, retrieved all of your belongings from the apartment you were sharing with your sister across town. Everything is in boxes upstairs."

They'd done what? Anya paused. "How?"

Once again, nobody answered her.

Zara looked at Ryker and then straightened her shoulders. "How about I take Anya upstairs and show her Heath's apartment?" She reached for Anya's arm with a soft touch. "You've been on the road for two days. The showers aren't luxurious by any means, but I've stocked them with very nice supplies."

"Good idea." Heath kept his veiled gaze on his brothers and then gave Anya a gentle nudge. "I'll be up in a few."

Anya looked around but couldn't think of a protest. They had every right to keep their lives private, but now she was part of this op. For the moment, part of the team.

Yet they didn't trust her. Her chest ached, and she lifted her chin, drawing on a calm mask. How nice would it be to belong? To really belong to a family again, like she'd been with her father? Her eyes were gritty, and her hair felt limp. Maybe a shower would wake her up. "Okay, a shower sounds nice. Heath, when you come up, I want to know what's going on. If I'm going to be part of this plan, then no more secrets."

Did Denver snort?

Anya swung her gaze to him, but his face remained expressionless. Just who were these people? Big badass blank slates, that's what.

But who?

CHAPTER
16

Heath waited until Zara had squired a bewildered Anya out of the parking level before facing his brothers. "All right. Let me have it."

Denver crossed his arms, which amounted to a full-out lecture of disapproval.

While Heath usually spoke up for Denver, this time Ryker jumped right in. "You told me she was all bruised up when you first met her, although she seems fine now. What the holy fuck are you doing?"

Heath sighed and dropped the bags. "What needs to be done. The bruises weren't from a man. Well, not a man she was involved with. This isn't about me or childhood scars. My past doesn't drive me."

Denver snorted.

Ryker interpreted. "Our childhood scars do more than drive us, and you know it. Own it before it gets you killed."

Ah. As usual, his brothers were worried about him and not themselves. Even so. "Anya was bruised training in self-defense. She's not a battered woman, and I'm not having flashbacks to my mom."

Denver cocked his head, his lip twisting.

Heath sighed. "Okay. I flashed back when I saw Loretta's body. But that's all."

Ryker's gaze delved deep. As with most of his gazes, there was a mixture of several emotions. Concern, caring, warning, questioning…

It was the questioning that provided warning. If Ry decided the op was too dangerous, mentally or emotionally, he'd pull the plug. Since he was the most mentally stable at the moment, he'd do whatever he had to do.

Heath sighed and continued. "I'm fine, so please don't plan to drug me and get me somewhere safe." Since he'd done so to Ryker years ago when things had gotten too dicey, he couldn't rule it out. "This is going to be dangerous, and I'm doing it. But I fully understand if you guys want to sit this one out. I can hire backup."

"Don't be a dick," Denver said slowly. "If you're in, we're in. It's not even an option."

Heath blinked. Heat flushed through him. Family. They'd formed it out of necessity, and they'd held on through the years because it was right. They were never truly alone, which was a hell of a mantra used by brothers across the genetic pool. He accepted the truth of the words. "Fair enough. What about Zara?" He looked at Ryker. The woman was Ryker's heart, and Heath would instantly die for her if necessary. "She could go to the Montana gang for safety."

"Won't go," Ryker said. "I could force her, but according to her, my being a throw-back dickhead asshole is not a good way to plan a life together."

Man, Ryker had found the exact prefect woman for him. "She does have a way with words." Heath grinned.

Ryker nodded. "She can work details from here in the safe house, and she's phenomenal with details, so she'll be a big help." His chest swelled, and his eyes glowed.

Zara was a paralegal originally out of Wyoming and probably the most analytical person Heath had ever met. Ryker had never smiled as much or been as relaxed as when she'd entered his life. Even so, if anything happened to the sweet woman, Heath would never forgive himself. "I appreciate everything you guys have done in such a short amount of time."

Ryker's eyes hardened. "We want to catch this guy, too. From the day we were hired and didn't find the girl in time, I've been waiting for a chance to take this bastard out."

"Damn, he's smart," Heath said.

"Yeah," Ryker said. "I'm worried how twisted you are about this job. This woman. If you need to talk, you need to talk."

Heath's lips twitched. "What are you, Dr. Phil?"

Ryker grinned and rubbed a hand through his thick hair. "Not even close. Not with these luscious locks."

"Luscious?" Denver snorted.

"Hey. Zara said my hair is luscious." Ryker frowned.

Heath coughed to mask a laugh. So that was why Ryker's hair was growing past his collar. "That's definitely the word for it."

Ryker brightened. "Exactly. For now, let's go inside to discuss the case. It's cold here in the garage. Follow us, and I'll show you the living quarters." He led the way toward the door. "We can have a brief meeting, show you around, and then get rid of the SUV on the way to the decoy offices."

"And shopping," Denver said.

"Shopping?" Heath retrieved the bags and followed his brothers through the doorway and up the stairs.

The landing was brick and bare...and four doors went in different directions.

"Three are apartments, and this one was a conference room that we turned into a war room." Ryker shoved open a new metal door to show a sprawling room with a conference table, a small kitchen to the side, a wall of windows, and a pool table by a bar. "The pool table was here."

His brothers had worked hard to get all this ready. After the past week, Heath was finally able to take a deep breath and fill his lungs. His neck and shoulders relaxed. Even as a kid, he'd known that family was all that really mattered. It was an easy lesson when you didn't have any.

Now he did.

Even though they were worried about him, they'd still cover his back and, by extension, Anya's. He was lucky to have them and that extra layer of protection for her. So many emotions slammed into him, he couldn't find the right words. His brothers not only had put themselves into the center of a serial killer investigation but also had made themselves far too visible for past enemies to find. For him.

"I like this place."

Denver nodded. "You're welcome."

Heath dropped the bags and crossed to a large board already filled with notes and pictures of the Copper Killer case. Next to the board was a long desk covered with several computers and monitors. Some showed the current building, while others surveyed another, newer-looking building near downtown. "Wow. You guys did a lot of work quickly."

"Yeah, and we really cut into our savings," Ryker said.

"Emptied them," Denver muttered. He shrugged. "We'll take more paying gigs after this and be okay."

Now they were broke. Heath scrubbed both hands down his face. They had to get back to business. "We have to talk about the asshole I fought with at the hotel. I'm not sure how he found us, and he's damn good," Heath said.

Ryker grimaced. "He must be one of Sylvia Daniels's—I mean Dr. Madison's soldiers. Did you get a look at him?"

"No, but he moved just like our, well, our brothers from Montana."

Recently, they'd discovered another group of created soldiers, who'd actually been raised by Dr. Madison and were brothers through a common sperm donor. Some of them might share maternal genetic material with Heath and his brothers, too. Who knew? They were deadly but family. Unfortunately, Madison—whom the three of them had known as Sylvia Daniels in their childhood—had some tough soldiers working for her who would have no problem kidnapping Heath or his brothers so she could keep experimenting on them.

Heath stretched his neck, his body urging him to take a run. Two days in a car and a too-brief tumble with Anya in bed had him rioting. He rubbed his forehead. "I feel like something's coming and soon."

Denver nodded.

"Ditto," Ryker said. "Of course, after Anya's press conference and our actually moving to her cited location, we've sent out full-on neon signs for the past to come and get us."

"Briefly. Just fast enough for this killer to make a move," Heath said, a rock dropping into his gut. "Timing is everything."

"Right." Ryker looked at the murder board. "We have a seventy-two-hour countdown. It'll take Madison and Cobb that long to organize a full-on assault on us here, so from the minute you go public with Lost Bastards Investigative Services and Anya, we start the countdown. If the killer hasn't struck by the time it hits zero, we move on and find another way to catch him."

"That's if Madison and Cobb haven't already set a plan in motion," Denver interjected. "After the press conference."

Ryker tapped on the murder board. "Chances are if Madison saw the conference, she figured it was a red herring. Oh, they'll be monitoring Snowville, but she doesn't think we're stupid enough to actually come here."

"She has no clue how stupid we can be," Denver muttered.

There was enough truth in the statement that Heath couldn't smile. Tension and stress bombarded him from every side, and he had to fight himself with Anya. He couldn't go near her again. "I'm in fucking trouble."

"No shit," Ryker said.

"She's stronger than she looks," Heath said, his body heating.

"No doubt," Ryker said. "I saw her with the reporters, remember? But you're on full protector mode, and when you get that way, you don't think. You don't cover your own back."

Heath frowned. "I'm solid."

Ryker shook his head. "Yeah, but I can see you looking at her like some wounded animal you need to fix. Her sister died. A serial killer is after her. She's tough, man. But you're going to screw it up and treat her like she's not strong enough for you."

What the hell? "You finally find a woman and now you have to give us advice? Knock it off, Ryker." Heath rolled his eyes. "While I admire you for taking a chance, let's face it. Our lives are so unsteady and uncertain, it's crazy. We have Sheriff Cobb and Madison after us, their psycho soldiers working hard, and now we're messing with a serial killer. I'm always going to be on the run, and that's no life for Anya."

Denver nodded.

Heath winced. Denver had given up the love of his life for the same reasons, and if his bloodshot eyes were any indication, he was still coping by putting way too much whiskey in his coffee. "I'll help you keep Zara safe, Ryker. But it's as far as I'll go for any woman until we're no longer on the run." If ever.

Ryker sighed. "Fair enough. Let's head into the secured apartments. They're small, just what we need for this op, and they have only one bedroom each." His smile made his eyes twinkle just like they had on last April Fools' Day, when he'd covered Heath's

Plymouth Hemi 'Cuda with feathers. "Do you want me to get you extra pillows to place in the center of the bed as a nice divider?"

Denver snorted.

Heath rolled his eyes. "A fence of down feathers. Yeah. That'll work." In bed with Anya again? His body heated, completely ignoring his brain.

CHAPTER
17

With blood dripping down his face, Daniel was the epitome of danger. Dr. Isobel Madison watched from the outskirts of what would soon be a well used training field as he methodically kicked the hell out of anybody who challenged him. A few of the soldiers had been with Isobel for years, like Daniel. Others were new to her employ, and if Daniel didn't cool it, a couple would be new to graves. "Daniel," she called out, trying not to wince when he drove two soldiers into the icy dirt.

Her boy turned to face her, bare to the waist, apparently not feeling the cold. Cut muscles rippled in his chest and down his arms. "Yes?"

His skin was so young and smooth. Strong. "Enough training. We have business to discuss." She turned on her high heel and strode back into the newly furbished laboratory building. While the fifteen-acre facility in Boise wasn't nearly as big or as well outfitted as the facilities and compounds in her past, it was a good start. There were barracks for soldiers, offices for medical personnel, a lab, and now a training field. She'd invested well through the years, as had Sheriff Cobb.

Heat filtered around her as she made her way down the fairly sterile hall to her office, which had a window facing the training field. Shrugging out of her jacket, she took a seat at her wide glass desk.

Daniel had followed her and stood at attention behind one of her two modern guest chairs. "Yes?" he asked, seemingly unconcerned by his bare chest or ripped jeans.

She swallowed, her abdomen heating. It would take an hour to kiss down that chest. "How has recruiting gone?"

"Not well." He planted both broad hands on the back of a chair. "We need to reach out to mercenaries for hire, and your boy is stopping me on that."

She arched an eyebrow. "The sheriff is stopping you?" Elton Cobb had better get on board with her plans.

"Yes. Said he only wants ex-military with honorable discharges." Daniel's voice was smooth, like honeyed whiskey, and his eyes were an intriguing brown veiled of any emotion. "I disagree."

"He's a sheriff and wants to stay within the law as much as possible." She let her gaze roam over Daniel's broad chest. "I wonder. Once this place is up and running, do you think the sheriff can run the military side as well as the commander did?" She'd begun her career in genetic research and manipulation with her one love, the commander, so many years ago. Now that he was dead, she needed to continue their work. "Is Elton Cobb up to the task?"

"No. The sheriff is soft."

She lifted her head. Daniel was nowhere near soft. Anywhere. "What about you?"

For the first time, Daniel's eyes flared. "Absolutely." His chin lifted.

"What drives you?" she asked, trying to probe into his head. Ambition looked good on him. She'd known him since birth, and yet she still didn't fully understand what made him tick. Many of her other highly trained soldiers were driven by family and the need to protect each other, which was why and how they'd escaped her for now. Daniel didn't have that. "What do you want?"

"A home," he said simply. "I grew up in a compound as a soldier, and that's all I know. This is what I want." He shoved a hand through his short hair. "If I'm in charge, this is my place, too. It's mine."

"I see." She crossed her legs, showing plenty of leg. Half naked, he made her mouth salivate. When was the last time she'd been taken and hard? Oh, the sheriff was getting into shape and had a nicely sadistic bent, but there was something about a dyed-in-the-wool soldier—one who rarely let go—that was truly unique. The commander had been like that, and he'd trained Daniel on how to kill and control his emotions. Would Daniel be as good in bed? Her last wild time with a man holding frighteningly absolute focus had been way too long ago. "You said something last time we spoke about me being the closest thing you have to a mother. Do you really see me as a mother?"

His head lifted slightly. "Not mine. No."

Interesting. She stood and crossed around the desk, her heartbeat humming nicely. "No?"

"No." He looked down several inches at her, his gaze sweeping her entire form and making her breasts tingle. "I've never seen you in that light."

Fair enough and very good news. "Do you have a woman?" She had made sure her boys had the best training in sexual techniques from many experts, so he definitely knew how to please a woman in a thousand ways. "Are you attached?"

"No." He kept her gaze, one of the few soldiers who apparently did not feel the need to turn away. Was that curiosity in his eyes? "It's hard to maintain a relationship with secrets. I prefer casual."

"As do I." She'd have to tread softly, but she could have both Daniel and Elton Cobb. Maybe. Just imagine the churning depths beneath Daniel's calm exterior. "Don't you want more? A relationship of some sort?"

He frowned. "Not now. I like sex, and women have their place, but I don't want the picket fence." He gave a mock shudder. "Although…"

She paused. "Although what?"

"I'm interested in the command here. I wouldn't mind something, someone, who was just mine. Even secretly. But mine." He brushed her long hair away from her shoulder.

She shivered. They were definitely on the same page. "I'm glad to hear that."

Daniel leaned into her space just enough to catch her breath. "You said we had business to discuss, which always comes before pleasure."

She swallowed. "Good point. I want you to find Heath, Denver, and Ryker now. Report only to me and not to Sheriff Cobb." While Elton wanted those boys dead, she wanted them alive, well, and donating sperm for her experiments. "Have you studied the news conference given by Anya Best?"

"I have." Daniel crossed his muscled arms and stood straighter. "When Anya Best gave her little impromptu news conference, she lied."

"Agreed." Isobel's hands itched to touch his chest. "Do you think she was lying about the engagement, the move to Snowville, or both?"

"Both." Daniel shook his head. "No way would Heath allow her to announce their engagement or, more importantly, their location. She set herself up for the serial killer who had taken her sister, and she set Heath up at the same time. My guess is that he told her to give Snowville as a location and then headed right for Florida."

Isobel sighed, her mind spinning. "I agree. Yet I think we should check out Snowville just in case."

Daniel lifted an arched eyebrow. "If that's what you want, I'll head there tomorrow morning."

Her smile even felt catlike. "What in the world will we do with tonight?" Were his sweats tented? Why, yes. Excellent. Heavy footsteps sounded down the hallway, and she hustled back around her desk to sit. "We can talk about it later."

Elton Cobb strode into the room and stopped instantly at seeing Daniel. "You put three of my men into the infirmary," he barked.

Daniel just looked at him with no expression on his face.

Isobel watched both men, reminded of a film of fighting tigers she had watched years ago. They were both deadly and most likely sociopathic. While Daniel had more training, Cobb was seasoned and lacked remorse. It'd be an impressive battle, and she wasn't sure who'd ultimately win. Daniel could probably take Cobb in a head-on fight, but Cobb would come at the younger soldier from behind.

She smiled. Things were certainly getting interesting.

* * *

Sheriff Elton Cobb stared at the bare-chested man eyeing him with no expression. Daniel Brown was the scariest motherfucker Cobb had ever met, and that was saying something. The guy was a deadly machine completely lacking in emotion, and he'd been created by Isobel to be just that. "My men?" Cobb probed, struggling to keep the man's gaze.

Daniel shrugged. "The missions we'll send them on when we're back up and running aren't like a typical milk run, Sheriff."

Had there been a snide edge to *Sheriff*? Cobb glared. "Train them. Don't kill them." If he had to teach both Daniel and Isobel a lesson in not to mess with him, he would. A bloody one. His hand itched to hold his gun. Not because he was afraid, of course. Just equipped.

"If your men die in training, they weren't prepared anyway." Daniel turned toward Isobel. "I'll put together a plan for tomorrow and then run it by you later." He moved past Cobb to the door.

Cobb instinctively pivoted to keep the man in his sights until he'd disappeared down the corridor. He was tempted to smother Daniel with a pillow one night. After drugging him. "That man is crazy."

Isobel chuckled. "No. He's just the perfect soldier. I worked hard to create him, you know."

Cobb shut the door and moved to drop into a chair. "You've lost too many of your creations, and I think you need to offer more incentives for the remaining ones to stay. Especially Daniel." Oh, Cobb might not like the asshole, but the soldier certainly got the job done. For now, Danny-Boy could stay—until Cobb figured out a suitable death. Something that would make Isobel eye him with alert contemplation, like she did Daniel. He could be deadly, too. "An incentive for Daniel should be one of your top plans." Maybe if Daniel found an interest beyond Isobel, Cobb wouldn't feel so off-center.

Isobel arched a finely plucked black eyebrow. "Interesting. Like what?"

"A woman," Cobb said flatly. One that didn't belong to Elton Cobb.

Isobel sat back. In her pressed white dress shirt and slim skirt, she was the epitome of a businesswoman. But Cobb knew what she liked, and he had plenty of mental images of her hair down and wild…around all that bare skin.

"Meaning?" she asked, her eyes like a cat's.

Oh, she knew what he was saying. "Hire somebody to work here and seduce him." It was all so simple, really. "Many men are led around by their dicks, as you know. That guy has never been in love, and when he falls, he'll topple hard and fast. Let's take advantage of that." Cobb picked lint off his dark jeans. If Isobel thought she was leading *him* around, she had it wrong.

Some women needed to feel pain, the real kind, before succumbing to love. His Isobel was one of those, and he hadn't shown her enough to truly bind her to him. Yet.

Isobel tapped red nails on her glass desk. "Daniel is not interested in love."

The dickhead probably had no clue how to love. "All the better." Cobb narrowed his gaze. "Unless you're saving him for some reason."

Her tinkly laugh eased something in him. "Are you joking? I was there when that boy was born. Ew." Her eyes were overbright and the tone of her voice was calm. Did she really believe those words? Was there a line she wouldn't cross?

"Sorry." Cobb glanced at the snowy field outside. "All men need sex."

"Oh, I'm sure he's getting sex." At the word, Isobel's blue eyes flared. "I had the best whores in the world teach those boys about sex, and they learned everything from seduction to technique. The way to motivate Daniel is by offering him a permanent home in the form of a job with our new facility. That's all he has ever wanted."

Well, the woman was brilliant and probably did know her creations. So long as she didn't want to keep this one as a pet. "All right. What's this plan he's coming up with tomorrow?"

"He's going after the Gray brothers," Isobel said, slowly unbuttoning her shirt, her gaze remaining steady on Cobb as she referred to a group of brothers with gray eyes whom she'd created in test tubes and trained to be killers. "It's time we hunted them down and brought them home."

Cobb shook his head. "You said they escaped and have formed attachments." He paused. "Or do you want your daughter back?" One of the Gray brothers had apparently married and knocked up Isobel's only daughter.

"I'd love to see Audrey again, especially since she's pregnant. Just think. Another generation of supersoldiers is now in the works." Isobel's eyes gleamed as she shrugged out of her shirt, revealing a lacy tan bra.

Cobb's dick hardened. Was she seducing him because she wanted him or because half-naked Daniel had just revved up her engine? His chest prickled.

"I am so excited to see if the genetic alterations I made have been transferred to the kid. My grandbaby," Isobel continued.

The woman did not look like a grandmother, that was for damn sure. Cobb's groin tightened, and he took note of how easily she affected him. "What about Heath, Ryker, and Denver?" It was time for Cobb to finally catch up to them and kill them, like they'd murdered his brother. It was time for them to suffer, and now that Ryker had a woman, he would get to see her die first. Should Cobb feel badly about betraying Isobel? She wanted them alive.

Their deaths were more important. This battle he'd win. And instinct told him that to keep Isobel's interest, he had to outmaneuver her. On every front. His chin lifted. Causing her pain would force her to bind to him. To want him only. Oh, she was going to know pain and soon. She'd love it.

She smiled. "We'll find Heath and the boys, I promise. In fact, if I can get the Gray brothers to cooperate—"

"They're gone." The Gray brothers had escaped years ago.

Her lips thinned. "I'll find them. They're our best bet for finding the Lost boys." She stood and reached behind her for her bra clasp.

"I hate it when you call them that." His dick was going to punch through his zipper.

She shrugged. "They lived plenty of their lives at the Lost Springs Home for Boys, so it fits. But I won't use the nickname if it upsets you." The bra dropped to the floor, and her still-pert nipples hardened before his eyes.

Cobb stood, unable to sit any longer. With his gaze trapped by her tits, he yanked off his shirt. If she was manipulating him, he didn't give a shit, so long as she used her mouth first. "I'm tired of hunting them. It's time for blood."

"Agreed." She smiled and shimmied out of her skirt. "Look at the wait as a positive sign. If Heath truly is working with this Anya, and if they're pretending to be engaged, maybe they'll develop feelings. How nice will it be to torture and ultimately kill her with Heath watching?"

Cobb's dick hardened further. He felt eighteen years old again. Stronger and younger than Daniel by far. "Good point," he grunted, on full alert as she drew down her thin panties. He had an affinity for torture, and one of the things he appreciated most about Isobel was that she supported him in that need. "You're an amazing woman. Are you all mine, Isobel?" Sometimes he still wondered.

Her smile filled the whole room. "Of course, Elton. How could there be anyone else?"

Good question. He was smart enough to know he didn't have all of her. To get that, to own her, he had to let his true nature forth. She responded to darkness, and he could be darker than even she imagined.

He reached for the button on his pants.

CHAPTER
18

Anya stepped out of the shower, more than a little pleased with the water pressure. The shampoo and conditioner supplied by Zara were high-end and smelled fresh. The bathroom was a little old but functional, and the walls were the same cool tattered brick.

She tugged jeans and a shirt from her bag and quickly dressed before finger combing her hair and clipping it at her nape to dry. Finally, she swiped mascara across her lashes and smoothed lip gloss over her lips. Just to be presentable, of course. She wasn't trying to look pretty for Heath.

Not at all.

Right. She sighed and headed for the bedroom. She stopped cold, and her entire body went into overdrive. Heath sat on the bed, his shoes and socks off, his hair ruffled. "How's the shower?"

Her mouth dried up. She cleared her throat. "Great water pressure." He was on the bed. The king-size bed with obviously new sheets and a black comforter, between two simple wooden nightstands. A luxurious shag rug covered the worn wooden floor and provided warmth. No other furniture had been placed in the room. "So. One bed." Again.

He nodded, looking beyond sexy and rumpled. "At least for tonight. We can figure out the rest tomorrow." His polite tone was going to get him punched in the throat.

"What's the plan?" Her stomach rumbled.

He stood and stretched, revealing smooth, long lines. "There's a diner across from our soon-to-be decoy place of business, so we thought we'd all grab something to eat and then look around."

She frowned, her heart thrumming. "Decoy business?"

"Yeah. This is the safe house, and the decoy building is across town but not close to your and Loretta's temporary apartment, in case the killer is watching that. He'd be suspicious if we let you go back there. We'll use the decoy offices to draw in the killer but we'll stay safe here in the meantime, and definitely at night. Well, until we don't want to be safe at night."

"Oh." It was her first undercover op. "Makes sense."

He jerked his head to the bathroom. "Are you finished? I could use a quick shower."

"Yes." She waited until he'd taken his bag into the bathroom and shut the door before grimacing. Why did she have to pretty much attack him in bed earlier? One kiss from the guy and she'd forgotten her entire existence. Man, he knew how to kiss. Warmth spread throughout her belly at remembering.

But now he was as distant as he'd been the first time they'd met. All because of a couple of bruises on her ribs. Was that it? There seemed to be secrets upon secrets surrounding him. If he wasn't wanted by the law—which made sense since Reese hadn't mentioned anything—then what was the deal? Why wouldn't he level with her?

How could she be so attracted to somebody she didn't know? Her father, her hero, would be so surprised. And yet she needed Heath to do the job—to avenge her sister. That was what she had to remember. The rest could take a backseat.

She set her suitcase on the bed and reorganized everything, trying to press out some of the wrinkles. Then she reached for the stack of files below the clothes and started reading through her profile of the killer, adding a couple of notes. She sat, her mind spinning. Who was he?

Too soon, the bathroom door opened, and Heath stalked out. He wore faded jeans that cupped his muscled legs and a dark T-shirt that stretched nicely across his tight chest. His wet hair curled toward his neck, and he'd left the shadow on his jaw. His greenish brown eyes were back to being alert and distant.

Even so, her breath quickened a little. Just from one simple look at him.

Why did he have to be so good-looking?

"Ready?" he asked.

She set the files down and followed him out of the bedroom and into the wide, currently empty living room, which was adjacent to the open-concept kitchen. "Zara said we probably won't get more furniture for the apartments."

Heath shook his head. "We're not gonna be here long enough to get furniture, and we don't have the funds right now anyway." He strode around the granite-covered kitchen island and opened a cupboard above the fridge to take down a mean-looking black handgun. He checked the clip and slammed it home. He stuck the gun into the back of his waistband. "I always carry."

She shook her head. "You didn't at the funeral in DC."

He tilted his head. "I figured the FBI might want to chat. Maybe even check out my rig. So you're right…No gun in DC."

As she watched, he reached to the top of the fridge and drew out a fighting knife to place near his calf. "Knife, too?" she croaked.

"Yes."

"We do seem to have enough enemies, now, don't we?" She ran through events. "Besides the Copper Killer and the fake marshals, you think the guy who attacked us at the hotel will find us again."

"Yeah. The guy at the hotel could be one of the fake marshals, but I'm not sure," he returned. "They're associated with another case, which I can't tell you about. I'm sorry, but that's the way it is."

She understood patient confidentiality, so she kind of understood this. Her temples twinged with the promise of a migraine, and she brushed it away. If that's how he wanted it, they'd keep it distant and professional. So much for being friends. Something told her he'd be a good friend to have, but apparently he limited the people he let in to his brothers. And Zara. There had been definite fondness when he'd introduced Zara. As twisted as it was, Anya wanted that trust and loyalty from him. She wasn't going to get it.

A lump filled her throat. "Fine."

His eyebrows rose. "Many an expression crossed your face for nearly a whole minute for you to end with a good old 'Fine.'"

She strode for the apartment door and yanked it open. "It sucks to be on the outside looking in, you know?"

He reached her in seconds and slid his palm down to clasp her hand, enclosing her with warmth and strength. "I didn't mean to hurt your feelings."

There he went, being sweet. She tried to keep her hand stiff in his, yet her fingers relaxed right into his hold. "I'm trusting you to come up with a plan to catch a serial killer and keep me safe at the same time." She wasn't delusional enough to believe she could take on the Copper Killer on her own, and Heath definitely had experience she lacked. "I understand confidentiality for other cases, but this guy came after you with me there, too. Tell me something about him."

"All I can tell you is that he's a hired gun for somebody I'm hunting down, and he's trained. If he finds us and comes at me again, you have to run away as hard and fast as you can."

A shiver wound down her back. "Who are you hunting, and who's your client?"

He leaned over and pressed a kiss to her forehead. "Sorry. Confidential."

The soft touch warmed through to her heart. He might act like a distant badass soldier sometimes, but Heath Jones sure liked to kiss. At least his cold attitude was warming toward her. "All right. Let's get something to eat."

Denver was waiting for them in his Jeep. "Ryker went early to return your rental." He smiled at Anya.

She smiled back while Heath held open the passenger door. She jumped in and buckled her belt. The drive across town took twenty minutes, and Heath remained silent in the backseat. Snowville was an older town with mom-and-pop stores, bigger department stores, and tons of fast-food restaurants.

Neon lights proclaimed the diner as Hal's Diner, which sat directly across from another older brick building.

"Decoy offices," Denver said quietly as he pulled up to the curb.

Heath jumped out and opened her door to assist her out. "I've never asked."

She kept hold of his hand for balance and looked up. "Asked what?"

"About dietary restrictions. I should've asked. I don't think they have vegan options here." He led her through the snow to the door. "I haven't dated in a long time. Not that this is a date. I mean, you know."

God, he was cute when floundering. "I like meat, Heath." Warmth flooded her face. "I mean. Well, you know."

He chuckled and opened the door for her. She spotted Ryker and Zara in a back booth and quickly made her way past faded red booths and a fairly quiet crowd to slide in toward the window. "Hi."

Zara grinned, and Ryker nodded. "The food here is okay, but it's a great vantage point and place to plan."

Heath slid in next to her while Denver grabbed a wooden chair from another table and sat at the head. "The steak is okay."

A gray-haired waitress showed up with glasses of water. "We have wine and beer but no hard stuff." She tugged out a green order pad.

"The Wallace pale ale is really good," Zara said.

The waitress's blue eyes sparkled. "I wouldn't recommend the wine. The box has been kicked a few times and stored outside for a bit."

Anya bit back a grin. "I'll go with the pale ale."

"All around," Heath said.

The waitress smiled. "Be right back."

Ryker leaned in, looking positively hulking next to Zara. "I think we go public tomorrow. The mayor is throwing a gala for new businesses tomorrow night, and there will be press. We can register the business in the morning and finagle an invitation."

Heath drummed his fingers on the tabletop. "Are we ready?"

Denver nodded. "The killer is gonna take another woman soon, so if we're gonna do this, we have to get going."

Heath turned and studied Anya until she wanted to squirm. "Are you sure you want to do this? I'll try my best to keep you safe, but I don't like it."

"I'm sure," she murmured, hoping she appeared confident. Her stomach cramped. What if the guy actually found her? He'd been watching her for so long.

Heath covered her hand with his. "I won't let him get anywhere near you."

"I know," Anya said.

"Excellent," Zara said, smiling when the waitress brought the beer.

They all ordered and waited until after the waitress had left.

Zara took a drink. "You'll attend the gala. The killer will be pissed after the press coverage of you being with Heath, right? We'll all be at the office the next day, then act like we're going to bed and wait."

"Agreed. The killer won't like seeing me with Heath." Anya reached for her glass. Tension rolled across the table, and she looked up, frowning. "The guy will make a move soon. He has to."

Ryker nodded. "His compulsion is getting stronger, as you can tell from the crime scenes."

Heath grimaced. "He'll make a move—he has three days, and then we go."

Anya sipped the delicious brew. "Why give him just one chance? I mean, shouldn't we stay here until he makes a move? That's the entire reason for being here, right?"

Nobody answered her.

She leaned back and eyed Zara. "Why did you all leave Cisco?" She understood the need to move, but now questions kept bombarding her.

"Fresh start," Zara said with a smile. Somewhat of a smile. "It was time to go."

Smooth but not quite the full story. Anya turned toward Heath. "Does this move have anything to do with your other case and the guy who attacked us? Is that why you've left Cisco?"

Heath shook his head.

More secrets, and she was on the outside of this tight group, peering in through veiled windows. It hurt. Anya forced a smile. "Excuse me." She waited until Heath slid out of the booth, then, keeping her head high, she went to look for the restroom, finding it past the entrance and the cash register. Once inside, she washed her hands and took several deep breaths.

Being on the outside looking in really sucked. The group was so tight, so protective. Her father had been like that, and then she'd been alone until finding Loretta. Family mattered. Zara was so lucky.

Yeah, Anya understood confidentiality, but still. She patted her hair into place and calmed herself. She'd be with these people just until the case was over, and then she'd go find her own life. Yeah. Good plan.

Steeling her shoulders, she walked out into the alcove and into a body. "Oh, sorry." She looked up and gasped. Her knees weakened. "Carl?"

He smiled and grabbed her arms. He wore a heavy ski jacket, and snow was still evident on his thick blond hair. "I've been following you for two days. Finally, we're alone and can talk." His gaze darkened. "Please. I really need your help."

That quickly, heat flushed through her entire body until her skin ached. "You are such a dick." Reeling back, she swung and hit him right in the gut.

CHAPTER
19

Heath's nape tickled, and he turned around in time to see Carl Sparks stagger into the entryway as if he'd been kicked. What the hell? Heat slammed into Heath's solar plexus. He sped past the line of booths and grabbed Carl by the coat, steering him easily through the door and out into the chilly night. Keeping his momentum, Heath shoved the bastard down the sidewalk, turned him into the nearest alley, and threw him up against a metal door.

"What the fuck?" Carl tugged down his coat, his face a mask of fury. "Who the hell—"

There was only one reason the asshole was in town. Heath swung and punched Carl in the face, sending his head back into the door. It protested with a loud clang. A round red circle appeared on Carl's cheek. "I pulled that punch, dickhead." Heath flashed his teeth, anger ripping through him. "The next one's going to break something."

"You don't understand." Carl charged him, grabbing him in a bear hug.

Heath's ribs protested, and he reacted instantly. He dropped onto the icy snow and threw Carl over his head to crash into the opposite building. Then Heath stood, turned, and strode toward the guy groaning and rolling in the snow. He picked Carl up and planted him against the brick.

Carl's eyes narrowed and he kicked uselessly, his boots sliding on the ice. Heath kept his hold strong. The guy needed to learn what happened to men who hurt women.

"Heath!" Anya skidded around the corner, with his brothers and Zara right behind her. "What are you doing?"

He released Carl and took a step back. Forcing calmness into his movements, he wiped snow off his hands and took a good look at her. Pale, eyes wide, no bruises. His muscles vibrated down his back, and he reminded himself he was in control. Fully. "Did he hurt you?"

"No." She shook out her right hand. "I punched him."

They'd have to work on her fighting skills, because Carl had still been standing. "You want to knock them down fast and hard, sweetheart," Heath said, turning his attention on the bully breathing heavily against the wall. The man thought he could stalk an innocent woman and get away with it. Somebody needed to teach him differently.

"I tried to knock him down," she grumbled.

Heath stiffened. A bully needed to be put down and swiftly— it was the only way he'd stop. If Carl didn't learn a lesson tonight, he'd never leave Anya alone. "Ryker? Take Anya back inside, would you?" He didn't think she needed to see any more violence.

She set her boots in the snow. "I'm not going anywhere." She stomped toward Carl, and Heath halted her with an arm around her shoulders. "How did you find me? You said you'd followed me, but we didn't see you."

"I had been getting to that questioning," Heath said, his temper fraying. How *had* Carl found them? What if the jerk had gotten Anya outside before Heath could've intervened? Images of Loretta in death and his mother on the floor filtered through his mind. He gently pushed Anya toward Ryker, who planted a hand on her arm. "Get her out of here."

"No." Anya shrugged off Ryker's hand. "How did you find me, Carl?"

Blood dripped from Carl's lip. Snow slid down his face to mingle with the red. "I need you."

Heath pivoted and kicked Carl in the gut. "Wrong fucking answer."

Carl fell back, his arms spreading wide before he leaned over with a pained *oof*. Even then, he chuckled. "You are such a Neanderthal. Anya? You are better than this. We are better than this."

Heath kept the entire group in his sights. Denver hissed out breath and looked both ways down the street. "We're clear."

Ryker just studied the scene, even as Zara paled next to him. "I suggest you give a good answer, buddy," Ryker said calmly. "When Heath starts kicking instead of hitting, usually people end up drinking through straws for the rest of their lives."

Heath straightened. Yeah. His brothers had his back. But he needed to calm down.

Carl straightened and spit out blood. His eyes hardened, and his welling lip curled. "I understand Anya on an intellectual level you'll never reach." The absolute tone held as much arrogance as determination. "I've decided I will never let her go. She doesn't want to go anyway. She knows we belong together." He feigned right and punched left, hitting Heath in the ear.

More heat rushed through Heath, and he nailed Carl in the chin with a quick front kick.

Carl's head cracked against the brick, and blood pooled from his ear.

"Might want to cool it a little," Ryker warned.

Heath's hands clenched. If the asshole claimed Anya one more time like that, he'd lose all his teeth. "We're not going to ask you again. How did you track Anya?" Heath knew without a doubt that nobody had followed them. Neither he nor Carl was leaving the alley until the truth came out.

Carl wiped blood from his chin and set his feet on the ice. His chest puffed out, and his smooth blond hair was matted to his head. Fury and an odd gleam lit his eyes. "You're temporary, you know that? We share a connection based on psychology and the human mind. You're all sorts of screwed up, and she knows it. We all know your violence is a mask, whack-job." He turned toward Anya. "I'm sorry about what happened, but you have to claim some responsibility. There was a reason I turned elsewhere."

Anya snorted and moved forward. "You're such an idiot. Now go home." She turned for the restaurant.

"No." Carl grabbed her arm and jerked.

She yelped, her arms windmilling as her boots slipped on the ice. Landing with a crunch of ice, she winced and shoved to her feet.

The pained look on her face snapped the leash Heath had kept on his control. Drums sounded in his head, and his vision went black. He moved then, all muscle, no thought.

Sounds barely permeated his punches, his kicks, until strong arms wrapped around him from behind and threw him to the side. He grunted and pivoted back to his goal—a predator with no conscious. Images of battered and bloody women flashed through his head, from his mother to Loretta to others he'd tried to save over the years, adding a desperate strength to his hits. His fist plowed into Carl's gut, and he felt a rib break across his knuckles.

Even then, he couldn't stop.

"Heath!" Denver grabbed him again and yanked him away, while Ryker stepped in front of him, hands out, gaze concerned.

Heath growled and struggled against his brother.

"Stop," Denver murmured into his ear, dragging him across the icy alley. "You need to stop now. Focus and breathe."

Heath blinked. Pain exploded in his hand suddenly, and he glanced down at his battered knuckles. Blood flowed over his fist... most of it not his. He shook his head. Jesus. He'd lost his mind for a moment.

Ryker still faced him, blocking Carl, who was on the ground breathing heavily. "Get Heath out of here," Ryker ordered Denver.

Heath froze. "Anya?" Slowly, he turned his head to see her next to Zara, her eyes wide and her face paler than the snow around them. Her lips quivered, and Zara put an arm around her shoulders to draw her away from the alley.

Oh God. What had he done? His body started to shake, and Denver loosened his hold.

Carl spit blood to the side and shoved to his feet using the brick building behind him. His face was already swelling, and blood flowed from his nose. A cut above his eye also bled profusely. "I hope you enjoy jail, dickhead," he slurred through purpling lips.

Heath settled. What the hell had he just done to his entire family? If Carl turned him in, Sheriff Cobb would certainly find him. He partially turned toward Denver, his mind spinning. They barely had enough time to get free. This was his fault, and he'd deal with it. "Phoenix."

Denver's head jerked.

Ryker snarled. "We're not to that point yet."

"Yes, we are." Heath shook his head. "You guys go, and I'll wait for the cops with Carl." His brothers had only minutes to get out of town, but they could do it. It was the first time he'd given the code word to run and now, and he meant it. He'd take the fall for this, even if it meant facing Cobb and Dr. Madison on his own. Hopefully the psychos had enough pull to get him out of jail before killing him. "Go ahead and call the cops, Carl."

Anya shrugged off Zara and moved forward.

Heath pivoted to halt her. "I'm sorry, Anya. I really am." He'd give almost anything for her not to have seen him in a violent rage. Carl wasn't even that dangerous. This was on Heath. Only Heath. The pressure had been building since he'd found Loretta's bruised and battered body, and now it had just exploded. In front of Anya. "This is rare. I promise I don't lose it like this often."

"Not ever," Denver said grimly. He reached out and awkwardly patted Anya's arm. "Honest. He's usually the one in control around here. Smooth and smart."

Ryker nodded, his alert gaze sweeping the alley. "This is new." Apparently seeing no additional threats, he focused on Anya. "It won't happen again. Heath won't ever lose his control like this again."

Man. His brothers sounded like they were covering for him with a school principal. Even now, after Heath had put their lives in jeopardy, they had his back. God, he'd miss them, but they had to go. His only options were to kill Carl or let the moron call the cops. "You're lucky I'm not a killer, Carl," he muttered.

Denver shrugged. "I'd be okay with it."

Carl sucked in air.

Heath fought a grin. Denver let spiders go if he caught them inside. Yet the man gave a good bluff. "I guess we could consider it," he said amenably.

Apparently Heath didn't bluff as well.

"You're full of shit," Carl said, glancing from Heath to Anya. "Do you see what kind of man he is? Calmly talking about killing."

Heath shook out his smarting hand. "You know we ain't gonna kill you, dickhead. So go ahead and call the cops." He cut his gaze to Ryker. "You all need to go. Now."

"No." Anya paused, her gaze on Carl. "Carl, if you turn Heath in for assault and battery, I'll call the dean of the college right now and give him a full account of you sleeping with a student. Then I'll let him know about this stalking issue. You've stalked a woman, another professor, across the country. The college won't let that slide. You know it." Her voice quivered, but she held her ground.

Carl's bloodshot eyes widened. "You're joking."

She shook her head. "I'm really not."

Heath tried to make sense of the conversation. The little redhead was defending him? Why? Hadn't she just seen the real him? She didn't owe him anything, damn it.

Her ex gaped, and then his gaze hardened. "Go for it. I have witnesses as well, and I'll say your statements are retaliation for my turning in your boyfriend here. I'll have the dean convinced in a minute that you invited me here."

Oh, the man needed another beating. Heath breathed out. "Ryker? Get Anya out of here, please."

Ryker studied him and then turned toward Anya. "We need to go."

She shook her head, her gaze remaining on Carl. "You know what? Something tells me that student wasn't the first you've slept with."

Carl flashed bloody teeth. "Of course she was."

"No." Anya arched a fine eyebrow. "You just went pale. That's a sure sign." She turned toward Heath but kept her distance. "Carl is already in trouble, but I could certainly add to it. In fact, maybe I should call the dean right now."

"You have no right," Carl snapped. "You said you cared about me. You're so alone, you've forgotten what that means."

Stupid psychologist. Anger ripped through Heath again, and he turned for Carl.

Ryker stepped toward him. "Knock it off. You beat him. Walk away before we all get caught up in a shit-storm."

It was too late to worry about that.

Anya stood taller. "I mean it, Carl. We're even—blood for blood right now. You call the police, and I'll take you down." Her eyes blazed a stunning green, and pink tinged her cheeks in the cold. The woman was magnificent, facing down a jerk. "I'll lead the investigation into your past myself instead of staying out of it." Her smile showed she thought he'd get nailed anyway.

"You're committing extortion," Carl snapped.

Anya nodded. "That's a fair characterization." She shivered in the cold air.

Heath shook blood off his hand. Then he moved toward her. They needed to get out of the alley.

Her eyes widened, and she took a step back.

He paused. She'd just backed away from him? He'd scared her. *He* was the thing in the darkness that instinct told her to run from. That quickly, she ripped out his heart.

CHAPTER
20

Anya's knees wobbled. She hadn't meant to back away. Yet when Heath had turned, so much anger had still crossed his expression that she'd just reacted. Plus, he'd been spraying blood a little. Anyone would back away from flinging blood. She was wearing her good coat. "I'm not afraid of you," she whispered for them both, not caring who was around them.

The green in his eyes seemed to burn brighter. "I know."

Yet he didn't. She could tell from the tense line of his long body that he didn't believe her. How she'd fix that, she had no clue. But for now, she still needed answers. "Carl? Last chance to tell me how you found me."

"Or what?" Carl tilted his head to the side in the way he had during their relationship that had made her think he was so much smarter than he really was.

Not this time. She stepped to the side at only about five feet from Carl. Then she drew a small handgun from her purse and pointed it at his head. "Or I shoot you."

He blinked.

Heath sucked in air. "Where the hell did you get a gun?"

Not exactly the supportive remark she would've appreciated. "Doesn't matter. Carl, I'd really like to shoot you." She lowered her aim to his groin. "In the balls."

Carl pressed back against the building. "You wouldn't."

The man didn't sound so sure this time, did he? Anya steadied her aim. "Oh, I would. Believe me. I'd really enjoy it." To think she'd actually dated this dipshit. He'd seemed so intellectual, and he'd come from a law-enforcement family, just like she had. Man, she'd been fooled.

Heath studied her and then shrugged. "Your call, darlin'." He stepped out of the way.

Carl sputtered. "You can't be serious."

"I am." She inhaled and carefully exhaled. "Sure, I might get in trouble. But since you stalked me across state lines, I think I can convince a prosecutor that I was just protecting myself. You know?" Maybe she could. Her finger tightened on the trigger. Perhaps she should just shoot above his head? "Last chance."

"Fine," Carl spat. "I tracked the GPS on your phone. I've always tracked you that way."

Heath closed his eyes and shook his head. "Shit."

Anya slowly lowered her hand. "We'll have to fix that." Her heart pattered wildly. Um, what now? Should she just leave? Or should she wait for Carl to decide not to call the police? She bit her lip.

Heath must've caught her uncertainty. "Let's get out of here." He glared at Carl. "This is a one-shot deal. Come near her again, and I'll end you." He strode forward and grasped Anya's arm, gently turning her toward the street. "Let's go."

She stumbled next to him, her knees still shaking, while everyone else followed. The altercation had been bloody, and yet with Heath at her side her body felt alive in a way it never had. Awake and tingly. "This is weird," she murmured.

"Where did you get the gun?" he asked quietly.

"From me," Zara said from behind them, accepting the gun when Anya handed it back.

"Great," Heath said as they reached the vehicles, his gaze scanning the empty street. His shoulders appeared to be drawn back, and he didn't meet her eyes. While he seemed to be on high alert, there was a tension—almost a sadness—that all but rolled from him. Something in him—in it—touched her. "You can drive with Ryker if you want," he said.

Anya turned and faced him squarely. What was it deep inside her that wanted to soothe him? "I'm riding with you. We need to talk." Without waiting for an answer, she reached for the door of the Jeep. The guy had gone nutso to defend her, and something about that electrified her entire body. She was crazy.

He beat her to the door, holding it open until she'd jumped inside.

"We'll settle up with the waitress," Ryker called out by the diner door. "Denver is with us."

Heath nodded, crossed to the other side, got in, and ignited the engine.

What should she say? The man only sat at the other end of the seat from her, but the distance felt immense. A sense of safety wrapped around her just from his nearness, and she wanted more. Her body definitely wanted more, and she had to fight herself to keep from scrambling right into his lap.

He drove down the lonely street, and snow began to fall on the windshield. "Sorry you had to see that."

She studied his strong and capable hands on the steering wheel. His knuckles were bruised, and one had split. The idea of those hands touching her, really touching her, caught her breath in her throat. "This is my fault, not yours." She was an educated, intellectual woman. Violence wasn't a part of her life. Yet there was something so primitive about Heath losing it to protect her, to defend her, that ignited her. Why was that? Were baser feelings like that a preview for a disaster? Or for something deep and inexplicable? God, she wanted him. Now. Without thinking and rationalization. "I should've gotten a new phone." She had to concentrate on the conversation.

Heath nodded. "We can get rid of the GPS tracking on it. No need for a new phone."

"Oh." There was so much she didn't know about the world—a place that Heath seemed to navigate easily. Why that turned her on, she'd never understand. The adrenaline still coursing through her made it difficult to concentrate on anything but burning it off. The best way would be with his strong body. What was going on with her? "You kind of lost your mind back there."

"Yeah." He sighed as he made a left turn. "My temper is usually much better controlled, but I have definite triggers. I'll do better next time."

How could she explain how much she wanted to reach over and soothe his hurts? She was so tired of not following her feelings. If they got her into trouble again, did it really matter? Would a night with Heath be worth it? Probably. Or she'd get her heart broken. Yet after losing Loretta, did that matter? "I'm sorry I backed away from you," she said softly, her hands in her lap. "It was just a moment, you know?"

"Yeah. I get that." He flipped on the windshield wipers as the snow increased in force.

Was there a way she could help him? "Have you talked to anybody about, well, triggers?"

"Yep. My brothers and a shrink a few years back. Ryker all but forced me there, but I'm glad he did. I'm usually better than this." His greenish-brown eyes caught her gaze. "I'm worried about you, Anya. Everything about you is soft and sweet and smart, and I want to put you somewhere safe now. It eats at me that I can't."

Yet he could. There was no doubt he was bigger, stronger, and meaner...and he could probably easily secure her safety against her will. The fact that he wouldn't do that warmed her chilled body. Heat flushed through her, and she crossed her legs. "I like you, too," she said. Yeah, she'd just opened herself up. Perhaps she was crazy.

His upper lip quirked. "You're dangerous, lady."

She blinked. Was that a dimple in his right cheek? Her pants were suddenly too restrictive. "Huh?"

"Ah, sweetness, the real kind, is more dangerous than an armed weapon to a guy like me." He rubbed a hand through his ruffled hair, turning back to the road. "Temper or not, I'm not completely un-self-aware."

She'd noticed that about him. He'd been incredibly violent with Carl, and yet she wasn't afraid of him. Not one inch of her feared him, and wasn't that interesting. "Who are you?" she whispered, her instincts humming right along with her body.

He breathed out and shook his head. "Hell if I know. Sometimes I think I didn't even exist until I found Ryker and Denver." He lifted his hand to show her the long scar down his palm. "We cut ourselves when I was eleven, mingled blood, and became family." His brows drew down. "I don't think I was really *me* until that moment, you know?"

She was more than a little intrigued. She'd felt adrift since her father had died and left her alone. Nobody really *knew* her. Not until Loretta had gathered her close. How sad and scared those three boys must've been to have needed each other so badly. More than ever, she wanted to ease him. Why was that? They'd only just met, and yet something in him called to her. "I began to find parts of me I'd forgotten existed when Loretta and I reconnected, so I think I understand." Her chest ached, and she absently rubbed it. They had needed more time together.

"I promise we'll find the guy who killed her." He reached across the seat and gently took her hand. His thumb brushed along her knuckles.

Warmth and power burst across her skin. She ran her finger along his blood brother scar. "I know." While she sensed a land mine, she couldn't help herself. "Where did you guys all meet up?"

His body didn't stiffen, and he didn't draw away. Yet a tension—one she could feel—rolled through the Jeep. "At a boys home." He released her to press a button above the mirror, and the garage door to their building slid open. "We didn't come up with a plan tonight or check out the decoy offices, so we'll do so tomorrow morning. You and I have to go public soon, or we'll miss the window to catch this guy."

This time. The words went unspoken, but she could feel them. The killer would go after somebody very soon, whether it was her or not. There was a chance—a small one—that the killer would actually get her. If that happened, she'd see Loretta again. But what about this life? The Jeep stopped, and she unbuckled her belt to jump out. Had she really lived? As she walked around the vehicle, she was struck again by Heath's size. He could crush her in a second, and he had way too many secrets.

He gently took her arm and led her toward the door.

Gentle. He was always so gentle with her. The same way Ryker was with Zara while still being on full alert.

Tension still cascaded from Heath, probably from the fight.

Adrenaline rolled inside her, too, sparking in her veins.

God, she was tired of thinking. Tired of being scared. So tired of being alone. For a while, she didn't have to be. Heath had been up-front with his offer of taking them to another level. That level would probably be explosive. Would he let her know him? Really know him? "I don't want to leave this life without really living," she murmured.

He opened the door and escorted her to the stairs. "I get that."

She climbed two stairs and turned to stand in front of him, stopping his progress. Two steps up and she could meet him eye to eye. She pushed her shoulders back and tried to look confident. "I'm done analyzing everything to death. At least for tonight."

His eyes darkened. "All right."

Courage. She could do this. "You're attracted to me."

One of his dark eyebrows rose. Fire flared, hot and bright, in those stunning eyes.

She swallowed. Her knees still felt weak. "I'm attracted to you, too."

He drew back slightly. "Anya—"

"You already made the offer." She planted both hands on his broad shoulders. "Life can end very quickly. We both know that."

He stiffened and very slightly shook his head. Something that looked suspiciously like panic lit his eyes. "Anya—"

"Wait," she burst out as she curled her fingers over his shoulders and dug in. "I know all the reasons we shouldn't." What if he no longer wanted her? She hadn't quite considered that. He'd called her *dangerous*. What if that didn't mean desirable? Heat climbed into her face. "I'm just saying, since we're pretending to be engaged, maybe we should act like it." Okay, that was lame.

"Anya, listen. I want you so badly I ache, but I'm not the guy for you," he said calmly.

"Enough of that crap," she snapped. "I don't want to hear how dangerous you are or how you're not good enough. It's all just so stupid."

His chin lifted enough to give her pause. "I'm not talking about worth, darlin'. I'm saying that I'm not a permanent type of guy and probably won't ever be. The more I get to know you, the more I see a picket fence and a happily-ever-after."

She rolled her eyes.

His hardened.

"I'm not asking for forever, you idiot. I just want to burn off some of the energy from tonight." Her tone remained perfectly exasperated, even as she kind of lied. Oh, she knew they didn't have forever, but she also knew herself. One night, and her heart would get involved. It probably already was after he'd defended her so violently in the alley. But the idea of a touch from him, a night with him, was worth it. It had to be. "No strings, Heath."

His jaw tightened. His gaze probed deep. The second he made a decision, one to protect her for her own good, she saw it clearly.

So she moved into him. Her mouth slid against his, and she sighed at the contact. Closer. She wanted to get closer. Pressing against him, she kissed him. His lips were firm, and he tasted somehow of chocolate.

He stiffened even more.

It took her a second to realize he wasn't kissing her back. His body all but vibrated beneath her palms, but he didn't move. She drew back, explosive heat filling her cheeks. Well, crap. "I'm sorry." She released him and began to turn away.

A low growl from him was all the warning she got. He grabbed her, hard, and slammed his mouth over hers. One arm banded around her waist, and the other cupped her head. The strength in his mouth overpowered her, and she opened hers. He took advantage, sweeping his tongue inside.

Sparks flew throughout her body, and she kissed him, becoming lost. Her nipples hardened, and her sex pounded instantly. When her lungs had all but burst, he let her breathe. She panted, her eyes opening wide to look at his face.

Holy crap. His eyes had turned a dark green, and lust was stamped hard across his strong face. His hold remained implacable, and he looked as unmovable as granite and as wild as the wind.

What had she just unleashed?

CHAPTER
21

Heath studied her and tried to yank back control on his raging libido. Her soft lips had nearly pushed him over the edge, but he'd been able to keep his mind. Yet the moment hurt had flared in her soft green eyes, he'd been lost. Drawn in so quickly he hadn't had time to stop himself—even if he had wanted to do so.

Desire darkened her eyes to the color of a lake bed beneath a winter sky, and a pretty pink filled her smooth face. Her upper lip curved. "So you do want me."

"With everything I am." He'd always give her the truth. She was sweet and kind…and she had a fairness to her that appealed to the better part of him. Even her obvious intelligence spurred him to be better. To want more. "But it's a mistake." Didn't mean he wouldn't make it, though.

Her smile widened, and she planted her hands on his chest. His heart thundered against them. "I appreciate the warning, but it doesn't have to be a mistake. We're both adults, and you've properly warned me about your penchant for taking off."

Her humor caught him off guard and ratcheted up his lust to a near painful level. Humor was a challenge, as was getting her out of her very smart head. A part of him—one he wasn't sure about— wanted to claim her on a level that wasn't funny. It was absolute, and that should concern him. There was no road map for what she brought out in him, and he liked to navigate. He needed to know his path. He tilted his head. "Be careful, baby." It was fair to warn her, right?

Her chuckle bounced through his body and landed squarely in his groin. "Oh, we're way past careful," she breathed, leaning in to press her lips against his again. She stretched up on her toes for a better angle and tilted her head, her softness against him a temptation he'd never be able to resist.

Her confidence awoke something in him. This time he went slow in taking over the kiss. He let her play for a few moments, let her set the pace and feel powerful. Fire shot through his body to heat his groin, making his jeans too tight. He grasped onto self-control with everything he had when all he wanted was to flip her around and take her down to the steps.

Not Anya.

He needed to be gentle. As his muscles tightened, he leaned back and studied her. Intrigue and need crossed her pretty face, and her breath came rapidly. Oh, she wanted a walk on the wild side—that was for sure. He'd give her what she needed without losing control or scaring her. He could do this. It was too late for him to turn back and it had been since the first time he'd met her. He hadn't considered she'd give him a chance. "You sure?" he asked.

She rolled her eyes again.

"Don't challenge me, baby. Trust me." Before she could give a smart-ass reply, he bent and smoothly lifted her over his shoulder.

Her answering laugh held both glee and need.

He held her legs to keep her in place and make sure she didn't fall. The woman weighed nothing over his shoulder, so he climbed the stairs carefully to keep from jostling her.

She sighed and slid both hands into his back jeans pockets. And squeezed.

His vision went black. He halted and then continued on, his cock all but bursting from his jeans. The woman was a temptress who had absolutely no idea who she was dealing with. Control. He needed to keep control of himself. While she might think she wanted passionate and crazy, she had no idea of the wildness living within his skin. The primal being deep inside who wanted her sighing his name. Begging for more. Becoming his.

But it couldn't happen. This was casual and this was fun. Maybe if he repeated the mantra enough in his head, he'd actually believe it.

He made quick tracks through the vestibule and into his temporary apartment, reaching the bedroom in a couple of heartbeats. Taking care, he flipped her over to sit on the bed.

All that glorious red hair flew back. What would it be like to have the mass wrapped around him for life? An impossible dream.

She laughed and settled herself. "Thanks for the ride."

"Smart-ass." He grinned and bit back the order he wanted to give her. Instead of commanding her to undress, he reached for her buttons. Slow and gentle, damn it. His hands stiffened, and he had to concentrate.

She hummed and reached for his belt.

Heat swept through him. *Basketball scores. Golf courses. Baseball teams.* He tried to take himself out of the moment...and she unzipped his fly. "Whoa." He finished the buttons and jerked her shirt down, capturing her arms at her sides by tying the loose ends in front of her belly button.

"Hey." Her hands dropped, and she lifted her head.

God, what he wouldn't do to have her tied up, completely at his mercy. There was a power in having a strong woman like her give complete trust. But such power held two prongs. She'd own him. What if something happened to her? He blinked and shook his head at the uneasy thought. "Slow down," he murmured, his gaze caught by her frilly pink bra. "Pretty." Yeah, he'd been expecting something cotton and simple…Just how many layers did this woman have?

"Thanks." She struggled against her shirt. "I can't move."

"That's the idea." He gave in and flicked the front clasp of the bra, springing it open. Her breasts were small and firm, with pert pink nipples. "Beautiful," he breathed, easily tugging the bra straps down to join the shirt. Slowly, he dropped to his knees between her legs. "Behave yourself and slow down, or you're about to see how easily I can use this pretty bra to contain you."

Her breath caught.

No. Definitely no. She might think she wanted all of him, but no fucking way. He reached out, almost reverently, and cupped one breast. At the touch, his entire body shuddered. "God, you're beautiful."

"Heath," she murmured.

Yeah. *Heath.* He leaned in to kiss her between the breasts.

She sucked in air, and her abdomen rippled. He smiled and kissed his way around both breasts, finally taking a nipple into his mouth. Her gasp moved her deeper into his mouth. Then she started to struggle against the shirt again. He growled and released her nipple, leaning back. "Knock it off."

"No." She moved to kick him, and he pressed her to the bed, keeping her knees spread on either side of him. Her snarl was more of a growl.

He grinned, light careening through him. Was that happiness? "You are so cute."

She rolled her eyes. "Somehow I just went from beautiful to cute. Would you please free my arms so I can touch you?"

Hmm. He would like her hands on him now that he was back in control. And she had said *please*. "Fine." He released the tie and pulled her shirt and bra free.

"Better." She licked her lips and grabbed the hem of his shirt. "Duck."

He had just enough time to duck his head before she ripped it off.

"Nice," she breathed, flattening her hands over his abdomen. "Ridges and packed abs. You're like a cologne advertisement."

Who cared about his abs or cologne? Her breasts were within his reach.

She stayed away from his stitches and his newest bandage. Her hands flitted across the scars on his left side, and she frowned. "I hadn't taken time to inspect these."

"Whip and belt," he confirmed, pressing his hand between her breasts. Man, she was small.

The sound of protest she made filled his heart. When was the last time a woman—and somebody not his family—truly cared? His touch turned reverent.

"Who hurt you?" Anger rode her words.

"Doesn't matter." And it didn't. "Was a long time ago." Although danger still hunted him, and he needed to remember that fact. "Enough talking." He grasped her waist, lifted her, and moved them both to the center of the bed. Then he tunneled his hands into her hair and kissed her, putting all the words he couldn't say into the kiss.

She moaned and kissed him back, rolling onto him. The second her chest slid against his, he nearly lost his mind. Then she moved to the side and tried to shove down his jeans.

He helped her and then added hers to the pile on the floor, leaving them both nude. She was beyond perfect, and his insides rioted. He had to protect her.

She chuckled and moved back on top of him. Her thighs spread and her knees dropped to either side of his hips. She leaned down and nipped his chin. "Although I feel like I'm on a boulder right now. I mean, I don't even press you into the bed, do I?"

He tried to concentrate on her words and not on the wet heat coating his dick from her sex. Figured she'd be a talker. Why he liked that about her—a lot—he'd never know. "No?" He ran his hands down her back, to the dip in her waist, and finally to her butt. The woman had an ass on her, and he could spend days learning each curve and dimple.

She wiggled against him, and he saw stars. Then she fingered a scar along his right pec. "Knife?" Her eyebrows drew down.

"Yep. Bad guy I had to find for a Lost Bastards case." The scars from adulthood he bore proudly, while the ones from his childhood he just wanted to forget about. Yet sharing them with her freed something inside him. Maybe he didn't have to be so alone. At least for the moment. He flitted his fingers across her rib cage. "Does this still hurt?"

"No." She leaned down and kissed him. "The bruise is almost gone, too."

"Good." He'd need to be careful not to bruise her tonight. They could go slow, and he'd make sure she was safe.

She shook her head. "You're thinking too much." As if to stop him, she leaned down and bit his lip.

Hard.

* * *

Anya knew the second she drew back that she had gone too far. Heath's eyes flared, and he grasped her waist, flipping her onto her back. Then his powerful body rolled over her, easily bracketing her in place. "Anya," he murmured, warning in his voice. Warning for her or for himself?

"I would love to make you lose control," she said, letting her mouth get ahead of her brain again.

His head tilted in a curiously threatening way that somehow turned her on even more. "No, you would not. Trust me." He held his weight up on his elbows but still somehow pressed her into the bed. "No more biting, and no more trying to catch me off guard." To soften his order, he pressed his lips against hers.

She opened her mouth to argue, but he took her under, shoving the words back down her throat. His chest flattened her breasts, and his mouth destroyed hers.

Deep and hard, he kissed her. Her vision fuzzed, and she shut her eyes just to feel. So much and so fast. He clasped the back of her neck, massaging with a gentleness that only hinted at his strength. Her clit pounded against his engorged penis, and she shifted restlessly against him. Big. He felt too big.

The idea gave her a thrill.

Then he nipped her lip, and she dug her nails into his back. He released her mouth to trail kisses along her jaw and then bit her ear-lobe.

Sensations hurtled through her. Her eyelids fluttered open, and she widened her legs. Her body ached, empty and needy. But the emptiness went deeper than the moment. He could fill her. Make her complete again. "Heath."

"Not yet." He licked beneath her jaw, and she shivered.

"When?" Her entire body was alight with fire, and only he could soothe her. She'd never wanted sex this badly in her entire life, and they were just getting started. It wasn't only his body, although that was spectacular. It was the way he protected her—the way he'd defended her. As if she was more important than anything else. She wanted all of him—and with him inside her, she'd have him as close as possible for now. "Heath?"

"When you're ready." He kept moving, licking along her collar-bone, touching her everywhere.

She scraped her nails across his lower back. Her entire life she'd been waiting for such an incredible feeling. "I'm ready."

"No." He nipped her abs and then settled farther down on the bed, his breath heating her sex.

Oh. A thought crossed her mind that she should be embarrassed at the blatant intimacy in the act. Yet his tongue swirled around her clit, and she forgot all feelings but the one centered right on him.

He did it again, and she almost came off the bed. Chuckling, he clamped both hands on her thighs, spreading her open and holding her in place. Cool air brushed her sensitive parts, and she bit back a moan.

He was going to kill her.

"Finally," he breathed against her. One hand released her to trail along her thigh and then her labia. His touch gentle, he slid a finger into her. "Ah, baby. You're so wet." His pleased rumble heated her, even as he continued to play, as if memorizing every inch of her.

His mouth and fingers were taking control, and all she could do was dig her fingers into the bedspread on either side of her. The intimacy of the moment ratcheted her need even higher. Her thighs quivered, and she tried to tighten them. Her eyelids closed, and her body stiffened on its own.

His nip to her clit nearly sent her into an orgasm.

Another finger joined the first, instantly hitting a spot inside her that made her arch. "What the hell?" she sputtered.

"Your G-spot," he said, sucking her clit into his mouth.

The room tilted and then spun. Shock held her for a moment before the orgasm rushed through her, flicking arcs of pure pleasure through her entire body. She cried out and rode the waves, knowing nothing for a few minutes except delicious ecstasy. She came down with a soft sigh, her body melting into the bed.

He lifted his ruffled head, the rogue in him showing in his smile. "Let's do that again."

Empty. Even though that had been spectacular, deep inside she still felt empty. Going on instinct, she reached down and grabbed his hair. "Up here," she barely got out.

His eyes narrowed.

She was past caring and gave him a hard tug.

He winced and grabbed her wrist, quickly securing the other one, too. "Now, that wasn't nice." Easily keeping hold of her, he moved up her body, his heated skin brushing over hers.

Too much and too wonderful. She let her thighs open more. "Now." Who needed sentences? God, she wanted him inside her. Wanted to be with him…surrounded by him. Wanted, for a small sliver of time, to be part of him.

He held her hands down on either side of her head with enough pressure that she couldn't move. "Stay here."

She blinked. "I didn't know I had a G-spot."

He halted, poised above her, and then threw back his head and laughed, the sound a little pained. "You're gonna kill me. I just know it."

She basked in the idea. To think that studious Anya Best could affect a man like this in such a way. With very quick motions, he grabbed a condom from his wallet on the bedside table. Within seconds, he'd sheathed himself and moved over her again.

He looked back at her hands, still flat against the bed. "Good girl."

Okay. That was kind of sexy. It shouldn't have been…but it was. She smiled.

He paused, his gaze darkening. "Dangerous," he murmured, positioning himself at her entrance. "We need to go slow. You're tight."

And he was huge. Definitely well endowed. She slid her hands over his massive shoulders. "Tonight would be nice," she said on a breath.

He grinned and dropped his head to her forehead. "It's like you want to be spanked."

Her body spasmed. "Wh-what?" Figured he was into kinky games. "I do not." Yet the idea made her even wetter.

"Liar," he whispered, slowly entering her. The pace cost him, and she could feel it. His skin dampened, and his taut muscles all but vibrated as he controlled himself.

Inch by inch, he moved inside her, taking possession. Her eyes widened as he more than filled her, stretching her in a way she'd never experienced. He was so large as to be everything.

"You feel so good," she whispered, feeling taken over. "There's just so much of you." He touched every nerve inside her.

He chuckled, a vein pulsing in his neck from the tension of going so slow. "You are a sweetheart, Anya Best. You truly are."

She didn't want to be sweet. She wanted to be dangerous and irresistible. In fact, she wanted to be wild enough to make him lose control. Needed to be his match. So she ran her hands down his torso, feeling his scars and strength. Maleness filled her palms, and she moved around to lightly tap his muscled ass. "Maybe I'll spank you."

He shoved harder, breaking all the way in.

She arched and cried out as pleasure and pain melded into one. "Heath."

"Yeah." His head dipped, and he kissed her hard on the mouth. He went deep, taking her with him, shooting liquid fire throughout her body. Finally, he let her breathe. "Stop challenging me."

Challenging him? Her lips tingled and her breasts ached. Her body was alight…beneath his. She couldn't even think. Yet there was an answer she had to give. "No."

"Hmmm. I think I know how to quiet you." He began to move

inside her, pulling out to thrust back in, quickly gaining pace and strength.

She couldn't concentrate. Sensations rose inside her, a series of lightning storms over churning water—all electricity and danger.

He manacled her thigh and tugged. "Wrap your legs around me."

She obeyed, clasping her ankles at his back.

"Good." He shoved in harder, going deeper than she would've thought possible.

She arched against him, taking everything he had. The strength and the power of him—coupled with the gentleness—was more than she'd ever be able to fight. She gave her body to him, memorizing every second. "More," she said, her fingers clutching the top of his butt.

He kissed her again, going deep, hammering into her with longer strokes. His cock slammed hard and fast, his entire body one muscled machine around her.

The raw flames inside her uncoiled, and she detonated, shutting her eyes and crying out his name.

He pounded harder, prolonging her orgasm. Only after she'd wound down with a whimper did he press his face into her neck and latch on with his mouth. He didn't bite her or break the skin, but his mouth was attached to her neck as absolutely as his body was taking hers. With a massive shudder against her, he stopped moving.

Her eyes opened, and she ran a soothing hand down his heaving back. God, that had been amazing. Her heart turned over.

All the way.

CHAPTER 22

Heath shoved his hands into his jeans pocket and hunched further down into his leather jacket as the morning threw snow at him. "You sure it's safe to leave them?" he asked Ryker again.

Ryker glanced down the quiet street and continued walking. "The alarms are set, and the booby traps are activated. If anybody tries to break into the building, we'll know it instantly. Plus, Zara is armed and out of bed doing some weird yoga-Pilates DVD."

"Okay," Heath said. "We have thirty minutes to shop, and then I want to check out the decoy offices." They'd be back at the safe house within two hours. That was okay.

"Did you take care of the GPS tracker on Anya's phone?" Ryker asked.

The mention of her name jolted his system. "Yeah. Last night after she fell asleep," Heath said. "Didn't want her to worry about it." He'd left Anya sleeping peacefully in bed after their night together. After sex, she'd pretty much fallen into sleep immediately, which he'd appreciated. He'd never been good with the after-coitus talk. The night had been special and beyond his experience. Were there words for that? And how could he tell her that the second she was safe he would leave her to hunt down the people who wanted him dead? He couldn't promise her he'd make it back. There was a good chance he wouldn't.

Denver paused next to a jewelry store. "Wanna talk about it?"

Heath frowned, his body feeling heavy. "Talk about what?"

Den rolled his eyes. "Forget it."

Ryker looked from one to the other of them. His eyebrows slashed down. "What? Heath? Oh, come on."

How did Denver always know everything? Heath glared at his brother.

Denver winced. "Sorry."

Yeah, he probably was. "Don't worry about it, and I do not want to talk about it." Right now, anyway.

"You slept with her. I knew you would." Ryker sighed. He paused to lean against a brick building, his gaze darkening.

Heath straightened. "I've got it under control."

"I'm sure you do." Ryker stretched out his hands in his gloves, obviously looking for the right words. "I've been there. Hell. I'm there right now."

Heath paused. "Where would that be?"

Ryker straightened. "Realizing that we have something great but that everything we love is under threat."

Heath swallowed over a lump in his throat. "It's not the same. I mean, as you and Zara." Ryker was going to propose again with ring and bended knee. That was real.

Ryker lifted one massive shoulder, and snow slid down his leather jacket. "Maybe, maybe not. But Anya is special, and you know that, and there's only one chance for you to even think of having a life with her. Hell, having a life at all. We can't keep running."

Realization slapped Heath in the face. Yeah. Ryker did get it. "We take the fight to them. To Madison and Cobb…after we finish the Copper Killer." The wind slid beneath his collar, and his skin constricted. Facing monsters was something he could do. But monsters from the past? The ones who'd known him when he was weak and scared? He swallowed. "We can to this." Together, they'd make it.

Denver nodded. "It's time to stop running. We're ready now."

"Yeah," Heath said softly, his gut churning. He wanted a life not only for himself but also for his brothers. They deserved peace. "It'll be bloody."

"Always was," Denver said.

Heath studied his brothers. They'd gotten a raw deal from birth, and yet they'd found each other. They'd formed a family—and they weren't alone. Not when they had each other. That meant something. In fact, that meant everything. That's why they'd win. "Let's deal with Madison and Cobb after this case. I'm not sure what to say about Anya, so let that lie for the time being."

"Fine." Ryker's eyes crinkled but didn't lose their worried gleam. "I'm here for you. Also, we need to talk about last night at some point. You could've killed Carl, and I'm not sure you would've stopped if we hadn't been there."

Heath winced. His ears heated. His rage could've brought the cops, and then he would've harmed his brothers. "Sorry about what happened. I'm all right now. Lost it for a moment, but it's all good."

"You're forgiven." Ryker rubbed the scruff on his jaw. "That's great about being fine and all, but when one of us loses it, we talk it out." He winced. "I'm sure I saw that on *Dr. Phil*."

Warmth burst through Heath, and he chuckled, really feeling the amusement. Man, he loved his brothers. "We're all so good with the feelings, right?"

Denver frowned, his blue eyes darkening.

"Exactly," Ryker agreed. "Later over beer?"

"Over beer," Denver said.

Heath gave in. "Yeah. Later over beer." He sighed. Ryker was right. They all had scars from the past, and when the old pains boiled up, they talked it out. That's what family did. Well, if they really wanted in, the busybodies, then…"I need more condoms, I think."

"Too much information." Ryker shook his head and shoved open a glass door. "Let's be quick about this. Though the apartments are secured, I don't want to be away for long."

Neither did Heath, although he had no clue what to say to Anya, especially when all he wanted was to put her right back into bed where they could both stay. He followed Ryker into the jewelry store and was instantly hit with the soft scents of lemon and cinnamon. As an air freshener, it wasn't bad.

The store was small with long glass counters running alongside all three walls. The door and windows took up the fourth wall and let in plenty of natural light. No other customers had braved the storm to buy baubles.

Ryker made his way over to the wide counter to the right. "I'm thinkin' that one." He nodded down at the case, his gloved fist clenched over it.

Heath stepped up to one side of him with Denver on the other. The three of them took up the entire length of the counter. "Which one?"

"It isn't obvious?" Ryker tilted his head to study him.

Heath frowned and looked at five rows of sparkly rings. Some were diamonds, some pearls, even some sapphires. "Uh."

Denver bent closer to the counter. "That one." He pointed to a stunning ring with a large square diamond surrounded by deep blue sapphires. "Matches her eyes."

Ryker grinned, his entire body relaxing. "Yeah. That's the one."

"It's perfect." Denver straightened and wandered over to another counter, tension rolling from him.

As usual, Denver had seen through the question to the answer. Too bad he couldn't do that in his own life—especially when it came to the woman he'd left behind in Alaska for her own good. It certainly hadn't done Denver any good.

Heath studied the ring. "It's beautiful." At his words, an elderly man who'd been hovering on the other side of the room made his way over, his eyes gleaming with a promised sale.

"I'm Ernie, and I own the store." The guy pushed back his thick gray hair. "Can I help you gentlemen?"

Ryker pointed out the ring. "I'd like to buy that one."

So much for haggling. Heath lost interest and wandered around the store. What kind of jewelry would Anya like? He paused by a section holding emerald jewelry. In the center sparkled a square-cut emerald of the deepest green he'd ever seen. Two bands were set along each side, each containing several square diamonds.

The image of it on her finger wouldn't leave his mind. He tore himself away and walked over to where Denver was staring into another counter. "What did you find?"

Denver didn't move. His body was tense in his faded jeans and worn black leather jacket, and the snow had melted away.

Heath followed his gaze to a series of rings with diamonds and a pretty light green stone. "What is that?"

"Alexandrite," Denver said quietly, his hands shoved into his pockets. His eyes shuttered, and his face lost all expression. But his jaw remained set, and a vein pulsed down his strong neck. Even standing next to Heath, he looked...alone.

Heath studied the pretty designs. The only time Denver had that look was when something reminded him of Noni, the woman he'd left behind a year ago. "I know you don't want to talk about it, but—"

"Then don't." Denver turned to go.

Heath grabbed him by the shoulder, and Denver stiffened beneath his touch. "If I have to chat about my feelings, so do you." They'd let him stew long enough. "For a while, I thought you'd work her out of your system, so I gave you space." Yet Denver seemed to be getting worse. "I can smell the booze on your breath from your coffee," Heath said quietly.

Denver turned and faced him directly, his deep blue eyes all but glowing. "We all drink."

Heath knew how hard it was for Denver to speak, so he rarely forced him. But this wasn't getting better. "Not the way you've been drinking." He nodded as Ryker strode up with a bag in his hand. "Denver is ready to talk about Noni. Apparently she likes alexandrite."

Ryker stopped short. "Who is Alexandrite?"

Denver rolled his eyes. "It's that jewel." He pointed to the light green stone. "Turns purple sometimes. It was Noni's favorite. Her grandpa was Russian, and it's found in Russia."

"Okay." Ryker cut Heath a look. "Apparently we have a lot to chat about tonight."

Denver shook his head. "I just chatted. Am done now."

Ryker lifted one eyebrow at Heath.

Heath shrugged. He had no clue whether they should push Denver or not.

Ryker narrowed his gaze but didn't say anything.

"You gonna buy a ring?" Denver asked, his lips twitching.

Heath shuffled his feet. "No."

"Why would you buy a ring?" Ryker asked, his gaze going from Denver to Heath.

Because it was perfect for Anya? "They're pretending to be engaged. She needs a ring." Denver turned away from the green stone as if the movement hurt him.

Heath moved toward the emeralds just to get his brother away from the alexandrite and back to the other counter. "I'm not getting a ring."

Ryker started to argue, but something stopped him. Heath partially turned to see Denver with a hand on Ryker's arm. Denver shook his head and then said to Heath, "Do the ring. If you're pretending, do it right. Maybe have fun with it."

Heath lifted his head in surprise. Have fun with it? What would Denver give for a fake engagement to Noni, even for a short time? Maybe he wouldn't be able to let her go again.

Ryker kept his mouth closed, but his eyes broadcast genuine concern. Different expressions crossed his face, ending with acceptance. And amusement. "All righty. Dig out what little cash we have left. Might as well go completely broke." He leaned toward Denver. "You're right. He should get the ring. This might be fun to watch."

Denver nodded, his eyes twinkling. Finally.

Heath would do anything to keep Denver amused, and getting Anya a ring did seem like it'd be good for the case. He dug out the last of his cash, which would just cover the bauble. "You guys. It's just for the case. I like her, and she deserves a ring. Maybe a memento of us. Yeah, that's it." Heath motioned for the proprietor. This was just for appearances…and Anya would like the ring. She should have some sort of souvenir from their time together after he'd gone. "I'd like the emerald ring, please."

* * *

Anya finished taping up her notes of the Copper Killer case on the wall to create a new murder board in the empty living room, wincing again at her sore body. She had tingles and reminders of the night with Heath pretty much everywhere, which only made her want him again. Like now. He'd left a rather short note saying that he'd taken care of the GPS tracker on her phone, that he was going on an errand with Ryker, and that she should stay in the apartment building until he returned. It hadn't been phrased as a request, either.

She glanced at the clothing in the corner. While she'd had a lot of items in the temporary apartment, she missed her apartment on the coast. Hopefully her neighbor was still gathering her mail.

A soft knock sounded on the front door. "Come in," she called.

Zara opened the door and poked her head inside. She'd piled her dark hair up. Without makeup, her skin was smoothly flawless and her eyes were a sparkling blue. "Nice murder board. Denver has a similar one. Now you're surrounded."

"Good." The more she saw the ties between victims and times, the more her mind would work on the case. "We have to figure out who this guy is."

Zara nodded. "Fair enough. For now, I've made breakfast, if you're hungry."

"Starving." Anya launched herself toward the doorway but paused as she drew closer. "Is that a hickey?"

Zara rolled her eyes as she gingerly touched her lower neck and the clear mark there. "Ryker is such a dork."

Dork? Not a word Anya would've considered for the strong and silently moving badass. "If you say so." She glanced toward the empty kitchen. "I take it you keep the food?"

Zara chuckled. "I pretty much do all the cooking, so I usually have the food."

Anya frowned as she followed her new friend, who'd so nicely loaned her a gun the night before. "That doesn't seem fair."

Zara let her into another apartment, this one just as empty except for what appeared to be a fully stocked kitchen. "I enjoy cooking quite a lot, and I also like to eat." She walked around an island to grab a couple of plates piled high with scrambled eggs, bacon, and pancakes. "When those guys cook, we starve."

Anya accepted a plate and took a seat on one of the two barstools. "None of them can cook?"

Zara munched on a piece of bacon, her blue eyes thoughtful. "Well, Denver can cook. In fact, he's a pretty good cook. But he's just fine with somebody else taking control in the kitchen."

Anya took a bite of the eggs, and wonderful tastes exploded in her mouth. She swallowed. "I see why. These are delicious."

"It's my grandma's recipe." Zara grinned.

Anya faltered. "Oh. Where does she live?"

Zara sampled her eggs. "She's in Montana with family right now." Her gaze remained on her plate.

Ah, the mysterious Montana contingent. "I'm so tired of secrets," Anya murmured.

"I totally understand. I really do."

"But you won't tell me what Heath is hiding, now, will you?" Anya asked, digging into her pancakes.

"Nope." Zara swallowed and turned to grin. "What fun would that be? You need to get Heath to give you all the dirt. Wouldn't you rather he told you everything anyway?"

Anya tried to keep her expression stoic and then gave up. "I would really like that." She scrunched up her nose. "But we're just working together for this case. After that, he's back on the run. You know. You're all running?"

Zara opened her mouth and then shut it again. After several seconds, her smile returned. "Says who?"

Anya couldn't help it. She smiled back. Here was a woman she could befriend. She had many acquaintances and a few friends, but it had been easy to go on sabbatical for a year. Or it would've been, anyway. Zara would be hard to leave. "You're not a very good liar."

"I know, right?" Zara chuckled and then ate more of her pancakes. "It sure is nice having another woman around, though."

"What about Denver? Is he dating anybody?" Anya considered the quiet brother. "He seems so sad." Big, broad, dark, and sad.

"I think he is sad. He was in love with a woman and he left for his own reasons. But if you ask me, I don't think he's over her," Zara said.

"Please don't tell me he left for her own good." Anya shook her head.

Zara grimaced. "I think something like that may have happened."

"Moron," Anya murmured, anger for the abandoned woman filtering through her. "They're all kind of like morons."

"Most men are, honey." Zara threw back her head and laughed, the sound tinkly and full of humor.

Anya joined in for a moment. Then she sobered. "What's so different about you?" Yeah, her mouth was ahead of her brain again, but she didn't care. There had to be a good explanation.

"What do you mean?" Zara asked, finishing off her eggs.

"Well, Ryker didn't leave you behind. Heath won't take a chance, and that's fine, because I'm not sure what I want right now anyway. But Denver left some woman, and he's sad. So what is it about you? Why are you on the run with these men and not safely hidden away somewhere?" It probably wasn't fair to ask the woman such intimate questions, but Anya couldn't help it. She was so curious about this too-good-looking, dangerous band of men. What would it be like to be included with them? "I'm sorry to be so nosy."

"Don't worry about nosy—that's the name of the game here. We're few, but you're in the fold, Anya."

Anya jolted. She was in the fold? Her body warmed, and tears pricked her eyes. From simple words. "Now I'm the dork."

Zara snorted. "I get it. These guys have a strong bond, and being included within such a bond means something. It can mean everything." She leaned close, her gaze soft. "Heath cares about you, and that makes you family, like it or not."

Anya cleared her throat. "That's the sweetest thing I've ever heard. Thank you." She lifted an eyebrow. "Again…how are you here on the run?"

Zara thoughtfully put her napkin on her plate. "Well, I guess I didn't give Ryker a choice." She hopped off her stool and strode around the island again. "Once I knew the full truth, I had a decision to make, and I made it. Wherever this life takes us, I'm with him. No matter what."

Anya polished off her pancakes. How amazing would it be to be so sure about where you fit in life? Zara knew she fit with Ryker. "You're in love."

"Yep." Zara waved a wooden spoon in the air. "Did you and Heath get busy last night?" Her eyes gleamed with curiosity.

Anya bit her tongue and then grimaced. "I guess that's a fair question since I just grilled you."

"Well?" Zara tapped her foot. "He has had some serious tension, and I'm hoping it all exploded into ecstasy."

"Nicely put. We got very busy." Nothing in the world could've stopped the smile that spread across Anya's face.

Zara grinned. "Oh man. You've got it bad."

"It was incredible," Anya whispered. Then she gave in to the nagging voice in the back of her head. "But I think he held back, you know?"

Zara nodded vigorously. "They have hang-ups about hurting people, and Heath totally has issues with any woman being harmed." She leaned forward a little. "If you care for him, if you want a future, you have to do two things."

"I just got out of a relationship," Anya protested. Yet her curiosity kicked in. "What two things?"

Zara set down the spoon. "First, you have to get the whole truth from him about his life. There's no going forward without that."

Anya had already figured that one out, and she hadn't needed her degree in psychology to do it. "I'm not saying I want a future with him. But just in case. What's the second thing?"

Zara glanced at the empty living room and then back at Anya. "You have to show him it's okay to lose control and be himself with you. That he won't break you."

Anya's mouth gaped. She quickly shut it. "That totally makes sense. How would I do that?"

Zara bit her lip. "Heck if I know."

Wonderful. Just wonderful. Anya cleared her throat, not wanting to push too hard. But she had to ask. "Is Heath in danger? I mean, I can tell he's running from something or somebody. Is he in danger?"

Zara studied her for a moment, her gaze intelligent and knowing. "Yeah. Danger is coming from several directions. Soon."

CHAPTER
23

Zara had been kind enough to cook a late breakfast for the brothers after they finished shopping, and now she'd disappeared into her bedroom. His belly pleasantly full, Heath glanced over at Ryker, seated with him at the small kitchen island. When was his brother going to pop the question? By the strained look on his face, he was trying to figure out a good time.

The room felt empty without Anya. She'd gone into their apartment to shower pretty much the second Heath had arrived.

Sweat dotted Ryker's forehead.

"Are you all right?" Heath asked, leaning back on his stool.

"Yeah." Ryker used his sleeve to wipe his head. "I'm fine." His hand shook.

Denver's eyebrows rose as he stood near the sink on the other side of the island. "Dude."

"I'm fine," Ryker snapped. He shook out his shirt. "Is it hot in here? It feels really hot in here."

Heath coughed away a laugh when Denver turned around, his shoulders shaking.

"You're dicks," Ryker said without any rancor.

Denver turned back around, his face in calm lines. "I don't know what you mean." His voice had risen a little on the last words.

Amusement bubbled up again, and Heath burst out laughing.

Denver joined in.

Ryker took a deep breath and stopped shaking his shirt. "She'll say yes again. It's not like she's waffling. I have no idea why I can't breathe. She'll say yes. *Again*."

Heath forced himself to stop chuckling. "Not necessarily. I mean, you are the ugly one."

Ryker glared at him.

Denver nodded solemnly. "And the dumbest."

"That's accurate," Heath said sadly, shaking his head. "Maybe she'll take pity on you."

"Plus, the ring is pretty," Denver said, grabbing a kitchen towel off the counter. "She'll like the ring."

Ryker breathed out. "You guys suck."

"See?" Heath asked. "What woman would want to be around such a negative attitude?"

Denver bit his lip. "So true. I mean, that's just true."

Ryker slowly turned his head. "Heath? Why don't you stop worrying about me and go give your woman the fake ring. I mean, the real ring for the fake engagement. Let's see how that goes."

Heath lost his smile.

Denver snorted.

Heath turned on Denver just as Ryker did.

Denver backed away, hands up. "Hey. You're the ring buyers."

Heath rolled his shoulders. "I've got this." He needed to talk to Anya but had no clue what to say. "Thanks for breakfast." He handed his plate to Denver, who'd offered to clean up. "Let's meet in ten minutes in the war room to finalize the plan to go public later today."

His brothers failed to hide amused expressions—this time at him. Yeah, they all knew he was dragging his feet. He wasn't good with the mushy talk, and Anya deserved all the gooey words.

He steeled his shoulders and moved for the door, quickly leaving and heading back into his silent apartment. Victims and timelines were spread across the room's northern wall. Anya had been busy.

Making his way to the bedroom, he stopped short at hearing Anya singing quietly. What was that? "Any Man of Mine." Interesting. He bit back a grin and moved into the room.

She jerked in surprise and then finished making the bed. Apparently she'd already showered, and then she dressed in form-fitting jeans and a green sweater that matched her eyes. "Um, hi."

The woman looked good enough to lick inch by inch. His mouth watered. "You have a lovely voice."

She blushed a pretty pink. "Thanks."

The bed lay before him, big and inviting. She'd piled her rich hair atop her head, and with her freshly scrubbed face, she looked to be about eighteen. A purple mark on her neck caught his eye. "What the fuck?" He reached her in a second and grasped her chin.

"Hey." Her eyes widened.

He slowly tilted her head to see the round bruise on her neck. Where he'd almost bitten her. "Shit."

She rolled her eyes. "It's just a hickey. Apparently it's a family thing."

Man, she bruised easily. He wanted to apologize, yet the sight of his mark on her filled his chest with heat. He straightened his shoulders at the primitive rush of possession that took him. He wanted to mark the other side of her neck. What was going on with him? "Did I bruise you anywhere else?"

She pulled her face free and met his gaze. "Guess you'll have to find that out on your own."

Moxie. The woman definitely had moxie. The challenge shot through him, hit all the erogenous zones, and landed in his heart. She was one of a kind.

He grinned. "Is that an invitation?"

Her gaze strayed to the bed and back. Then she shrugged. "Should we, ah, um, talk about last night?"

Instinct ruled him, and he took her shoulders as gently as he could. "It was wonderful."

"But it doesn't change anything," she said quietly.

"No." Why did his chest hurt suddenly? "We're working this case together, and then I'll be moving on once we track down the killer. It isn't safe to come with me." Especially since his plan was to run right into danger and toward people who'd kill him if he didn't give them what they wanted. Somebody had to die, and he hoped it wouldn't be him. But it was entirely possible it would be.

Her green eyes studied him. "I'm not saying I want to come with you, so don't think that, but what about Zara? She's on the run with you."

"She isn't mine," Heath said simply. "That's Ryker's decision, and I follow his lead with his woman." Heath's emotions were so damn jumbled that he wondered if he could make Anya his when he couldn't guarantee even his own safety. He felt more for her than he should after knowing her such a short time. "I want to be honest with you."

She leaned in. "That's fine, but you should be honest with yourself, too."

He drew back. Her words pricked and impressed him at the same time. Maybe it wasn't just threats against him he worried about. Maybe it was just him. Was he afraid of the risk? Afraid of having her and losing her? Life was full of losses, and he knew that firsthand.

"Fair enough," he said. "For now, are you ready to go hear the plans?"

She paled. "Yes. For a minute—a nice one—I'd forgotten all about the killer. So much for a relaxing day."

"Exactly. Are you sure you still want to do this?"

Her chin snapped up. "You bet your ass."

Courage impressed him. He'd keep her safe, no matter what. With one last, longing look at the bed, Heath reached for her hand. "Then let's go make a plan." What was he thinking, letting her be part of this? As he moved through the living room, the faces of the victims taped to the wall taunted him.

He'd failed at saving any of them so far. He led Anya from the apartment, fighting every basic urge he'd ever had. "I'm not sure I'm comfortable putting you in danger," he murmured, pushing open the war room door.

"I put myself there," Anya said. Her hand felt small and way too delicate in his, even as her voice was strong. Determination darkened her emerald eyes. "And I'm not yours to worry about, remember?"

His head jerked back, and his gut felt like she'd kicked him. "Yeah. I remember."

On the room's walls behind its bank of computer monitors, Denver had set up whiteboards that held the pictures and timeline of the entire Copper Killer case.

Heath whistled. The setup looked similar to the one Anya had created in their apartment. "Nice command room."

"Thanks," Denver said, moving in from the room's small kitchen. He looked at Anya. "Hi."

"Hi," she said, releasing Heath's hand.

He clenched his fist, feeling empty. "Where are Ryker and Zara?"

"Checkin' out the decoy offices and installing the security measures. More of them, anyway," Denver said, moving to another whiteboard with the words CURRENT OP at the top. "We did research."

Heath quickly read the notes. "All right. So we're in play."

Denver nodded. "Yep."

"Play?" Anya asked, looking around.

In the sterile room, she was all light and color. Heath fought the need to reach out and take her hand again. "That means we've started the op. Denver is hacking or has hacked into the state database as well as the county's one, and we're now a legitimate business with public records and an address. In other words, we've gone public."

"The decoy address," Anya murmured, squinting to read the board. "We're going to a cocktail party for new businesses hosted by the mayor tonight?" Her voice trembled on the last words.

"Yeah, and Denver has probably already petitioned the state bar for my law license to be valid here?" Heath asked.

Denver nodded. "Yep. Reciprocity is easy with Washington, so you'll get it."

Anya started. "You're a lawyer?"

Heath grinned. "Sometimes. I went to law school and did pass a bar exam, but it was just for the background information for the detective agency. I don't want to really practice law."

He sobered. By the time he was granted reciprocity, they'd be out of Washington State. Who would protect Anya then? Although the woman was resourceful and spunky. "We need to brush up on your self-defense skills. Keeping training fresh is important," he mused. Yeah, that might be a weak excuse to get his hands back on her body, but he would feel better leaving her if she could kick ass if necessary.

"I've been thinking the same thing." Her phone buzzed, and she drew it from her pocket to read the screen. Her breath whooshed out. "It's the FBI. Reese is back in town, and he said if we don't meet with him, he's going to put a BOLO out on both of us."

Shit, damn, and fuck. "I figured he'd be in touch again soon,"

Heath said calmly before focusing on Denver. "Are our identities strong enough here?"

Denver eyed the monitors. "Doubtful."

Anya gasped. "Why is that?"

Heath naturally stepped in to explain Denver's response. "Denver can keep adding to our backgrounds, but if the FBI decides to dig, they're gonna see the problems. If they get suspicious and start to investigate us, we'll need to leave town sooner than planned. It's the FBI, you know?"

"You don't have genuine IDs?" she asked.

"Not really. Long story," he said.

She shook her head, her lips thinning. "I'm sure, and I know you won't share. For now, what do you want to do?" she asked, staring at the phone like it might bite her.

There was only one option, really. "Call Reese and tell him we'd love to meet with him." Heath didn't need this complication. "Maybe we can appease him a little so he'll worry about the killer and not us right now." The need to run away hard and fast tensed every muscle in Heath's body.

Anya swallowed. "Before I call, I have to know. Are you wanted by the law? Is the real you, whoever you are, running from the law?"

He winced and glanced at Denver, who shrugged like normal. No help there. "The FBI is not after us, and neither is any state agency," Heath said. That was absolutely true. "We are being hunted by somebody who wants to kill us, and that person does have ties to the law enforcement community but has not to this point used those contacts. If, or rather when, he chooses to do so, we're in trouble."

Denver pursed his lips. His eyebrows rose. "Nicely put."

"Yeah." Heath relaxed. He'd told her the truth without putting his brothers in danger.

The nearest computer dinged. Denver stilled and moved for it. "Wait a sec," he said as Anya reached for a phone.

Heath tensed. "What?"

Denver sat on a rolling chair and started typing rapidly. "Anya just got an e-mail on her university account."

Anya stiffened. "You hacked my account?"

"Yeah," Denver said absently, hunching over the keyboard. He sat back. "Oh."

Heath moved to stand next to him and leaned down to see a series of pictures of Anya flash across the screen from different locations and during different seasons. Her hairstyle was different in some of them. The pictures probably spanned a couple of years of her life. His shoulders went back. "Anya?"

She stepped closer to him. "That's from last June," she whispered, pointing to a picture of her laughing with a group of people at a café. All the color drained from her face and neck. "That one is from last Christmas—a year ago." Her voice trembled.

Heath looked at the Christmas picture. She was walking down an icy sidewalk with colorfully wrapped packages in her hands and snow on her pretty hair. Her eyes were bright, and her face was relaxed. She'd obviously had no clue somebody was watching her or taking her picture. How vulnerable she'd truly been.

Heath put an arm around her. Fury rippled through him, tensing every muscle. The killer had stalked her for a very long time. He could've taken her right there and then. He only hadn't because he wanted to play the game longer. Heath bit back a snarl.

Then pictures of the Copper Killer's victims flashed in between pictures of Anya.

She gave a small sound of distress.

Heath tugged her closer, his breath heating. "You don't have to look at these." He tried to turn her away.

She held fast, her body shaking.

The slideshow abruptly stopped. The screen went white, and black letters slowly faded in.

SEE WHAT I'VE DONE FOR YOU? IT'S TIME FOR US.

Then a picture of Anya at the diner from the night before flashed hot and bright, burning at the edges.

"Oh God," she whispered. "He's here."

CHAPTER
24

Anya tugged her seat belt more comfortably over her chest as Heath drove through the billowing snow on black-ice roads. "We're not going to argue about this."

His hands were steady on the steering wheel, and he handled Ryker's truck as if he'd done so his entire life. "You're right. No arguing."

She watched him from the corner of her eye. His rugged face remained stoic, his gaze concentrated, his body on full alert. He hadn't said much after seeing the pictures from the e-mail beyond calling and letting the FBI know they were on their way in. "I need to know what you're thinking. You're too hard to read."

He didn't so much as twitch. "I'm thinking about how to get you out of town and to safety without pissing off the FBI or alerting a serial killer." His voice was even. Too even.

A shiver tickled down her spine, and she hugged her arms to her body. "The pictures scared me, too." The rock in her stomach wouldn't stop aching. "To know he's been watching me for a couple of years. Maybe longer." One of the pictures had been from four years ago at a Halloween party. She couldn't remember who'd taken it, and there was a chance the killer had just found it on the Internet. Or not. Had he been there?

Heath finally glanced her way. "You're safe, Anya. We'll get you out of town." His tone remained low and calm, while his eyes glittered a heated fury.

"No." She faced him fully and swallowed over a lump in her throat. Chills swept along her arms. "This is what we wanted, right?"

"No." He continued to concentrate on the road, his tone firm.

"Yes," she countered, her hands too cold. "We're here to draw him out."

Only a slight tightening of Heath's jaw showed any reaction. "Well, he's here. So no need."

"That's not it," she burst out. "Don't you get it? He knows that we know he's here. *That's* part of the game." Her throat hurt.

"This isn't a game," Heath snarled.

"I know." She breathed out, trying to focus. Trying to think and plan when all she wanted to do was hide. "But this is a game to him—one that just got even more interesting because we're here in Snowville. He thinks he's smarter than we are, and the more we goad him, the more we act like we're not frightened, the sooner he'll make a move. The sooner he'll make a mistake."

Heath took a left turn toward town. A vein pulsed down his strong neck. "Gee, Doc. That sounds textbook."

Anya reared back. "Sarcasm isn't necessary."

Heath's broad chest shuddered. "Sorry."

Anya's temples started to ache, and she rubbed the right one. "Listen. I don't want to face a serial killer. I really don't."

"Good." He was back to an even tone.

She shivered from the anger just under the surface of that tone. "But he'll just keep killing. He won't stop, and now he's making a move against me. Let's let him come while we control the situation." Her vision blurred. She had to find Loretta's killer and make him pay.

Heath turned down another road, this one busier than the rest. He glanced her way, one eyebrow rising. "You okay?"

"A migraine may hit. Could go either way." She pinched the pressure point between her thumb and forefinger. She sighed and looked back at him. "I'm right about this."

"Probably." Heath eyed the gray sky outside. "You challenged him on television, and he has responded by following us here and sending you those pictures." His knuckles turned white on the wheel.

"Exactly." Anya rolled her neck, trying to ease the pressure. "So we make a move, and he'll have to respond." She swallowed and tried to sound brave. "He's a psychopath with a good side of narcissism. He won't be able to help himself."

"He's also unpredictable," Heath countered. "The guy could just walk up and shoot you."

"No," she said, trying not to tremble. "He wouldn't do that. He has a ritual, and he'll have to follow it with me. But he might just walk up and shoot you." Her chest ached at the thought.

"Great." Heath parked outside the long brick building that held the FBI field office and Copper Killer Task Force before reaching for the printouts of the pictures and e-mail they'd just received. "We'll talk it through later. For now, let's go see what good ole Special Agent Fred Reese thinks about this. My guess?"

"He'll try to put me into protective custody," Anya said, her shoulders straightening. "It's not going to happen."

"Agreed." Heath moved around the truck to open her door and then held out a hand for her. She took it without hesitation.

The FBI's offices in Snowville were well protected behind several layers of security, which included cameras and armed agents. After going through the checks, Anya smoothed her hands over her jeans in a chilly conference room, complete with oil paintings of bison and deer. Heath sat quietly at her side, and Special Agent Reese sat across from her, no expression on his face and a stack of manila folders in front of him.

"Thanks for finally coming in," Reese said, looking impeccable in a black suit with a shiny blue tie.

"Sorry about the delay," Heath said smoothly. "Anya wanted to hurry here to Snowville and set herself up as bait."

Anya barely kept from flinching at the rough words. "I chose Snowville because this is where you are stationed." Where her sister had often visited and worked from as well. "I want to work with you, Reese."

"I'm glad to hear that." Reese turned his attention to Anya after having flipped through the pictures the killer had just sent to her. His jaw had hardened toward the end. "You have no idea who this guy is."

"No." Anya coughed, her mind reeling still. "I can't believe he got this close so many times and I had no clue."

"These types of psychos are good," Reese said. He turned toward Heath. "How's the engagement going?"

"Great," Heath said.

Reese glanced at Anya's hand on the table. "Don't most engagements come with a ring these days?"

Anya stiffened.

"I've been looking for just the right one," Heath countered easily.

Anya felt like she was in the middle of a tennis match. No, not tennis. Maybe a duel. Yeah. A duel with knives in the forest, surrounded by wild creatures. She shook her head to regain reality. What the heck was wrong with her brain? "I'm not a big jewelry-type girl," she said quietly. What kind of ring would Heath buy, anyway? Not that she'd ever wear his ring, of course. Still. She wondered.

Reese tapped a file. "I have my techs looking into your background, Heath."

"Fine by me." Heath slid an arm across Anya's shoulders, providing instant warmth and a sense of safety. "My life is an open book."

He lied so well and so easily. Anya couldn't help but relax into his solidness, even as her brain issued warning after warning. What kind of guy could lie easily to an FBI agent trained to detect such lies? She was so far in over her head it wasn't funny. "Heath has been investigating the Copper Killer for months, Reese. He just wants to catch the guy."

"As do I," Reese said. "I'm doing you a favor out of respect to your sister by allowing you two to be questioned together. Please run me through your movements during the entire case, and then tell me everything you know, Heath."

Anya leaned into Heath as he methodically recounted his agency's work and movements with the case as well as his personal movements, sounding honest and factual. Damn, he was good.

Reese took careful notes and asked a question or two. "Why did you leave Cisco?"

"We were in Cisco just to trap the killer and figured Snowville would work better," Heath said.

"Uh-huh," Reese said, looking up from his notepad. "Why don't you have an actual and permanent address or place of business?"

Heath shrugged. "We like to travel, and we get plenty of work via computer inquiries. These days I don't think anybody needs a permanent address, you know?"

"No." Reese studied Anya. "I believe plenty of people do need a permanent address."

Heath didn't so much as twitch.

Anya cleared her throat, her stomach hurting a little. "Is there anything else?"

"Yes." Reese reached for a folder from the bottom of the stack. "When was the last time you saw Carl Sparks?"

Anya blinked. "Why?"

"Because he also has ignored my directives to come in for an interview," Reese said evenly, his gaze piercing. "Why do you think that is?"

She shifted in her seat, and Heath tightened his hold. Whether she wanted to feel protected or not, she did. His strong form next to her, bracketing her, gave her a sense of security she'd always wanted. "I don't know why Carl is ignoring you. However, he does seem concerned with tracking me down and did so last night."

Reese stilled. "Did he, now?"

She shivered from the tone. "Yes. Apparently he had a GPS tracker on my phone and found me in Snowville at a diner last night." Should she tell the whole story? Something whispered throughout her brain that she'd already said too much.

"What happened then?" Reese asked.

She swallowed. "I confronted Carl and told him to leave me alone. Later Heath got rid of the tracker on my phone, and that's about it."

Reese lifted an eyebrow and glanced down at Heath's bruised knuckles. "I'm thinking there was a bit of a discussion between your fiancé and your ex. Heath?"

Heath shrugged. "We had words."

"Just words?" Reese asked.

"That's all I'm willing to say," Heath said evenly. "If you're out of questions, then…"

"What time did you have words with Carl Sparks?" Reese persisted.

Heath sighed. "Around suppertime. Why?"

Reese flipped over the cover on the file to reveal a picture of Carl lying on red snow, his neck a bloody mess, his eyes open in death, aimed at the sky. "Because we found him early this morning with his throat slashed to his spine."

CHAPTER
25

Heath finished beating the hell out of the punching bag Denver had strung up in a corner of the garage. His knuckles ached and his temples pounded. He finished unwinding the tape from his hands just as his phone rang. Tossing the tape aside, he grasped his phone to see who was calling.

He paused for a second and then pushed a button to allow for a video chat. "Hi, Shane."

Shane Dean's gray eyes narrowed. "Why are you all sweaty?"

"Was workin' out." Heath tapped the birthmark beneath his left ear—the same one that Shane had. He stared at his brother in Montana, the one he'd first met just weeks ago, and searched for words. "What's up?"

Shane's gray eyes narrowed. "You're not okay. Why not?" The tone, full of concern and determination, was low.

Heath breathed out. "A lot going on, man."

Shane nodded. "I get that. You need me?"

Yeah. Definitely. This new brother had already worked his way right into the small circle of people Heath trusted—which mainly consisted of his other brothers. He and Shane needed time to really get to know each other. Soon. "Not with this case."

Shane studied him. "Got it. We can connect after the case. But if you need me, I'll come. You get that, right?"

Heath nodded, his chest filling. Bonds mattered, and he knew it. So did Shane. "I get it. Ditto, by the way."

"Yeah," Shane said with a short nod. "For now, there's a new Internet search on the dark web looking for the Gray brothers and the Lost boys, which is apparently your moniker now." He shook his head. "Dr. Madison is getting desperate, I think. She listed our first names along with the stupid group names she gave us."

Pinpricks set up along Heath's skin. Madison called the Gray brothers that because of their gray eyes, and the Lost boys must be from the name of the orphanage, the Lost Springs Home for Boys. "We all knew she'd be coming for us." Heath eyed the closed door in the far corner, his muscles tightening. "We're deep into the Copper Killer case right now."

"Yeah. We're trying to trace Madison now, but no luck so far. You know, my wife lived in Snowville. That's where I caught up to her."

Heath didn't bother asking how Shane knew where he was. Shane's intel was probably better than the NSA's. "Snowville's a nice town. How is everybody in Montana?"

"Just fine, but I still wanted to contact you." Shane sighed, his jaw hard even through the phone camera. "I had a dream the other night, and I don't want to push you, but I've been kind of wondering about her. About our mother."

Ah hell. Heath felt the question like a punch to the gut. "She was, ah, pretty. Bluish green eyes, blond hair, and kind of slender."

"Yeah?" Shane asked softly. "Was she nice?"

"Soft and nice," Heath said, leaning against the door and watching the very quiet box covered with a blanket in the far corner by a space heater. "But she was scared and on the run. Now I know from whom."

"Dr. Madison and the commander," Shane said, his eyes going slate hard.

Heath rubbed the center of his chest. "She started taking drugs and went down the wrong path with the wrong men." Damn, he wished there was another way to tell any of this to Shane. Just remembering those days hurt, and so did sharing them. "Died at the hands of one of her lovers—a man named Spyder, who got away before the police arrived. That's all I know. We've been trying to track down Spyder for years without really knowing his name, and we can't find him. He's probably dead or in prison." Heath waited a beat, failure rushing through him. If he'd been stronger or faster, then maybe Shane would've had a chance to meet his mom. "I'm sorry I let her die."

Shane blinked. "Dude. You were a kid. Don't take that on."

"I know," Heath said. But knowing and feeling were different.

"Let it go, brother. Trust me," Shane said.

"I'm trying."

"I'll help," Shane said. "That's what happened to her. But I want to know her, you know?"

Heath scrubbed a hand across his jaw. "Yeah. I know. How about I finish this case up, and then we meet in person? Have a few bottles of Jack, and I'll tell you everything I remember." He just couldn't dig deep right now. Not here. "I have no clue how she ended up being our mother or how Isobel Madison got her hands on her. More importantly, how our mother got away from Madison and ended up on the run. But I'll tell you everything I do know when we sit down together."

Shane nodded. "That's a deal. Why don't you come to Montana? You know we're going to get you guys up here at some point. Might as well take a look around now."

"We'll see," Heath said as the box moved and its occupant began to twitter.

"Call the second you need help. Or want to talk."

"I promise, and you, too," Heath said. "Later."

"Later." Shane clicked off.

Heath exhaled slowly.

"They're persuasive, right?" Ryker asked from the shadows by the door. Heath barely kept himself from jumping in surprise. "I have a feeling when we go to visit we might just end up staying in Montana."

"Yeah," Heath said. "I didn't hear you come in."

"You were beating the shit out of the bag." Ryker's gaze went to the box. He moved that way and gingerly lifted the blanket draped over the top. "Is that a pigeon?"

Heath snorted. "No. It's a mourning dove."

Ryker leaned closer and stopped when the bird fluttered one brown wing. "Seriously?"

Denver walked in, papers in his hands. "Hey—" He stopped. "Is that a bird?"

"Yeah," Heath said. "Found him outside earlier. He hit the window, and I was just keeping him warm until his head cleared."

Ryker looked over his shoulder at Denver. "He actually brought in a bird with a broken wing. A real broken wing."

Denver's cheek creased. "Yep."

Ryker shook his head. "I mean, we've had wounded dogs, scratched cats, a couple of dinged up squirrels—"

"Don't forget that pig in Daytona," Denver said dryly.

Heath sighed. "I found him outside, and he doesn't have a broken wing. He's fine."

"Just in case." Denver reached into his back pocket and drew out a folded piece of paper. "All local vets, Fish and Wildlife, and wildlife rehab centers."

Heath looked at the yellow legal-size paper. His chest burned. "Numbers?" He looked up to meet Denver's startling blue-gold eyes. "You looked up all the numbers for me?" Taking the paper, he slowly unfolded it.

Denver shrugged. "Always do when we hit a new town."

Heath cleared his throat over the lump. Denver must've been carrying the paper around the whole time. "Thanks." Who knew? That might come in handy.

"No prob," Denver said.

Ryker moved in closer, his face losing all amusement. "Anya told us about Carl being dead. What is happening?"

Heath shook his head and shoved the paper into his back pocket. "Hell if I know. I've been going around it in my head, and I just don't know."

"Denver is doing a full background on Carl, his partners, his life. If there's any clue in that, we'll have it by tomorrow morning," Ryker said, his eyes blazing. "I've got you covered here. I promise."

His big brother had been covering him since the first day he'd arrived at the boys home. Heath wasn't alone, and they'd figure this out together, like they always did. God had done him a solid by giving these men to him as brothers. He slid his phone into a pocket in his jeans and reached for the shirt he'd thrown to the ground earlier. "Any ideas?"

"None you're gonna like," Ryker said. He moved for the door and pulled a cooler into the room.

"Considering I'm the prime suspect right now, I'd like just about anything," Heath muttered.

Ryker's lip curled back. "That's exactly the kind of attention we *don't* need."

Heath yanked on his shirt. "Yep."

Ryker reached into the cooler and withdrew three beer bottles. He handed two over.

Heath took a deep pull of his. "Thanks." Then he studied his brothers, who both were staring at him intently. "Oh. We're having our feelings chat right now?"

Denver shrugged.

"Seemed like a good time," Ryker said, taking a slug of his beer, amusement creasing his cheek. "Zara and Anya are trying on cocktail dresses for tonight. Zara had a bunch of them delivered early this morning. I have no clue how she does that."

Heath winced. "I guess I need a suit."

"She ordered a bunch of suits, too—all on credit, by the way." Ryker shook his head. "Apparently she wants to attend, so we'll be joining you."

Heath turned toward Denver. "You coming?"

"Hell no." Denver tipped back his head and almost downed the entire beer.

Ryker watched him and then turned back toward Heath. "One problem at a time. So you lost your mind last night, and now the guy is dead."

"I didn't kill him," Heath burst out.

"No shit," Ryker said, gesturing toward the brown bird watching them so intently. "Maybe Anya wasn't the only woman he was stalking."

"Good point," Heath said thoughtfully. "There's another possibility."

Denver finished his beer. "The guy slept with a student, right?"

"Yeah," Heath said, taking another swallow of the local brew. "I guess he could've pissed the wrong daddy off. But this feels almost personal. Like somebody is fucking with us, you know?"

Ryker nodded. "Yeah, but who? If Madison or Cobb had found us, they wouldn't mess around. They'd come at us head-on."

"What about the Copper Killer?" Denver asked.

Heath thought the issue through. "Doesn't make sense, either. The guy kills redheads and is obsessed with women. There's no way Carl tracked him down or was any sort of a threat to him. Or them. Current thought is that there might be two killers."

"Feels like one to me," Ryker countered. "Somebody brilliant with fighting skills. Maybe ex-military?"

"Agreed," Heath said. He played through the day in his head. "Do a search on FBI Special Agent Frederick Reese, too. He seems personally involved in this case."

"His partner was killed," Ryker said. "But that's a good idea anyway. We need to know if there's anything in his past we can use if necessary." He cleared his throat. "You're gonna have to talk to Anya about Carl. See if she has any clue who would want to kill him. Besides you, of course."

"I know. Just wanted to work off energy before I did," Heath said. The last thing he wanted to discuss with her was an ex-boyfriend who had cheated on her. "Shane called and wanted to know about our birth mother." Heath finished his beer and let the bottle dangle between two of his fingers. "I don't have much to tell him."

Denver lifted a shoulder. "Just tell him what you remember. That's all you have."

Heath nodded. "Then I guess we're good here?"

"No. Why don't you tell us what happened last night?" Ryker asked quietly, determination threading through his tone.

Heath drew up short, and it took several seconds for him to realize Ryker was asking about the fight, not his sexual escapades. "Oh. Well, you already know. Carl was mean to Anya, it triggered memories of my mother, and I saw black."

"It was different," Denver said. He cleared his throat. "Different."

Heath replayed the night in his head. His rage had felt personal...and painful. In the moment, all he could think about was protecting Anya from pain. Any pain. It wasn't about women or bullies. It had all been about Anya. Only her. "Yeah, I guess it was. Anya is different." He sighed.

Ryker cut a look at Denver. "That's what we figured."

"I don't need another warning," Heath said, his chest heating.

"Not gonna give you one." Ryker drank his beer. "If you want to tell her the full truth about us, it's okay. We talked about it earlier while you were at the FBI."

Heath blinked. He coughed out. "You did?"

"Yep," Denver said.

No. Definitely no. "I'm not looking for a permanent relationship, you guys. This is temporary, because as soon as we're done here, we're going after Madison and Cobb. To the death." The words burst out of him in a rush, and he quickly calmed himself down. A part of him wanted to tell Anya everything, but then she'd be smack in the middle of his fucked up world. Could he keep her safe from Sheriff Cobb? How could he take a chance like that with her life? "I appreciate the support, but I can't do a relationship now."

"Sometimes they grab you by the neck, toss your ass on the ground, and grind your heart into pulp until you give in," Ryker said, flashing a dimple.

Heath snorted. "Graphic." His brother had a way with words. Had he been tossed on his ass? Sometimes it felt like it.

The idea of letting Anya go curled his fingers into a fist. So he controlled his voice. "I'm fine. Stop worrying."

Ryker rolled his eyes. "Don't be a dork. We just wanted to give you the all clear in case you wanted to tell her the truth." His phone buzzed, and he glanced at the screen. "They're ready to go to the cocktail party. We'd better get a move on."

Heath glanced at the bird.

"I'll take him outside and let him free," Denver said. "No problem."

Heath settled into the fact that his brothers would back his play, no matter what it was. Even if it put them in danger. "Thanks, guys." He led the way through the garage and up to the apartments. "I need a quick shower and will be out in a few minutes."

"I'll be ready in a few." Ryker disappeared into his apartment.

Hey. They hadn't talked about Denver's drinking at all. Being silent was sure working in his brother's favor. Heath shook his head and shoved open his door, then stopped cold at seeing Anya in the middle of the room. He whistled.

She turned. "Like it?"

His heart rolled over, and his cock sprang to attention like he'd swallowed an entire bottle of those blue pills advertised on television late at night. "Yeah." A deep green dress stretched across her high chest and fell to almost her knees. The back was bare. Her stunning back was revealed…with no bra. "I like it a lot." His voice turned hoarse.

She smiled, and her entire face turned pink. Deep smoky eye shadow brought out the amazing hue of her eyes, and a muted pink curved along her pretty lips. "Thanks."

"You're missing something, though." He wandered around her, pretending to take note.

"What?" She messed with her hair, which fell in long curls to her shoulders. "What did I forget?"

He reached for the box in his jeans. "This." His hand almost shook as he held out the square velvet box. None of this was real, but still, he held his breath. "It's yours."

CHAPTER
26

Anya's nerves fired, and it wasn't just from alertness about the case. She blinked rapidly, trying to focus. "What is that?" she asked. She couldn't look away from the velvet box. A small box—small enough for a ring. Was it a ring? What was going on? Her heart clamored.

For an answer, Heath flipped open the top. "It's your engagement ring."

She gasped. Diamonds surrounded the most stunning emerald she had ever seen. "It's beautiful," she breathed, almost afraid to touch it. Wait a minute. Confusion clouded her mind. She focused on his face and not the rampant emotions running through her. Those were totally out of place. "I don't understand."

"You need an engagement ring for this op," Heath said, his eyes a burning green. "I thought this was pretty."

"Pretty?" She shook her head, fantasies of this very moment running through her brain. But *this* wasn't a moment. Not the real one. Why did her body feel like it was real? "It's incredible. Have you lost your mind? You didn't have to spend a fortune for an op."

He pulled the ring from the box and took her left hand, a slight flush emphasizing his strong cheekbones. "This matches your eyes." Without giving her a chance to protest, he slid the ring onto her finger. Satisfaction curved his lips. "Fits perfectly."

Her body short-circuited, and her lungs compressed. The beautiful ring did fit perfectly. Heath's ring. She was wearing Heath's ring, and he'd purchased it especially for her. Her heart warmed while her adrenaline spiked. Panic? Did she want this to be too real? Was she getting lost in fantasyland? "I, ah—"

He brought her hand to his mouth and kissed it. "I guess the world will know you're mine for now."

The words. Possessive and determined—and way too appealing. He was too appealing on so many levels. She coughed. Reality. Grab on to reality. "I hope you saved the receipt," she said weakly.

He nodded, tension rolling from him. "This is dangerous tonight, so get your head in the op. Give me ten minutes to get ready, and then we'll go over the plan. I want you armed at all times."

She shook her head. "There will be metal detectors protecting the entrances of the building." With almost desperate relief, she concentrated on the job at hand and not her actual hand. The ring caught the light and sparkled, nearly mesmerizing her. Tempting her. Making her want things she shouldn't want. "Denver checked out the security, and no weapons allowed tonight, since the mayor will be there."

"Oh." Heath frowned. "All right. Then you don't move more than two inches from me all night. I haven't had a chance to train you yet." Without waiting for an answer, he turned and hurried into the bedroom.

Anya looked down at the ring again. God. It was incredible. Why had he done it? Her heart lurched, and she had to stop that right now. This was work related. The beautiful emerald didn't look work related. Why was he confusing her like this? A sweetness lived in Heath Jones that drew her as much as his strength. It hadn't been a real proposal, and yet he'd chosen the perfect ring for her. That had to mean something. Right?

She continued to worry the issue over in her mind, her legs all but glued in place. Finally, she heard him moving throughout the bedroom.

"Which suit should I put on?" he called. "There are five of them here."

"The black one," she said automatically. The man looked sexier than hell in black, so why not enjoy that fact? "Put on the dark green tie with it." It would bring out the green in his eyes. "And Zara said no boots with the suit. There are very nice Italian leather shoes by the suits."

"Okay," he called back.

They were acting like a couple, even without the ring. She had to get a grip on herself before she started daydreaming like a teenage girl. The beautiful ring on her finger felt like a claim, and a part of her, deep down, reveled in the fact. What would it be like to truly belong with a man like Heath? Pretty exciting, she imagined.

A knock sounded, and Denver opened the door to poke his head in. "Hi."

She turned. "Hello."

He straightened and opened the door wider, one arm banded around a cardboard box holding a wide-eyed bird. "You look beautiful."

Heat filled her face. "Thank you. Um, who's your friend?"

Denver looked down at the little guy. "He's Heath's friend. Guy rescues hurt animals everywhere we go." Denver shuffled his feet. "Let him know I took the little guy to the park down the street to let him free." He shut the door.

Her heart pounded. Hard. Heath saved lost animals and lost people. She glanced down at the sparkling ring again. How could she not care for him? He was amazing. Unreal. Honorable and dangerous at the same time.

"You ready to go?" Heath prowled into the living room.

Her body short-circuited again...head to toe. Her mouth went dry. Talk about spectacular. Heath in a full suit with a power tie, his hair brushed back, his hard face cleanly shaven, was the sexiest man she'd ever seen. In real life or on television. The suit emphasized his broad chest and powerful legs, fitting him perfectly. A wild animal minimally contained within its expensive folds. "You're beautiful," she breathed.

His face creased in a smile. "I think that's my line."

"No." She shook her head. If masculinity could be beautiful, he was. She'd never equated power and strength with beauty before right that second. There was a danger to his beauty, and that drew her inexplicably. "No matter what happens, I'll never forget you, Heath," she murmured.

He paused, his gaze sweeping her. "You're a sweetheart, Anya. The truth of you—all kindness."

"No." She barely smiled. "I was just stating a fact." Okay. Enough with the raw emotions. She steeled her shoulders. "All right. Let's go." She hustled over to the coat closet by the door. "Zara purchased coats, too."

"She loves Internet shopping—especially on credit," Heath said over Anya's shoulder, helping her into a soft wool coat. "Are you ready for tonight?"

She thought she had been ready, but now she wasn't sure. The very real truth was she was playing a game of chess with a brilliant killer, and there was no guarantee she'd win. Not really. Her knees wobbled. "I'm ready for the party. It's just a meet and greet. No worries." She kept her voice light to hide her doubts.

"Good." He gently pulled her hair out from under the coat's collar.

She shivered, more than tempted by his nearness. A knock on the door kept her from making a fool of herself and turning to kiss him.

Ryker opened the door. He'd shaven, revealing a strong jawline. In his gray suit with a striped blue tie, he looked tough and fit—and more than a little dangerous. "You guys ready?"

"Yeah." Heath lifted an eyebrow in what looked like a clear question.

Ryker shook his head. "Not yet."

Anya turned toward Heath. "Huh?"

Heath leaned in to whisper, "Yours wasn't the only ring purchased today."

His breath brushed her neck and ear, sending spirals of energy through her body to land in personal places. Then her mind went to Zara, who would be so happy—with her real engagement. "Oh," Anya said. "If she sees my ring, she'll know you guys went ring shopping." Maybe she should take off the emerald.

Ryker grinned. "Let her know. It'll build the anticipation." He lost the smile. "Just checked in with Denver, and he took your bird to the park. Then he plans to watch a special on last year's Superbowl while doing Internet searches. He seems...sadder than usual."

"It was probably the ring shopping." Heath winced. "Enough is enough, Ryker. We have to do something. Maybe even kidnap Noni and bring her to him."

"One disaster at a time. For now, we have a serial killer to find," Ryker said evenly, a muscle twitching in his strong jaw. "You guys come up with any ideas about who killed Carl?"

"No. We'll need the research from Denver by tomorrow," Heath said, turning Anya toward the door.

"We'll have it. Even distracted, Denver is the best. He also called in a few favors he's been storing up from online hacker buddies." Ryker stepped back into the hallway, where Zara met them, dressed in a simple black sheath that showed off toned arms and legs. She and Ryker looked like they belonged on a magazine cover.

She smirked. "Anya said you'd end up wearing the black suit. It's perfect."

"Thanks. You look lovely," Heath said before turning serious. "All right. There are no weapons, which means we keep a line on each other at all times. Anya, you're on my arm the entire night."

Anya gulped. There was nowhere else she'd rather be. Things were getting way too complicated, and from the tension emanating from the man occupying her every thought, it was about to get worse. What if the killer made a move? What if somehow she got Heath hurt? Or Zara? She was a criminal psychologist, not a covert operative. What if she'd overestimated her ability to handle this case? "I need to do this for Loretta, Heath."

He gave a short nod. "I know, but we'll have to talk about the next few days. The plan of ticking off the killer and using you for bait after tonight doesn't work any longer."

She stilled. "Why not?"

"It's too dangerous."

"It has always been dangerous." Her mind spun. The only thing different was that they'd slept together. "We need to go forward and not just with tonight." Right? She owed that much to Loretta.

He ushered her toward the stairs. "We'll talk about it later."

Oh, he could bet his very fine butt they would.

* * *

Heath barely kept himself from tugging on his tie and shrugging out of his suit jacket. People milled around the simply decorated first floor of the county building dressed in bright colors, as if defying the gray night outside. All of the reception area had been cleared to make room for high-top tables, a smattering of chairs, and a long counter of appetizers. A bar had been set up discreetly in the corner.

Ryker and Zara worked one side of the room, while Heath and Anya took care of the other side, introducing themselves and their new detective agency to the local business members.

Christmas lights were strung along one wall, with a sparkling tree taking up another corner. It was mid-December, and the mood was festive.

Where would he be when Christmas arrived? More importantly, where would Anya be? If they were still together, he'd bombard her with presents. Jewelry, clothes, and shoes. Women liked shoes, right? There was no chance they'd still be together at the end of the month, however. Maybe if he took care of Cobb and Madison, he could come back. If he lived. But she didn't trust him—not completely—and he couldn't blame her. He hadn't told her everything. A woman like Anya wouldn't trust without having it all. Could he ever give her it all? His chest ached, and he absently rubbed it, surveying the crowd to see if they'd missed anybody.

"These canapés are delicious," Anya said, sliding a mushroom-looking thing into her mouth, her gaze darting around the room. "You should try them." Her voice trembled, and she looked like a doe frozen in some headlights.

"Relax, sweetheart," he whispered, eyeing two guys near the bar. "You need to take a deep breath and forget you're undercover. There are cops over there."

She turned and crumpled her napkin in her hand. Her pale face made her eyes look like a rocky riverbed. Green and deep. "How do you know?"

"Check out the way they're standing and watching the crowd. They're alert and paying attention."

She studied them for a moment. "Just like you."

He stiffened. "True."

One of the guys caught their eye and said something to his buddy.

"Here he comes," Heath said, relaxing his body.

Anya took a sip of her champagne. "I don't like undercover. It's too hard to pretend." Then she shivered. "I feel like everyone is watching me. Or maybe it's just him—the killer."

"Just pretend you're shy," Heath murmured, smiling as the man approached. "Heath Jones from Lost Bastards Investigative Services." He held out a hand.

The cop shook it, his brown eyes shrewd, his brown suit wrinkled, and his yellow tie shiny. "Detective Malloy from Snowville PD." He turned his attention to Anya to shake her hand in what looked like a gentle grip. "I'm very sorry about the loss of your sister, Miss Best."

Anya lifted her chin. "Thank you. I'm surprised you put that together so quickly."

Malloy studied Heath over Anya's head. "Let's just say we have a friend in common."

Awareness cascaded through Heath, and he drew Anya to his other side. "Do we, now? Somehow, I doubt that. My agency just arrived in town, Detective."

Malloy rolled his eyes and suddenly appeared much more approachable. "Shane and I have worked together and still keep in contact."

Heath drew back. "Is that a fact?" Why did it surprise him that yet another brother wanted to meddle in his life? He was used to Ryker and Denver interfering, and he loved them for it…usually. But Shane could've at least started slowly. Maybe with a fruit-of-the-month subscription or something. "You're friends with my brother?"

"Well, I'm not sure I'd call us friends." Malloy snorted. "I did try to arrest him for murder once. But we reached an understanding, and he's a good guy. So long as he takes care of that Josie, we're on the same page."

Jesus. Heath kept his smile in place. It figured his brother would fall for a woman who'd wrap a cop around her little finger, even while said cop was investigating her man. "I really don't need my brother or the local cops interfering." There was no reason to pretend he was in town for anything other than an op, obviously. "I'll give a call to Shane later tonight to make sure he understands that clearly." In fact, he'd make his point loudly if necessary. Shane was safe, and he needed to stay that way.

Malloy's eyes lit, and he chuckled, the sound surprisingly deep. "Shane mentioned you were still getting to know each other." He held up a hand when Heath started to speak. "I don't really care about your family dynamics, but you should know that even I could see how tight those men were. If you're family, they're definitely gonna interfere." He leaned in, his cop face back in place. "If you're running an op in my town, I'm involved as well. Shane assures me you know what you're doing, but I rarely take anything at face value."

Fucking great. Now they had the local cops on their asses. If Sheriff Cobb found these men and reached out for help, Heath and his brothers were screwed. "I'd surely appreciate any help you could provide, Detective." Damn it.

Ryker caught his gaze from over by the Christmas tree, and Heath imperceptibly shook his head. No need for Ryker and Malloy to meet. Yet maybe Heath could take advantage of the situation. "Have you found any leads into the murder of Carl Sparks?"

Malloy shook his head. "Besides you?"

Heath lost his smile. "I didn't kill Carl."

Malloy didn't twitch. "Miss Best? Who do you think killed your ex-boyfriend?"

Heath fought a growl. "This isn't an interview room."

"You brought it up, buddy." Malloy smiled at Anya. "Well?"

She eyed the detective, looking beyond stunning. Curiosity and sadness filtered through her expressive eyes. "I truly don't know." She pursed her pretty pink lips. "Carl had inappropriate relations with one student, which I assume you already know. Perhaps there were others and somebody didn't like that fact?"

"Hmmm." Malloy studied her for a moment and then turned his focus on Heath. "So that's only one case file currently occupying my desk. We're also looking into the Copper Killer case, of course. Are you really comfortable setting this sweet girl up as bait?"

"No," Heath said simply. The hair on the back of his neck rose. He looked around the room and then stepped closer to Anya. Something was off, but it might be his feelings. He had to get himself under control.

Anya frowned. "I set myself up, Detective Malloy."

"I saw the news reports," the detective said evenly. "While I understand your need to avenge your sister, I don't think this is the way to do it. Let the FBI and local police do their jobs and catch this guy."

Sparks flew through Anya's eyes. "If the FBI and state cops were doing their jobs, then my sister wouldn't be dead."

Heath winced.

Malloy nodded, his eyes hangdog. "We're just as frustrated as you are. Special Agent Reese has started meeting with state and county law enforcement, and he met with my precinct yesterday."

Heath lifted his head, his body going on alert. "Were we mentioned?"

"Yes," Malloy affirmed. "Miss Best's stunt was obvious to all as an invitation for the Copper Killer to make a move, especially since she's his main obsession anyway."

Well, hell. Heath calculated how many cops now knew he was in town. When would word get to Sheriff Cobb? How far was his reach? The walls started closing in, and only his training and strong sense of self-preservation kept him from giving away his emotions.

"I'm so glad that we're on your radar, Detective Malloy. I will take your advice and see how we can get Anya somewhere safe while we finish this op."

She lifted an eyebrow that promised a fight later.

Malloy grinned again. "Good luck with that."

They needed to get out of town and now. There was way too much focus on them, and Cobb and Madison might catch their scent. The op had just turned unsafe for all of them. Plus, Heath needed to get Anya out of danger so he could think again. His attention was too fractured. She could fight him all she wanted, but he knew when to go underground.

Now was definitely the time.

Malloy's phone buzzed, and he drew it out of his jacket pocket to answer a text. The cop went stiff, from head to toe. His soft eyes went rock hard and sharp.

"What?" Heath asked. He looked around for a threat but didn't see anything out of place.

Malloy glanced at him and held up the screen to show a picture of Anya near the Christmas tree in the corner, taken probably within the last half an hour. As Heath watched, the picture morphed into one of Special Agent Loretta Jackson, nude and dead on the barn floor.

Heath's ears burned, and he quickly scanned the busy party. He went on full alert, adrenaline flooding his system.

Anya sagged into his side, and he tucked her close, fury slicing through him like a sharp knife.

"Lock the room down," Malloy told his partner. "Now."

Heath motioned for Ryker to hurry their way. "It won't do any good. He wouldn't have sent the picture unless he was walking out the door." This time. The need to cover Anya, to protect her, was beyond overwhelming.

Anya breathed in as she allowed him to support her weight.

This was way too close. The fucker was definitely playing with them and had no problem involving the local cops.

Heath eyed the exits and tried to calm himself down. They had to get out of there. Now.

CHAPTER 27

Anya tossed her purse across Heath's empty living room, her temper finally springing free after a too-silent drive home. She'd spent nearly two hours answering police questions while keeping herself from freaking out, and her nerves were beyond frayed. The killer had wiped the cameras from the party remotely, and even though the police were going through everyone's camera phones, they hadn't been hopeful. The killer had escaped. "We are not running away," she hissed, fighting a very real urge to throw something at Heath's stubborn head.

He crossed his arms, which did nothing but flex his impressive chest muscles. "I didn't say a word about the op."

No, but she could read his face as well as the tightness of his body. The image of Loretta kept flashing into her mind. Yeah, she was scared. But at the moment, she was more pissed. Loretta had deserved so much better, and that asshole had to pay. "So you're *not* thinking of abandoning the op?"

"Of course I am." His jaw appeared made from granite. "This guy is good—even better than I thought. He sent an untraceable text to a cop, for God's sake. After disabling cameras and being within what looked like three feet of you."

"That's the point," she spat. "He's playing this game. He will keep playing until we catch him." She put her hands on her hips. "He took an FBI agent. He won't be able to keep from making a move on me, and that will make him sloppy."

"This guy doesn't get sloppy," Heath returned evenly.

God, she hated how in control he was, while her temper was spooling completely away from her. Or was that fear?

It was true. The killer didn't get sloppy. But he'd go kill some other young girl or woman soon, and right now they had a window of time when they might catch him. The only window. "All I'm asking for is enough time to play this out. We work in the fake offices, we sleep in the fake apartment, and we wait just a few more days. Stick to the plan."

He swept his arm out to encompass the entire apartment. "All of this is fake," Heath snapped, red spiraling through his high cheekbones.

The words were a slap, and she shocked herself by not recoiling. "You're right. Every single bit of this *is* fake." The ring on her finger mocked her. But this was her one chance to avenge Loretta, and she was not quitting. It was her fault Loretta had even been involved. She'd have to live with that her entire life. She *refused* to live with running and hiding. "I'm not giving up on the plan," she returned, her voice lowered.

"I am," he gritted out, "because while this damn apartment is fake, last night was not fake. You and me, it was real, and I'm not letting you be another fuckin' failure in my life." He reached her in two strides and grasped her biceps. "I can't put you in the path of a serial killer smart and strong enough to take down an FBI agent and smart enough to say 'Fuck you' to all of us tonight. Don't you get that?" The sparks in his eyes glowed hard and bright.

"No," she all but shouted up into his face, twisting against his tight hold. "I'll do this with or without you, Heath."

His smile was mocking. "You're underestimating my determination here."

Oh, he did not. She settled down. Heat filled her chest. "I understand there's too much focus on you right now. Whatever or whomever you're running from might catch up. So leave. Just get out of here and leave me to do the job I vowed to do." She could work with Malloy and the FBI. Heath could get to safety.

"I don't care about the focus on me, and you'd better understand that right now." He leaned down, his nose just inches from hers, his anger riding the oxygen around them. "The second I discovered the FBI was warning law enforcement about your crazy plan, I realized it had gotten too big. Too dangerous."

"How?" she snapped. "The more cops, the better."

"Wrong." He shook his head. His hold was unbreakable yet somehow still gentle. "I've studied this asshole for months, Anya. He's calculating and willing to mix things up. Oh, he has his ritual, but I can see him giving another big old 'Fuck you' to the FBI by shooting you from afar. This. Is. Too. Dangerous."

"He's not going to shoot me," she said quietly, giving up on breaking free. "I understand him better than you do, and he needs his routine. I challenged him. You're not the only one who has studied him, and I even got my hands on the reports from the other profilers. He won't be able to turn away from the challenge—especially since I've always been his end goal." A shiver chilled her spine at the thought.

"All the more reason to get you out of town," Heath said quietly.

She shook her head. "No. I'm staying." Her words were brave, but her chest hurt. No way could she deal with a serial killer all on her own. She could train every day for the rest of her life and not end up as practiced or as deadly as Heath already was, and she knew it. "I understand you have other cases and people after you. So leave, and I'll handle this myself."

"Those are big words, baby," he said softly.

Her lip quivered, and she bit down on it. "I know. I promised her, Heath. It's all I have left to give to her."

He paused, understanding crossing his expression. "Ah, sweetheart. Your sister wouldn't want that for you." His voice turned velvety and soft. Soothing.

Anya nodded. "I know. But she was my sister. We shared blood and part of a childhood. She took me trick-or-treating when I was five, and it's one of my best memories. Then when I needed help as an adult, she didn't hesitate. She came to me right away, like family. She was the first person I really cared about in far too long, and it hurts like hell that I got her killed."

He breathed out, the emotion in his eyes deepening.

She swallowed. "I have to do this for her. Either you understand that or you don't."

"Why don't you just let us handle it?"

She pressed her point. "I could, but you need me. I'm the bait." Inwardly, she winced at the description. That wouldn't help her to convince him. "Also, here's the deal. This could be a long op. At some point, you have to leave and deal with whatever is haunting you from your past. When you do, I'll just challenge him again, and next time you won't be around to assist."

"That's extortion," Heath said, amusement curving his lip.

She grinned. "Apparently I'm getting quite good at it."

Heath shook his head. "You're putting me in an untenable position, baby."

"No, I'm not." She shrugged out of his hold. Finally. "I'm not yours to protect, Heath. We're not together, and we're not responsible for each other." The words sliced through her even as she said them. "You've been more than clear on that score."

"There's something here, Anya. Maybe something real and lasting, if I get everything done I need to do."

She blinked. "What's that?"

"The less you know the better. Believe me."

"What a bunch of bullshit. Go back to your 'This is fake' proclamation," she all but yelled. "Your position is one of work…and this is just work."

His chin lifted. "You think this is just work?" The tone—low and filled with tension—zinged through her body.

Her legs trembled with the urge to take a step back. "Yes."

"Want me to prove otherwise?" His eyes darkened to the color of the sky right before midnight hit.

As a threat, as a warning, it was damn good. But she'd gone too far to give in now. "You can't." Yeah, she'd just waved a red flag in front of a bull.

He didn't move a muscle. His focus on her was so absolute, she wanted to squirm. "You're into challenging dangerous men these days, aren't you?"

She kept her stance. "You're not all that dangerous, Heath."

His smile stole her breath. Then he moved. Faster than she could track, he had her by the armpits and up in the air as he carried her toward the bedroom with such speed that her legs automatically wound around to clasp his rib cage. By the time she sucked in air to protest, her butt was on the bed, and he was flattening himself over her.

She struggled, her body on fire, fighting the urge to laugh out loud.

His mouth crushed hers, and she stilled.

Heat.

Fire.

True danger.

He held nothing back, kissing her hard, pressing her head into the comforter. His tongue worked hers, his powerful body plastered against hers, and his hands dug into her hair to hold her in place.

Desire spun so quickly into need she couldn't breathe, even when he wasn't controlling her mouth.

She shifted against him, closing her eyes to kiss him back. This was what she'd wanted. All of this.

He nipped her lip, soothing the slight pain with another kiss. Then he traced along her jawline, kissing and nipping, finally reaching her earlobe, where he bit.

She arched against him, letting out a soft sigh.

"Anya." His fingers tangled in her hair, and erotic pain tingled down her scalp. One of his strong arms slid around her waist and then down. His palm spread across her butt, and he ground her against his hard cock.

Pleasure swamped her, and mini explosions flew through her sex. The idea passed, somewhat fleetingly, that he wasn't playing. Not at all.

Yet she couldn't stop herself. Her knees widened, and she rubbed against him. "This feels real," she whispered.

*	*	*

Heath fought to hold himself back and be gentle. Oh, the woman liked a bite with her kiss, but even so, she was damn breakable. At her sigh, his cock hardened, so full and ready that he might erupt. So much for soft and slow.

He'd go fast and then take his time with her later.

He could be fast and gentle. It might hurt him, but he'd do it for Anya. Keeping his mouth plastered to hers, enjoying the way she returned his kiss, he stripped her. The dress sparkled through the air before it hit the floor. Her tits sprang free, and the thought that she'd gone braless all night stirred him even more. He released her to look at her. Small breasts, tight abs, and a curvy ass.

He could get lost in her forever.

Where had that thought come from? Could they have a forever? If he beat Madison and Cobb, it was possible. But he had always been a realist, and his chances weren't good—death or capture were definitely possible. As was running again, in case they regrouped.

Getting rid of useless thoughts, he shucked his own clothes, taking little care with the suit. It landed somewhere out of his way, which was all that mattered.

Her nipples were pink and tight…fuckin' perfect. He leaned down and brushed his lips over them, and a gasp rolled from her lips. So honest and so true. For the first time in his life, he felt like himself. Like the man he could be.

This woman wouldn't know how to be coy if her life depended on it. She was responsive and honest, and those traits alone wrapped around him and held tight. Her skin was like silk, and as she moved against him, he felt surrounded by softness. So sweet. So real. So his.

He propped himself up and cupped her breasts, wanting to study her but needing to get inside the wet heat rubbing against him. Pink filled her cheeks, and her pupils had widened, swallowing the green of her eyes. Need, desire, hope—all three flashed hot and bright in those stunning orbs.

He'd never wanted a woman more. "You're everything, Anya. Everything good."

Her expression, taut with need, smoothed out. "You are, Heath. I wish you believed that." Her touch was sweet as she brushed back his hair.

Go slow. Be gentle. His hands kneaded her breasts, and his fingers plucked. She sucked in air as her eyes widened along with her thighs. Okay. Not too gentle.

The bruise from the night before still glowed on her skin, on her neck, and damn if that didn't please him. If he truly made her his, he'd probably keep her marked at all time. Maybe on her thigh instead of her neck.

"What are you thinking?" she whispered, her hands sliding down his bare back.

"You don't want to know." The touch went deep inside him, where a part of her would always be. No matter what. He leaned down to lick her breasts again, taking his time and making her moan. Her breaths panted against him, and her fingers dug into his shoulder blades, causing a slight pain that only turned him on more.

She arched against him. "Now, Heath."

Now would work. His teeth scored her skin, and he fought the urge to mark her breast. Instead, he fumbled in the nightstand and drew out protection, which he quickly rolled on. She was wet and ready against him. He levered up onto his knees, grabbed her ass, and drove into her as deep as he could go.

Her body tensed, and she breathed out. Shit. He held tight to his control, keeping still. Hurting her wasn't an option. Darkness drew down over his vision. He needed her. Now. "You okay?"

"Don't stop." Her voice sounded pained, and her internal muscles clamped down hard.

With her sex all around him, holding him in, he nearly lost his mind. Heaven. All around him, caressing him. "You sure?" His voice sounded like he'd eaten glass.

"Yes." She locked her ankles behind his back as if to keep him with her. "Please don't stop."

Thank God. He thrust into her, driving as deep as possible. The woman was tight and slick around him, and he took advantage, hammering forcefully out and back in. The physical pleasure was incredible, and yet nothing compared to the rawness of the emotion. The purity of it. She spurred him on with gasps, her fingers, and soft words.

Her thighs trembled against him and then tightened. Her entire body seemed to quiver. Her climax hit, and she cried out, shutting her eyes. Her inner muscles squeezed tightly around his cock.

Holy hell.

He shut his eyes just to feel, letting the sound of her gasps fill him. Her muscles vibrated, and he let himself go, pumping hard into her. Electricity danced down his spine to land in his balls, and he exploded. The orgasm took him, every bit of him, and wrenched him quiet. God. He stopped shuddering and all but rested against her, his muscles weak.

"Amazing," she murmured, caressing his back and shoulders with a soft touch.

So soft.

He couldn't lose her. She had to survive and live, be happy. He lifted his head, feeling like he could sleep for hours. "Amazing, baby."

She stretched, and a small smile played around her slightly swollen mouth. "You've ruined me for all other men."

He chuckled, but the words slammed into his gut. Anya and another man? Oh, hell to the no. He'd had plenty of women through his life, and he'd never had a problem leaving. Pleasure wasn't new to him...but this was. Only this woman. He pressed a kiss to her mouth, naturally going deep when she accepted him. Her hum of pleasure whipped through him, and his dick started to harden again.

She broke free, breathing rapidly. Her eyes rounded. "Are you a machine or what?"

"Nope." He grinned and nipped her cute nose. "You do that to me."

Pleasure spread across her face. "I do, huh?" She wiggled wetness against him, and he hardened completely. "Look at me, all flush with power."

"Hmmm." He pressed her into the bed. "Power, huh? You might

want to watch the attitude, or I'll make you beg." He was teasing, but interest leaped into her eyes.

She levered up and sank her teeth into his bottom lip before dropping back down. "I do love a good threat."

Oh, she was asking for it. But he gave her a smile instead, determined to be careful with her. She deserved everything sweet in life. Even so, he grasped her hands and flattened them beneath his on the bed. The ring on her finger slid against his, and he caught himself. His ring. Her finger. His woman. "Keep your hands here."

She grinned. "I could go another round."

So could he. Problem was, he wasn't sure he could stop at one. Then she rubbed her hard nipples against his chest, and he forgot all about thinking.

CHAPTER
28

Anya dropped a blue file folder into the tallest cabinet, humming softly to herself. "Whoever organized these files for the move might've had OCD."

Zara laughed from across the wide room. "That would be me. I love organizing."

To each her own. Anya grinned at her new friend and surveyed the open floor plan of the fake office. Desks and chairs made up the space, set at different angles through the area. There were no individual offices, but the layout still seemed cozy. Maybe it was because the reception area held plush chairs right next to a television and a sofa.

If it were a real office, it'd be an awesome place to work.

Wide windows fronted the quiet, snowy street, and Heath had somehow managed to place her desk out of any line of fire. Apparently he really did think the killer would take a shot. He wouldn't. The guy had a ritual he had to follow. Anya noted that Zara's desk was also in a safe zone.

Zara moved toward a small kitchen area in the back.

Denver walked into the room from a side entry that led up to the fake apartment, which took up the entire second floor. "Heath is almost finished with the surveillance equipment upstairs, and Ryker is checking all the cameras outside."

"Sounds good." Anya studied this quiet brother of Heath's. Denver's eyes were a startling blue that contrasted nicely with his black hair and rugged jaw. He reminded her of a wild wolf she'd seen once on television. His movements were quick and economical as he checked the connections to her computer and made sure the cords were safely out of the way. "Thank you," she said.

He looked up. "Sure." For a minute, he seemed to be considering her. "I, ah, I'm sorry about Carl dying. I know it was bad between you, but you still knew him."

She caught her breath as warmth infused her. "Thank you." Heat climbed into her face, and she tried to unravel some of her emotions. Carl had hurt her, but he hadn't deserved to die. "I feel badly that he died, and I hope it wasn't because of me. Because he followed me." Though it didn't seem to be the Copper Killer's M.O., it was still possible.

Denver shook his head. "Feelings are never one way. It makes sense for you to be sad." He stood and looked around the room, his gaze seeming to take in everything at once. Apparently satisfied that the room was secure, he focused back on her. "Ah, it's okay to feel bad that he died." Almost awkwardly, Denver patted her shoulder, his voice soft.

She smiled at him while tears pricked the back of her eyes. Being accepted felt as good as being understood.

He turned to double-check the security measures at the front of the office.

She watched him and made note of the camera locations. What would it be like to have a family again? To belong to this family? So much support and protection and safety all around.

She started as Zara stepped up next to her with a cup of tea.

"It's blueberry. My favorite." The woman handed over a fragrant cup.

Anya accepted it and blinked away tears. "What did you do before, ah, this?" she asked.

Zara blew on her steaming cup. "I was a paralegal. That's how Ryker and I met. My law firm hired him for a job, and we took it from there."

"Love at first sight?" Anya asked.

Zara pursed her lips. "Well, definitely lust at first sight. We moved into the love part later."

"How did you know?" Anya asked. Could she sound any more like a dork? Maybe Zara would pass her a note in gym class about boys. "Dumb question, right?"

Zara shook her head, and her dark hair flew out of the clip that had held it. The clip bounced on the desk. "That isn't a dumb question. I guess I realized it was love—the real kind—when I thought about never seeing him again, and it made me want to throw up."

Anya burst out laughing.

Zara grimaced. "Okay. That doesn't sound very romantic. Um, what I meant was that the idea of not sharing every day with Ryker made life seem endless and gray. Boring and sad. Lonely."

Anya sobered, her heart touched. "Much better. That's sweet."

"It really is," Ryker said, approaching from the back kitchen area.

Anya jumped.

Zara pressed a hand to her chest. "For pete's sake, Ryker. Would you stop being so quiet when you enter a room?" She shook her head. "I'm going to die of a heart attack. I just know it."

Ryker grinned. He wore his customary faded jeans, motorcycle boots, and black leather jacket. As rebels went, he was definitely one. He reached Zara in several strides and drew her in for a hard kiss.

Anya looked away, her cheeks heating just as Heath prowled into the room from the stairs. He moved with purpose, a hard mask of determination on his face. With a black T-shirt and ripped jeans on, he looked more dangerous than any rebel, especially with the gun casually tucked into his waistband.

His eyes glittered, and he surveyed the room much like Denver had. "Anya? You understand where you can go and where you cannot?" The command in his tone pricked through her, bringing with it the urge for her to rebel.

She bit her lip. "Yes." If they were going to fight again, she didn't want witnesses. After the amazing night of sex, she thought they were of like minds. But unease still whispered in her. Even though he'd enjoyed himself, had he been holding back? Something told her he had kept his control in check. What would it be like to make him lose that? To be the only woman who could? Every instinct in her sensed that he'd never lost that control in bed before.

Ryker cleared his throat and nodded at Denver, who was heading toward the kitchen area "I thought we'd all take a moment before opening the doors for business." He paled a little beneath his normally bronze face.

Anya stilled. Was he okay? As she watched, he wiped his brow.

Zara leaned back. "What's wrong with you?"

"Nothing." Ryker cleared his throat again.

Anya looked toward Heath. He stood near the door, arms crossed. No expression. What in the world was going on? Was Ryker okay?

Ryker took several deep breaths. "So, hmmm." He took Zara's hand in his. "Here's the deal. I love you, you love me, and I think we should make it permanent." He pulled out a ring box and flipped it open. "Figured I'd do this in front of family. I called your granny and got her blessing last week." His voice trembled just a little, and he dropped gracefully to one knee. "You're the entire world to me, Zara. I'll never be worthy of you, but I'll do my damnedest to be my best. I already asked once, and you said yes, but I wanted to do it right. Marry me?"

Anya leaned closer to get a look at the ring. Diamonds and sapphires. Beautiful.

Zara breathed out. "Ryker." Tears filled her stunning eyes.

"That's another yes. The final yes." Ryker took the ring from the box and slid it onto her finger. "Good. That's done." He stood.

Zara laughed, love in the sound. She held out her hand. "It's stunning."

"You are." He leaned in and kissed her, his large body all but dwarfing the woman.

Denver hustled up with a tray of champagne and glasses. "It's five o'clock somewhere," he said, handing them out.

Zara laughed again. "How many proposals are you going to give to me?"

Ryker paused with the glass halfway to his mouth. "Two. That's it. We're final."

She smiled, happiness cascading from her. "Perfect."

He grinned. "Nailed it." Then he drank down his entire glass and wiped off his forehead.

Anya snuck a peek at Heath. He held his champagne and took a quick drink, his gaze blazing over the glass and focused on her. The ring on her finger felt like a boulder, and she refused to look. Their engagement wasn't real, and having just witnessed the real thing, she wanted nothing more than to take off the beautiful jewelry.

Only the hard look in his eyes stopped her.

This time.

* * *

Heath shifted the knife against his calf and tried to appear interested as the elderly lady across the reception desk in the decoy office finished describing her lost dog. "We'll get right on it, ma'am. As soon as you send us a picture of Snuggles." For Christ's sake.

Mrs. Burnaby squinted through thick glasses, her painted pink lips trembling. She clutched her flowered purse to her chest. "Do you need a retainer?"

Denver snorted somewhere behind Heath.

Heath forced a smile. "No, ma'am. As a new business, we're happy to find lost dogs free of charge. Just tell your neighbors and friends about us if any of them require a private detective." Even though the offices were just a decoy, he'd be out looking for that lost dog as soon as humanly possible.

Her massive purse buzzed, and she rummaged around to tug out a flip phone. Her arthritic hands shook as she opened it. "Hello?" she yelled into it.

Heath fought a wince.

"Gerty? Really? Oh my. Thank you." She hung up and dropped the ancient phone into her purse. "I'm so sorry."

Heath stood and came around the desk to help her from the seat. Relief loosened the knot of tension in his gut. "I take it Gerty found Snuggles?"

"Oh my, yes." Her tiny arm felt like a twig in his hand. "Snuggles went visiting, I guess." She tittered and smiled up at him. "You are quite a handsome young man."

"Thank you." Heath helped the lady outside and across the sidewalk to a battered Buick. He'd seen her drive up. Making sure she didn't slip on the ice, he got her safely ensconced in the vehicle. "Drive carefully."

"Thank you, good lookin'," she said, flashing new-looking dentures. "I'll be back if I need help."

"Excellent." He shut the car door and stood on the sidewalk to watch her drive away through the snow. Keeping his smile in place, he looked around. A bar sat next to a recreational outfitting store across the street, and both were lightly busy this afternoon.

His nape prickled, and he looked around again. Nothing. Yet he couldn't shake the feeling that somebody was watching him. Tuning in with his odd senses, he still couldn't hear anything out of the ordinary. With another hard look around, he turned on his boot and reentered the agency. "Something is off," he said quietly.

Denver looked up from his computer. "What?"

"Dunno." Everything in him wanted to force Anya to safety. "Just a feeling."

Denver stood and stretched his back. "I'll go for a quick walk and see if I sense anything." Drawing his coat from the chair, he loped for the front door. "Ryker and Zara went upstairs to review surveillance tapes from the area around where Carl was murdered. Don't ask how we got our hands on those."

"No problem. Watch your back, Denver." Heath eyed Anya, who sat at her desk finecombing through her entire life again, trying to find any connection to the serial killer.

Her dedication was absolute. Every time he learned something new about her, she became even more intriguing. She glanced up. "I think we did a good job with the reporter earlier."

Heath nodded. A local reporter had shown up to interview them about the new business, and Anya had discussed the loss of her sister and their determination to bring the killer to justice. "You said everything you could to challenge the Copper Killer to make him come after you—especially that you're going out of town in two days."

"Yep." She met his gaze evenly. "The reporter said the article will hit the local business page tomorrow. Should be online late tonight— we've given the killer a short window to make a move."

"Are you ready for when he comes?" Heath asked.

"No. There's no way to get ready for a nutjob." She pulled her shoulders back. "But with the security around here and your weapons, I think if he makes a move here, we'll get him. Loretta's mistake was working alone, and I'm not making that error."

That was true. In addition, Anya had obeyed every direction he'd given. "No plan is a hundred percent sure." He'd scare the hell out of her if it'd get her to go somewhere safe, but he knew better. Her motivation was pure, and her need to avenge the sister she'd loved was understandable. He'd go out of his freakin' mind if anything happened to Denver or Ryker. Or the Gray brothers, for that matter. Even though he'd already yelled at Shane earlier for getting Detective Malloy involved, he'd do anything to protect the brothers he'd just found. He tugged a Lady Smith & Wesson 9 millimeter from the reception desk and crossed the room to hand it to her. "Have you ever shot a gun?"

She took the silver gun. "I've never shot one, but I can handle them. I like how this one fits my hand."

"Yeah. It's designed for a smaller hand." He pointed out the safety. "Keep the safety on, but remember to flip it off when you want to shoot. The clip is filled with hollow-point bullets, and there's one in the chamber right now. If you point the gun, you shoot. Don't play chicken, and don't point unless you fully intend to shoot." They had to get out and have some target practice somehow.

"Okay." She gingerly hefted the gun. "It's heavier than it looks." Swallowing, her face pale, she set the gun in a drawer in her desk.

The woman shouldn't have to worry about the weight of a gun. Heath shook his head.

"I know, it's scary," she countered before he could say anything. "He's upping his moves every day, and the next one has to be an attempt."

"I know," Heath said softly. "We have the doors rigged so we can lock him in the second he makes a move. The obvious move will be in two nights at the hospital charity Christmas party, even though that's after the window I'd like to have left town." They'd received an invitation as a new business in town. He'd already started going over the schematics for the hotel where it would be held.

"We're probably safe until then?"

"No. Taking you at a gala or party is an obvious move. Going for you here in the office or in the upstairs decoy apartments is less obvious. He might make a move at any point." His gut ached. "We're covered here, but still." She'd be in the thick of danger again at that party.

She twirled the ring around on her finger. "I should give this back. There's no need for it now."

He liked the ring on her finger. "Keep in character, Anya. The ring stays on."

Her brows drew down, and her stubborn chin firmed. "You think he's watching."

"Yeah. Keep the ring on. I feel like we're being watched, and if you want to appear engaged, you have to keep it on. In fact…" He reached for her and picked her up, planting his mouth on hers.

She struggled for about two seconds and then kissed him back, shoving her tongue into his mouth and her hands through his hair. He growled and went deeper, bending her back over the desk.

"Whoa," Denver said, jerking Heath out of the kiss.

Heath turned, his chest rioting.

Denver held up his hands. "Sorry. I, ah…"

Heath scrubbed a hand through his hair. "No worries. Was just kissing my fiancée." Giving her a look to behave tinged with wiggling his eyebrows to make her smile, he maneuvered back to the front door. "Did you see anything?"

"No." Denver rubbed his neck. "But I'm with you. Somebody is watching, somehow, and I couldn't hear a thing. No heartbeat, nothing out of the ordinary."

"Ditto," Heath said. "What does that mean?"

Denver shrugged. "Not sure, but I can tell you that something or someone is definitely coming for us."

Yeah, but that was nothing new. Heath straightened his shoulders and again surveyed the icy street outside. The question was…who would get there first? The Copper Killer or Dr. Madison and Sheriff Cobb?

CHAPTER
29

The decoy apartment was cold for some reason. Anya sat on the bed with papers in front of her. Heath hadn't been to bed yet, and she couldn't sleep. He was scouting the neighborhood under the cover of night, hoping to find what his subconscious was trying to tell him.

The apartment had three bedrooms, a sprawling great room, and an updated kitchen. The walls were brick, the floors wood, and the fixtures antiques. Ryker and Zara had retired to the farthest bedroom from the front door, while Denver was still downstairs working on the computers. He seemed to rarely sleep.

She'd spread papers across the bed. Copies of the FBI file along with her profile. Notes from her past. Anyone she'd dated, been friends with, or just had met. Dossiers on all of them.

"You're in here," she muttered, looking through the lists again. The killer was there.

Her eyes blurred. She yawned and looked around. The bedroom held the bed, covered with a deep green comforter, two nightstands, and an antique dresser. They had to make it look authentic for the killer, just in case he got in somehow when they weren't there. She shook her head as her stomach cramped. The plan was a good one, and there were cameras and guns all around. Yet she couldn't help but feel like she was playing a game of chicken with somebody making up new rules.

Her phone buzzed, and she grabbed it, startled to see Carl's number come up. What in the world? She shook her head and read the phone again. It rang insistently. She stopped breathing.

Wait a minute. That couldn't be right. Her vision blurred. She ground her palm into her right eye and then blinked until she could see clearly. It still showed Carl's name.

A metallic taste filled her mouth. Her heart rate sped up. Adrenaline. She could taste it. Her breath panted out, and her head swam. She gulped down air. God. The thing kept ringing. She had to answer it. Her hand trembled, but she answered the call. "Hello?"

Silence.

"Who is this?" She scrambled out of bed and hurried from the room, glad she was wearing yoga pants and a T-shirt. Her ears rang. Who was calling? Did the killer have Carl's phone?

Nothing. Maybe breathing.

She ran out of the apartment and hustled down the stairs to find Denver at his desk with a soft light glowing. He looked up, his eyes quizzical. She handed over the phone. "Carl's phone," she whispered.

Heath moved in from the kitchen area, and she jumped. He'd been in the building but hadn't joined her in bed? He grabbed the phone and turned it over to press the speaker. "Who the fuck is this?" he growled, his body one lean line of sizzling anger.

An audible click echoed over the line.

Anya leaned against the nearest desk, her heart clamoring. "That had to be the killer, right?"

"Can you trace it?" Heath asked.

Denver looked at the phone, pushed a couple of buttons, and read the screen. "No. The phone is now off, and any location-tracking elements are disabled."

Anya swallowed. "The only reason Carl's killer would call is to mess with me. To scare me." Chills swept her, and she wrapped her arms around herself.

Heath reached for her and drew her into his body. She wanted to protest, but he felt too good around her. Solid and safe. "The killer might've been going through Carl's contacts, or he might be somebody you know from your time working with Carl," Heath said, his voice a reassuring rumble.

Good. Heath was calm. Somehow that calmed Anya. She looked up at his face and nearly stopped breathing. Furious. His eyes glittered with a dangerous rage, and his jaw looked like it was made from pure rock. "Or?" she asked.

"Or the Copper Killer is messing with us," Heath said in a gravelly voice.

Denver placed his hands flat on the desk. "How does that make sense? The killer doesn't mess around. He kidnaps, tortures, and kills. Why would he be messing with us?"

"With Anya," Heath said. "She challenged him, and he's having way too much fun playing."

She thought through all her research. "Killing Carl doesn't make sense for a serial killer. He has a type and a routine." She shook her head. "But…this has been about me since the beginning. You're right. He's playing a game, and he's having fun."

Heath placed a kiss on the top of her head, his movement controlled and gentle. "I can have you out of here within an hour. Please." The *please* was said in a low rumble, one with contained emotion.

She could nearly feel the fight going on inside him to even give her a choice.

For the first time, she actually considered running. She'd received a phone call from a dead man's phone. Her body trembled. She'd honestly considered Heath and his brothers almost invincible, and how foolish was that? Nobody was invincible. "I'm not sure."

"We can sleep on it," Heath said, turning her toward the stairwell. Her phone buzzed again.

Heath's entire body tightened next to her, and he looked down. "What the hell?" He pressed the speaker button so they could all hear. "Reese?"

"Anya? You sound, um, funny," Agent Reese said, his words slurred. "You been takin' testosterone?"

Anya's mouth dropped open. "Are you drunk?"

"Yeppers." Reese snorted. "I loved her, you know. Loved Loretta. Pretty Loretta. She's gone."

Anya coughed. The man had definitely loved her sister, and Loretta had felt the same way. Her heart ached for them both. For what they might have had...for what they could've created together. It was all lost. Tears filled her eyes. "Where are you?"

Reese sighed. "I don't know. In my car outside the Red Bonnet Bar. I guess I do know. Loretta and I used to drink here sometimes and hash out cases." He belched, his tone low. Angry and beyond sad. Maybe desolate. "You know. We worked together."

Heath shook his head, glaring at the phone still in his hand. "Did you just call from a different phone?"

Anya gasped. That had not been Reese. She'd bet her life on it.

Reese snorted. "Called who?"

Heath drew in air, obviously trying to hold on to his patience. "Did you just call Anya from a different phone?"

"Nope. Only have one phone. How many phones you got, Heath?" Reese went into a coughing fit.

Heath pinched the bridge of his nose. "You can't drive like that."

"Who cares? You know? At this point, who really cares?" Reese sighed, his tone hollow. "She's, uh, she's gone. All gone." His slurred voice broke. "She loved you, Anya. So much. Was so proud of her baby sister."

Tears welled in Anya's eyes. "We'll come and get you, Reese. Just stay warm in your car, and we'll be right there." She ignored Heath's harsh look.

"Hold tight," Heath said into the phone. "Okay?"

"Okay." Reese sounded drowsy this time. "I'll hold tight. Nothin' else to do anyway." He clicked off.

Heath slipped the phone into his jeans pocket. "Anya, go back to bed. Denver, stay on guard. I'll be back after I take care of the agent."

"No." Anya grabbed his arm, her mind spinning. "I want to go with you."

Heath looked down at her. "No way. You stay here and stay safe."

"No." She wanted to stomp her foot…right on the flat of his damn boot. "I told Reese I'd come, and he needs help. I can help him." Anya tugged on Heath's muscled arm.

Heath frowned. "You are not going."

Denver sighed. "I'll go."

The phone rang again. With a snarl, Heath jerked it free of his pants, looked at the screen, and pressed the speaker button again. "What is it, Reese?" he barked.

"Um, hi. This is Special Agent Dingman. I have his phone." Her voice was quiet through the speaker.

Heath's shoulders settled. "I take it you found Reese?"

"Yeah. He called earlier waxing poetic about love. I tracked him to the bar," Dingman said. "Thought I'd let you know he's safe. I'm sorry he bothered Anya. He was very much in love with her sister."

"Make sure he gets home," Heath ordered.

"No kidding, buddy. Anya, I'll call you tomorrow," Dingman said, clicking off.

Heath shoved the phone back into his pocket, his movements smooth and a little too controlled. "We need to return to the chain of command here, Anya. Get in line, or I promise I'll lock you down thousands of miles from here."

Her head snapped up. Awareness lit her skin. Anger and an odd intrigue rushed through her to steal her breath. "Knock it off, Heath. I'm not in the mood."

With no warming, he moved against her, his shoulder to her stomach. She flopped over and instantly kicked out. Her body jolted, and blood rushed through her head. She kicked again, heat washing through her. Hard. He manacled her legs and all but jogged through the office and up the stairs to the apartment.

She couldn't move. He was so freakin' strong. "Heath. Let me go." She could barely struggle, and her anger rose.

Several steps later, he tossed her onto the bed. Her files and notes scattered in every direction.

She scrambled back, her hands clenching with a new need to punch him in the face. Just who did he think he was?

He stared down, anger burning in his eyes. "You understand that we are dealing with killers, right? One, maybe two?"

"Yes," she snapped.

"Good. Keep your ass in this room and get some sleep. Baby, you definitely do not want to cross me on this." Without waiting for a response, he left the room and shut the door none too gently.

She stared at the closed door, her mouth gaping. With her own version of a snarl, she yanked off the emerald ring and threw it at the wall. It hit the brick and dropped, bouncing twice on the floor. She winced. Her hands shaking, she pushed off the bed and bent down to retrieve the ring, studying it.

Her mind instantly battled with her emotions, digging into Heath's psyche and motivations. Oh. She knew enough about Heath already to understand he was coming from a place of worry and concern. Seriously deep and justified concern.

But he could've handled his emotions much better. She sighed. Whatever was in his past seemed to have created those rough edges. He really needed to learn a better way to communicate.

The ring glittered, stunning and vibrant, in her hand. Both the band and the gems were perfectly fine.

God, it was beautiful.

She placed it carefully on one of the nightstands. Her limbs felt heavy, and her body was chilled. The pretty bauble didn't belong to her. Not really.

* * *

Dr. Isobel Madison leaned over her keyboard, typing furiously. Code flashed across her screen, and she squinted to read in the dim light. It was well after midnight, and her neck ached. She'd skipped her exercise session earlier, and she could feel it.

Yet...she was close and getting even closer. Finally.

She sat back and stretched her arms while her computer went to work. "Ah, Detective Malloy," she murmured. "I knew you'd come in handy someday." A short time ago the Snowville cop had worked with some of the other boys she'd created before they'd gone underground again.

A snowstorm rattled against her windows, and she turned to stare into the darkness. Night had masked the training field, which would be littered with ice and snow in the morning.

Elton Cobb strode into the room, sweat across his brow and workout shirt.

She hummed softly to herself. Since they'd started living together full time, he'd made an impressive effort to get in shape. Oh, part of his effort was for her, she knew. The other part was in preparation for finally finding the Lost boys...if he got to them first. "How was training?" she asked, letting her gaze linger on his broad chest.

He dropped into a guest chair, his electric blue eyes focused. "Boxing matches went well. There's a definite difference between your soldiers and the new recruits."

"Of course," she said as she stretched her left trapezius muscle, keeping the pride she'd earned out of her voice. "Mine have been trained since birth." By her beloved commander, may he rest in peace. She winked at the man now occupying her bed most nights. "The rest of the soldiers will be trained well enough, Sheriff Cobb."

He grinned like a wolf. "Are you flirting with me?"

"Yes." All men liked their titles used. He was on leave from his job and needed to be reminded of his status more than most would. "I feel like things are finally coming together here." In mere weeks her lab would be fully functional, and she could start a new reproductive trial. She still had genetic samples from her other lab to use, but she didn't fool herself into thinking they were still viable. The sperm was old and had been moved around. She needed new samples.

The Lost boys would provide those first, she decided. If they refused to jack off for her, then she'd just knock them out and take sperm the old fashioned way—with syringes.

Elton twisted his neck. "What are you working on?"

A little truth would appease him. "I've had somebody watching a Detective Malloy in Snowville ever since Shane lived there. I'm fairly certain the cop helped Shane get out of town." Shane had been one of her supersoldiers—one of the Gray brothers—and he'd deserted her. How could he not understand the importance contained in his very genes? She sighed.

Elton cracked his knuckles, his gaze narrowing. "And?"

She lifted a shoulder. "The cop has been doing some odd Internet searches into the Lost Bastards detective agency, and he has been attending local meetings and get-togethers that he has never attended before. I'm trying to hack into his phone, but it's surprisingly secure for a cop from eastern Washington."

"You think he's in contact with Shane?" Elton asked.

"I do not know." Which was why she was trying to hack into his phone. "I keep an eye on Detective Malloy, and whenever he does something out of his normally very boring routine, I figure out why. So far the only interesting thing about the guy is that he's dating a veterinarian who likes to buy him flashy ties."

Elton eyed the storm outside. "It seems like a lot is going on in Snowville. Has our soldier reported back?"

Now Daniel was *their* soldier? Interesting. She hadn't decided to share him. "Yes. He's searching new rentals in Snowville as we speak but so far hasn't found Heath, Ryker, or Denver. I still think Snowville is a red herring, and they're somewhere else here in the Pacific Northwest. Seattle would be my bet," she said. "It's a big enough city, they can get lost but still have access to mass transit to flee if necessary. I believe the Gray brothers are somewhere in the West, too, and now that they've all connected, I surmise they'll stay close to one another." Which was nicely convenient for her.

"Makes sense." Elton plucked a framed picture off the desk. The silver frame looked delicate in his beefy hand. "This is new."

"I finished unpacking and found it in some boxes. She's beautiful, right?" Isobel glanced at the photograph of her daughter, Audrey. It had been taken during Audrey's graduation from high school, where she'd earned straight A's in advanced classes.

"She looks just like you. Blue eyes, black hair, flawless skin," Elton said, turning the photo around in his hands. "Different expression in those eyes, though."

"Really?" Isobel watched his movements, curiosity rising. "How so?"

"She looks a little lost, whereas you always look determined." He gently set the picture down on the desk again. "She has to be about seven months along now, right?"

"Yes." What Isobel wouldn't give to test that baby. A cross between Audrey and one of Isobel's genetically enhanced soldiers might be something new. Something incredible, really. The hair on her arms stood up. "Audrey and one of my creations are giving me my first grandchild."

He cleared his throat, scrutinizing her. "Do you feel love like other people?"

She tilted her head to the side. Interesting question. "I don't know how other people feel, but I do feel love. It's probably more cerebral than most." Of course, most women would probably be hurt that their only daughter had fled with a man who hated her mother, but not Isobel. It was what it was, and she'd get what she wanted in the end. "I do love you, Elton." He provided her with a service, and that was love as far as she was concerned.

He steepled his fingers at his chin. "I love you, too."

She smiled and double-checked the code on her computer. It seemed important for him to be able to say those words, so she lingered in the moment. "I'm glad we're finally together. We're almost family." His chest swelled at the words. Yes. They had been the right words. She allowed her smile to widen.

"Speaking of family. About your daughter—you'd be sad if she died, right?" He frowned as if trying to read her mind.

Why was he questioning her? "I'd be devastated." For goodness' sake. Audrey was carrying the first baby born of Isobel's creations. If that baby died before she could examine him or her, it'd be a scientific loss of epic proportions. "I can't even imagine something so terrible."

She caught herself and slumped her shoulders a little. "Not to mention the loss of my sweet Audrey. It's hard to explain a mother's love for her daughter."

Elton relaxed. "Yeah, that's what I figured."

Isobel nodded solemnly.

"I was wondering. When you get the lab up and running, what if you and I had a kid?"

She blinked. "What?"

"A kid. You and me and a surrogate. It could happen, right?"

She sat back, her mind spinning. She hadn't hit menopause as of yet, so she might have viable eggs. Elton was strong and smart...and slightly sociopathic. Her breath burst out, surprising her. "You want a child?"

He shrugged, his skin flushing. "Yeah. I think I'd like a son to name after my dead brother. The one Heath and his brothers killed." Defiance crossed his broad face, and a softer light than usual glimmered in his eyes. Vulnerability?

"You want this," she mused, calculating the possibilities.

"Yes." His chin lowered, and he met her gaze directly.

A child would certainly bind Elton to her for the rest of his life. It also seemed a shame to waste Isobel's intelligence; maybe she should pass that on to another generation like she had with Audrey. Through the years, Isobel had considered creating more children, but her secret hope had been to have one with the commander. That hope had only recently been destroyed by his death. "You're sure?"

"Yes," Elton said.

With some splicing and careful work, she might be able to create the perfect soldier using her own genes. Perhaps she should harvest *several* of her eggs.

What would combining her genetic material with samples from one of her earlier creations do? Heath's extraordinary reflexes, self-control, and raw size would be a nice combination with her intelligence. Elton could never know that her thoughts were going in that direction, however. "I'm very intrigued by your idea, Elton."

He smiled. "I thought you would be. Just think of the kid we'd have."

"I am," she said softly, donning a sweet smile as her mind went to work. The new lead with Detective Malloy had her instincts humming and her spine straightening. Oh, she was so close to finding them.

It was time. The Lost boys would be back home within the week. She just knew it. Codes started to stream across her screen. "It's time to send a force to Snowville."

CHAPTER
30

As dawn tried to usher in the morning against the grim night, Heath prowled around the decoy office, making sure all the cameras were on and capturing the entire area. This was the last day his brothers could stay in town. Madison and Cobb would be closing in.

So was the serial killer. He could just feel it. Sensors had been placed in the floor, so they'd know instantly if anybody breached the perimeter. The locks would then engage. "This is a bad idea," he muttered. The walls started closing in, making it hard to breathe.

The stairwell door opened, and Denver stumbled into the office.

Ah hell. Heath took in the dark circles beneath Denver's eyes. "What are you doing up?"

"Can't sleep," his brother muttered, stalking over to his desk. "Thought I'd grab a drink."

"You've been drinking all night." It was a guess but not a tough one. Denver's eyes were bloodshot, and his movements were a little slower than normal. Oh, Heath would take a drunk Denver to cover his back over most men, but even so. "Dude. Your liver is going to start rebelling."

Denver rolled his eyes and yanked out his desk drawer. The pain gripping him wasn't going to let him loose.

Heath moved toward the kitchen. "Maybe I'll join you." It was time they talked. Ryker usually handled the emotional stuff, but he had his hands full with keeping Zara safe and now planning a wedding. What was a chocolate fountain, anyway? Heath grabbed two coffee mugs off the counter and approached the desk. His heart ached to see his brother hurting. There had to be something he could do.

Denver pulled out a bottle of Jack to pour into each cup. "No talking." He dropped into his chair.

Heath rolled a chair over, frustration sharpening his movements. He was being a crappy brother, and he needed to help Denver now. "Wrong. There will be talking."

Denver sighed and tipped back his glass.

Heath shook his head. "I'm barely holding on here, man. You've got to tell me what's eating you up so badly."

"Nothin'. Just life." Even after a full night of drinking, Denver sounded stone-cold sober. That had to be a bad sign. "I feel like a sittin' duck here."

Wasn't that the truth? Heath eyed the walls again. "Yeah. I get that." When the newspaper article hit the paper that morning, they would have all but sent an invitation to Sheriff Cobb to track them down. "We're stronger than Cobb is, you know." Together they were stronger than any enemy.

"Yep." Denver poured more booze into his cup. "Though monsters from your childhood always seem bigger in your mind."

"True," Heath whispered. Denver could be the quiet philosopher when he wanted. Heath had always liked that about him. Heath took a sip and let the liquor burn down his throat, the feeling sharper than the guilt of letting his brother get to this point. "I've been lax." Too caught up in his own issues.

"You're fine. We're fine," Denver said somberly. "Stop blaming yourself for everything."

"I don't."

"Sure you do. Probably something having to do with your mom dying young." Denver turned the cup in his hands, his gaze becoming thoughtful.

Now even Den was a shrink. Heath opened himself to the possibility. "You're probably right." Yet he still owed Denver his best, and seeing the guy hurting slammed a helplessness into him that actually ached. He set his cup down and absently rubbed the scar on his palm. "Ryker and I were good friends before you showed up at the boys home."

"Yep." Denver studied him.

Heath shifted in his seat. "We became a family when you joined us."

Denver looked at his own scarred hand. At the line making them brothers. Officially. "I know."

Heath fought for patience. He could do this. "Are you regretting leaving Noni behind?"

"Are you going to leave Anya?" Denver asked quietly, his shoulders slumping.

Heath jerked back. "This is about you."

"Nope. I had to leave Noni. We're not normal, Heath."

No, they weren't. They'd seen the darker side of life—they'd embraced it and made it their own. Most people wouldn't get that. "You're right. Anya has no idea. I can't take somebody that delicate on the run from Cobb and Madison. That'd be crazy."

Denver nodded. "So you get it. You're wrong about her, but you do get it." He scratched his chin. "Plus, you and I know we're waging a war, and we're going to try to keep Ryker out of the line of fire."

Heath blew out air. "Yeah. I know." Ryker had proposed and was getting married. He needed to be protected for Zara. "I'm okay with it. Are you?"

"Absolutely," Denver said, his gaze flaring. "I want him happy. In addition, I want you happy and safe."

Heath's shoulders jolted. "You're not going after them alone. Don't even fucking think it."

Denver remained silent.

Damn it. "Listen. They have trained soldiers, and Cobb wants us dead, whether or not Madison needs us alive. Either way, it ain't gonna be good."

"I know. That's why I left Noni." Denver took another slug.

"If we beat them—if we end Cobb and Madison—are you going back for her?" Heath asked quietly.

Denver stared into his now-empty cup. "I don't know."

Yeah? Well, Heath sure as hell knew. If they lived through taking out Cobb and the psycho doctor, he'd kidnap both Denver and Noni and put them in a mountain cabin somewhere they couldn't leave. Yeah. Good plan.

"Whatever you're thinking, stop it," Denver muttered.

Heath grinned. "Okay. Let's go back to agreeing about Ryker, okay? He stays safe when we go."

"I have super-hearing, you dumb-asses." Ryker strode into the room, bare chested and with his jeans unbuttoned. His hair was ruffled, and his eyes concerned. "I heard you guys."

Heath reached for his glass. He would've heard Ryker had the guy not gone stealth on them. "The downside of having superhuman, genetically altered hearing. Shit wakes you up."

"I'm not being left behind. Ever." Ryker eyed the bottle. "You guys putting one on?"

"No. Too much to do still before we invite a killer into our little nest." Heath took another drink. "Just having a bit of a chat."

"Good." Ryker scratched his whiskered chin. "You're both dumb-shits."

Denver set down his cup, and Heath jerked his head toward his brother. "Excuse us?" Heath drawled.

"I'm done, Heath," Ryker said, his gaze softening. "I have a woman in my bed muttering about place settings, I have Denver here losing his ass in a bottle, and now I have you, the normally reasonable one, being dishonest with himself. Not to mention you two just made a tacit agreement to go after killers without me. Not happening."

Heath pushed his cup onto the desk and partially turned to face Ryker, his chest heating. "You're gonna want to clarify the dishonesty statement, brother."

Denver pushed away from the desk, no doubt to intervene if necessary. Always the peacemaker, wasn't he? Heath took note of Denver's movements while keeping his gaze on Ryker, who did look like he was done. His chest was out, his chin was up, and his eyes said he was pissed. Even with interesting little scratch marks across his battle-worn chest, which showed he'd probably just gotten laid, his temper was clearly present and ready to go.

"Cool it," Denver said.

"No," Ryker said. "You love her. Stop lying to yourself and deal with it." He partially turned toward Denver. "I'll deal with you next."

Fire flashed in Denver's eyes. "Looking forward to it."

Heath shook his head. "I just met the woman."

"Who gives a fuck?" Ryker snapped. "Time doesn't really have constraints in our world, and you know it. There's no reason to stop livin' just because we're being hunted. We've run long enough, and it's time to end this. I agree it's time to take the fight to Cobb and Madison."

"You're prepared? You know what we have to do?" Denver asked.

"There's only one thing to do," Ryker replied just as tersely.

Heath breathed out. "Shit, man." Yeah, he could probably put a bullet in Cobb without breaking a sweat. But Madison? A woman?

"I'll do it," Ryker said. "I'm not asking you to."

No, he wasn't. But Ryker couldn't cold-bloodedly kill a woman any more than Heath could. Not even that woman.

"Could go to Montana," Denver said. "Go off the grid like the Gray brothers have."

Heath rubbed his chest. "There's no *off the grid*. They're safe now, but they won't be forever. There's no way they're not having this same conversation on a regular basis, especially now that our brothers have taken in the next generation and started having their own kids."

Ryker nodded. "Exactly my point. There's no future and no safety as long as Cobb and Madison are breathing. We want a future, and we have people to share that with. There's only one way it can happen." His gaze was stark. "It's our only option, as much as I hate it."

"Fine. I agree that we're all in if we go," Denver said. "We don't know where they are."

"We can find them," Heath countered. "We can find Cobb, and I'm sure he'll lead us right to Madison, even though he's on sabbatical from his sheriff job." He eyed Ryker. "You brought Zara into it, and we're fine with that. But you should stay safe."

"No. We're all in—together. Period." Ryker reached for the bottle and tightened the cap. "I won't let you guys down. I'm not distracted."

"Didn't think you were," Heath countered.

Ryker cut him a look. "Really? Part of the reason you won't go for it with Anya is that you don't want to have your attention split when we rush into hell. I'm not better than you."

Huh. Heath frowned, his mind spinning. "I know, but—"

"No buts. If you had a future, a good one, would you keep Anya?" Ryker asked.

"She's not a puppy," Heath muttered.

Denver snorted.

It was a good question, though. Forget reality and timelines. Could he imagine a future without her? His chest hurt again.

Ryker kept the bottle. "I say we finish this case and cut off the Copper Killer's head. Then we take out Madison and Cobb."

"Aren't we macabre tonight?" Denver asked, eyeing his bottle.

"Yeah." Ryker glanced toward the door to the stairs. "If that's what it takes to protect Zara, I'll do it."

Denver nodded. "Agreed. One case at a time, though."

The idea of anything harming Anya propelled Heath right back to the current issue. "All right. We have to get back to work. A serial killer is planning his next move, and everything in me says it's gonna be soon."

The words hung in the air like an icy omen.

* * *

Anya finished wiping up in the kitchen, her nerves almost frayed. Tension hung over the office, heavy and ominous. Ryker and Zara scouted outside as if they were going for a walk, Denver typed furiously on the computer, and Heath checked the motion sensors set into the office for about the millionth time. What if the trap sprung and locked them in instead?

The waiting was going to kill her. Forget about the bad guy.

Was it possible her impromptu news conference had been only last week? If so, that had given the guy enough time to scout Snowville and find a good killing spot. There were tons of abandoned barns throughout eastern Washington. "He should be getting antsy from seeing me cozying up with Heath."

Heath rubbed the back of his neck. "Agreed, but he's smart. He may have a different victim already chosen, and he's taking her while we're waiting with a trap."

"Yeah, but Anya's challenge would be hard for him to resist," Denver said, not looking up from his computer.

"Yeah. He's locked on." Anya placed the dishrag over the faucet. Denver had begun speaking more freely around her, and that warmed her thoroughly, even as Heath appeared to be more distant than ever. He hadn't joined her in bed all night. She tried to make herself okay with that fact. They weren't a couple in real life. This was make-believe for a killer. But one more night with Heath would've been nice to keep her mentally warm in the future.

She ran her thumb over her naked finger where the ring had been—an obvious connection to Heath. It represented a feeling of security and protectiveness that she missed. Man, she had it bad.

Why wouldn't he trust her with everything about himself? She would be able to handle it. Trust was the only way they could go forward.

If that's what he wanted. Maybe he truly didn't want more than right now.

If so, after they caught the killer—if they did—she'd go on a cruise. Somewhere warm, all by herself, to figure out her life before she went back to work at the college. Then maybe—in the far, far, far future—she'd be able to forget Heath Jones and find somebody else.

Yeah, right. Plus, she wanted to stay in touch with Zara. The former paralegal had an infectious laugh and such a brave way of facing life. They'd formed a good friendship already.

"Anya?" Heath asked. "Did you hear me?"

"No." She turned and smoothed down her dark jeans. His eyebrows were drawn down. "Sorry. I was thinking too hard."

He waited a beat before speaking again. With his faded jeans and dark green T-shirt, he looked powerful and masculine. "You don't have to be here if you're scared. I can put you somewhere safe while we wait for this guy."

"That's not the plan," she said. Plus, wasn't it the girl off being safe who always got kidnapped? Seriously. Had he never watched *Buffy* or *Angel*? "We agreed the guy has to see me in here working and going up to bed." She frowned. "But he'll see you, too. All of his victims were taken when they were alone." Although…wasn't that even more of a challenge?

Heath nodded. "I'm betting something will happen to draw me away. This isn't the type of guy to walk in shooting."

"Wish he were," Denver said.

"Definitely," Anya agreed. "He shoots, we shoot back, and it's over." It definitely wouldn't be that easy.

She wandered over to her temporary desk, sat, and reached for a stack of files. Victim files. She filtered through them, rereading the killer's moves, seeing the damage he'd created.

So much blood, fear, and death. Her mind fuzzed while she tried to focus. Smart. She needed to be smart here. Taking several deep breaths, she opened the file she'd copied from the profilers. "The profilers disagree. One thinks the killer is two men, while the other is sure it's one brilliant psychopath."

Heath was using some handheld device while wandering around the room. Every once in a while, the box would ding in his hand, and he'd nod. "I read those. My guess is it's one guy. Makes more sense."

Anya kept reading. "I still agree. Midthirties, white, highly educated but isolated." Weren't many serial killers in that demographic? She kept reading, not finding anything concrete to use in trying to find the guy. "I went through my notes and files again. I just can't figure out who he is. How I met him."

Heath kept moving around the room. "If you met him. It could be somebody you passed on the street who formed an obsession. Right?" A low thread of tension was in his tone, and his energy rolled through the room, taking over the entire atmosphere.

"Yes. These guys live in their own fantasy world." Anya shifted her body on the chair. Goose bumps rose along her arm. She tried to calm her breathing and fight the sensation that she was about to crawl out of her own skin.

Zara entered the front of the office with Ryker covering her back. She held several copies of the newspaper. "Well, you made the front page of the business section." Dusting snow off her shoulders, she continued to Anya's desk and dropped the business page in front of her. "With a full picture of Anya and Heath in their happy engagement glow along with clear directions to Lost Bastards Investigative Services."

Heath swore quietly but kept moving around the room with his device.

Anya looked down at her friendly expression staring back as the new face of Lost Bastards. Heath had his arm possessively around her shoulder, and they looked happy. Well. That was that, then. "The reporter made a big deal about our engagement. Oh, the killer is going to take this as a slap in the face—and now with a countdown because I'm leaving town and he won't be able to find me."

Zara breathed out, lines fanning from her eyes. "That was the plan, right?"

Anya swallowed over a lump in her throat. "Yeah. That was the plan."

CHAPTER
31

After Zara cooked blackened salmon for dinner, Heath finished checking the sensors one last time. There wasn't anything else to do but wait.

He hated waiting.

Ryker and Zara then headed to bed for a few hours of sleep before things heated up, while Denver jogged around the perimeter to make sure everything was still in place. Cameras, sensors, and escape vehicles. Anya had gone upstairs to continue reading her files.

The picture of them in the paper should've pushed the killer hard—but the timeline of her leaving town...Well, now. That set a deadline.

The itch between Heath's shoulder blades wouldn't ease. As always, instinct ruled. Something or somebody was coming. Either that or he'd keyed himself up so much that he was losing his edge. Considering all he could think about was the woman upstairs preparing herself to be hunted by a killer, that was entirely possible.

Denver shoved the door open and shook his hair. Snow went flying. "FBI and local cops are staking out the business."

"I figured." Heath frowned. "Have we made it too hard for the guy to get inside?"

"No. He likes a challenge." Denver locked the door and moved past the reception area. "My guess is he'll make a move early tomorrow morning. When we're strung tight and tired of waiting."

"We're missing something." Heath moved to the window and stared into the darkness outside. He could sense the cops out there. "I don't know what it is, but I feel it. We're missing something." Maybe he should've put Anya and Zara in the hidden headquarters with Ryker as guard. But the killer would've seen them leaving the building. This was a good plan. It had to be.

"Stop second-guessing. The plan is good," Denver echoed.

Heath looked at the stairs.

"Go calm her down. She was nervous as a cat facing a squirt gun earlier." Denver sat at his computer.

Heath swallowed. "I know. Make sure you pretend to head to bed by midnight just in case the killer is ready to roll."

"Yep."

Heath strode for the stairs and quickly entered the sprawling apartment to listen. Heartbeats in the other room, Ryker's low murmur, Zara's laugh. The electromagnetic buzzing from sensors surrounded him, and he mentally checked their frequency. Perfect.

He flexed and relaxed his hands several times before crossing the living area to Anya's bedroom. His bedroom, too. He knocked and waited for her call to enter.

She sat on the bed, her glorious hair pulled up and her face freshly scrubbed. In her yoga pants and Wonder Woman T-shirt, she looked fresh and innocent. Fragile. The bed spread in every direction, way too big for her, making her seem even smaller. She looked up and shut the file she was reading. Her lips were a white line, and stress had drawn dark circles under her pretty eyes. "The wait is killing me."

Bile rose in his throat at her terminology. If anything happened to her, he wouldn't be able to breathe ever again. "Do you understand the plan?"

"Yep. Zara and I wait in her reinforced room. You guard the door while Ryker and Denver position themselves downstairs. You gave me that Lady Smith & Wesson, and Zara has a Sig. Cool-looking gun, by the way." Even though her tone was light, her eyes were dark. Fear. There was definite fear glowing in those green orbs.

"I won't let anything happen to you, Anya." As a vow, he meant it to his soul.

"I know," she whispered. "Just don't let anything happen to you either. I couldn't stand that." Her eyes glowed a soft green in the dim light. So sweet and pretty.

Ah man. She just reached right in and grabbed his heart. "Okay."

She swallowed. "Listen, Heath. I know we haven't been together long, but I want to say thank you."

He leaned against the door and tucked his thumbs into his pockets to keep from reaching for her. He needed to hold her. Tight. "For what?"

She lifted a small shoulder. "Everything, I guess. For not treating me like some weak woman who could never stand on her own two feet and for letting me be a part of this op."

Heath breathed out slowly. "You're the brains here, baby. The one with the degree and knowledge." He stretched his neck. "But you're human and very fragile." She couldn't argue that one with him. Her very bones were small and easily breakable. Especially for somebody much larger than she was—which the killer certainly had to be.

"I'm strong enough to do this."

Yeah, she was. But it still wasn't right. "You're made for the white picket fence and PTA, sweetheart."

She rolled her eyes and glanced at the silver gun on the nightstand. "I don't think so. In fact, after this, I think I might go into the field. Use my degree for profiling—not just teach about it." Slowly she tilted her head to the side and studied him this time. "We're ready for him, right?"

He gave her assurances he didn't really have. "Definitely. Plus, we have traps in place that we'll remove at midnight. No way can he get in here until we're ready."

She smiled and batted her eyes. "It looks like we have a few more hours together, Heath Jones. What do you suppose we do with those precious minutes?"

Cute. Definitely cute. Her words licked along him and danced around his dick. "We should probably focus." His voice came out painfully hoarse. Or they could get lost for a few minutes and forget the danger stalking them. He fully understood her need to escape reality for a few moments.

"The security is still on, and Denver is downstairs." She smiled, a siren's dare. Tossing the folders onto the table, she stood and moved toward him. "Why don't we focus on each other?"

The blood rushed south of his brain. Way south. She'd never played the temptress with him, and he had to force himself to keep still. "I appreciate the thought, but maybe we should celebrate tomorrow." If they lived.

She reached him and slid both palms up his chest. "I want to *live* tonight."

His mouth watered as she read his mind. "Living is good," he agreed, like a hungry puppy. Then he shook his head. "Honey, I really need to be on edge tonight."

"Oh, you're on edge." She caressed down and cupped him through his jeans.

His knees almost gave out. His muscles started undulating on their own, every instinct in his body clamoring for him to take her to the ground. His cock pulsed against her palm as if trying to get to her. Now.

Okay. Calm. He could be calm and gentle.

Yet the stress around him, the tension inside him, clenched his hands into fists. "Anya? Baby? This probably ain't a good idea."

Her eyes flared, and her hold tightened.

God. He sucked his stomach in. All right. Focus. Reining in control with everything he had, he slowly lifted his hands to her hair. One pinch of the clip, and the colorful waves cascaded down in a fluff of strawberry scent. He inhaled sharply, taking as much of her in as he could.

Gently he cupped the back of her head and leaned in to brush his mouth over hers. She sighed and opened to him, welcoming him.

His body hitched, while his heart rolled. Without a doubt, he'd never again meet a woman like her. He'd never thought to find some-body who belonged next to him, who felt right. Oh, their timing sucked, that was for sure. But he'd take this night. Before everything went to shit again, he'd take this night.

His way. He'd protect her, and he'd keep her whole. No bruises this time.

Yet as she stroked him through his pants, the primitive male at his core bucked, wanting to meet her challenge.

God help them both.

* * *

Anya could feel his body vibrate, his cut muscles hold themselves in check as he tried to be gentle. She didn't want gentle. Not in the slightest.

Kissing him harder, she stroked him beneath his pants, hard and fast.

He grasped her wrist, and she murmured a protest into his mouth. She needed her hands on him. If their plan worked, this might be their last night together.

She wanted all of him, and she'd get it. Gathering courage, pretending she was some sort of femme fatale, she pushed away from him. Well, she did have a gun. That made her somewhat dangerous.

He leaned back against the door, his nostrils flared, his lids heavy over glittering eyes.

She swallowed and took another step back. To maintain control. Not to get out of his reach. Nope. Her chest heaved with her breaths, and her nerves zipped lines through her skin while her knees trembled. Now she knew what a trapped rabbit felt like. The way he looked at her...like he could eat her whole.

She was brave, and she could handle him. Gone was the woman who'd let anybody treat her like less than she was. While Heath was trying to protect her, he still wasn't seeing her strength. It was time to show him she was enough for him. More than enough. Keeping his gaze, she grasped her T-shirt and slowly drew the soft material over her head.

Did he groan? She thought she heard a slight sound.

Gaining courage from that, she slipped her thumbs into her pants and shimmied out of them. Her lace panties went with them, leaving her nude.

Yep. Definitely a groan that time.

She smiled. "So—"

He was on her. Faster than any wolf, he had her up and then on her back on the bed, legs over his shoulders. The first touch of his mouth on her sex wasn't gentle. Not even close.

Oh God.

His broad shoulders kept her thighs apart, and his fingers did magical things along her labia.

She arched into him, her mind fuzzing. Wait a minute. Hadn't she been in control? She lifted her head to protest, and he swirled his tongue around her clitoris. Ecstasy sparked through her, and she fell back down. She could control the situation...in a minute.

He chuckled against her sex.

She cried out, pushing toward him. It was too much and not enough at the same time. Need burst inside her, clawing with hunger. Only for him. "Heath," she moaned.

He settled and went at her with teeth, tongue, and fingers. As her need built, as she writhed against him, she could almost feel him becoming calm and more in control. But she couldn't stop him at the moment. He sucked hard on her thigh, no doubt leaving a mark. *His* mark. The thought sent her spiraling a second before his tongue lashed her clit again, throwing her into an orgasm so wild she could only gasp and hang on.

She came down, her body still on fire for him. She rose up onto her elbows, feeling almost drunk. "Nice start."

He stood, need etched into the lines on his face. Trapping her in place with his gaze, he drew off his shirt.

Man, he was beautiful. The scars only enhanced his wild masculinity.

His jeans hit the floor next, and his penis sprang free. Whoa. She hadn't been imagining his size. He moved toward her, and she swallowed, holding up a hand.

He paused, his head cocking slightly to the left.

She got the feeling, the very strong feeling, that if she ran, he'd chase her down. That alone gave her the courage she wanted desperately. "No holding back, Heath."

His brows drew down as if her words were unclear.

"Did you hear me?" Her voice was way too breathy, but she couldn't control it.

He leaned over and ran his big palms down her legs. "I won't hurt you, Anya."

"I know." She settled her hands over his and squeezed. "But you don't have to hold back. I want all of you tonight."

He studied her, and she fought the urge to fidget. "You want me to fuck you."

The crassness turned her on. She drew in air, more than sensing the edge he rode. Yeah. The atmosphere around them swelled like the quiet before a storm broke. "Yes."

"Say it."

She stilled, instinctively knowing the words would have power—and not only for her. "I want you to fuck me." Her voice was low but strong.

If she thought he'd just pounce, she was wrong.

In fact, he straightened up and walked, all grace, to the nightstand. "Then you're wearing this while I do." He held the pretty green ring.

Vulnerability whispered through her. She held out her hand, and he slipped the ring on, his gaze keeping hers. It felt like more than a piece of jewelry. It was a claim…and a promise. For the moment, she let those become her reality. God, it felt good. Real and strong.

By the flaring of his nostrils, he knew it, too.

She had to regain control somehow. Surprising herself, she flipped her legs around and rolled to the other side of the bed to stand. Anticipation and warmth burst in her chest.

His chin lowered. "What are you doing?"

Was that a tremble in his voice? She smirked, adrenaline flooding her system. "You want me? I think you need to catch me."

He gave a sharp shake of his head. "Enough, Anya. Come back here." No tremble—just raw gravel.

Ah, the warning. Sure, he gave the order as a command, but it was said as a warning. One she had no intention of heeding. "No."

He moved.

She jumped out of the way, scrambling across the bed. He caught her with one arm around her waist and threw her down, face first.

Yelping, partially laughing, she struggled against him.

He grabbed her hips and pulled her onto all fours.

She tossed her head, and her hair fell down her back. A condom wrapper crinkled. She started to move forward, and he yanked her back against him. She had one second to appreciate him at her core, and then he shoved inside her so hard she nearly exploded in raw pleasure.

Pain and pleasure rippled through her in unison, and she arched her back from devastating sensations. He filled her completely.

Then he was over her back, his mouth at her ear, his hand along her neck, forcing her head up. "You wanted this," he whispered, his voice dark and deep.

She shivered in his absolute hold. Her back was to his heated front. "Then give it to me.'"

His hand slid down, his palm flattened over her collarbone with a thumb and a finger on either side of her neck. The strength in that one hand should've given her pause. Yet it was way too late to stop. She clenched her internal muscles.

The sound he gave was more of a growl than a moan. He tightened his hold, pulled out, and shoved back in, using his hand to keep her upright. "Ah, baby. You're feeling so brave."

"Yep." She tried to sound flippant, but her voice was breathy with need. When he moved like that, he touched every nerve that existed inside her. Twice. She wanted to lower her head, but his hand prevented that, leaving her back elongated and her body slightly off balance.

"Hmm." His free hand tweaked a nipple—not gently—and then he tapped down her abdomen.

Her eyes widened. "I—" She dissolved into a gasp as he plucked her clit. Sensations bombarded her—too many all at once. She bucked against him.

And he kept her perfectly in place.

She started to protest, and his hold around her neck tightened just enough for her to realize her position. Even her air depended on him. The thought should scare her, but mini explosions rocked her core.

"I see you're getting it." His warm breath brushed her ear right before he bit down on her lobe.

She gasped again, leaning into him, wanting more. He was everywhere, and she couldn't think. So she just stopped thinking to feel, relaxing into his hold.

"There you go," he rumbled, kissing her ear.

Holding her tight, not letting her move, he started to thrust. Deep and hard, keeping her back arched, he pounded into her. The first orgasm barreled through her, and she shut her eyes, crying out his name.

Yet he didn't stop. If anything, he hammered harder, taking her, taking everything. Sparks uncoiled inside her. Heat flashed through her, driving her high, so close to the edge of a cliff. Need cut sharp. She opened her eyes, not understanding. Minutes passed, maybe hours, and he slid his fingers against her clit again. She gyrated against him, holding her breath, detonating into a million pieces.

With a garbled whimper, she settled down, realizing seconds later that he wasn't done.

"You want me?" he asked. "You're gonna take all of me. We're just getting started."

CHAPTER
32

Heath kept his back to the door and his gun in his hand. The only way into Ryker's reinforced bedroom was through him, and that wasn't gonna happen. Even the window had been outfitted for protection.

He'd faced danger, and he'd defied death. But with Anya counting on him, with her needing him, his concentration held a sharp edge. A new one. He shut his eyes and listened.

Two heartbeats behind him and two downstairs.

Midnight had come and gone. With dawn's approach, he didn't feel danger near. The sense of air changing or the presence of somebody who shouldn't be there was definitely absent.

But the morning was young yet.

He tried to banish thoughts of Anya from his mind and focus, but he couldn't. He'd been way too rough with her, and there was no excuse. Yet she'd sighed his name and had been right with him until they'd gotten dressed and she'd taken position with Zara in the bedroom. She truly was stronger than he'd given her credit for. Damn, he wanted to be back in bed with her, and now.

It had to be about seven in the morning. He drew Anya's phone out of his back pocket, checked the callers, and dialed Special Agent Reese.

"Yeah?" Reese answered, sounding fully alert. "Anya?"

"No. It's Heath. Are you still watching the agency?" Heath asked.

"Affirmative. No movement out here. I don't think he's coming for her." Reese sounded relieved.

"Agreed. He'll see there's no way to get her, so he might get sloppy. Maybe make a mistake. Do you have that covered?"

"Of course," Reese said evenly. "We have agents on the families of law enforcement personnel within a two-hundred-mile radius of Snowville. If the guy is here, and if he has a backup plan for another victim, we'll get him."

That's what Heath had been counting on. "Good. Keep surveillance on us."

"I plan on it, but you need to do the right thing for Anya. Convince her to go into protective custody with us. We're the best."

Not in a million years. They'd let Loretta die, and the image of her lifeless eyes would never completely leave him. "I can keep her safe. Trust me." Heath clicked off, shaking his head. Those were words he'd never planned to say to a cop. But they'd ride out the day and then get out of town and off everybody's radar. Whether Anya liked it or not.

He'd give her this day to participate, and then she was done. Of course, he'd made it so there was really no way for the killer to get to her.

Movement sounded, and the door unlocked. He slid to the side so Anya could tiptoe out. She was still in the jeans and sweater she'd worn when they'd taken positions at midnight, and her hair was back in a spunky ponytail. After shutting the door, she settled against the wall. He studied her. Whisker burn on her cheeks and maybe a slight bruise on her neck. "I'm sorry," he whispered.

She turned toward him. "One should never apologize for amazing sex." Her voice was low and soft with a hint of amusement.

He noted her sparkling green eyes and pleased smile. Any lingering doubt in his mind disappeared. "I really don't understand you."

Her quiet laugh eased the knot in his chest. "I can live with that." She stretched her neck. "It's morning time. Shouldn't we go downstairs and act like it's a normal day? Almost taunt the killer with that, since he knows we're waiting for him? I can act like I'm all packed and ready to go on my vacation and out of his reach."

Heath shoved his gun into his waistband. The woman had gotten into the killer's head, now, hadn't she? Impressive, and yet he still wanted to shield her. "I could use coffee."

She frowned. "I don't see how he can make a move with all of us here."

"Agreed." Which was exactly how Heath wanted it. "My guess is that he can't make a move, so he'll get frustrated and make a mistake."

Her voice lowered. "But what if he takes another victim?"

"The FBI is covering potential victims." Although it would be impossible for them to protect everyone.

Anya slipped her hand into his. "Coffee. Please, coffee."

Her hand felt small and right in his, and he settled himself. So many thoughts and emotions careened through him, he couldn't find one to use. They had to talk, but they'd be a lot more focused after the day passed. Then they'd figure out what was next with them. "Is Zara sleeping?"

The door opened. "Nope," Zara said, tying her hair atop her head. "I heard the word 'coffee.'" She brushed past them, hurrying for the stairs.

Anya's eyes lit. "Let's go."

Heath allowed her to lead him down to the main office, where Denver had already started a pot. "I guess we try to act normal."

Ryker unlocked the front door. "Everyone stay on alert. If he strikes, it'll be when we let our guards down."

There was no way Heath would allow that to happen. He couldn't remember the last time his guard had been truly down.

Denver tossed some premade breakfast sandwiches into the microwave, and several moments later, they all dug in. Within thirty minutes, everyone had settled at their desks to try to get some work done.

Before nine in the morning, Zara had fielded five calls from potential new clients. "We'd actually make some decent money if we ran a detective agency here."

Maybe someday they'd come out of the darkness and into a real day, but not while Cobb and Madison still breathed. Heath continued conducting Internet searches to trace Cobb's movements. The guy had purchased plenty of property through the years.

The front door burst open, and Heath jumped to his feet, reaching for his gun.

"I wouldn't." Special Agent Frederick Reese pointed his weapon at Heath while several other FBI agents, all clearly marked by their jackets, stormed into the room. "Anya Best? I have a court order here allowing the FBI to take you into custody as a material witness."

Anya stood, her mouth dropping open. "Are you on drugs?"

The dick had waited until the courts had opened to get the order. Heath reached for it.

Reese handed the paper over with a smile on his face and his gun hand steady. "Sorry about this, but I promised Loretta I'd keep Anya safe if anything happened to her. We don't have the manpower to keep watching your offices like we did last night. Anya is much safer with us than with you. Let her go."

He'd never fucking let her go. Fire swept through Heath so quickly he almost swayed. He started to move.

"Heath," Denver said from his desk as he stood. "No."

Heath counted agents and weapons. Oh, he could take Reese down and press the gun to his jugular, but if somebody started shooting, Anya or his family might get hurt. "What is she a witness to?" He edged toward her. With all the guns out, adrenaline pumped through him with the need to cover her.

Reese shrugged. "Her sister was taken. She's a witness."

"Bullshit." Heath crumpled the paper, wanting nothing more than to punch Reese in the face. "There's nothing she can personally testify to, and you know it."

Anya cleared her throat. "I agree. I'm not a witness, and I do not want FBI protection."

"Which is why we obtained a court order first thing this morning," Reese said. "Don't make me handcuff you."

Fury boiled through Heath.

Ryker instantly made it to his side. No doubt to keep him from doing something disastrous. "This won't work, Reese."

"It already did." Reese motioned for Anya.

She faltered and looked at Heath.

Heath counted agents again. If he and his brothers moved at the same time…

Ryker put a hand on his arm. "We'll fight this the right way." His voice vibrated with anger and determination.

Heath settled himself into battle mode and calmed down before he did something that got Anya hurt. Anger burned him from within, and even his breath heated. The idea of her out of his sight flowed lava-hot adrenaline through his veins. "If anything happens to her, I'm coming after you, and I'm gonna take my time."

Reese paled just enough to be noticeable. "You just threatened an FBI agent."

"Yeah, I did. And I meant every fucking word," Heath said, his voice deadly soft. The need to grab her and run nearly pushed him into doing something stupid. Ryker clapped a hand on his arm as if knowing exactly what he was thinking.

Anya hurried toward the agent. "It's okay, Heath." Her voice warned him not to do anything at the moment, and panic had filled her pretty eyes. "Reese loved Loretta. I'll be safe."

Reese nodded. "I'm glad you're seeing reason."

"Where are we going?" she asked, looking uneasily at the surrounding agents.

"To my office for a couple of hours and then to a safe house," Reese said, gesturing her toward the door.

She paused and gave Heath a nod. Her eyes clouded, and her lower lip trembled. Then her shoulders went back. "I'll be fine."

Rage and helplessness kept him rooted in place. "I'll come get you," he said, his throat hurting and his voice sounding like his vocal cords had lost a fight with a blade.

Her gaze softened. "I know." Then she walked right out the door, surrounded by FBI agents.

* * *

Anya's mind spun as she was hustled into the back of a black SUV with Reese at her side. She had to get out of there. This was wrong. She needed to be with Heath.

"Go," Reese ordered a blond man in the driver's seat. The guy smoothly pulled away from the curb.

The leather was new, and the side doors were solid. Anya looked out the rear window to see three other black vehicles move into place behind them. "All for little ole me?" she muttered, her lungs compressing.

"I promised your sister," Reese said, holding the mic of his wrist comm unit to his mouth. His gaze was serious and his body tense. "Status?"

He seemed to listen to somebody, and Anya peered at his ear to see a white earbud like Secret Service guys on television shows used.

"What did they say?" she whispered. She looked frantically around.

"No movement following us." Reese peered out the window before reaching into the far back for a bulletproof vest. He tugged it over Anya's head and quickly fastened the straps.

Anya coughed out and allowed him to finish. The vest was heavy around her sweater, and the sense of danger pressed in. The vest was like a vise. "You think he'll try to shoot me?"

"No, but I'm not taking chances." Reese sat back, scanning the buildings flying by outside, his jaw hard. "We'll be at our offices in a minute, and there's a procedure for taking a witness from the car inside. I have the back parking lot secure, but we'll still jump out and get into the building immediately. Once inside, you'll wait in my office until we take you to a safe house. It's being readied and secured."

The world tilted. Anya shook her head and tried to focus. "I don't have a say in any of this?"

"Nope. That's why I acquired a court order. Unless it gets stayed or overturned, you're mine for the time being." He kept his focus out the front window, his voice full of authority. "Take Pine Street, Kent."

Kent didn't speak as he made a sharp right turn.

Anya shivered, remembering the look in Heath's eyes. He wouldn't give up on finding her, and things might get bloody. This was a disaster. The day narrowed, and she tried to concentrate. Damn adrenaline. "I'm not a witness, and you know it."

"Don't care."

"Figures my sister would fall for somebody like you," Anya muttered, anger taking her. The FBI had no right to do this. "I loved her, but she was pushy, too."

Reese stiffened. "I'm doing this for her."

"She's not here, and I can make my own decisions. I was safe with Heath and his brothers." She missed him already. They hadn't had time to say good-bye. She glanced down at the sparkly ring still on her finger. It felt right. Maybe she could draw some sort of comfort from it. "Heath will find me."

Reese snorted. "I don't care how good of a detective he is. There's no way he'll find you if we don't want him to."

She shivered, caught by the ominous tone. Nothing in her could imagine never seeing Heath again. "How long is the order for?" she asked.

"It's open-ended, since you're in so much danger. Until we catch this guy, we have the right to treat you as a material witness." Reese checked the clip on his gun and then talked into his comms mic again. "One minute out. Have the rear door open."

Why hadn't she brought her gun? She'd left it on the nightstand. "There has to be some way I can fight you legally on this."

"There isn't. With a court order, I have all the power." Reese placed a hand on her arm, his gaze direct and his voice low with authority. He looked like a capable lawman. Just like her father had. "We're almost to the office. Are you ready?"

She swallowed over a lump in her throat. Her breath came shallowly, and she tried to calm herself. "No."

CHAPTER
33

Two hours exactly after Anya had walked out of an area he could control, Heath pounded his fist on the metal door of the FBI offices.

"They're in lockdown, hence the barricaded metal door." Detective Malloy chewed on peanuts next to him. "Calm down or they won't let us in."

"Can I help you?" came a tinny voice from a speaker set above the door.

Malloy grabbed Heath's arm before he could answer while also looking up into a camera above the door. "Detective Malloy from the Snowville PD. I'm here to see Special Agent Reese, and it's urgent."

Heath barely kept himself from smashing a shoulder into the door.

"Credentials?" the voice asked.

Malloy sighed and reached for his wallet, which he flipped open and held up. "You should know my face by now, Shanella."

"We have procedure, handsome." The voice had warmed. "Who's your friend?"

Malloy tucked his wallet away. "This here is Heath Jones from the Lost Bastards detective agency in town. He's got news on the Copper Killer case."

There was a pause, and then a buzz went through the door.

"Let me handle this," Malloy muttered to Heath, pushing open the door.

Heath kept silent and flexed his hands into fists.

He followed Malloy into a reception area that led to another door. Shanella buzzed them into a long hallway.

Reese strode through the matching door at the other end, his face pissed, a gun visible in his shoulder harness. "You have news?" The heavy door clicked shut behind him.

"Yeah," Malloy said, reaching into his coat pocket for a folded piece of paper. "Consider yourself served with a writ of habeas corpus for Anya Best. She's free until a hearing next week."

"Next week? That's too late." Reese snatched the writ and quickly scanned it. A vein bulged in his head. "How did you get this so quickly?"

"I'm good at my job," Heath said, flashing his teeth. "Sometimes I'm a lawyer." The second Anya had left, Heath had gotten Denver working on reciprocity while he called Malloy for help and the name of a good judge. "Next week, during the hearing, the judge would like to hear from you how Anya is a witness. How do you feel about perjury charges, asshole?"

Reese's lips peeled back. "You do know that taking her from here makes her vulnerable."

Heath leaned in. "You fuckin' cops. Think you can use the law any way you want and then also enforce it?" Past hurts and fury bubbled up, and he had to struggle to force them down. "Taking her from *me* put her in danger. Use your fuckin' head." If he didn't see her soon, he was going to lose his damn mind.

"You let her set herself up as bait," Reese exploded, his cheeks turning a dark red.

Heath got into his face, enjoying his two extra inches of height. Rage caught in his lungs and squeezed. "There was no way he could get to her, and you know it. I kept her safe and made it so he'd make a mistake and you could catch him, dickhead. She was secure until you moved her."

Reese shook his head. "We're the FBI, dumb-ass. We can keep her safe."

"Like you kept her sister safe?" Heath snapped.

Reese grabbed Heath's shirt and shoved him against the wall. Heath reacted, breaking the hold and punching Reese full-on in the face. The agent stumbled back and then threw a punch of his own, nailing Heath in the jaw.

Stars exploded behind Heath's eyes, and he struck out, smashing his fist into Reese's gut. Releasing the anger felt good.

The agent doubled over with a strangled *oof*.

Almost casually, Malloy stepped between the two men. "You guys might wanna knock it off. There are cameras, and I'm sure—"

The door at the end of the hallway burst open, and two male agents ran in, both with their guns out.

Reese held up a hand to stop them. "We're fine," he panted out, straightening.

The agents looked from him to Heath.

What the hell was he doing? Heath tucked his aching hands into his jeans pockets. His knuckles really needed a break. "Just had a difference of opinion on defense techniques," he said smoothly.

Reese rolled his eyes. "Yeah. We're fine, men. Stand down."

The two agents holstered their guns but didn't retreat.

Malloy munched contentedly on more peanuts out of his pocket. "If you'd just get Miss Best for us, we'll be on our way."

Heath breathed in sharply. He had to see her for himself right now. Needed to make sure she was okay.

Reese snarled. "You're going to get her killed. Stay here." He turned on his heel and stomped down the hallway to the closed door, shutting it with a bang. The sound echoed throughout the hallway, and then silence descended.

Heath could barely breathe. Trying to concentrate, he pulled his phone from his back pocket and dialed Denver.

"Did you get her?" Denver asked without preamble.

"I think so. Reese went to get her. At least, he better be on the way." There was something off with the FBI agent. Maybe it was just losing Loretta, or maybe not. "We need a deeper background on him. I want to know everything he's ever thought."

"I already ran him. He's clean." Even so, the sound of Denver typing came over the line. "Of course, the killer is good. Really good. I'm on it." He clicked off.

Malloy lifted both eyebrows. "You're a suspicious son of a bitch."

Heath stared grimly at the closed door at the end of the hallway. "You have no idea."

Malloy's phone rang a funky tune, and he took it out. "Malloy." He listened, his gaze narrowing on Heath. His face went cop hard in an instant. "Interesting. All right. Tell him I'll call him back in a few moments."

Everything in Heath stilled. He swallowed, edging to the left to free his right hand in case he needed to strike out. "What?"

Malloy leaned back against the wall, somehow still on full alert. "Have you ever heard of a Sheriff Cobb?"

Run. Fucking run. The order rushed through Heath's head. Had Cobb found their location already? Heath only needed a few hours to evade them. Where was Anya, damn it? Heath swallowed rapidly, forcing his face into merely interested lines. "Sounds vaguely familiar. Why?" His words had come out harsher than he'd wanted.

"Guy called the office and wants to talk to me about you. As soon as possible, actually," Malloy said.

"Huh." The world narrowed and dimmed. Heath shook his head. "Why?"

"Dunno. But I'm going to find out."

The door at the end of the hallway opened.

* * *

Anya tried a deep-breathing technique a friend at school had taught her to keep from having another panic attack. She shook her head and kept breathing, following Agent Reese through the bullpen to where he said Heath waited. Without the bulletproof vest, she felt twenty pounds lighter.

"I'd like for you to reconsider staying here with the FBI," Reese said once again, his broad body blocking her view of the hallway.

She gulped. "I know you want to protect me, but I'm going with Heath."

"You're making a mistake that will get you killed." He opened the door and started moving again. Anya trooped behind him, almost holding her breath now as they walked into a long hallway.

The second she saw Heath, she launched into a run. Instinct ruled her, and she had to get to him.

She barreled right into Heath's waiting arms. Tears stung her eyes. "I'm sorry. I didn't know, so I left, and—"

He kissed her.

Her entire body centered. She kissed him back, letting him take her weight. Sensations bombarded her, from need to want to a sense of safety. Away from him, she'd been so alone and vulnerable. Lost. Now, finally, the world righted itself. She could do this.

He released her. "Take a breath."

"That's what I've been doing." She stepped back and wiped her face. "Sorry. Emotional overload." Heat flooded her face. She didn't know where to put her hands.

"It's okay, baby." His touch was gentle as he smoothed back her hair. Determination glinted in his brilliant eyes. He still wore the faded jeans, boots, and T-shirt from earlier. He stood so tall and strong, all she wanted to do was burrow into him for protection. "I'll get you to safety."

Fury and something else glimmered in his eyes? Panic?

"No," Reese said from behind her. "Be smart. She needs to stay here."

Heath met the agent's gaze squarely, even as he moved Anya between himself and Detective Malloy.

Anya forced a smile for the detective. "Hi."

"Hi," Malloy said, his gaze watching the two other men with interest. "I guess we're lucky neither one of them has tried to pee on you yet."

Humor shot through her, and she burst out with a laugh. Yep. Emotional overload. "Reese, I'm sorry. But I'm leaving."

He opened his mouth to argue and then shut it abruptly. "Your sister was stubborn, too." His phone buzzed, and he lifted it to his ear. "Reese." His shoulders stiffened. "What? Say that again."

Anya stilled.

"Goddamn motherfucker." Fury flew across Reese's face, and another vein bulged along his neck. He turned and threw the phone against the far wall. "Fuck." He kicked out and turned to punch the wall. Sheetrock flew. Reese turned, a wild glimmer in his eyes.

Agents poured from the far doorway, already armed and suited up. Heath shoved Anya all the way behind him. "What the hell?"

Reese took a shuddering breath and flexed his bloody hand. "Killer took another victim."

Anya pressed a hand to her shuddering chest. "Oh God. Who did he take?"

Reese shook the white powder off his hand. "Ex-wife of a local cop. She's more a brunette than a redhead, but I guess she could count."

"She wasn't under surveillance?" Heath asked.

"Yeah, she was," Reese said. "The killer somehow got into her house and got her out, even with a car on her door. He's good." Reese turned for the door. "We've been dicking around with this, and he took somebody else."

Anya's legs wobbled.

Reese turned toward Heath. "Stay in town, and keep her in town and safe. I'll deal with you next." He glanced at Anya. "The second you realize you need protection, you call me."

Then he sprinted toward the door with his agents on his heels. "Let's find this guy."

Heath grabbed his phone and quickly texted his brothers. Anya leaned around to read what he sent.

Phoenix. Cobb called cops. Vacate. Now.

CHAPTER
34

Heath drove quickly and kept an eye on the world outside as the winter storm increased in strength. Wind threw ice and sleet at the borrowed Jeep, and the whole day had turned a stormy gray. Malloy had taken his own car—probably back to his station to investigate Heath. Cobb had called Malloy. Was he fishing, or had he found them?

Anya sighed next to him. "Thank you for coming to get me."

"Always." His heart had all but leaped out of his chest. Even now, he just wanted to gather her close and hold her for good. "We need to talk as soon as we get to safety."

"I know." She settled back down. "I'm done with secrets. It's you and me, and I'm finished acting like it isn't. You're going to give me all of it."

"Yeah." He'd never cared for a woman like he did for her. Was that love? Hell, he didn't know. He always figured he loved his brothers, but this was different. More primitive. It ate at him. The truck skidded on the ice, and he corrected, leveling out.

What was he going to say to her? He didn't want to hurt her, but he wasn't sure about taking her on the run for the next several years. The thought of leaving her made him want to punch through the window. For now, she was still in the serial killer's mind. She wouldn't be safe from him until he was taken down.

Heath's phone dinged, and he pressed the speaker, needing both hands on the wheel. "Denver? What do you know?"

"Got your message—we're mobilizing. Do you have Anya?" Denver asked.

"Anya is with me now, and we're heading for the safe apartments to pack. We're getting out of here," Heath said. Damn, it was getting hard to see through the storm.

"I'll meet you there," Denver said. "Ryker and Zara are finishing closing the decoy offices, and I'll help you close down the main apartments in a few minutes. Should take about thirty minutes, and then we all head separately for safe house Alpha."

Anya lifted an eyebrow but didn't speak.

Heath nodded. "Copy that. Don't only worry about Cobb. You guys stay alert in case the killer makes a move now."

"He's got his victim, Heath. He'll stick to his pattern," Denver said.

Yeah, the guy did like to sneak in and out without a trace. It was too much to hope that he'd try to take Anya right in front of them. Heath gripped the wheel tighter. "I know. Speaking of which...what have you learned?"

"Victim's name is Jolene Landers. Twenty-six, brunette with possible red highlights, and ex-wife of a cop in town. She lives in a bungalow on the west side, and the killer got in through a backyard entrance and took her around dawn." Denver typed some more. "The FBI and local police are coordinating to find her."

"Agent Reese said a patrol car was on her street," Heath said, maneuvering carefully around a corner. The truck fishtailed, and he quickly regained control.

"Yeah. They didn't see or hear anything," Denver said.

Heath slammed his fist on the steering wheel. His temples pounded, and his stomach rolled over. "We have less than a week to find her." As soon as they got to a secure location and Anya was safe, he'd start working the case. But Cobb was definitely breathing closer, if he wasn't already in town. Anya was safe for now, but there was still a chance to find the victim before she was killed.

Denver said, "I'm still running a deeper check on Reese, but so far nothing has popped."

Anya shook her head, sending her pretty red hair flying.

Heath ignored the clear message. "Keep digging. There's something I don't like about him."

"You don't like that he took Anya from you," Denver returned evenly. "But I'll dissect his entire life. See you in about ten minutes."

"Drive carefully. This storm is strong," Heath said, ending the call.

Anya held her hands closer to the heater vents. "You can't suspect Reese."

"I can." Heath turned the final corner and pressed a button to allow entry to the parking area of the apartments. "Okay. We're in and out in thirty minutes."

She grabbed his arm. "We can't leave town, Heath. Agent Reese pretty much ordered us to stay here."

"We're leaving." Heath didn't have time to explain. "It's time to go, sweetheart."

"Why?" She crossed her arms as they drove into the quiet garage.

Heath pressed the button again, and the garage door closed, leaving the world silent. The windshield wipers finished removing the rest of the ice and snow. "Just because he didn't try for you this time doesn't mean you're safe." Heath couldn't guarantee her safety over the long haul, unlike during the last day. So she had to get to safety, whether she liked it or not. "We go."

"I'm bait, damn it."

Oh shit. She really didn't get it. "You weren't really bait, darlin'." Did she truly believe he'd let her just wait around for a serial killer to take her?

"What?" her voice trembled. "Sure I was."

"No. You were covered at all times, Anya. We let you be seen just so he'd get frustrated and maybe make a mistake. But the FBI dropped the ball." He didn't want her to think he'd ever let her put herself in danger like that. "I'm sorry, but I'd never let you take such a risk."

She drew back. "It isn't your decision."

"I believe it is," he said evenly.

Her chin went up. "Oh yeah? Then it's time you leveled with me. Why else are we getting out of town so quickly?" Her lower lip pouted.

He frowned. She liked to push, and her tone was almost a dare. But it was time to give her the truth. She deserved it. "Ryker, Denver, and I were raised in a boys home where the owner liked to beat the shit out of us. You saw the scars."

Her eyes glowed in sympathy. "Yeah. That's terrible."

"Well, the owner's brother was the sheriff, Sheriff Cobb, and he liked to get in on the action, too. Had a nightstick he really loved." Heath kept his voice level, but his ribs ached in memory of that damn stick.

"Oh, Heath." She released her seat belt and scooted toward him. "I'm so sorry."

"We lived," he said grimly. "Then one day the owner killed a kid right in front of Denver. Tried to make me and Ryker say that Denver had done it, we said no, and he rushed us. Both of us swung bats we had, and his head exploded like a melon." Nausea wound down to his gut. No matter how long he lived, he would never forget that sound. Sometimes he heard it in his nightmares.

"Oh." She leaned into him and flattened her hand over his chest. "I'm so sorry. But I'm glad you survived."

"Yeah." He breathed out, allowing her touch to seep inside him and warm where he'd always thought he'd be cold. "Me too. Well, we set the place on fire and got out. The sheriff has been chasing us ever since."

She patted right above his heart as if she couldn't hold still. "You said the law isn't after you."

"No." He swallowed. "He wants revenge, not justice. And there's more."

She blinked. "Really. Wow. Okay."

Somehow he knew, right then and there, that she'd accept all of him. So he gave himself to her. "You've noticed my reflexes and super-hearing?"

She nodded. "Yeah. Ryker and Denver seem to have those skills, too."

It figured she would've already noticed their oddities. "Yep. The three of us ending up in the home together wasn't a coincidence. We were created in test tubes, separated at birth, and then put back together in the boys home to be studied. We're not genetic brothers, but we actually do have some in Montana. We are brothers, though. All of this was engineered by a doctor named Isobel Madison, who has also been hunting us since we got free. She and Cobb are together now, like they were then, and they're never gonna stop coming for us." There. He'd told her everything. His chest felt lighter.

Anya was silent for a moment, her eyes wide. "That's a lot to escape, Heath. I'm so glad you did." Her mouth opened and closed. Her eyes blinked several times. "That's just so…much."

"I know." He put his hand over hers. There wasn't time to ease her into the truth or let her absorb it. They had to go, and now. "They're rebuilding their labs, and they have extremely well trained soldiers working for them. We're in danger and will be so long as Madison and Cobb are alive." Would she still care for him if he decided to kill in cold blood? He wasn't sure he'd like himself any longer, but he was struggling to find another way out of this life. There wasn't one. Cobb had to die.

"Why are you telling me all of this finally?" she whispered, her hand so perfect right where it was.

"I love you." He dug deep for the right words. "I mean, I love you. This is new, and it's everything, and all I want is to hold you tight. Keep you close, protect you. See you grow and get old. I mean…all of it. I've never felt that kind of love. I mean—"

The outside door opened, and Ryker's truck roared into the garage with Denver behind the wheel.

Heath coughed. "How about we have the talk once we're back on the road? We really do have to get out of here." Then maybe he could find the right words. She deserved the right words, and he'd give them to her.

She squeezed his hands. Tears filled her eyes, and she looked away. "All right. We could both use a reprieve from emotion for a moment, I think." Then she paused, not looking at him. "I love you, too."

God. The words hit him harder than a blast of C-4. He swallowed several times over the rock in his throat. "I—"

"Yeah," she whispered. "We have to go. Let's talk later."

Definitely. The world was closing in on them. His chest heated. He moved from the truck and helped her out. "We need to hurry. Just grab what's essential, and we'll get on the road." His nape tickled, and he wanted nothing more than to toss her into the Jeep and speed away from danger.

He nodded to Denver, who had just jumped out of the truck.

"Boxes upstairs," Denver said, tucking a gun into the back of his waistband. "Security is still in place here."

"Okay." Heath ran through the schematics in his mind as he jogged up the stairs with Anya following. Seven cameras and eight booby traps needed to be fetched. Even though Denver had checked the security, Heath scouted the entire apartment before letting Anya retrieve their personal items from their bedroom and bathroom.

"I'll get the cameras in here," Denver called from Heath's kitchen. "You get the security items and personal stuff. We have to get out of here before the storm gets worse or the FBI discovers we have two buildings here in town. We're on their radar now."

"We're on Cobb's radar." Heath hurried to the camera hidden inside a sconce in the corner, grabbing a backpack out of the coat closet on his way. Quick movements had the device removed and tucked into the pack. "Number three camera secure," he called out to Denver.

A wisp of sound caught his attention, and he paused. A slight buzz turned his focus. Was that one of their devices? The frequency was off—way too slow.

Anya moved out of the bedroom with a laptop bag in her hands. "I think I got it all."

Realization slapped him. "Back!" he yelled, going for her.

An explosion rocked the floor right where he'd been, throwing him sideways toward the granite island. Pain ripped through his side. Fire bit at his arm, and he fell hard, his ears ringing.

Canisters seemed to drop from every direction, gas spewing.

A figure crashed down through the wooden beams, barely discernible through the gas.

"Anya!" Heath croaked, shoving himself to his feet and holding his breath. His right arm hung uselessly at his side, and his shoulder felt like it had been wrenched off. None of that mattered. Where was she? The smoke completely blocked his vision.

An explosion rocked near the fridge, and Denver roared in pain.

Oh God. Heath turned back but could only see smoke. A tremor rippled through his rib cage. His heart clutched.

"Heath!" Anya screamed.

Damn it. He pivoted and ran toward her voice, his heart thundering, his lungs exploding. Tears filled his eyes from the gas. A man in head-to-toe black pulled a struggling Anya out of the bedroom. The guy had on a gas mask and moved with graceful purpose.

Heath fought the need to breathe and rushed the assailant.

The guy lifted an arm and pressed some sort of device.

The floor blew, and Heath crashed across the room and back into the kitchen, where Denver was sitting up. Agony bore into Heath's head, and fire burned his chest. Denver frantically patted out fire along Heath's shirt, his own jeans a smoldering mess.

"Anya," Heath croaked out.

Denver nodded, blood pouring down his face. He jerked Heath up, and they both tried to make it through the smoke. Pain made Heath's body try to shut down, but he used every genetic advantage he'd been given to fight it and carry on. He had to get to her. She was all that mattered.

The guy had Anya over a shoulder, and she was out cold.

Heath's legs weakened, but he pushed on. Denver fell next to him, his head thunking on the destroyed floor.

The gas surrounded Heath and finally got inside. He gasped for air, and his lungs detonated. The last thing he saw before dropping into unconsciousness was Anya's beautiful red hair hanging down the back of the Copper Killer.

CHAPTER
35

Anya opened her eyes, her body a dead weight, mist still hovering around her head. She lay on something soft, but she couldn't see what it was. Sounds came to her. Sleet against a windshield. The hum of a heater. Windshield wipers. She tried to lift her head and drifted back into the darkness.

Something drew her awake again, and she tried to focus. Movement. She was moving in some sort of vehicle. A song on the radio crooned around her. Her brain was fuzzy, and she couldn't make out the words.

She couldn't feel anything. The darkness surrounded her again, and she fell into it.

Another song. More movement. She blinked to see broad hands on a steering wheel. Somebody whistled with the radio. She fought to stay awake, but she fell again.

She jerked awake. How much time had passed?

The air chilled her, and her eyelids struggled to open against some type of cloth. Fear slammed through her, and she bit her lip to keep from screaming. She sat on what felt like a sofa with her hands tied behind her back and a blindfold covering her eyes. A fire crackled and provided heat in front of her.

Memories of the attack flashed through her mind in rapid succession. God. Was Heath all right? He'd been blown across the room.

What about Denver? Tears pricked her eyes, and she willed them back. She had to think. It had to be the Copper Killer. Or maybe it was Cobb and that crazy doctor who'd created Heath. But why would they take her? No, it had to be the killer.

Her nerves turned raw. Where was he? Terror filled her. She opened her mouth and screamed.

A large male hand clamped over her mouth hard enough so she couldn't bite. Her jaw protested, and pain slashed into her temples. When she stopped trying to scream, her heart ramming her rib cage, he removed his hand. "Scream again, and I'll cut out your tongue."

She whimpered.

"I like that sound." He spoke near her ear, his voice low.

She tried to focus past the blood rushing through her head. Did she recognize his voice? Maybe a little? "Wh-what do you want?" she asked.

He chuckled. "I think you know."

She swallowed. "Why am I blindfolded?" That hadn't been in any of the reports.

"I find it enhances the experience," he said, moving away from her.

Chilled air swept around her. Terror caught her in such a strong grip her limbs felt frozen. Her entire body shuddered.

Pots and pans clanked over in what sounded like a kitchen. She quickly took inventory, noting she was still wearing her jeans and sweater, although he'd taken her socks and shoes. She curled her toes into a roped rug. When did he put the women in the burlap? Static buzzed through her brain. Concentrate. She had to get him talking. "What kind of gas knocked me out?" she asked.

"A special concoction," he said. Another pot clanked. "I hope you like steak."

Should she say yes or no? Criminal psychology textbooks didn't

account for pure terror. "If I don't, would you let me go? Find somebody who does appreciate a good steak?" she asked, her voice trembling.

"No." His voice was at her ear again.

She yelped and tried to jump away from him.

He squeezed her shoulder. "I like that you talked to me through
the news people. It's as if you also knew we belonged together."

She shivered. "How do you move without making a sound?"

"Maybe you're not listening well enough." He released her.

She tilted her head but couldn't hear anything. A second later,
more noise came from the kitchen area. "My name is Anya." Didn't
she read somewhere that personalizing oneself to a killer might forge
some sort of connection?

"I know." The sound of chopping emerged next.

"I know you know. We've met." A scream rose up inside her, and
she ruthlessly shoved it down. He had a knife. But he was just making dinner. "Right?"

"You know we have." He chuckled.

God. Who the hell was he? "Are we having salad?" she asked, trying to balance the conversation with politeness.

"Of course," he replied. "Anya is such a pretty name. As is Loretta."

Pain filled Anya's chest. "Why did you kill her?" she asked, her
voice breaking. More fear swept ice through her. This man had killed
her sister. Her trained, tough, kind, FBI agent sister.

"Because she wasn't the one," he said, his voice catching.

God, when had she met him? Shouldn't she recognize his voice?
"Why me?"

"You know why. We're soul mates and have been since that first
touch." His voice was gravelly.

First touch? This guy had touched her? She tried to remember
anyone she'd dated who sounded even remotely like him. Everyone

had been cleared, but maybe the FBI had made a mistake. "You sound odd," she said.

He laughed again. "Some of the gas got into my mask. I'll be back to myself in no time, don't you worry. Have I told you how lovely you look here in our mountain hideaway?"

"Um, thank you." There had to be a way for her to get free. "I think this would be more fun if I could see you, too."

He kept chopping, each slice of the knife a reminder of what he'd do to her later. "You will in good time. For now, let's chat while dinner cooks."

How could she convince him to let her live? Nausea boiled up inside her, burning her throat. "I don't want to die," she whispered, her eyes filling beneath the blindfold. A tear slipped out and ran down her cheek, cooling it.

"None of us wants to die," he said conversationally. "We're meant to be together. We'll live forever."

Crazy. The man was freaking crazy. "Why did you kill those other women?" she asked, her voice trembling. God, she needed to get her hands on that knife.

"They reminded me of you," he said, stopping his chopping. "I thought I could be happy with them for a while, maybe. I don't know. Each time I wanted them, but then they weren't really you, and I was so sad. So very sad. I took their pictures to show you that you were special. Better than any of them."

She bit back a sob. He'd always be sad because he was freaking insane and would never find what he was looking for. No way would she live up to his fantasy of her. She had to think, but images from the previous victims kept flashing through her brain. Okay. She had to set herself apart. "You wanted me from the beginning."

Silence for a moment, and then, "Of course. It has always been you." He was right at her ear again.

This time she didn't jump. If she confessed she couldn't remember him, it might set him off. He might say he wanted a soul mate, but he was playing with her like a bully torturing ants with a magnifying glass. This is what he got off on. She had to actually engage him. "I called you out, remember? I was tired of you playing this game."

He settled a hand on her shoulder. "Games are so much fun, though. Did you like the pictures I sent to you?"

"No," she said, knowing to go with honesty. "They scared me." *Don't flinch. Don't flinch. Don't flinch.* Her mind tried to take her away, and she forced herself to stay in the moment. It was her only chance to get free. She was strong enough to do this. "I knew you'd find me," she said, keeping her voice calm when all she wanted was to scream her head off and struggle against the bindings at her wrists. She hadn't thought he'd get to her—she really hadn't. "I didn't expect the full-on assault, however."

He laughed, the sound throaty. Then he released her, and soon the chopping commenced again. "Those private detectives are pretty good, actually. Your fiancé just didn't expect anybody to find your real headquarters. The decoy was very convincing, I'll admit."

Anya breathed out. He was again a short distance away. She tried to blink beneath the blindfold to dislodge it. Nothing. "What about the other woman you took earlier today?" What was her name? "Jolene? Jolene Landers?"

"Ah, sweet Jolene. Now, she was a screamer," he said amicably. "Didn't even have pretty hair like you do. She was a red herring, Anya. I just took her to throw off the wolves, you know." The knife scraped across wood, probably a cutting board of some sort. Did he kill his victims with the same knife he used to cook dinner?

"Where is Jolene now?" Anya asked, unable to keep her voice from trembling this time.

"Not sure. Do you believe in heaven? Or hell?" he asked.

Terror exploded in her chest. She took several deep breaths to calm herself. God, she had to hold it together. "Yes. Do you?"

"Not really. I figure we're already there. This is hell for some, heaven for others. Sometimes it switches."

Her mouth went dry. "Where are you?"

"At the moment, now that I've found you? I'd say heaven. How about you?"

She ran through what she knew of him. He was brilliant and no doubt read people very well. Lying to him would be a mistake, and yet she didn't want to provoke him. "I'm not sure yet. Being blindfolded doesn't help me to decide."

"That's a fair point."

She wanted to know more about Jolene, but he seemed disinterested. "My favorite color is green." She had to personalize herself.

"I know that." A pot clanged. "You wear green a lot, and have for years."

Years? God. Who was he? "What was I wearing the first time you saw me?" she asked, her voice trembling.

"You don't remember?" His voice lowered.

"My clothes? No. I don't keep track of clothing," she burst out.

More chopping. Each slice cut through her, and she had to force herself not to jump each time.

"You were wearing a small blue skirt, white T-shirt, and girly flats," he said.

Small skirt? She blinked. Nothing came to mind. "What's your favorite color?" she asked, trying to listen for any other sounds. Nothing but the wind and an occasional rattle of ice against the windows.

"Red. The color of your stunning hair."

Nausea rolled through her stomach. "Favorite television show? Video game? Movie?"

Something slammed down on a counter. "If you would've been true to me, you'd know the answers to those questions."

True to him? "Sorry," she said, tears filling her eyes again. "I just wanted to talk about something, and being blindfolded is confusing."

"Why are you making me doubt you?" he yelled.

She cringed. Her mind spun so quickly she could barely catch a thought. "I told you to come get me, remember?" That had to make some sort of difference.

He remained silent for a few moments. "That's true. You did." Now he sounded thoughtful.

"We haven't really talked in a while. You know that." She pressed her advantage. "I like *The Big Bang Theory* on television. Sheldon is hilarious." She cleared her throat, her stomach cramping so badly she wanted to bend at the waist. "I don't have a favorite video game, but I love the X-Men movies."

"Those are fun to watch," he admitted.

Was there any chance the FBI had a clue where she was? If Heath had survived, he and his brothers would be looking for her. She just knew it. Her only goal, her only chance, was to stay alive until either they found her or she could make a break for it. Loretta was a trained agent, and she hadn't escaped. Anya had to use her one advantage. "I thought you'd come for me earlier than you did."

"I wanted to play the game for a while. It's fun to build the anticipation." His voice was almost familiar as it lost the hoarseness. How much gas had he taken in? Apparently not enough to make much of a difference.

She cleared her throat again. The guy wanted to impress her. She could use that. "How did you find the safe-house apartments tonight?"

"I piggybacked the GPS tracker on your phone initially," he said conversationally. "I saw Carl Sparks with you at the funeral in

DC, and I quickly learned everything about him. It was easy from there."

Who was at the funeral? She went through everyone she could remember. "Did you, ah, kill Carl?"

"Of course."

Adrenaline flooded her system, making sitting still difficult. "Why?" she croaked.

"I had reasons. For one, he was in the way. Two, it'll come in handy."

What did that mean? Poor Carl. Sure, he made a lot of mistakes. But he didn't deserve to die like that. "Did I know you were at the funeral?" She brushed aside thoughts about Carl and her sister's funeral and tried to focus.

"I think you've always known where I am. You feel me, right? Always with you?" he asked.

She faltered. Though lying would be a mistake, the truth might get her stabbed. "I don't think I'm as intuitive as you are." Probably true. "I like to study and learn, which is why I went into psychology. But that's statistics and knowledge...not instinct."

"What do your instincts say?" He was back at her ear, his voice a low drone now.

That there was no way to keep up with his fantasy. She coughed out, "I'm foggy from the gas. Kind of confused."

"I'm sorry." His sigh was regretful. "Also, I guess I should say I'm sorry I killed your sister. That was wrong of me."

The words sliced right into her. Her body jerked as if she'd been hit. Her stomach cramped hard. "Loretta was a good person. I loved her."

"Until I started our game, you only talked to her periodically—maybe once a month," he said, his breath brushing her face. "Only saw each other once a year."

Anya jolted. "That's true." How long had he been watching her?

"So I brought you back together—got you close again. You owe me," he said.

She tried not to edge away from him. "Yet you killed her."

"I said I was sorry," he bellowed right into her ear.

Pain filled her head, and she cringed away from him. A sob escaped her.

"My poor girl." He brushed hair away from her face. "You need to learn not to make me angry."

Right. She tried to see past the blindfold, but there was nothing. "You've obviously been keeping track of me for years. Why start up the game this year? Why start taking redheads and playing the game now?" It was a risky question, but she had to know.

"Would you like a Shiraz or a Cabernet?" he asked.

She didn't press or ask how he knew she liked both vintages. "Shiraz." She held perfectly still. "I do have another question." Maybe he'd answer this one.

"You can ask me anything."

She swallowed over a lump in her throat. "The explosions back at the apartment. You could've killed Heath and Denver, and you didn't. I'm sure you have guns."

"That would've been no fun. If this works out, they need to see my happiness."

If it didn't work out, he needed them to be tortured by her death. Her nerves jumbled inside her with the urge again to scream. "I see. Thank you for the honesty."

"No problem." He shifted against her, and suddenly she was in his arms being carried. His very strong and fit arms. Who was this guy?

She gave a small yelp. "Where are we going?" Kicking wouldn't do any good.

"To dinner." He set her down on a hard chair and fastened what felt and sounded like handcuffs around her ankles. Seconds later, he sliced through the bindings around her wrists.

She stilled. "Are those handcuffs?"

"Yep."

Okay. Cops had handcuffs. So did FBI agents. Was his voice becoming more familiar? Oh God. It couldn't be. "Reese?" she asked.

The blindfold was whipped off.

She faced an empty chair over a table set with fine linens and crystal. A wooden counter ran along the wall of the kitchen, holding a sink and two plates. He moved then into her view, and she could see his broad back. He transferred the plates to the table and sat across from her. It took her a moment for her vision to focus on his face.

He smiled.

She blinked. "I know you." He looked different without the colored contacts and weird putty along his chin. Her mind scrambled. He was the fake marshal who'd tried to kidnap her from her apartment before Heath had rescued her. "Marshal D. J. Smithers."

He laughed again, his brown eyes twinkling. "Just a cover."

"Oh?" Her hands were free, but no weapons were within reach. "Not your name?"

"No. You've met me before, however. My name is Daniel."

CHAPTER 36

Heath came to as he was being loaded onto a gurney. Pain filled his entire body, so he dug deep and tried to expel it. When that didn't work, he just ignored it. "Anya?" he croaked as he was lifted. Sounds bombarded him—surrounded him—the sound of too many people breathing and moving around.

"Hold on, sir," said a younger male voice. "You have pieces of wood embedded in your body, but you'll be okay. You need to hold still until we get you to the hospital."

He struggled. "What? Where?" He opened his eyes to see the smoldering ceiling flashing by. "Anya?" He tried to jerk up, and hands held him down. "Let me go."

God, he could barely move. Was his right side going numb?

"Denver?" he bellowed.

"You're all right," said a guy holding his gurney. "Just hold on. We'll get some pain meds into you shortly."

"No." Heath struggled to sit up. "Where's Denver? Anya?" he called. Snow and wind hit his face, and a gray day came into focus.

Flashes went off, and he closed his eyes. Voices rumbled, all shouting questions. There were reporters? What was going on?

Seconds later, he was loaded into the back of an ambulance. The door shut, and they started to move. Something pierced his arm, and hands started working on him.

Pain exploded in his shoulder, and he passed out.

He came to in a hospital bed and sat straight up. His shoulder burned like hot iron rods poked him from inside, and his chest felt like he'd filled his lungs with needles. He blew out and tried to control the pain. Machinery beeped behind him, and liquid dropped into him through an IV.

"Ah, you're up." A forty-something male doctor with bushy brown hair strode into the room in Reeboks, his eyes twinkling behind thick glasses. "You have three cracked ribs, a concussion, multiple contusions, and several healing wounds that required stitches. I also removed some home-made looking stitches from you. That wound is healed." The guy glanced at a tablet in his hands. "We have you on morphine and a saline solution. The irritation in your lungs from the gas should dissipate in a day or so."

Heath shook his head to focus and then winced as agony slammed through his temples. "Where's my brother?"

"The next room. He required stitches as well, but he's a little better off than you are, so long as he stops fighting his nurses." The doctor let the tablet hang loosely in his hands. "Agents from the FBI are interviewing him now, and I believe they'll be in to see you next."

"Anya?" Heath asked, his gut aching.

The doctor shook his head. "I don't know but am sure the FBI will update you."

"Great." Heath reached for the IV and yanked it out.

"Whoa." The doctor held out a hand. "What are you doing?"

Getting his woman back. "Where are my clothes?" Heath glanced around the room, chilled in the hospital gown.

"The FBI took them for evidence," the doctor said, his eyes wide behind the glasses.

Great. Heath turned and planted his bare feet on the freezing floor. The room twirled around him.

"I have to advise you to get back into bed," the doctor said. "You have a concussion, Mr. Jones."

"I've had worse." God, he had to get to Anya. Where was she? "Reese?" he bellowed.

Detective Malloy hurried into the room, his trench coat flying behind him. He flashed his badge, his brown eyes serious. "Need a minute, Doc."

The doctor pushed his glasses up his nose. "I'll go check on my other patient." He hustled from the room.

"Malloy? Where the hell is Anya?" Heath shoved off the bed and instantly went down.

Malloy caught him under the armpits and hauled him back onto the bed. "We have a problem. A serious one." The cop looked frantically around. "Where are your clothes?"

"FBI took them." Heath sucked in air. He needed to go find Anya. "Does he have Anya? The Copper Killer?"

"Yeah." Malloy shoved an arm beneath Heath's good shoulder. "We have to get out of here. Now."

As Heath stood, dizziness grabbed him around the throat and took his vision. "To get Anya."

"That too."

Heath tried to focus. "What the fuck is going on?"

"I'll explain in the car." Malloy all but carried him to the door and poked his head out into the hallway. "I'm risking my job and possible freedom here, buddy. I owe your brother Shane, and I trust him. But if you're a bad guy, I'll hunt you down and shoot you myself."

Heath leaned on the cop, not having a choice. He needed to get out of the hospital, so he went along with the guy. "Fine. We need to get Denver."

"Right now, if you want to save your girl, we have to get you out of here." Urgency deepened the cop's already deep voice. "I don't know why the hell I'm helping you. I don't owe Shane that much, damn it." Muttering to himself, Malloy propelled Heath down a fairly empty hallway to a stairwell. "If we get caught, I'm claiming you got my gun."

Heath had to concentrate to put one foot in front of the other and not fall on his face. "I need clothes."

"No shit." The cop led him into an underground parking area, grunting from the weight. "Brown car."

Heath tried to help. They reached a nondescript brown car with a few dents in the side, and Malloy shoved him inside. Within seconds, the cop was in the car and roaring out of the parking area.

"Wait," Heath said. "Your phone?"

The cop handed over his phone. Heath dialed Denver, holding his breath.

"Yeah?" Denver asked, his voice gravelly.

"You clear?"

"Affirmative. FBI just left to take a phone call. Where are you?" Denver asked, sounding like he was moving fast.

Heath set his head back on the seat. "We're outside to the west. Where's Ryker?"

"He and Zara just created another safe house in town. It was a rental, former drug house, and they paid cash. No trace to us. I told them I could get you there."

Heath nodded. "Good. They need a safe place until we can get them out of town."

"Agreed." Denver swore. The sound of a window being wrenched open came over the line. "I'll be right there." He clicked off.

"We can't wait," Malloy said urgently.

Heath opened his eyes and viewed the cop. "We're waiting."

There wasn't a need to argue further because the back door of the car opened and Denver jumped inside, still wearing a hospital gown. "Fuck, it's cold. I need socks."

Heath swallowed down bile. "Go."

Malloy was already pressing the gas, and soon they were speeding away from the hospital. "I hope my guy cut the camera feeds like he promised," he muttered.

Heath shook his head. "What is going on?" His chest started to hurt worse. Maybe the morphine had been helping.

Malloy twisted on the windshield wipers as the snow bombarded them. "Jolene Landers was found dead an hour ago near the river. Raped and strangled."

Heath made a low sound and fought nausea. "She was just a decoy."

"Yeah," Malloy agreed. "The kicker is that we also found a bag loaded with rocks in the river...hidden not too well."

Heath shook his head. "Don't tell me."

"Yep. Carl Spark's phone, another phone, and a wallet with a Wyoming driver's license for Kip Levy."

Heath settled back and shut his eyes again to keep from passing out. "Great."

Malloy turned the heat on full blast. "Yeah. Your face is on the license. I guess Kip is an alias?"

"Yeah." Heath slowly opened his eyes, and gray light pierced into his brain. Concussions sucked. "Was there a gun with it?"

"Nope."

The gun no doubt would show up since it probably had been used to kill Carl. Heath pushed that thought aside for now. "Does the FBI have the info?"

"They should by now," Malloy said. "My guys found the body and the sunken bag, and I had a friend hold off on contacting Special Agent Reese until I could get to you. But he couldn't have waited long."

Gratitude for the cop exploded through Heath. "We owe you."

"Damn straight." Malloy took a sharp left turn. "Your face is also plastered all over the news. Reporters were waiting when you were taken out of the bombed building. They have stills and video—clearly showing it's you. Shane told me to warn you about that for some reason."

Heath studied the cop. Cobb and Madison would be coming. Fast. "How much do you know?"

"More than I want to know. I ran into the force chasing you guys, and I know they're not really with the military. So I help Shane when I can," Malloy said. "This is above and beyond, however. I don't need the FBI on my ass. Or a Sheriff Cobb—whose phone call I still haven't returned."

"Agreed. Where are we?"

Malloy eyed the storm outside. "Headed to a hotel on the outskirts of town where the owner won't ask any questions."

"No." Heath tried to sit up, and his ribs protested. He sucked in air. Jesus. "Denver? Where's the safe house?" He needed to make sure Ryker and Zara were all right.

"Mulcolly Street," Denver said, working away on his phone. "Last house on the end. Cute blue bungalow."

Malloy shook his head. "Safe houses. For the love of pete."

"Take us there," Heath said, his body wanting to shut down. "Do you have anything on Anya? Anything at all?"

"Not yet," Malloy said grimly. "We have everybody working on it, and I'm sure the FBI does as well. Reese was bellowing into a phone the second she was taken. He's almost obsessed, which is good."

"Denver?" Heath asked, struggling to keep his brain working when his body wanted to freak the hell out. She was with a fuckin' serial killer. This was Heath's fault.

Denver tapped on his phone. "The quickest kill for this guy, besides the victim this morning, was three days. She's smart, Heath. She'll keep herself alive until we can get to her. Plus, she's the one he's always wanted."

"I saw the guy." Heath closed his eyes again and tried to see through the fog. A man coming toward him, more smoke, his lungs burning. Hours later he still coughed, and he forced himself to concentrate on the man. The guy was dressed in all black and wore a gas mask. A clear gas mask.

It had been difficult to see through the smoke, but Heath's eyes weren't exactly normal. "The way the guy moved. Smooth and graceful...and he knew all about explosives. In addition, he somehow found our safe headquarters."

"He's smart," Denver returned, still working on his phone.

Yeah. Definitely smart. "He tracked us, he blew the place up, and he took Anya." Heath rubbed at the stitches along his forearm. "I've seen him before." Where had he seen the guy? He needed to clear his head, and now. "How long till morphine leaves your system?" he muttered, turning toward his brother. His ribs protested, and he sucked in air as pain beat at his innards.

"With your metabolism, not long," Denver said.

"Good." Heath concentrated harder, and a face swam into his vision. He blinked. Wait a minute. Everything crashed through his head at once. "Ah shit."

"What?" Denver looked up.

"Give me your phone." Heath lifted a hand, and his chest compressed.

Denver handed it over. Heath quickly dialed for a face chat.

"Heath?" Shane swam into view. "Saw you on the news. We're loading up now and should be there in a couple of hours."

"No." Heath coughed and could swear he still tasted the gas. "We're heading to a safe house, and we have no clue where Anya is.

Right now, you're of more use to me by getting on the computers. Hack into every satellite and camera you can, and find this guy."

Shane's worried eyes turned a dark gray. "You need backup."

"I have it. Please. For now, hold tight. If we need physical reinforcements, I'll let you know. Right now I need your expertise, contacts, and prayers." Heath stored up his breath to talk. "The guy who took her, I saw him." The face cleared. Came into focus. Determined brown eyes and a hard jaw. That fucking fake marshal. The one who moved like he'd been trained his whole life.

Shane's eyebrows lifted. "Who is he?"

"Dunno, but he acted like a U.S. Marshal looking for us. I think he also attacked Anya and me at the hotel near DC." Facts started clicking into place. "He moved like you. Like he's been trained."

Shane drew in a breath. "You think he's one of Madison's soldiers?"

"That's what I thought when I saw him the first time—even though he wore a disguise." It made a sick kind of sense. "The way he fought at the hotel coupled with the knowledge of infiltration and the use of explosives tonight? He's one of her soldiers."

Shane frowned. "Shit. That's too much of a coincidence, Heath. Think about it."

"I am." He was trying to, anyway. His mind was still muddled. "This guy is a serial killer, and he's trained by Madison."

"How did you get involved in the case?" Shane asked slowly, his lips flattening out.

Heath rubbed his gritty eyes. "We were hired by one of the families."

Shane's eyes darkened. "Call them. Ask how they got your name or found you on the dark web."

Man, if the killer had engineered Heath's involvement in his crazy spree, the guy was beyond brilliant and psychotic. If he worked with Dr. Madison, he was playing a very twisted game. "I'll call the family."

Heath fought the anger burning inside him. He had to think and get into this guy's head. Finally there was at least a slim lead. "Forgetting that Anya is the key for a moment, is there any reason one of Dr. Madison's soldiers would have an obsession with redheads to the point of carving the word 'Mine' into their chests?"

Shane paled to the color of paste.

Heath sat up straighter, his instincts humming. "I'll take that as a yes."

Shane gave a curt nod. "Call me back when you're alone." He disconnected the call.

CHAPTER
37

Anya took a bite of her already cut up steak and gingerly tested the shackles around her ankles. A quick glance confirmed they were ordinary-looking handcuffs, which were also attached to big rings in the floor. Should she address the handcuffs? He seemed to be playing out some sort of fantasy with the dinner, and a reminder of reality might just piss him off.

Daniel sat across from her and poured more red wine into his glass. He wore dark slacks and a blue silk shirt, looking like he was out on a first date. His hair was thick and combed, and he'd shaven his face recently. If she'd just met him, she'd think he was extremely good-looking. She squinted. They had met.

He smiled. "You're remembering."

"Yes." But he was only vaguely familiar. "Why don't you refresh my memory?"

He sighed. "You were seventeen, and you thought I was maybe nineteen. We met at Sharon's Hometown Diner in Lake Wana-tanka."

She blinked. Memories, hazy, fuzzed through her head. "You bought me an ice cream." He'd been a cute boy sitting alone near the beach, and he'd approached her.

"Yeah," he said softly. "Even with that red hair, you were so pure. So sweet."

She struggled to capture more of the memory. "It was my last day at camp."

He nodded. "I asked you out the next night, and you said you had to go back home to school. You left me." His lips turned down.

He'd been so handsome, but the moment had been fleeting. Now, as it was, he looked like a monster. One she needed to get to trust her. "I didn't have a choice."

"Maybe. I was on a job and couldn't follow you." He sighed. "But I eventually did find you, and I've kept watch."

She took a sip. They needed some sort of connection. She'd have to go slow with the questions and maybe give him some admiration. "The wine is good. What is it?"

"It's a local blend," he said, smiling. "I like to buy local when I travel."

She tried to choke down some steak. It looked like it was cooked perfectly, but it tasted like exposed cardboard. Fear made everything bitter. "What kind of job were you on when we met?"

"I'm a soldier and was even then."

"With the U.S. military?" she asked, her mind rioting.

"No. With a private group." He munched on his steak, humming with pleasure.

She glanced toward the stormy evening outside and kept her gaze from the bed. All of the victims had been raped, but maybe the courting part of his ritual with her would last more than a day. She could only hope. "I've always admired soldiers."

"We do work hard," he confirmed. "I'm planning on taking command of the group I work for. It lacks military leadership right now."

What was his trigger? He'd obsessed about her for years but hadn't made a move. Something had forced him to start killing and sending her pictures. "Ambition is good." She tried to take a bite of the fresh salad. "You must have a lot of freedom with your hours to be able to, ah, keep an eye on me."

He nodded, his gaze still piercing. "I have more than I used to."

She needed some sort of plan. Getting into his head was like dancing around land mines. But she just needed to distract him long enough for her to make a break for it. The deadbolt on the door wasn't engaged. Where was that knife? "Loretta's death made me so sad. Have you been sad lately?" she prodded, her breath almost burning her throat and lungs.

His face darkened. "Yes. I lost my father."

"I'm so sorry," she burst out. "Is that when you started, ah, playing a game with me?"

He took another sip of wine. "I've done more than play a game. I arranged all of this." He paused. "Well, I hadn't thought you would sleep with Heath. You'll have to pay for that."

She shivered. Fear pricked along her back. "You, ah, know Heath?"

"Yes. Your boyfriend and his brothers are part of my job." Daniel took a healthy drink of the wine, and color burst across his chiseled features. "I guess I should say your ex-boyfriend now."

Anya tried to interpret his words. "I don't understand."

Daniel set down his glass. "You're not dating him now. That makes him your ex, and me your future. Or do you disagree?" His chin lowered, and his voice flattened out.

She sucked in air. Warning tickled through her. She couldn't promise something she didn't mean, because he was smart enough to read her, without question. Yet she really didn't want to disagree with him yet. "I would only date one man at a time, Daniel. I've never played the field. It's just not me." God, she hoped that appeased him. She added some strength into her voice. "It hurts my feelings that you'd think otherwise."

He blinked slowly. "Don't try to play with my head."

"I won't," she said, trying to put them on a level field. "It's not fair for you to play with mine, either."

His lip twitched. "Your sister was smart, too."

Oh God.

She needed to turn his focus. "I don't understand how Heath and his brothers are part of your job." Her hand shook around her fork, so she set it on the plate and reached for the wine. "You said you were looking for Heath when you came to my apartment and tried to kidnap me."

"Yes." He cut into his steak again with a small steak knife. "I was hurt. You didn't recognize me."

"You were wearing a disguise of sorts." She'd had no idea she was meeting a serial killer in that moment.

"True."

"Was the other soldier with you that day part of your job? The other fake marshal?" None of this was making sense.

"Yes," Daniel said.

"I don't get it. You work alone with your, ah, hobby with redheads." God, that sounded so wrong. "Why did you try to kidnap me with that other marshal. Wait a minute. Do you have a partner?" She looked frantically toward the door.

"No." Daniel chuckled. "I partially told you the truth. We were bugging your phone because of your connection to Heath, and it made sense to approach you after that phone call. The other soldier was with me."

She swallowed. "But you tried to kidnap me."

He lifted a shoulder. "I know. At first, I just wanted to be in the same room with you. Touch you somehow. Know that I'd killed your sister and you had no clue. Hence the disguise."

Bile lurched up into her throat, and she forced it back down. That was so sick. "That's mean."

"No. It's part of the game. Then I just couldn't help trying to take you." He sighed. "This has worked out better."

Man, he was crazy. "How are both Heath and I involved in your work and love life?" She had to play along to get answers. "That can't be a coincidence," she said softly, trying to keep her voice from shaking like her hands. The wineglass was heavy enough that she had to concentrate to lift it to her face.

"Per my orders, I found Heath and his brothers right about the same time I started the game with you, but I didn't want to bring them in yet. I would've lost some freedom if I'd succeeded so quickly. So I suggested to one of the families of my redheaded dates that they hire the Lost Bastards to find their daughter, to keep Heath close and on the case, where I could watch him and his brothers." He grinned. "She was already dead at that point, and I was just maneuvering pieces into place like in chess."

Anya gagged.

"Are you all right?" he asked, his gaze on the sloshing wine in her glass.

She nodded. "I'm still feeling the effects of the gas you let loose. It's made everything fuzzy and my muscles weak."

"Oh. I do apologize for that." Concern filtered through his eyes now. "You should be all right by tomorrow."

His calm concern made her want to throw up. She couldn't breathe. "I'm trying to understand why you got Lost Bastards involved in your, ah, game. You wanted Heath looking for you."

"It was only fair, since I'd been looking for him." Daniel wiped his mouth, an odd glint in his eyes. "But I hadn't expected that you'd go to bed with him so soon after Carl had broken your heart. You'll have to purify yourself for me. Like you were when I first met you. Redheaded and oh so innocent." His lip twisted, and his eyes hardened.

Her stomach lurched, and she swallowed rapidly. If she threw up on the table, it'd probably piss him off. She had to take herself out of her own head and play the part right. "So you liked me because I was a pure redhead."

"Yes." His gaze dropped to her breasts.

Screams rose inside her, wanting out. She bit her tongue, and the coppery taste of blood centered her. "Was there a redhead in your life who wasn't pure?"

His gaze hardened to flint. "Watch yourself."

Her legs went weak. "I'm sorry."

His chin lifted. "Apology accepted."

"Thank you," she whispered, pressing her knees together to keep her legs from trembling. "Why were you looking for Heath and his brothers?"

"Now, that's a smart question." Daniel dug into his salad. "Heath, his brothers, and I were made by a woman named Isobel Madison. She spliced and diced genes to create us. I'm supposed to bring Heath home."

Anya choked on her wine and coughed, setting the glass down. "What?" she asked weakly.

Daniel frowned at her wineglass. "You heard me."

How was that possible? "You're one of those supersoldiers?"

"Yes," Daniel said smoothly. "Yet now I'm faced with a dilemma, right?"

"What is that?" she asked weakly.

"Now that you and I are together, I can't have Heath at the new compound all the time, can I?"

If she could just get him to trust her in some way, maybe she'd get a chance to escape. Somehow. "What's your alternative?" she asked, trying to appear curious and not scared shitless.

"I can call Sheriff Cobb instead of Dr. Madison, considering Sheriff

Cobb wants Heath dead." Alertness lit his gaze. "What do you think I should do?"

She sensed the trap and scrambled to think of a way around it. "I thought they worked together."

"Heath told you about them?"

She numbly nodded.

"I didn't figure you were that close." Daniel set his knife on his plate. "That's unfortunate."

Panic pricked along her skin. She had to bring the conversation back to him. "Is my intel wrong? Don't Cobb and Madison work together?"

"Sheriff Cobb and Dr. Madison. We use manners here," Daniel said, his voice hard. He lifted his knife and pointed it at her. That knife had probably carved letters in women's chests.

Her hands went clammy. She couldn't help but pant. "Of course. Sorry."

He waited a beat. "That's the last apology I'll accept from you tonight. They do work together, but they have different motivations regarding Heath and his brothers." Daniel took another drink of wine. "The sheriff wants to torture and kill them, while Dr. Madison wants to bring them home to work for her and donate genetic material for the next generation of enhanced soldiers. It is a conundrum."

"I see," Anya murmured weakly. She couldn't let Cobb get to Heath. Her shoulders straightened. She'd do whatever she had to in order to protect him. "Do either the sheriff or the doctor know about your, ah, search for me? Your game?" Was that how she should put it?

"No." Daniel shrugged. "I need something that's just mine."

Mine. There was that word he'd carved into his victims' chests. Anya rubbed her collarbone, her mind blanking. She couldn't continue to act normal.

A phone trilled. Daniel pulled it from his slacks. He glanced at the screen and stood. "Finish your dinner so we can get on to the next part of our date." Walking by her, he paused. "Try to escape, and I'll make you pay in ways you can't even imagine—and I have no intention of letting you die. Though you might beg for death." He strode behind her, and the front door opened and closed.

Cold air whispered around her, and she shivered. He wanted to hurt her. To make her pay for forgetting him and taking up with Heath. Anticipation had filled his voice.

Tears blurred her vision, and she let herself shudder this time. How badly hurt was Heath? He'd been in the middle of an explosion, and it was unlikely he was even walking already. Nobody was that tough.

She was on her own.

* * *

Daniel scouted outside the cabin, paying no heed to the snow pelting down on him. Yet he didn't want to appear disheveled during his date, so he pressed himself against the cabin and out of the wind. Threadbare eaves slightly protected him. "Dr. Madison. How may I be of service?"

"What is going on in Snowville?" she asked, her voice higher than normal. "I saw Heath and Denver being carted out of a burning building—I watched it on the news. Where are you?"

He kicked snow out of his way and angled further back to keep somewhat dry. "I saw the news but don't know what happened. My guess is that they were messing with explosives they couldn't handle and made a mistake." It wasn't as if those three had the lifelong training he'd enjoyed. They were amateurs. Strong and genetically enhanced amateurs, but still.

The doctor seemed to hold her breath for a moment. "Can you get to them in the hospital?"

"Negative," Daniels said smoothly, wondering what Anya was doing at that very moment. Hopefully finishing her wine. "The FBI and local police are all over the hospital. Apparently Heath has been linked to the murder of his girlfriend's ex-boyfriend. It's all so reality television here in the Pacific Northwest."

The doctor didn't laugh at his humor like she usually did.

Daniel stood straighter, and his head brushed the eave. He ducked down lower to keep his hair smooth. Anya seemed to like him well groomed. "I'm outside the hospital right now, monitoring the situation. If you want me to conduct a full assault, I'll do so. But I don't know where Ryker is. Only Heath and Denver are being treated by the doctors." Probably. He'd monitored the police scanner on his way out of town.

She was silent.

He shuffled his feet. "Dr. Madison?" He hated how tentative his voice sounded. If he wanted to take command of the military side of the compound, he needed to show her he could do it. "I think the better plan is to wait and see if Ryker shows up. Perhaps even the Gray brothers will arrive here to assist, considering they've connected." No way would she be able to ignore that dangling carrot. She wanted the Gray brothers as much as the Lost boys.

"Daniel, have you reported in to the sheriff?" she asked.

"No. If he shows up here, I need directions from you." Daniel eyed the snow-laden trees surrounding the summer cabin on the river. There were other cabins close by, but they were deserted for the winter. "Doctor?"

"Whatever do you mean?" There was the calculating tone he was accustomed to hearing from her.

It was time to show her his loyalty and acumen. "Sheriff Cobb wants to torture and kill those brothers. You want them alive. At some point, you are going to have to make a decision. The sheriff or the Lost boys?" Daniel had planned to end the sheriff sometime, anyway, but it'd be easier all around if she ordered the kill.

"I'm not ready to give up the sheriff, Daniel. If you truly want to run this compound, you need to give me what I want." Her voice firmed like it had when she'd studied him as a child.

Right now she wanted the impossible. "Only you can control the sheriff." Daniel felt like he was nine years old again and had just disappointed her. He didn't like to think how she controlled the men around her, although he'd probably have to satisfy her in that way at some point. He swallowed down nausea. If Anya turned out to be his soul mate, maybe he should just take her and start over like the Gray brothers had.

He'd finally found his love. She was his and his only. Yet could he truly leave home? He growled and scrubbed a hand through his hair.

His head hurt.

"I know this is difficult, my boy," Dr. Madison crooned. "We'll figure it out."

He focused, and his headache whispered into nothingness. "Dr. Madison—"

"Isobel. It's time you called me Isobel, don't you think?" she asked.

He gulped. Desperation tore through him. He needed a redhead and now. That's how he asserted control and became the man he was always supposed to be. "Isobel," he repeated dutifully, feeling like a child again. His shoulders thumped against the icy log cabin as he tried to shrug away the sensation. He was a man, not a helpless child. There was a woman inside the cabin who made him feel like a man. His woman. She was made just for him.

Isobel chuckled through the phone. He instantly went from thinking of her as Dr. Madison to using her given name, even in his own thoughts. His shoulders slumped. "What are your orders?"

"Keep an eye on Heath and Denver, and try to find Ryker. I'm sending backup your way. Once they arrive, I want you to take all three men into custody, regardless of collateral damage or casualties." Something clacked over the line, and he realized she was using her fingernail on a tablet. "Be vigilant, and if the Gray brothers make an appearance, let me know immediately." She'd always valued the Gray brothers over all her other soldiers. That fact had stopped hurting him years ago.

Mostly.

"Understood." Daniel wondered once again what type of skills they had that he lacked. He could create an assault plan in seconds, and he was brutal with a knife. Yet they'd always had something more. Did Heath and his brothers have more? Daniel rested his head back. He'd have to ask Anya. "If it comes down to your order or Sheriff Cobb's wishes, what do you want me to do?"

"We don't have a new facility and compound without the Lost boys, Daniel. They are your primary objective," she said.

She was so matter-of-fact, having just given him the green light to kill Sheriff Cobb if necessary. Daniel let the cold air soothe his skin. He should probably be put off by her callousness, but he didn't feel anything about killing her current lover. Oh, he had feelings, but they were all for the woman inside the cabin.

All the good and all the bad feelings that bombarded him were hers. Only after finally fetching his soul mate had that powerful barrage finally calmed.

Perhaps Anya could make his peace permanent. In fact, she would. No matter what he had to do to her.

CHAPTER
38

Heath's chest felt like he'd been kicked by an elephant, his shoulder burned, and the stitches itched at several places on his body. Nothing compared to the headache behind his eyes, however.

"You have quite the setup in such a short amount of time," Detective Malloy muttered, glancing at the computers in the bungalow's otherwise empty living room. He shook snow off his trench coat. "I'm running to the office to see what the task force has drummed up. If I get information, I'll make sure you have it." He opened the front door, where the storm threw snow around like a popcorn popper. "If you get any sort of lead, you call." The door shut quietly behind him.

Heath sat at a computer, his fingers feeling numb as he booted it up. "We need anything we can find," he said.

Denver grunted, already setting up the rest of the computers. "I called the family who initially hired us on the Copper Killer case. A U.S. Marshal had passed on our contact information to them. The killer, one of Dr. Madison's soldiers, set us up to be involved from the beginning."

A door opened to show a dingy kitchen, and Ryker strode inside with Zara on his heels. "We got all the computer stuff we could but now can't get into either the real offices or the decoy ones. The cops are going through them both," Ryker said grimly. "Anything?"

"No," Heath said, his gut churning. The killer had Anya. His arms felt paralyzed. "Denver?"

"I'm accessing our main server," Denver said tersely. "Don't need the files from the office. Got them here." He swept his hand across the screen, and all the files came into view on Heath's screen. "Checking satellites and local cameras now."

"Thanks." Heath still had Denver's burner phone in his hand. "First send the surveillance video of Smithers and his buddy to Shane, would you? If Smithers is one of Dr. Madison's soldiers, then Shane might know him. Any insight will be helpful." He waited until Denver nodded. "I'll be right back." He stood and moved toward the kitchen.

"Copy that," Ryker said, taking his seat.

Zara hovered at Ryker's shoulder. "I don't have anything to do. Give me something to do." Her face held no color, and she worried her bottom lip with her teeth.

Ryker pulled a chair out. "Sit here and go through the map of the town, making notes of banks and anywhere else there might be a camera. We'll try to trace her that way."

Zara sat, her face pinched. "We'll find her, Heath."

Heath limped through the kitchen and into the garage, where a rusty old heap was parked. He and his brothers couldn't get access to their vehicles, damn it. He pressed a button on his phone, and within a second Shane's face came into view. "I'm alone," Heath said.

Shane visibly took a deep breath. "Me too. Everybody knows about this, even Josie, but I don't like talking about it."

Heath leaned against the door and tried to keep from falling on his ass. "Thanks for trusting me."

"We're brothers." Shane's eyes darkened to a gray storm cloud. "Part of our training growing up was in how to seduce women and what to do with them after that." He cleared his throat. "They had whores—a lot of them—meet with us a couple of times a week."

"Jesus." The boys home had been horrible, but at least Heath and his brothers hadn't gone through that. "I'm sorry, Shane."

"Don't worry about it." Shane's jaw hardened. "One of the women was named Cinnamon, and I figured she used that name because she had red hair. Real red hair." He blanched. "She was rough and really liked her job—and she often sighed the word 'Mine' during the, ah, the training."

Bile rose in Heath's throat. "That is so fucked up."

Shane forced a smile. "No shit. But it's a weird coincidence."

Heath nodded. "That at least explains why, I guess. The killer hated redheads and then met a sweet one, Anya, and he fixated. Denver is sending you a video of the killer. He masqueraded as a U.S. Marshal who was looking for us. He was caught on video."

Shane started moving, and the screen blurred. "Is Denver sending it right now?"

"Should be there," Heath said.

Shane clomped down some stairs. "Hey, Mattie? Did you just get a video from Denver?" Shane held out the phone, and Matt, the oldest Gray brother, came into view.

"Hey, Heath," Matt said, his hard jaw set. "We're ready to roll the second you need us."

Warmth bloomed through Heath. They weren't alone—not by a long shot. Although Anya was. Fury cut through him. "Right now, I need intel. We have no clue where she's been taken."

Matt turned to a computer screen and punched a couple of buttons. "Holy shit," he muttered, his eyes widening.

Heath dropped to sit on the stairs and fought the chill in the air. The garage was freaking cold. "I take it you know the fake U.S. Marshal D. J. Smithers?" he asked.

Matt lifted the phone so only his face was visible. "Yeah. His real name is Daniel, and he's still working with Dr. Madison, it looks like."

"He's a lunatic," Heath said.

"Jesus," Shane said, taking the phone. "He worked undercover with my wife for a while before I found her. God. To think he's the Copper Killer."

Josie didn't have red hair, and that alone had probably saved her life. "He just started killing recently, I think."

"Oh fuck," Shane said grimly. "Doesn't something trigger serial killers?"

"Yeah. Why?"

"The timing of this whole case," Shane said, his eyes burning. "We killed the commander, and Daniel was always close to him. That had to be the trigger."

"Shane?" Matt said urgently. "If Daniel is working with Madison, then…"

Shane gasped. "Maybe?"

Heath leaned in. "What? Tell me. What?"

Shane's expression turned thoughtful. "Dr. Madison has always liked to keep track of her soldiers. She tagged us. If Daniel is working for Madison, she has him tagged somewhere. A microchip…under the skin. The guy probably doesn't even know it's there."

For the first time in hours, hope rushed through Heath. "If he's gone off the grid, as we know he has, maybe she activated it?"

"Definitely," Shane said. "Listen. An activated tracker has a frequency, and we can find it. The signal would use radio-frequency identification. I mean, it's a long shot, but a tracker would send out a signal. We just have to find the right frequency and hope it's activated."

"I'm familiar with RFID," Heath said, his chest compressing. "We'll need to increase the sensitivity of Denver's antenna to pick up the frequency, if there is one." The killer usually stayed close to the abduction town, so it might actually be possible. "You guys work the problem from your end as well. Please send Denver all the data you have on those chips, especially frequency."

Shane sat next to Matt, their faces taking up the entire screen. "I'm on it right now."

Heath clicked off and ran through the old kitchen to the living room, quickly explaining everything to his brothers and Zara.

Denver scratched his head. "I need supplies to increase the sensitivity, and the storm ain't gonna help the antenna any." He stood and grabbed his jacket. "I'll be right back."

Heath dropped into a chair. His mind kept going to what was happening to Anya right that second as he sat on his ass. He curled his hands into fists, and his lungs seized.

"We'll get her back, brother." Ryker reached over and clasped his good shoulder. "I promise we'll get to her in time."

Heath nodded, knowing full well his brother couldn't make that promise.

Zara kept making notations. "Some of the smartest people in the world are trying to find her, including us. We'll get her." A fine tremor threaded through her voice.

"I can't lose her now," Heath whispered, dark clouds falling through him. The idea of a life without Anya cut deep and festered. He stood. There had to be something to do. As he looked around the dismal room with the storm billowing outside, he realized there was nothing to do until Denver got back.

God. Where was Anya?

* * *

Sheriff Cobb hitched up his jeans and waited until his one true love exited her office and barreled right into him. He grasped her shoulders and held her at arm's length. "Where are you going, sweetheart?"

Isobel pushed her dark hair away from her face. "On a mission, love. It concerns the lab and not you."

He pivoted and put her back to the wall. His chest burned, and his gut ached. "I can't let you go alone. It's a dangerous world." How far would she take the charade?

Her stunning blue eyes narrowed. "I can take care of myself. Thank you, though."

Oh, she was a damn good liar. Of course, that was one of the many traits he loved about her. Why did he have to hurt her to fully gain her love? There was only one way to do it, which was to finally kill those boys. Then she'd respect him. She'd have no choice. "I saw the news, Isobel." Heath and Denver were being treated at a hospital in Snowville, which meant they were weak. Vulnerable.

She sighed. "I want to bring them home before you kill them. Is that really too much to ask?" She slid her hands up his chest and leaned closer to bite his chin. "Just think how much fun you could have with them here, in secluded cells, if you got the chance to take your time."

He looked down at her smooth face even as his blood started to pump harder. "I could make them watch me torture their brothers. Maybe their women." The idea did have merit. "What do you want from them?"

"Genetic material." Her smile brightened even the dark night outside.

He grimaced at the idea of their sperm. "I don't think I can keep from at least one kill." He'd waited so long to avenge his brother. Maybe he could kill just one of them and cooperate with her.

Her pretty blue eyes filled with what almost looked like understanding. "How about you kill the redhead, if Daniel hasn't already done so? She's under Heath's protection, and he yelled her name as he was loaded into an ambulance. There are feelings there from him, and that would certainly make an impression."

Cobb frowned. "Why would Daniel kill Anya Best?"

Isobel rolled her eyes. "Oh, sweetheart. Think about it. The explosion and the damage to Heath and Denver? Only one of my soldiers could've done that. The second I saw the news, I put things together."

Cobb took a step away from her, his mind working furiously to catch up. Realization smacked him on the forehead. "Daniel is that serial killer?"

"I'm afraid so." Isobel shook her head. "It's so sad."

Cobb threw back his head and laughed, all but basking in the delicious humor. "I knew he was a psycho. I just knew it." What a fucking relief. "We need to take him out."

She sighed. "Yes. He's too much of a liability."

It would be a pleasure to cut off that asshole's head. "I will take care of him for you."

"I know." Faith in him lit her beautiful eyes.

His back straightened, and his newly sculpted chest puffed up. "I need to find him."

"No. I have a tracker. In fact, we need to get going to fetch him." She grasped Cobb's hand and started to lead him outside the building.

"What about the girl?" Cobb asked, already knowing the answer.

Isobel paused. "I already said you could have her."

"Maybe I'll put her dead body in the same cell with Heath." He smiled.

"I do like how you think." Isobel chuckled. "But it's imperative you gut her like a fish with Daniel watching—right when we arrive. It's the only way to catch him off guard."

"No problem." Cobb opened the door for her. "I'll get my hunting knife."

CHAPTER
39

Dinner had taken several hours with many different courses, including an apple pie. Anya was seated again on the sofa, this time with her hands and feet free. Daniel whistled from the kitchen as he cleaned up the dinner mess.

"I said I'd be happy to clean up," she said, her gaze on the fire. If she somehow could shove him into the fire, could she keep him there long enough for him to weaken? Probably not.

"I invited you to dinner, thus I clean up." His back was to her as he finished drying the plates.

She eyed the door. It was as if he wanted her to make a move. Most women at this point would run for the door. She measured the distance between Daniel and the exit. If she could get it open, she might have a chance. But he was fast and trained, and he had taken her shoes. He'd reach her within seconds, and she had no clue what waited outside.

Her mind would get her out of this, and she had to bide her time.

He set the towel on the counter and took out two thick glasses. She couldn't see what he poured, but he turned and walked gracefully toward her. The liquid was a deep copper. He handed one over. "After dinner drink?"

She took it and sniffed. Smelled strong. "Thank you."

"Of course." He sat next to her and sighed. "This is nice."

"How long do you think we'll stay in this cabin?" she asked, swirling the liquid around in the glass.

He slid an arm around her shoulders. "Until I know you're committed to me."

Her skin crawled, but she forced herself to remain still. "Which would take what?"

He squeezed her. "You're a smart girl. You'll figure it out."

Where was that knife he'd used at dinner? She swallowed. "I don't know what you want from me." Was there any way to reason with the guy?

He set his head back on the sofa and shut his eyes as if relaxing at home after a hard day's work. "My lungs are still irritated from that gas. I can't imagine what yours feel like."

"They hurt." That was true, but she'd thought it was terror. His touch on her shoulder made her want to smash the glass into his face and run like hell. Could she manipulate him into telling her if there were guns in the house? She didn't think so. Skirting the line with honesty had been working so far.

"I figured you'd try and run," he said almost absently. "Why haven't you?"

She couldn't think of an answer.

"It's okay, Anya. I know it'll take time." His body tensed. "I hope I don't have to hurt you too badly to get you to understand. I love you. You're mine."

She tried not to stiffen.

"Drink your drink."

The guy hadn't poisoned her so far, so she took a sip. The alcohol burned her tongue, and she coughed. "Wow. That's strong."

"It's a good liqueur." He emitted a pleased hum. "Finish yours."

She shivered.

"It'll warm you up before I do."

She took a deep breath and swallowed the shot. Heat did explode in her stomach.

"Good girl." He opened his eyes and took her glass, placing it with his on a side table. "I think the date is going well. Don't you?"

She nodded but couldn't find the right words.

He sat up a little and faced her, his gaze dropping to her sweater. "Maybe we should get more comfortable." His fingers started playing with her ear.

Her stomach heaved. "I am comfortable."

He laughed. "You're smart and funny. I like that."

She bit her lip to keep from screaming. "We should go slow in getting to know each other."

He leaned in, his breath too strong against her face. "I've been trained by the best in pleasing a woman. Don't you want to see what I've learned? Isn't that what you all want? That's what she told me."

Anya swallowed, her legs shaking. "I'd rather talk to you. Find out what makes you tick, you know?" Her voice trembled. "I don't care about other women or what they told you."

"You should." He pulled on her hair. Hard.

Pain jerked through her scalp. She gasped but refrained from crying out. "That wasn't nice." Tears filled her eyes.

"Oh, we both know you don't like 'nice.' No woman likes 'nice.'" He pulled again, this time even harder. Then he released her. "I'll pretend for a while, if that's what you want."

What she wanted was for him to have a heart attack and die right then and there. She couldn't do this. Unease filtered through her stomach and turned to an ache. Survival was what mattered. She had to survive and get back to Heath. "I like to watch television after dinner." Were the news stations running her picture? Could there be a report on Heath and Denver? "I don't suppose you have a television here."

Daniel shook his head. "We can entertain ourselves."

Anya tried to breathe normally and not show the panic spiraling through her entire body. Her legs twitched. The door was so close. God, she couldn't do this.

He smoothed the hair away from her face. "The color is so vibrant, and it's genuine. I can tell it's real." He clasped her nape. "Only one to two percent of the population has true red hair."

"Oh," she said, her body stiffening.

"Yes. Also, did you know that redheads feel pain stronger than other people?"

She gulped. "No. I didn't know that."

"It's true. Scientifically proven." He leaned closer. "I've conducted my own research as well."

She closed her eyes.

In one smooth motion, he grabbed the bottom of her sweater and yanked it over her head.

Her mind revolted.

"That's a pretty blouse," he whispered.

She shivered as cold went through the thin cotton. His hand wandered down and around to grasp her breast.

She jolted. Pressure built inside her, and her ears rang. Panic took over. Twisting, she threw an elbow into his nose. It cracked. She jumped up and skirted the couch, her chest heaving. "This isn't going to work." Think, damn it. "I'm not that type of girl, so you need to show respect now." She could make it to the door.

He stood and faced her, his expression dark. Blood dribbled from his already swelling nose. "I knew you would take convincing. Pain works with women. Trust me."

"I'll fight you," her voice quaked, even as she edged toward the door.

"I know." He shook his head, his too-handsome face in grim lines.

"You're spirited, and I like that." He almost casually moved around the sofa toward her. "I'm prepared to make you love me."

She made it closer to the door, her panicked senses tracking his every twitch. "Not a chance," she spat.

He smiled. "Please fight me."

She didn't have a choice. It'd be a fight to the death. "There has to be a third alternative."

He tilted his head to the side, his gaze voracious. "What's that?"

"We get you help." There was something so sad about the lunatic. Her legs trembled, and chills engulfed her shoulders. "You made a nice dinner, and you're trying too hard to make a connection with me. Don't you want to be able to do that? A good shrink could help you." The words burst out of her. She didn't see one weapon anywhere near.

He sighed. "I'm about to make a connection with you."

There was no reasoning with him. She bolted for the door and yanked it open. Wind and snow burst inside, and she rushed out onto an icy deck, her arms windmilling as she slid. Snow-covered trees spread in every direction, and the wind whipped up the snow in a frenzy.

A battered truck was over to the right, nearly covered with snow. She turned and ran for it with all her might. Snow and ice covered her bare feet, and she slipped, but she finally skidded to it. Gurgling almost uncontrollably, she tugged on the frozen handle.

"It's locked," Daniel called from the doorway. With the firelight behind him, his entire face was in shadow.

She gulped, the icy snow burning her feet, and turned to look at him. He didn't move. Why wasn't he chasing her? She looked frantically around for any other lights or sign of life. Nothing.

"I see you're understanding your position here," he said clearly, out of the storm. "I'm feeling generous toward you for some reason. Maybe because you called me into your life."

She swallowed down another scream. "I didn't really think we'd meet," she yelled back. "I thought I was just setting a trap for you, you fucking lunatic." The wind slapped her, and she shivered. The cold burned across her toes and up her ankles. The wet soaked her jeans. It had to be about ten degrees, maybe less with the wind. She wouldn't last long if she didn't find shelter.

"Anya? Last chance. Come meekly back here, and I'll let you warm up before we get started." He whistled a lonely tune. "There's nowhere to run, and you're only hurting yourself. We must do this my way."

What if she drew him out and then ran back inside? Had there been a lock on the door? Would a lock keep that asshole out? Probably not. A slap of water against a dock caught her attention, and she partially turned. Behind the cabin, there was a lake? She had to get to the water. Maybe there would be a boat or raft stored somewhere nearby.

God, she didn't want to die.

She must've broadcast her intention, because he suddenly launched into motion.

Shrieking, she turned and ran for the dark lake, kicking snow on her way. She tripped over some ice and went flying, tucking her body tight. She landed on hard ground, rolled, and desperately grabbed a huge branch that had dropped from a pine tree. Turning, she swung without even looking.

The branch hit Daniel right across the stomach, and he stopped cold, doubling over with a pained *oof*. Panicking, she slammed it down on his head and then kicked him as hard as she could in the balls. He squealed.

Run. Run. Run. Still holding the branch, she started crying as she ran through ice and snow toward the sinister lake. The storm threw wild whitecaps up into the air, tossing water in every direction. Sleet and snow smashed into her numb face. Her feet kept moving, but she couldn't feel them any longer.

He grunted and swore behind her, but she didn't turn to look.

The reeds and grass got taller, all covered in ice. She tried to shove through them and reached the lake. No dock. Panting, she looked in other directions. Just trees, mountains, and maybe a couple of darkened cabins?

She had to get out of the cold. Bunching her legs, she started to sprint into a run just as strong arms banded around her waist. She yelled and kicked out.

Daniel tackled her to the ground, face first.

She hit snow, and her forehead bounced against a rock. Stars exploded across her vision. She screamed, her head pounding and the world spinning.

He flipped her around and sat on her, slapping a hand over her mouth.

She punched out and struggled on the freezing ground, trying to dislodge him. Tears clogged her throat. He pushed so hard against her mouth that her head ground against the frozen dirt beneath the ice.

Pain fired along her jaw.

He tilted the angle of his hand, cutting off air to both her nose and mouth. "Nice hit with the board," he hissed, his hold absolute.

She clawed at his arm desperately, her lungs swelling in pain. Air. She needed air. Her legs kicked out uselessly.

"I knew you'd be a fighter." He wiped blood off his nose, his body almost relaxing. "You don't know the training I have. But it was a good effort." He squeezed harder. "Now we do things the hard way. Just the way I like it."

Darkness swirled across her vision. She needed to breathe. God. More darkness. Her body went limp. Helplessness forced a sob from her throat. She stopped feeling the cold.

"There we go." Daniel released her and stood, bending to lift her against his chest.

She tried to fight him, but her body hung limply in place. "Don't," she said weakly.

"Too late. I've known it would take time to earn your love. You have such a pretty voice." He laughed and carried her along the cabin toward the front door. "I bet you can really scream."

CHAPTER
40

Heath slammed the clip into his gun as Denver typed furiously on the keyboard. It had taken precious time to make the alterations to the antenna, and he could feel Anya slipping away from him. With every minute, he could sense his future becoming bleak. Why hadn't he figured out his feelings and put them into words for her?

Maybe there weren't words for how he was feeling. God. He was fucking losing it. Now he knew what the caged tigers at the zoo really felt like.

Ryker worked on another computer, and Zara was busy taping maps to a whiteboard. She started circling rural areas that held only a couple of structures, much like the ones Daniel had used in other states. There were too many circles already. They'd never have time to check them all.

"We need more to go on," Heath muttered, scraping a hand through his hair. "There has to be a way to find her." Maybe he should call Shane again to get more intel on Daniel, although his brother had told him everything he knew. Nobody had known that Daniel was a serial killer. Heath noted that Shane hadn't seemed all that surprised, however.

"Radio's ready," Denver finally said, even more quietly than usual.

Heath instantly sat and put the earphones over his head. Concentrate. He needed to focus and do the job. Shane had sent him the buzzing frequency of the tracking bug Isobel Madison had used before, and he'd listened to it for a good fifteen minutes. If he heard it again, he'd know it. So he started twisting dials and focusing on sounds.

Shane and the rest of the Gray brothers were hacking into satellites to see if they could track Daniel's movements, but the storm was making things difficult. Their ultimate goal was to track Daniel back to Isobel Madison so they could destroy any lab she'd created. But now was about Anya.

Just thinking her name made Heath's chest compress. What if he didn't find her in time? If this was love, it fucking sliced through a guy like a blade.

Ten minutes went by.

Then another twenty.

The frequencies started melding together, and he had to dig deep and remember the sound of the right one. She was waiting for him to save her and, damn it, he would. Somehow. God, he had to find her. If he didn't, he was done.

Ryker shoved away from his desk, lines cutting into the sides of his mouth. His hair was a disheveled mess, and whiskers covered his jaw. His eyes were bloodshot like he hadn't slept in far too long. "He disabled all the cameras in the neighborhood days before he planted the bombs. He's good."

"What about farther out?" Heath asked, hearing over the earphones. "There are several banks just three blocks away. He didn't appear out of nowhere." Anybody could be traced—with enough time. They didn't have time. But there had to be a way to find Daniel. The guy wasn't invincible. Heath's solar plexus pounded like he'd been punched with a brick. Anya. Where was she?

Ryker shook his head. "So far, I haven't found a thing on any of the cameras even close to our headquarters. My guess is he used back alleys and dark areas to get her out of town. He definitely knows how to stay under the radar."

If Isobel Madison hadn't tagged Daniel like a dog, then they'd never find him. How ironic that Heath's only chance of finding Anya rested with Madison being even more evil than he'd known.

A knock sounded on the door, and he took out his gun, not pausing in listening to different frequencies.

Ryker waited a beat and then turned to open it.

Detective Malloy came inside, covered with snow and ice. "The FBI has put out a BOLO on you, Heath, because of the fake ID near Carl's body. I'm gonna have to take you in. We'll get this figured out, I promise."

Something buzzed through the headphones. Heath sat up, his heart kicking into gear. That was it. The right sound. Madison had tagged Daniel. She had actually done it. "Got it." Glancing toward the radio, he rattled off the frequency to Denver, who was looking at the cop grimly.

"Denver? Get me the location," Heath said. He tossed the earphones to the side and stood, the need to run out the door and find his woman nearly making him insane. "Malloy? I'll meet you anywhere and anytime tomorrow. Got something to do tonight." He was so fucking close. Was she still alive? She had to be. There was no alternative.

Malloy winced. "I promised the FBI I'd bring you in to keep them from setting up roadblocks and plastering your face all over the television. I'm helping you out here." He put his hands into his trench coat pockets. "This was the only thing I could think of to help you for now. You have to come with me."

There wasn't time for this shit. "I don't want to shoot you, Detective." Heath glanced toward the shaded window. If Malloy had brought backup, they'd be already in position outside. He didn't have time for a shoot-out.

Denver started typing, his head close to the keyboard. "Got it," he muttered. "Found the asshole."

"Give me the address," Heath said, his body gearing up to run. He turned to Malloy. "I'm not going anywhere with you." His gun lay heavy in his hand. He couldn't shoot the cop, but he could knock the guy out.

Malloy shook his head. "There's no other option here, boys."

Denver shoved to his feet.

Heath noted belatedly that his brother's face had lost all color. "Denver?"

"I'll go in Heath's place and be arrested," Denver said. "Explain the mix-up later." He grabbed the desk and curled his fingers over it.

Ryker paused. "Den?"

"I'm fine." Denver wavered. Then he crashed to the floor, taking his keyboard with him. It clattered across the wood, several keys falling out to bounce away.

Zara rushed to him and slid to her knees. Her dark hair tumbled out if its clip. "Denver? What's wrong?" She patted his hand and then his face.

He was out cold.

Heath moved past Malloy to crouch and feel Denver's pulse at his neck. Weak but there. The scent of blood caught his attention. What the hell? He tugged up Denver's dark T-shirt. It was soaking wet. "Oh God." He pushed the shirt up more to see a festering wound below Denver's right pec. His stitches had popped wide open, and he was losing too much blood. "Call a bus, Malloy," Heath ordered curtly.

Malloy bent over and then whistled. "Got it." He moved to the side and yanked out a cell phone.

Ryker caught Heath's eye and then jerked his head toward Denver's console.

Heath's breath stopped. Indecision slammed through him. He couldn't leave Denver. Why hadn't the man said something? Because of Anya. Denver had ignored his pain to find Anya, working until he'd literally passed out cold. Now, that was a brother. One he loved and would die for. In an instant.

Heath dropped his chin to his chest. The world tore him in two.

"Get the girl," Ryker mouthed, tugging off his shirt. He pressed the worn material against Denver's wound. "We'll take care of Denver."

Heath's hands shook, but he stood and glanced at Denver's console. The address came up as 2121 Forsaken Lake Road. He faltered.

Ryker took Zara's hand and pushed it against the wound. Then he waited, his gaze on Heath. "Go," he mouthed again.

Heath took a deep breath. Then he pressed a button near the screen, and the screen went black.

"Now," Ryker whispered.

Zara held tight to Denver while Ryker leaped for the cop and took him down. Malloy shouted in warning, but Ryker slammed a fist into the cop's jaw.

Heath jumped over them both and ran through the kitchen and into the garage, his movements still a little shaky from his injuries. He yanked up the garage door. The car's crappy engine took two tries to turn over, and then he was speeding out of the small neighborhood and west. Nobody shot at him, so perhaps Malloy hadn't brought backup.

Man, he hoped the cop was all right and in a forgiving mood. If he arrested Ryker, everything would go to shit even worse.

If that were possible.

Grabbing his phone, Heath typed the address into his GPS with one hand. Shit. He was almost an hour away.

He quickly made a prayer to a God he wasn't sure about to save

Anya. She was good and kind and should be saved. He discarded thoughts about the other victims and how they were good, too. If God didn't save those women, why would he save Anya?

Heath's foot pressed harder on the gas pedal, and he slid through two intersections before he calmed himself down. He had one gun and one crappy car for this fight, but there hadn't been time to suit up with the cop there. Sirens trilled through the storm, and an ambulance passed him, followed by several patrol cars, heading for the blue house. Would Malloy turn him in?

He had to get to her. Now.

CHAPTER
41

The feeling came back into Anya's extremities with a rush of needlelike pain. She gasped while sitting on the couch, tears falling down her face.

Daniel stood near the fireplace in the cabin, watching her. "Hurts, huh?"

She tried to glare at him as her body thawed. "I'm going to rip you apart."

"Interesting." He crossed arms over his soaking-wet shirt. Apparently the cold didn't bother him. "They usually beg to live right about now. Promise me anything I want if I'll let them go."

"Oh, I promise you I'll see you dead," she spat, her body shuddering. Her toes felt like flames licked at them. Did she have frostbite?

"I wonder how long it'll take for you to beg." Red slid into his face, and his lips pursed. "I'm really looking forward to our life together." Almost casually, he leaned down and pulled up his pant leg to remove a wicked-looking knife. "You're going to pay for not seeing the real me."

Part of his game was to make her squirm, and she knew it. So she faced him as bravely as she could, unwilling to give him any satisfaction. "Fuck you, loser."

He threw back his head and laughed. "Your sister said the exact same thing to me."

Anya doubled over as if she'd been kicked in the stomach. Her poor sister. And Loretta had been seriously trained. How could Anya survive if Loretta hadn't?

Heath's face swam across her vision. Strong and handsome, he had given her himself. She knew he would come for her. All she had to do was stay alive until he found her. If she could get the knife from Daniel, she'd stab him right through the eye and go looking for Heath. Maybe he was still in the hospital. He had to be all right. He just had to be.

She shook her head to focus her thoughts when everything was so jumbled up inside her. "I don't suppose you'd believe I'm not a real redhead?" she asked grimly.

"Neither was your sister." Daniel shrugged. "It isn't that important to me. You're the woman for me. Maybe I'll tear your hair out to prove it."

"You're sick," Anya said, shoving to her feet. Pain prickled up her legs, and she winced. "You're a psychopath with delusions. A simple, run-of-the-mill serial killer." She eyed the distance between them. His balls had to still smart from when she'd kicked him. The idea of using her foot again made her want to cry harder, but she'd do it. If she could nail him, she could go for the knife.

Running for the door again held little appeal. But she'd take any opportunity.

Daniel sprang for her before she could move. Grabbing her hair, he jerked her forward and pressed the knife to her throat. "Don't even think of kicking me again."

She struggled against him, frustration welling up in her. At some point, he'd have to lower the knife. "Shouldn't I be getting a burlap sack by now?" she hissed, fury all but consuming her.

"You don't get to die," he said, sliding the knife down her neck.

She held perfectly still and tried to focus through the terror. Her mind tried to push her to fight what was happening. No. This was happening. A crazy man held a knife to her throat. She'd get an opening. Somehow.

He grabbed her breast again and squeezed. Pain detonated in her chest.

She screamed, long and loud, her instincts kicking in.

He laughed and tightened his hold.

The door burst open behind her. Taking advantage of it, she shot her knee up into his groin. He shifted at the last second, and her knee collided with his thigh. Without missing a beat, he turned her around, the knife still at her jugular.

She expected to see Heath.

Instead, a fit man wearing all black stomped into the room, brushing snow from his jacket. He had almost white hair, vibrant blue eyes, and a gun pointed at them.

"Who are you?" Anya croaked.

A woman followed the man, this one in her late forties or early fifties. Snow melted across her black hair, and she was dressed in nice pants, designer boots, and a fur coat. "Daniel, you didn't mention you had a hobby last time we spoke." Her voice was cultured and smooth.

Anya struggled in Daniel's hold, but he didn't relent. The night took on an almost surreal tinge. "I can see you all have things to chat about. I'll be on my way." Her voice came out hoarse.

Daniel sighed, his chest moving against her back. "How did you find me?"

"That's irrelevant. It's time to go home," the woman said.

The man kept looking at Anya. "You're Heath's." Satisfaction darkened his voice.

Anya shivered. "Nope. Not me. I'm just in the wrong place at the wrong time."

"You can say that again," the guy all but purred. "Daniel, buddy? Can I borrow your knife? I'd like to leave Heath a present."

Anya's legs went weak. She squinted. "Who are you?"

"Oh my, our manners." Sarcasm barely laced the woman's tone. "I'm Dr. Isobel Madison, and this is Sheriff Elton Cobb. Perhaps you've heard of us?"

A renewed panic washed through Anya. "No, sorry. Should I have?"

Isobel smiled, revealing perfect white teeth. "You're a terrible liar, dear." She clapped her rabbit-fur gloves together. "This is so good. If Heath confided his past to you, then he must truly care about you."

Anya tried to calculate a way out of this mess and came up with only one possibility. "Well, he did, and then Daniel came and found me. It has taken time, but I do think we might be soul mates. If you'd leave, we could continue getting to know each other."

Daniel stiffened behind her, but his hold didn't relent. "I need the night, Isobel."

Cobb pointed the gun at Daniel's head. "I want the knife and the girl. This one is my plaything, asshole."

Daniel pressed the blade into her flesh, and she shoved back against him. Her neck hurt, and blood started to drip down to her collarbone. "She's mine," he snapped.

Isobel rolled her eyes. "There are tons of redheads out there, and I'll help you find some. Let Elton have this one."

Anya coughed. "Who are you people?" she whispered. They were calmly discussing her torture and death as if she didn't matter in the slightest. "No wonder Heath hates you."

Daniel smelled her hair. "Heath was corrupted by being taking away from us. From the family. His mama was a stupid whore who stole him. Right, Isobel?"

"Actually, Heath's mother was a lab technician with a very high

IQ," Isobel said thoughtfully. "Ungrateful bitch, however. Escaped us with Heath and went on the run."

"I thought she was a junkie." Anya was willing to talk about anything but her imminent death.

"I heard that as well," Isobel said, eyeing both men. "She probably started using because of the stress of running from us. Trusted the wrong men, and one finally killed her. Of course, that's how I found Heath again and put him in the boys home."

Anya tested Daniel's hold, and it was firm. "Any idea what happened to that guy?" she asked.

"We engineered a car accident. Couldn't have him looking for Heath," Isobel said.

"What about Daniel?" Anya asked quietly. "Who was his mother?"

Isobel's smile widened. "Aren't you cute, trying to distract all of us."

Anya leaned back against Daniel and tried to stop shaking. Could she somehow convey trust to him? It'd be easier to manipulate him than the other two. "Don't you want to know who your biological parents were, Daniel?" she asked, very aware of the gun pointed just above her head.

"Not really," he said. "Though the commander was my father, I believe."

Darn it. "Fine. Then who is Heath's father?" She'd keep them talking all night if she could.

Isobel tugged off her gloves. "A soldier who died long ago, I assure you." She gently placed her gloves into a pocket of her mink coat and then drew a small pistol from the other pocket. "We need a decision here, boys."

"Give me the night, please." Daniel's voice rose in pitch. "I need the night with her. Just one." He held Anya's waist so tightly she couldn't breathe.

Oh, he had no intention of having just one night. But if they believed him, then maybe they'd leave and Anya could get free. "I agree, Daniel," she said softly. "Let's get rid of them."

Isobel turned toward Cobb. "We could let Daniel have the night, and then you could get a turn."

Anya sucked in air, her eyes widening. "You're a monster," she breathed.

Isobel lifted a small shoulder. "I've been called worse. You just don't matter. Elton?"

Cobb shook his head. "Daniel will probably kill her. I want the pleasure."

"What about using her to draw Heath and his brothers in?" Isobel asked, her hand steady on the gun. "I'm sorry to find Heath not here already, Daniel."

Daniel's chest heaved behind Anya. "You don't understand. I *have* to take the night with her. There's no other option. Afterward, I'll bring Heath, Denver, and Ryker to you. I promise. Give me this— since she's mine. Then I'll do whatever you want."

Cobb snorted. "You haven't succeeded in bringing those boys back yet. Why should we trust you now?"

"I *need* this," Daniel hissed. "She's my soul mate, and I have to make her mine. Have to hear her scream my name."

Blood dripped from Anya's neck to dot her white blouse. "Looks like a stalemate," she said. "Daniel? I want to stay here with you. Make them go away. Give me another chance. Please?"

He grabbed her hair and jerked her up onto her toes. The knife scraped against her skin. "I agree."

Isobel studied him for a moment. "Well, I think the redhead is correct. We're at a stalemate." She waved her gun toward Anya and stepped farther into the cabin. "One of you men needs to give in gracefully, or you need to fight it out. Either way, this is getting tiresome."

Cobb's lips peeled back. "Oh, I'd love to fight it out."

Daniel chuckled. "As would I. Isobel? Do I have your word you'll cover Anya?"

"Absolutely." Isobel pointed toward the handcuffs on the counter. "Just cuff her first."

Daniel's body moved against Anya's, and the knife finally left her throat. The wind burst out of her lungs. Okay. She took several deep breaths. He slapped a cuff around her left wrist and dragged her over to the sofa, where he fastened the other cuff to a ring set into the wall. "The rings will come in handy later," he said against her ear. "I'll be quick in killing him. You can always count on me."

She shuddered.

Isobel strode over to sit on the opposite end of the couch and pointed her gun at Anya's chest. "Make it speedy, gentlemen. Good luck to you both."

Cobb shoved his gun into his waistband. Before he had finished, Daniel was on him, propelling him outside in a harsh tackle.

"Makes sense," Anya said, her mind fuzzing. "Daniel doesn't feel the cold."

"None of my boys do," Isobel said, glancing at a diamond-encrusted watch on her left wrist. "What's it like to know you're going to die tonight?" she asked, her eyes gleaming.

Anya glared. "Excuse me?"

"I'm a scientist, dear. Curious about everything. So?" Isobel's gaze ran over Anya's body. "Answer me, or I'll shoot you in the foot."

Hatred burned hot through Anya. "I'm not planning on dying tonight."

"Oh. Denial. Interesting." Isobel lost the smile. "How is my Heath doing?"

"He's not yours, lady." Anya measured the distance between them. With her arm extended over the side of the sofa and attached to the wall, her other arm wasn't long enough to go for the gun. "In fact, none of them are yours. Why are you trying to get them back so badly?"

"My work isn't finished." A man's howl of pain echoed through the storm, and Isobel turned to look toward the open doorway. "I wonder who will win."

"Maybe they'll kill each other," Anya said hopefully.

Isobel turned back toward her with a scowl on her flawless face. "Be polite."

"All right." It was now or never. Anya balanced herself on the couch with her good hand and swung as far as the restraints would let her, kicking Isobel in the face. Anya's foot connected with Isobel's jaw, and then she brought her ankle down on the gun. It flew to the floor, spinning around and around.

Isobel screamed and leaped for the weapon.

Anya kicked her again, sending the woman crashing over the other side of the couch. Grunting, Anya dropped to the floor and reached for the gun. Her shoulder protested, but she ignored the pain. Her fingers closed over the weapon, and she drew back just as Isobel jumped for her.

Anya fired.

The bullet hit the doctor in the shoulder, and she fell toward the fireplace. Oh God. Anya pointed the gun at the cuff and turned her head before pulling the trigger.

The bullet hit metal with a sharp ping, and she fell away from the wall.

"What the hell?" Sheriff Cobb's big body blocked the doorway.

Almost sobbing, Anya pointed the gun and started shooting.

He bellowed and jumped out of the way as Daniel did the same.

Anya kept shooting and ran full bore for the doorway, clearing it and leaping from the porch. She partially turned and fired at both men, who stood on the porch and then ducked out of the way.

Her aching feet slapped ice and snow, but she turned and ran as hard as she could for the trees.

"Isobel!" She heard Sheriff Cobb yell, his boots stomping across the porch.

"Anya, wait!" Daniel bellowed.

Anya took a sharp left and then a right while the storm battled her. Somebody crashed through the forest behind her. She fought against snowy bushes, her movements panicked. She had to get out of there.

Daniel was coming.

Her feet froze, and her toes cracked. She halted, looking around. Where was the lake? She had to get back to the lake. The sound of water smashing into shore competed with the storm.

Too much sound swirled around her. She could no longer hear him coming. God. Where was he?

She turned toward the sound of the lake and barreled around a pine tree—right into strong male arms. Bouncing off a hard chest, she opened her mouth and shrieked.

CHAPTER
42

Heath grabbed on to Anya's arms before she could fall.

Her eyes widened. "Heath?" Sobbing, she rushed back into his arms.

In that second, his entire world settled. He breathed out. Snow and sleet pelted all around them, and the wind whipped the world into a frenzy. Yet he wanted to shout for joy. He'd had to circle around to catch her before Daniel did, but now he had her, and he was never letting go. His hands shook, and he probably held her too tightly. She was so fucking small. Her strawberry-like smell soothed him, and he calmed down. The snow reflected around them, and he could see her clearly. "Are you all right?"

She lifted her head, tears sliding down her pale face. Her eyes were a tumultuous green, and her pupils were wide open. Fright and shock filled her face. Even her lips were blue. "I shot Isobel Madison."

"I know." He hurried out of his coat and put it around her, helping her into the sleeves. He had to get her warm, and now. "I was outside getting ready to come in, and all hell broke loose. We have to run, baby." There wasn't time to take off his boots and give her his socks. So he lifted her up. She felt like a block of ice. "Hold on."

A force plowed into his shoulders, and he went flying. At the last second, he turned in the air and tucked his body around Anya's. He landed on his back and slid several feet, his head thunking against the rough trunk of a tree. Branches swayed and dropped snow and ice on him. He coughed. Pain attacked his eyeballs, and his stomach roiled.

Anya scrambled off him, a gun in her hand. Snow scattered from her. "Stop," she said, using both hands and settling her stance.

Heath shook off dizziness and stood, swaying. Pain still filled his body from the bombing earlier, and he had to concentrate to force it away. To not feel his nerves. The figure moving toward them was a haze and then took shape. "You must be Daniel."

The man strode through the trees, seemingly not bothered by the cold. His nose looked broken, and lacerations covered his jaw from his brief fight with Cobb. Heath had almost lost his lunch when he'd seen Cobb walk out of the cabin. Then the two men had started fighting, so he'd angled around to the kitchen window, planning to get inside for Anya, his nightmares doubling when he'd seen Isobel Madison again. Then Anya had shot her and run out the front door.

Daniel kept coming. His smile revealed bloodstained teeth. "You're mine, Anya. Time to go." His deep voice cut through the storm.

Anya paused for a second, her hair blowing wildly. "Fuck you, asshole," she yelled, pulling the trigger.

Nothing happened. Ah shit.

Daniel grinned. "I counted the shots. You're out."

She shook the gun out and then tried again. Panic spread over her wet face, and she gave a slight whimper.

The sound centered Heath. He had to concentrate and do this right. Anya was all that mattered. He reached for his gun in the back of his waist. "I have bull—"

Daniel leaped for him in a fast tackle, hitting Heath in the gut and sending them both crashing through trees. Fuck. Heath had forgotten other people could move as fast as he could.

His shoulders hit the ground first, followed by the rest of him. His gun went spinning through the snow and into a bunch of dead bushes, and his vertebrae compressed and then relaxed. He stopped breathing for a minute.

Daniel smiled. "Anya is mine."

Heath lost it. He clapped both hands to Daniel's ears and manacled his leg around Daniel's neck. Daniel punched Heath in the throat. Heath moved his neck enough to keep it from getting broken, but agony still rushed down his spine.

Daniel back-flipped off him, sliding in the snow and then gaining his balance. He shook out his hands, anticipation lighting his face.

Heath stood and wiped blood off his temple. Then he launched into motion, reaching the asshole and plowing a fist into his cheekbone. Daniel's head jerked back, and he retaliated with a front kick to the gut. Heath bent over, pivoted, and shot a side kick up into Daniel's jaw. All the hours of worrying, and all the pain the bastard had caused. "I'll kill you."

Daniel laughed, the sound high-pitched through the wind. "That's my job." He attacked with a series of punch-kick combinations that had Heath seeing stars and spitting blood. Everything from his jaw to his knees protested and wanted to give out. Pain centered in his gut and spread in every direction.

"Heath!" Anya screamed.

Anya. Heath shoved the pain away like he'd learned to do as a child at the boys home. No pain. Just think. Yeah. Ryker had taught him that.

Heath set his stance and focused. "Let's do this, dickhead."

Daniel smiled and whipped a double-edged blade from his ankle. "You've got it. When I'm done with you, I'm taking my time with Anya."

A helicopter rose high into the air, lights blinking through the murk. It turned and sped quickly away, over the lake and surrounding mountains.

Heath snorted. "Your ride just left."

Daniel angled to the side, the knife in his right hand and pointed for a fast strike. "Wasn't my ride. I'm sure the good sheriff is getting Isobel to a doctor." He cut a look to the side at Anya. "You shot her, and you will pay for that."

"I hope she dies," Anya spat, edging behind Heath.

Daniel shook his head, and snow went flying. "It was a shoulder shot. She'll live, but she isn't going to appreciate the scar. I assume she'll take it out on your brothers when I fetch them for her, Heath."

"Not me?" Heath asked, watching the smooth movements of the man and waiting for an opening.

"You're going to be dead," Daniel said easily. "But I do like giving people a choice. Leave right now, and I won't kill you. Anya and I have a date to finish."

The man was crazy-town. "I'll pass," Heath said, stepping closer.

Daniel held the knife like he knew how to use it. "I was hoping you'd say that," he said.

Heath angled more to the side to protect Anya. There was only one way this could go, so he settled into a mental place of action and no thought. It was too late to consider alternatives here. "I had a nice talk with Cinnamon while we were looking for you," he said conversationally.

Daniel stilled. "Excuse me?"

"The whore who trained you? I tracked her down." Heath set his stance. Good thing Shane had told him everything.

Daniel's voice hitched. "You did not."

"Sure, I did. She's living back East, still screwing for money. She told me you could rarely get it up, and she'd have to slap you around to turn you on." Heath made up the lie on the spot.

"That's not true," Daniel spat.

Heath eyed the man's legs. He could take out Daniel's knees. But the knife was key. He had to get that fucking knife. "Sure, it is. When I told her you were the Copper Killer, she laughed her ass off. Said you probably had to tie them up to get them interested in you. Also said you have a small dick."

"You bastard!" Daniel roared, running with the knife.

Heath pivoted, shot an elbow into Daniel's broken nose, and smoothly took the knife. Flipping it around in his hand, he kicked Daniel in the back of the knee. Daniel dropped, partially turning. Grabbing his hair, Heath sliced the knife across his neck, cutting as deeply as he could.

Blood arced as Daniel gurgled. His arms dropped to his sides. He pitched forward, his head hit the snow, and his feet flopped back. The snow all around him turned a deep red.

"Heath!" Anya rushed into his arms, tears falling down her face.

He dropped the knife and held her with one arm, tucking her close. "It's okay, baby," he whispered into her wet hair. "You're all right." Slowly, he moved her away so he could see her face. "How hurt are you?" He had to know. "Whatever it is, whatever you went through, we'll fix it together. I'll help you. I promise." The words rolled from his tongue and came from his heart.

She shuddered. "I'm fine." Her eyes darkened as she looked at the dead man. "In fact, I think I hurt him more than he hurt me." Her lips trembled as she almost smiled. "Broke his nose, you know."

"I saw his nose—didn't know you'd done it, though." Heath held her to him again, not liking her trembling. "You did good."

She sniffled against his chest, her body moving from trembling to full-on shaking. "I may have a nightmare or two later on, though."

"Me too." Heath picked her up, and the snow tried to fight him. They'd comfort each other in the nights to come.

She settled and pressed her freezing face to his neck. "What now?"

"I'll get you to the cabin and warm. Then I need to bring Daniel here to his truck, where hopefully he has the Copper Killer stuff he used."

She looked up at the sky. "What about Cobb and Madison? Shouldn't we get out of here?"

"We will. We're safe from them, considering you shot Madison." His heart swelled. His woman was quite amazing, now, wasn't she? "I'm so proud of you, by the way. You really are a badass, you know?"

She kissed his neck. "We can talk later. Let's get out of the storm now."

"Good plan." He turned and started slogging back toward the cabin. He had a lot to do. "I promise I'll get us out of this, sweetheart." They reached the cabin in record time, and he put her right next to the fire. "Stay here and get warm. I'll go fetch Daniel's body."

She nodded, her face contorting in pain from the sudden warmth.

His chest ached, and he pulled Denver's phone from his back pocket to quickly dial.

"What?" Detective Malloy snapped.

"Malloy, it's Heath. How's my brother?"

"Where are you, dickhead?" Malloy roared. "I'm going to arrest you for sure."

Heath winced. "Seriously. Denver?"

"He's fine. Doc patched him up again, and then guess what? He and your other brother disappeared. Gone. Cleared out of the blue house within minutes." Malloy's voice rose even higher. "You're on your own. I can't keep the FBI off you now."

Heath rubbed his pounding jaw. "Sure you can. Congratulations. You just caught the Copper Killer. Call Special Agent Reese and share the collar with him." After giving directions to the cabin, Heath clicked off. He couldn't help but place a gentle kiss on Anya's forehead. "Warm up, sweetheart, and I'll be right back. Then we're gonna talk."

CHAPTER
43

Anya looked out at the expanse of Lake Coeur d'Alene in northern Idaho, her feet up on a hand-carved coffee table and her butt cupped by a plush sofa. After a good night's sleep, she wanted to keep on relaxing without any deep thoughts or concerns. Being with Heath felt right, but everything had been so emotional and scary, she didn't truly know where they stood. Well, she knew how she felt, but what about him?

If he still wanted to keep her at arm's length while he confronted his past, he was in for a fight. She'd fight *for* him and this life. After she relaxed for a day, for goodness' sake.

Though she was no longer the scared girl hiding her feelings and keeping people away. She wanted a family, and she wanted Heath Jones. Patience was her friend, and she'd take her time if he didn't see things her way. They would end up together. She needed him, and she was fairly certain he needed her, too. Period.

Heath strode in from the kitchen, gripping two steaming mugs. He handed one over. "How are your feet?"

"Better." She took the fragrant coffee and wiggled her toes in the thick socks. No frostbite for her. Although her entire body was sore from the last few days. "How many safe houses do you own, anyway?"

He took a drink of coffee and looked at the lake. "Just this one and one in South Dakota. We rent the rest only when we need them." He winced. "We've needed them a lot lately, and I don't see that changing for a while. We're always on the move."

She sighed. "Where is everyone?"

"Denver is sleeping and recovering from the last set of stitches, and Ryker took Zara for a hike around the lake." Heath sat next to her and stretched out his legs.

"Is Denver going to be all right?" She glanced at the clock. He was due another antibiotic in an hour.

"Yeah, he's tough. Sleep will help him more than anything else. Speaking of which, are you sure you don't want to take a nap?"

"I slept all night, Heath." After meeting Detective Malloy and handing over the body, they'd driven to this comfortable house and fallen into bed. Zara had cooked a delicious breakfast, and here they were. She'd told him about her conversation with Isobel Madison, and he'd been stoic the whole time. "Are you all right about your mother's killer being dead?"

He breathed out. "Yeah, although I wanted to kill him. I believe she told you the truth, but when I find her, I want the guy's real name, and I want to see his grave. I only knew him as Spyder. Asshole."

She nodded. "Sorry your soldier dad probably passed on, if she was to be believed."

"She had no reason to lie this time." He shrugged. "I made my own family, and I'm happy. It's time to forget that part of my past and move on."

Sounded like a good plan. "Have you heard from Malloy?"

"Yeah." Heath settled an arm around her and tugged her against his hard body. "With the evidence found in Daniel's truck—mainly burlap, tape, and pictures of other redheads—the FBI has agreed that he was the Copper Killer. Carl's watch was found as well, so the FBI figured out that Daniel set me up with the fake ID at the crime scene.

They're pinning it all on Daniel, rightfully, and they all look like heroes. The FBI has stopped their search for me."

She winced. "What about that fake ID? Your real picture is on it, right?"

Heath grinned, flashing a dimple. "Apparently my brother Shane has sticky fingers. He's dropping by and filching the ID, and then he's coming here to meet you."

She straightened. "To meet me? Why?" she breathed.

Heath set down his coffee and turned to face her. "Because I'm completely in love with you and don't plan on ever lettin' you go."

Her chest heated. "Heath." Could fantasies really come true?

He cupped her face. "I'm still on the run, and you know the whole story. I plan on taking the fight to Madison and Cobb soon. If you want to wait for me at the ranch in Montana, where you'll be very safe, I'm fine with that. But you and I are the future."

She swallowed, almost afraid to believe the words. He was everything she'd ever wanted, and he came with a family that was pretty amazing. While he wasn't exactly on the right side of the law, she knew her father would've liked him. "I want to stay with you."

His body settled. "I should let you know that we're about broke after this last op."

She chuckled. "Figures."

He smiled again. "Yeah. If we can get the vehicles back from Malloy, we'll be better off. I think he'll turn those over since we didn't steal them."

Never in her life had she figured she'd fall for a guy who stole vehicles and played around on the dark web. She wasn't sure even how to access the dark web and only knew about it from television shows. "Malloy likes you guys and will try to help. Speaking of law enforcement, Reese called when you were making coffee."

"Oh?" Heath said, gently playing with her hair.

"Yeah. Told me good luck and to be careful. Also said you weren't such a bad guy." Reese had actually sounded like he grudgingly respected Heath. "Then he told me he was going on a monthlong vacation somewhere warm. I wished him well." Reese and Loretta would've made a solid couple. Anya missed her sister, and especially missed what they could've had through life.

Heath's thumb swept across her jaw in a comforting touch as if he knew her thoughts. "If we have a girl someday, we could name her after your sister."

Anya jolted. Whoa. "We're having babies now?"

"Not now." He leaned over and kissed her head.

Her heart rolled over.

He gently slid the ring off her finger.

She frowned. "Wh—"

"Doin' it right." He took her mug and placed it on the table before sliding down onto one knee. "I'll love you forever, Anya Best. Marry me, and I promise I'll protect you with everything I have and everything I am. No matter what, I'm yours."

Tears pricked her eyes. "Yes."

His face lit up in a way she'd never seen as he slipped the ring onto her finger. It felt right this time.

"I love you, Heath."

He leaned in and kissed her, going deep and taking his time. Finally, he let her breathe. "That's all I ever wanted to hear." He kissed the ring on her finger. "You and me, Anya. Always."

EPILOGUE

Denver redirected the Internet search for any new facilities built in the Pacific Northwest, concentrating on power requirements. He didn't know when, and he wasn't sure how, but he was gonna find Madison and Cobb's new facility. When he did, he had a decision to make. Could he take them out on his own?

Upstairs his brothers slept with women they'd found and decided to love.

That was a good thing.

Well, it might be disastrous. But he'd do everything within his power to make sure it wasn't.

Forces were closing in on them, and he could feel his heart rate accelerate in response. It was time to take the fight to his enemies.

But what about his brothers?

He wiped a hand across his brow, not sure what to do. If he could take care of the problem on his own, he would. Yet he'd need a good plan. Even a great plan... and he wouldn't make it back. That was okay. If his brothers lived... that was okay.

At the thought, he breathed himself into a relaxed state. The basement computer center suited him, with its quiet hum and low light.

For years he'd belonged in quiet and darkness, and he was fine with that. Once, and only once, had he found the chance to find anything else. He'd given that up—he'd given her up. Noni Sweeten was smart, kind, and way too gentle for a life with him. He'd spent three amazing months with her, and he didn't regret a second.

Well, until he'd ended things and left her. That...he regretted. But he'd had no choice. No way could he allow Noni into his life and into the danger.

He didn't blame Ryker and Heath for making a different choice.

But they had pain ahead, and if there was a way for him to shield them from that, he'd do it in an instant.

So he had to come up with a plan.

The door to the basement opened, and heavy footsteps pounded down the stairs. Two sets.

He quickly switched screens.

"Why aren't you sleeping?" Ryker asked, his voice gruff. "It's past midnight."

Denver partially turned to see his oldest brother in faded sweatpants...with a gun tucked into his waist. "Can't."

Heath was right behind Ryker, his brown hair tousled, his greenish blue eyes clear, and a knife in one hand.

When would they be able to leave bed without a weapon? Denver sighed. "You guys should be sleeping." With their women. Ryker was already engaged, and Heath was close enough, considering he'd already purchased a ring for Anya. "Go back to bed."

Ryker rubbed the dark scruff across his jaw and prowled closer, one long line of menace. "Have you found anything?"

Denver wanted to lie—but didn't know how to do that to his brothers. "Maybe."

"What is it?" Heath asked, his hard chest bare in the dim light.

"I've been following the money trail—" Denver paused as an alarm beeped from one monitor. His head swiveled, and he turned toward it. "What the fuck?"

Another alarm blared. His chest heated, and his breath panted out. He quickly typed in a series of commands. "Google search on us...detailed. Shit." He typed even faster, bringing up a picture of...him.

"What the hell?" Ryker leaned over his shoulder. "Denver?"

Denver stopped breathing. The picture was one of he and Noni over a year ago with the Portage Glacier in the background. He had been smiling, and he had his arm around her. The wind had tousled her long black hair, and her even darker eyes had sparkled with fun. "Noni," he breathed.

Heath pushed closer to him. "I thought you destroyed all pictures of your time in Alaska."

"I did." Yet he obviously had not. He clicked on the link to read:

"Denver: I need you and your detective agency. We're in trouble. Here's my updated schedule and where you can find me. Noni."

He stopped breathing completely. "Oh God." The woman had given her entire itinerary. Anybody looking for him, in any capacity on the Net, even the dark web, would find her instantly.

"What the holy hell is she doing?" Ryker snapped.

Denver shook his head. "I don't know." A fist dropped into his gut.

Heath leaned over to type in a series of commands. "She should be in Idaho tonight. Denver. Anybody looking for us, anybody with an iota of facial recognition, will see this. Madison and Cobb probably already have it."

Denver leaped from the chair as fury heated through him. "I have to go." He only had hours, but he had to get to Noni before his enemies did.

If not, she was dead.

Dear Reader,

When asked about extra content for the print edition of *Lethal Lies,* I thought instantly of the original first chapter. I often rewrite the beginning of a book after reaching the end, and this book was no exception. You'll see some similarities, but I basically rewrote the chapter because this beginning had ended up a little too slow. Having Heath watch the action through a camera isn't nearly as interesting as having him instantly in the scene being a tough guy. Also, Anya originally was a bookkeeper fleeing a bad relationship. She changed through the writing of the book to a criminal psychologist (which makes more sense in the plot and with her involvement in the case), but she's still leaving a bad relationship. Finally, in this first draft, Anya and her sister don't know each other very well. In the finished book, they know each other better.

I also deleted the second draft of chapters 1 and 2. Keep an eye on my newsletter and my FB page for how to get your hands on those once the book is released. You can find links for both at my website: www.RebeccaZanetti.com.

I hope you like the deleted content.

XO

Rebecca

LETHAL LIES
ORIGINAL CHAPTER 1

Present day

A flash of red caught Heath's eye as he was about to shut down the computer. He sat back down and squinted at the center monitor on the makeshift desk. Damn it. His instincts humming, he maneuvered the jewelry store camera he'd hacked until the red bloomed into shimmering highlights beneath the weakened sun. Son of a bitch. What the hell was she doing there?

He rapidly tapped keys to scan the street with a multitude of cameras—some he'd hacked and others he'd planted. "Anya," he muttered, shaking his head.

She drew a black wool coat tighter around her slender figure, stopping directly in front of the door to his former, short-lived detective agency. Drawing a card from her pocket, she read it and glanced at the now-scraped-clean window. Her shoulders hunched, and a winter wind lifted her hair.

"Go away, Anya," Heath whispered to the computer monitor, his body tensing.

She frowned and looked around the quiet street before pressing her face to the glass and cupping her eyes.

"It's empty." Heath punched up the camera feed from above the door, which he hadn't wanted to use, just in case others were surveying the area. It'd let out a signal they'd find at some point. But now he had no choice.

She backed away from the window and read the card again.

Heath zoomed in on her face. Delicate bone structure, green eyes, pale skin, and dark red hair. Oh yeah. And a black eye and bruises down her neck. They had faded since he'd last seen her—the only time he'd ever met her—but they were still visible.

Seeing them again pricked his temper just like last time.

A black sedan pulled to the curb, and two men jumped out, spraying snow.

Fuck. He'd known they were still watching the building. Heath reached for a Glock on the desk and tucked it into his waistband. He was three blocks down from the detective agency and could be downstairs in minutes.

If necessary.

He turned up the volume on the camera.

"Can I help you, miss?" The first guy had brown eyes and wavy dark hair. His smile was charming, and he walked like he could handle himself. A jacket covered his large frame, and a slight bulge showed at his waist.

Anya turned and took a step backward. "Um, I'm looking for the detective agency that was here last week." Her voice was low and tentative.

The guy looked at the blank window. "I think they moved."

She nodded, her gaze darting down the street. "The inside is empty."

The other man, a shorter black guy with adult acne, gave her a frown. "Do you know the detectives?"

She shook her head, her eyes wide. "Not really. But I heard they were well trained, and I need a detective."

The first guy smiled again, seeming to relax back against his car while motioning his buddy to cool it. The guy was good. "I've heard excellent things about them, too. Who did you talk to about them?"

Anya frowned as if knowing something wasn't quite right but unsure what. "Who are you?" Her chin lifted.

"Oh, I'm sorry." The guy laughed and dug out a badge holder to flip open. "U.S. Marshal D. J. Smithers. We're trying to find the detectives in connection with a current case."

Anya's eyes widened. "I hadn't known they worked with the FBI. I'm so glad. Do you have any idea where they've gone? Why they've left?"

Fuck. Heath groaned. The badge was a good one, but even through the camera he could see it was fake. Anya's sister was FBI Special Agent Loretta Jackson, and she'd been kidnapped by a serial killer nearly five days ago.

Smithers didn't miss a beat. "No, we don't. In fact, we're concerned about them. It looks like they've gotten caught up in a dangerous case with Colombian drug cartels, and we're concerned for their safety."

Colombian drug cartels? Seriously? Who the hell was this guy? Heath groaned and fought the urge to palm-smack his own head.

Anya rushed for him, waving the card. "I need to find them as soon as possible. I'll give you my information, and if you find them, please let me know."

Smithers handed over his badge. "Do you remember the name of their agency or any of the detectives?"

Anya glanced at his badge and then handed it back. "Um, no. Sorry about that. I met one of them, but I don't remember his name."

Heath winced. Guess he hadn't been that memorable. Of course, he'd only exchanged pleasantries with her before sitting down with Agent Jackson and exchanging information. Anya was supposed to be in protective custody by now, but with her sister taken, maybe that plan had been scrapped?

Smithers reached into his back pocket for a pen and handed it over with the card. "Write down your name and cell phone number." His tone was perfectly authoritative and polite.

Who was this guy?

Anya nodded and quickly wrote before handing back the card.

Smithers tucked it into his pocket. "We're investigating at the moment but would like to sit down with you later. Where are you staying?"

"At the Two Horse Motel just for the night," Anya said.

Heath gave in to the desire and smacked his hand against his forehead. Of course the woman had no idea she was dealing with trained killers, and one did have a badge, but even so. Though she must be desperate to find her sister.

"Okay," Smithers said. "Can we offer any assistance with your case? We're happy to help."

She faltered. "Maybe. How about we talk about it when we sit down? I'll get my files in order."

"Sounds good. We'll be in touch later today." With a reassuring nod, he moved back toward the car and the two men quickly drove away.

Heath sighed. Why hadn't she mentioned the FBI or her missing sister? Perhaps Anya had sensed something wrong with the guys, since they definitely weren't with any government. Today, anyway. They'd do a background run on Anya and then decide what to do with her—or come up with a plan to nab her. He couldn't take the chance they'd want to question her more about the guy she couldn't remember, considering it was him.

He glanced around the abandoned office he'd been using for a few days to see who came to check out his and his brothers' former business. Surveillance photos and videos lined the table, and he quickly scooped them up. There wasn't anything else for him to do in Cisco, and it was time to get the hell out of town.

After he picked up Anya.

* * *

Anya paced the counter of the car rental facility and tapped her paperwork against her leg. Why the hell was it taking so long? The blond kid behind the counter hummed while he typed happily on a keyboard.

There wasn't time for humming. Those fake marshals would've noticed her rental car decal, and she had to get rid of the car. She looked through the thick glass doors to the quiet car lot outside. Dark clouds barreled across the sky, and sleet slashed down. So much for the meager sunshine of earlier.

"All righty." The kid shoved glasses up his nose and smiled. "You're all set, and I waived the fuel fee."

"Thank you." She shoved the papers into her purse. Her phone buzzed, and she took it out to read the screen. Another message from her sister's partner, Special Agent Frederick Reese. The guy hadn't stopped calling since she'd headed out on her own the night before. She ignored him again and glanced up at the blond. "When will the airport shuttle arrive?"

The kid's Adam's apple bobbed. "Every hour. So it should be here in about fifteen minutes."

"Thanks." She forced a smile for him and then hurried for the door. "I'll wait by the sign."

"Sure thing." The worker followed her outside and locked the door behind her. "We close at five, and you were our only return today." He gave her a nod and strode around the building, minutes later roaring out of the lot in a lifted Ford with flames down the sides.

She grinned. Not in a million years had she pictured the guy wearing khakis and a button-down in such a flamboyant truck. Clearing her throat, she leaned back against the building, allowing the awning to protect her from the storm.

A heartbeat later, her stomach dropped as a familiar dark sedan pulled into the lot. Her legs tensed to run, but Marshal Smithers waved from the driver's seat.

She faked another smile, trapped in place. Her stomach rolled over.

An engine rumbled in the distance, and a battered Chevy truck careened across the lot, smashing hard into the sedan.

The sedan collided with several cars, and metal crumpled with a loud crunch.

The truck swung around, and the passenger door was thrown open. "Get in," bellowed a low voice.

She blinked at seeing Heath Jones, the detective from Lost Bastards. Her knees wobbled. D. J. Smithers jumped out of the totaled car, a gun in his hand. Her instincts told her she had about two seconds, so she yelped and ran across the snow, leaped through the passenger side of the truck, and slammed the door.

Heath punched the gas, and the truck fishtailed as it roared out of the lot.

Bullets struck the side of the truck with an odd pattering sound.

"Get down." Heath grabbed her neck and shoved her down, sliding down in the seat, too, but not losing any speed. His hand was rough and his voice tense, but he didn't hurt her.

She blinked, her heart thundering. The glove box slammed open, and a gun dropped onto her knee. She grabbed it and held on tight.

The truck fishtailed around a corner and then several more. Finally, Heath released her neck. "Are you okay?"

She nodded and straightened up on the bench seat. Her ribs hurt from the rapid beating of her heart. "How?" She looked out the back window at an empty and snowy road.

Heath glanced her way. "How what?"

She swallowed and surveyed him. At least six foot four, tightly muscled, definitely strong and fast. Light brown hair waved over his collar, and his greenish brown eyes pierced right through her. While the fake marshals had been shooting guns, there was no doubt this guy was twice as dangerous. What had she done, jumping into his truck? "Um." She fumbled for the door handle.

"I'm driving too fast for you to jump out." He kept his broad hands on the steering wheel.

She blinked, and her shoulders trembled. "Why are you here?" she breathed.

His frown drew down his dark eyebrows. "Me? Why the hell are you here?"

Okay. So he wasn't happy to see her. "Listen. I was looking through my sister's things and found the Lost Bastards card. I remembered meeting you the other week, so I thought I'd track you down and see if you were still looking for the Copper Killer." The words burst out of her in a rush. Damn it. She needed to seem in control and calm.

"Oh." His full lips tightened.

"Why were those men shooting at you?" she whispered, her mind reeling.

Heath glanced her way again. "They were shooting at you, darlin'. Chasing you."

She leaned her head back. That was true. "Why?" God. Were they somehow working for her ex? Would he send men with guns to bring her back? "Wait a minute." Her mind ran through likely scenarios. "I first met them at your former offices. They were looking for you, not me."

Heath's upper lip twitched.

She watched, not wanting to be fascinated. Then irritation took over. "You're a jerk."

He shrugged. "You're right. I'm sorry."

God, this was getting too damn confusing, and she was having trouble breathing from the fear of losing the sister she'd just found. "Why are those fake cops chasing you and now me?"

He looked at her again, really looked this time. "How did you know they were fake?"

"I didn't until I took a good look at one of the badges." Plus, her instincts were fairly decent at knowing when a man was lying to her. "There was something not quite right about them."

Admiration glimmered in Heath's stunning eyes for a moment. "Nicely done. So they followed you?"

"I guess." She sighed, warmed by his gaze. "I lied and told them I was staying at a motel, but apparently they didn't believe me. I also gave them a fake name and number." She eyed the snowy trees flashing by outside. "Why are they after you, Heath?"

"So you do remember my name," he murmured.

She frowned. "Sure."

"They're after me because of a different case of your sister's, and you don't have to worry about it." He turned down another road. "Since you were waiting for the shuttle, I'm assuming you have a plane ticket out of here?"

"Yeah. Back to Salt Lake City, where the FBI has a command center looking for Loretta." Just saying her sister's name made her gut ache.

"Okay, I'll drop you off, and you go right through security and get to your gate. The fake cops won't follow you." Heath's phone buzzed, and he glanced at the screen, his body tightening.

"What?" she breathed.

He looked at her, obviously weighing his words. "We have a lead on your sister. I have to go."

Hope exploded in her chest. "Not without me going."

He shook his head. "It's dangerous. I'll check in with you the second I know anything."

She sucked in air and pointed the gun at him. Not once in her life had she even held a gun in her hand much less threatened somebody with one. But she would find her sister, damn it. "I said we're going together."

Denver Jones walked away from Noni, his first and only love. With dangerous and deadly forces from his past hot on his trail, it was the only way he could protect her. But now, out of the blue, when Noni needs his help, he'll do anything to be by her side...even risk his own life to save hers...

A PREVIEW OF *TWISTED TRUTHS* FOLLOWS.

CHAPTER
1

Noni tossed her laptop and stack of maps on the faded patchwork bedspread, her eyes gritty and her temples aching. The battered electric heater rattled from the corner of the hotel room, providing a surprising amount of heat. Her fingers tingled as they started to warm up.

Winter blew snow around outside, and ice scattered against the window. She shivered and knelt one knee on the bed, spreading out the closest map. Where was her pen? Scrambling for her bag on the floor, she drew out a black marker and made several notations through the mountainous Pacific Northwest. Her heart raced, and her lungs compressed. She had to be closing in. Then she crossed out several towns, including Seattle, before pulling her phone from her pocket and hitting speed dial for number one.

Static crackled, and then an expletive echoed as it sounded like the phone was dropped. Something shuffled. "Eagle? This is Sparrow," finally came over the line.

Noni rubbed her aching head. "Hi, Aunt Franny. I thought we agreed to forget the nicknames."

"So did I, dear, but Verna likes being called Hawk Two."

Why would they have a Hawk Two when there wasn't a Hawk One? Noni swallowed down a sharp retort. "We have to get serious, Fran. This is dangerous." Though she'd done everything possible to make sure the two older women were out of the line of fire. "Where are you?"

"I just set up camp in Portland. Verna should be pulling into Salt Lake City any second now," Franny said. "I'm staying in the Motel Burnside just north of town. My meeting with the private detective is tomorrow morning—he has already left Seattle and is heading here."

"Good. I'm going to scout around here in Coeur d'Alene before backtracking to Spokane in a day or so." Though her sources, ones she hadn't revealed to Franny, had revealed her prey had friends in Coeur d'Alene. Now all she had to do was find them. Somehow.

"What about the FBI office in Snowville?" Franny asked.

Noni swallowed. "That's a last resort." If she contacted the FBI, the agents would immediately send out an Amber Alert for a missing child. If that happened, Richie might kill the baby. She couldn't let that happen. Plus, the law wasn't exactly on her side right now. God, she hoped she wasn't making the hugest mistake of her life by handling this herself.

"Any news from Denver?" Franny asked, sounding weary.

"No." Noni lifted her chin. "He gave me a fake last name, so all I have is his picture and basic information. But I've posted a search for him all over the Internet, even on dating sites. He has to see something." Her chest hurt to even think about the asshole who'd broken her heart so easily, but she needed his help, and she'd take the pain to save the missing baby. "I'll find him."

"Honey," Fran cleared her throat. "He's probably no better than that first private detective we hired. The one who stole our savings."

Noni's shoulders slumped. "Denver has to be better, and I'll get our money back. I promise." How, she had no clue. The first detective she'd found had been a fraud, and he'd taken their entire twenty thousand dollars. They'd been desperate enough to let him since Sharon's baby had been kidnapped after she'd died in childbirth.

Poor Sharon. The question of how she'd really died would have to be answered later—after Noni made sure her baby was safe from its dick of a father.

The second detective Noni had hired had at least traced Richie and the baby to somewhere in the Pacific Northwest. The PI was heading to Portland, but Noni's gut and source back home had told her to head to northern Idaho. "Get some sleep, Franny."

"I mean it. Let's forget Denver what's-his-real-name-who-the-hell-knows-because-he's-a-damn-liar and just do this ourselves."

"Let's go back to calling him 'dickhead,'" Noni said, even her arms feeling heavy. She'd met Denver while he was on a case, and he had seemed like a bloodhound. He ultimately found the guy he was looking for. Then he'd left. "We might be taking on an entire gang, Auntie. Denver is tough enough to do it."

"I don't know," Franny said, drawing out the words. "I guess, worst case scenario, we can just stand behind him if the bullets start flying."

"Absolutely," Noni agreed, pushing the map out of the way. In fact, she wanted to shoot Denver herself. "Get some sleep. I'll call in tomorrow."

"Night, sweetie," Franny said, disconnecting the call.

Noni set the phone on the nightstand and stretched out on the bed. She should get out her notes and maps and start working. Her eyelids fluttered shut.

A whisper of sound had them flipping back open.

Then he stood inside the room, quietly shutting the door against the freezing cold. The entire atmosphere electrified. Holy crap on a mutinous cracker. Denver was *there*. Really there. After a year of having no clue whether or not he was alive, the sight of him seemed surreal. Was she dreaming about him? Again? How could he really be there?

"Noni," he breathed, his gaze settling on her.

"I locked that door," she mumbled, shoving to sit up, her mind blanking to avoid the rush of emotion pouring through her.

"What the fuck are you doing?" he snarled, his eyes turning a furious blue.

She blinked. So much for her secret little fantasy of him finding her, begging forgiveness, and professing that his heart and soul belonged to her. Not that she'd take him back, anyway. But still. Her temper rolled from banked to a slow burn. "Excuse me?" She still sounded groggy.

"Pack. Now." He edged to the side and moved the heavy curtain out of the way.

She shook her head, trying to grasp reality. It had been so long since she'd seen him, and within seconds, her entire body had flared to life. Her heart thundered. How could he still affect her like this?

He turned back to her, his head moving slowly as he must've realized she hadn't jumped into action. Stress cut lines next to his mouth. "Noni. Now."

That dangerously deep and dark voice. She still heard the low tenor in the times between sleep and wakefulness…when dreams took her under. Like *he'd* taken her under.

Somehow, he looked even tougher than before. Even more remote and distant.

His black hair brushed the collar of his battered leather jacket over ripped jeans leading to snow-covered motorcycle boots. A shadow covered his square jaw, showcasing each hard angle. His dark brows were arched, his eyes a sizzling blue, and his full lips set into a thin line. Tension choked the air around them, rolling through the room with a discernible heat.

She couldn't stop looking at him, watching him like a starving woman would a cheesecake.

There was something unreal about *him*—an elusive, too-male, predatory quality she'd never been able to define. Yet she felt it. She felt him—the danger and the kindness, the complexity and simplicity. All characteristics he'd probably deny…if he bothered to talk at all.

"Noni," he snapped.

She came fully awake.

He was *pissed*?

Hurt shocked through her, and she shoved it away. "Sorry to bother you and whatever woman you're lying your ass off to right now, but I need your help." She pushed from the bed. Her knees wobbled, but she held herself upright.

He breathed out, and his nostrils flared. "Later." Angling for her, he shoved the maps and manila files off the bed and into her bag.

She'd forgotten. How had she forgotten how quickly he could move? "We're not going anywhere," she snapped.

He turned, and she instantly found herself up against the wall, his hand flat against her upper chest, his face leaning down toward hers. Different flecks of blue made up his spectacular eyes, each one glittering with an emotion she couldn't quite read.

She was pinned easily—too easily—in place. This close, she could smell him. Male and forest and leather and something that was all Denver.

He didn't speak again. No order, no sarcasm, no words. He just looked at her as if he could compel her into obedience with his intensity.

There was a time she'd responded to his looks. She'd read him, almost felt him. He wasn't much for speaking, and she'd learned to interpret his movements and expressions. Because he had mattered to her.

Apparently she hadn't mattered a whit to him.

At the reminder, her head snapped back. Her stomach clenched.

He had finally bothered to show up and now was giving her orders? Oh, hell no. She tried to struggle, and he kept her still and against the wall with one hand spread across her sternum.

His strength was unreal. There was a time she'd marveled at it. Not now.

His days of touching her were over. She pivoted and shot her knee toward his groin, fully intending to connect.

She failed.

His free hand grasped the back of her thigh, shoving her leg to the side and stepping into the vee of her legs. The full length of him, heated and hard, trapped her in place.

She gasped at the contact, sparks shooting through her. Her body warmed and then flashed to a boil, all from one simple touch. All from his nearness—something she'd so desperately missed. There were times she wished she hadn't even known him…that she didn't now know what it felt like to be protected by him. "Damn it, Denver."

His nose nearly touched hers. "Are you crazy?"

Maybe. Probably. She'd been off since he'd shattered her heart. "Let me go."

"Can't. You have no idea what you've done." A muscle ticked in his jaw, the fierce anger on his face making him look like a stranger. Not the man she thought she'd known.

Her mind spun. "What *I've* done?" Wait a minute. All of the thoughts, all of the fears of the last year, bombarded her. How many precious moments had she wasted wondering about him? Asking herself why he'd left without a word. Why would posting about him on the Internet cause problems? "Oh, God. You *are* married."

His gaze narrowed even further. "That's ridiculous."

All right. "Then wanted. You're wanted by the law."

He didn't answer.

That was an answer, wasn't it? Oh, man. What had she done?

"Leave now. Leave, and I'll take down all the posts about you." She didn't know him. Maybe she never had. For the first time, fear—the real kind—shivered down her spine. He was certainly more dangerous than anything else out there.

"Too late," he gritted out.

"I-I'm…sorry." The words breathed out of her as self-preservation took over. The man was one long line of coiled strength, and she didn't stand a chance in a fight, even on her best day. They were alone in her hotel room, and she had no friends near. Could she scream?

He blinked. His eyes darkened, and somehow, his jaw hardened visibly. "Don't be afraid of me."

"I'm not," she shot back, lying instantly. "This was a mistake. I know that now." It wasn't her first time trying to survive danger, and it probably wouldn't be her last. "Just leave. Please." She'd find the baby on her own.

"Too late." Regret twisted his lip.

Oh God. What did that mean? *Too late?* What would he do? Adrenaline jolted through her veins. She opened her mouth to scream and had barely sucked in air when his mouth crashed down on hers.

His touch was too carnal to be called a kiss. She fragmented, splintering into pieces. Fire swept her, lighting her body on fire even as her mind rebelled. Her nipples sharpened, and her knees weakened, but alarm bells clanged throughout her head. The disconnect between her feelings and her thoughts nearly dropped her to the ground.

He held her upright and in place.

His touch, his taste, his smell was so familiar her mouth moved beneath his, and her hands rose to his chest. Instead of pushing him away, her fingers curled into the leather jacket. It had been *so long*. Her body separating from her brain, she kissed him back, tilting her head to take more of him.

He growled low, and the sound reverberated into her mouth and down her body.

Her abdomen rolled and clenched, need flaring through her so quickly she gasped. What was she doing? No. God. She had to end this. With a muffled sob, she wrenched her head to the side. "Stop," she breathed.

He stiffened, his head lifting very slightly. Grasping her chin with a firm grip, he turned her to face him again. "No screaming."

She gulped.

"I won't hurt you." His eyes had darkened to the hue of a night sky right before the moon softened the dark. Now lust glimmered there along with the anger that hadn't disappeared.

She swallowed, trapped. Her lungs completely gave up the fight and stopped working. She couldn't breathe. God, she couldn't breathe. "Okay." Tears filled her eyes.

"Noni." His voice gentled to the tone she remembered. "I promise. You'll be safe."

Her mouth went dry, so she just nodded.

"We have to go. Now. Tell me you get me." His hoarse growl rumbled between them, his breath brushing her lips.

A shiver took her, head to toe, while all the areas in between heated. "Why?" she breathed, not nearly as forcefully as she'd like. He brought out a vulnerability in her that she had explored while in the safety of his touch, and then he'd left. The vulnerability remained, and she tried to hide it, even though he'd just become the thing to fear. Her chin lifted. There was strength in survival, and oh. She knew how to survive.

He jerked his head to the side, his attention focused on the door. His body stiffened, and he released her suddenly, moving back for the window. "Get your bag."

What did he hear?

The urgency in his voice propelled her toward the laptop and bag. Her stomach cramping and her breath quickening, she grabbed them and moved toward him. If she got outside, could she get away from him?

The window burst open with a loud shatter, spraying glass.

Denver turned and leaped for her, tackling her to the floor. She hit with a hard thump, struggling against him. Pain flashed from her hip.

He covered her, and the entire room exploded.